ROCK AND ROLL VOODOO

MARK PAUL SMITH

Virginia

Published in the United States by BQB Publishing
(an imprint of Boutique of Quality Books Publishing Company, Inc.)
www.bqbpublishing.com

978-1-945448-32-4 (p)
978-1-945448-33-1 (e)
Library of Congress Control Number : 2018966620

Book design by Robin Krauss, www.bookformatters.com
Cover design by Rebecca Lown, www.rebeccalowndesign.com
Cover photo and author photo by Michael W. Poorman
Editor: Caleb Guard

This book is dedicated to the world's greatest living artist,
my wife Jo Ellen Hemphill Smith.

SPECIAL THANKS

To Terri Leidich of BQB Publishing, who made this book happen. To Caleb Guard, my insightful and inspirational editor. And to Brenda Fishbaugh, beta reader extraordinaire.

PROLOGUE

"Life is a spiritual obstacle course, designed to see if you can get over your self."

Rock and Roll Voodoo

Mark Paul Smith

TABLE OF CONTENTS

CHAPTER ONE

MAGIC MUSHROOMS

February 12, 1977

The early morning fog was thick as Jesse drove carefully across the Huey P. Long Bridge in New Orleans. Visibility was less than twenty feet. Turning on the headlights made it worse. The only thing he could see in the reflective glare was the rounded hood of his beat-up Volkswagen Beetle.

A foghorn blasted from a barge on the Mississippi River below like an angry troll protesting his passage.

"How can that boat be going anywhere?" he asked Casey, who rode shotgun. Jesse turned off the headlights and braked to a crawl. "He can't see any better than we can."

"Keep going, man," Casey said. "There's nobody but us on this bridge."

"We won't even be on the bridge if I drive off it," Jesse said.

"Want me to get out and walk ahead?"

Jesse accelerated slightly. "No. I'll keep it slow. We'll be okay as long as I stay close to the side."

A tall, box truck exploded out of the fog, headed straight for them. It didn't have headlights on. Jesse grabbed the steering wheel and closed his eyes. The truck skidded and swerved and started to tip over on top of the Beetle.

Jesse inhaled and stiffened. He braced for impact. He tried to scream.

There was no collision.

The truck somehow regained its balance and missed the car by inches in a wail of screeching tires and screaming horns. A gush of displaced air shook the Beetle off its over-worn tires and moved it slightly to the right. The blast slapped Jesse in the face through his open driver's window.

Then, everything fell quiet, as though nothing had happened. The truck had roared out of the fog and disappeared back into it before the danger could fully register.

Jesse brought the car to a complete stop. The fog enveloped them. His eyes teared up from the pungent, stinging blast of burned rubber. Casey's eyes were wide and his mouth was open.

"Did that just happen?" Jesse asked.

"Man, I thought it was all over," Casey said. "All I saw was the grill of that truck, up close and personal. How did he miss us? That was so close it banged my head into the window."

"I think you banged your own head."

"Maybe," Casey said. "That thing was right on top of us."

"We should turn back," Jesse said. "That was way too close. It's a bad sign."

"No way. He missed us. It's a good sign, or maybe even a wake up call. Probably means we should start paying better attention to what's coming next. Yeah, that's it. I can feel it. Something big is going to happen on this trip. Keep going. We must be halfway across. Come on, we're sitting ducks here."

"That, my friend," Jesse said, "is an insanely positive spin on us nearly getting squashed like bugs."

"Call it what you want but let's get moving. Come on, I'm the navigator in charge."

Jesse inched the car across the bridge, sounding the Beetle's squeaky-toy horn every few seconds. Casey kept encouraging him to go faster. After a few nerve-wracking minutes, they reached the other side without further incident. Back on solid ground, it was still impossible to see anything but fog. Jesse drove resolutely, creeping along the highway, still shaken by fear.

"That could have been it for us," Casey said, backing off his previous bravado.

"Did you smell the burning rubber?" Jesse asked.

"Feels like tiny bits of rubber are lodged in my nose hair. I can't stop shaking. How about you?"

"I'm over it. Good to go." Jesse said. "I live for those existential moments."

Casey laughed loudly. "You and your existential moments. One of these days an existential moment is going to be your last."

"Not today."

"Not yet."

The fog evaporated as Jesse drove further away from the river. The rising sun peeked through a dense layer of low hanging clouds. It was going to be a hot and humid day on the bayou. Jesse couldn't help but make the obvious comment. "It's comforting to know that we're out of the fog and still have no idea where we're going."

"Of course we do," Casey said. "The magic mushrooms are on Bayou Lafourche."

"Do you have any idea where that is?"

"Head south. It's the bayou. How hard can it be?"

"The bayou is thousands of miles of waterways and swamp. Bayou Lafourche is only one of those rivers." Jesse glanced at Casey. "Did you think to bring a map?"

"That would take all the magic out of it. Keep going south." Casey pointed out the window.

Jesse checked the rear view mirror. "We're headed west."

"How can you tell?"

"Look behind us."

Casey turned around. "I don't see anything."

"The sun rises in the east?"

"Oh, yeah, I see what you're talking about. Don't worry about it. Just keep following the road. My guys say cross the bridge and follow the road."

"You keep calling them your guys. Do you even know them? Jesse asked.

"I don't know their names, except for the one who calls himself Gypsy. I buy psychedelic mushrooms from them. They've got the best shrooms around. Gypsy says they come from Bayou Lafourche."

"And did this Gypsy of yours tell you exactly where to find the shrooms?"

"What's with the cross examination?" Casey asked. "Obviously, they didn't give me a treasure map with an X marks the spot. They can't be that hard to find. From what I gather, they're everywhere."

Jesse kept driving west on Highway 90, feeling more and more like he was on a wild goose chase. It wouldn't be the first unsuccessful drug run they'd made. One mission to Ohio State in 1969 had seen them pay $2,000 for 500 worthless pills.

Jesse and Casey had been close friends since they were ten years old. They grew up together in Indiana and had both graduated from college five years earlier. They were now twenty-seven years old. Casey was a second year law student at Loyola University. At 6′2″ tall, he was a ladies' man with California-surfer good looks. He had a strong chin with a big smile, playful eyes, and curly, blonde hair. Jesse was playing in a four-man, acoustic-rock band on Bourbon Street. He was

6'3" tall with a full beard and frizzy hair that flowed over his shoulders and halfway down his back. The one-inch difference between Jesse and Casey's heights had always been a factor in their never-ending competition with each other.

Casey had helped convince Jesse to bring his band to New Orleans. "It's the perfect place for a musician. Tourists come from all over to hear the music of Bourbon Street and New Orleans. They do the traveling. You stay in one place and make the money."

Despite finding somewhat steady work in the bars on Bourbon Street, the band hadn't exactly hit the big time. Jesse was in the process of learning, the hard way, that New Orleans is not Los Angeles. Nonetheless, he was determined that his band would find a drummer and hit the road to rock and roll stardom.

"I'm telling you, Jesse, if we find shrooms, we can make a fortune. Let's face it. We could use the money."

"If we can find them."

"Don't be so negative," Casey said. "What's the worst that can happen? We get a tour of the bayou."

"If we can find the bayou."

The sun kept rising to disappear into the clouds. It looked like the day might be rained out. Jesse drove on with continuing misgivings. He didn't know where they were going but he knew where the conversation was headed.

"You know, if the band thing doesn't work out, you can always go to law school," Casey said.

"That's not going to happen." Jesse slapped the steering wheel with both hands. "I knew you were going to bring that up again."

"Why not?" Casey asked. "Your father's a lawyer. You two get along great."

"I do love my father. But I don't want to end up in a suit and tie, upholding a system that throws people in prison for doing what we're doing now."

"What are you talking about?" Casey asked. "There's no cops on the bayou."

"I'm not quitting my band to sell out and go to law school."

"You always say that. Going to law school doesn't mean selling out. Once you get your degree and pass the bar, you can represent all the revolutionaries and rock poets you want. You can change the system from within."

Jesse slowed down the car. "What a load of bullshit. The system's going to change you more than you will ever change the system."

Casey leaned forward to stretch. "Why not give law school a try? You don't have to make any career decisions. Just try it. You could still play in a band."

Jesse took a deep breath. "How many times do I have to say it? I'm not going to law school just because you did. And I'm not going because my father wants me to. I'm a musician, and I'm going to make it in the music business or die trying."

Casey didn't respond. Jesse decided not to rehash the argument. At the moment, he was more worried about getting hopelessly lost on a mushroom mission.

The Beetle had no air conditioning and no radio. The only sound during the conversational lull was the hot air gushing through the open windows.

As the road headed south again, an oncoming Louisiana State Trooper slowed down and looked them over carefully as he passed. Jesse's VW Bug was a car any self-respecting law enforcement agent would want to pull over and search. It had a banged-up front hood held down by a bicycle chain. The rear bumper had been beaten into a wavy shape from multiple accidents. The red paint job had faded into a rusty-orange color. Two decals of Goofy were pasted on the front. Jesse called them his twin Goofys like they were some kind of fuel injection system for his little cartoon of a car.

Jesse had named the car, Harley, after the motorcycle he could never afford.

"What were you saying about no cops on the bayou?" Jesse said. "Shit, he's slowing down. He's going to turn around."

Casey turned around to look. "Wow. What's he doing down here?"

"Apparently, we're still in Louisiana."

"Are you holding?"

"Nope," Jesse said. "They can search me all they want. You?"

"I'm good. Or bad, depending on how you look at it."

"It's a rare moment in sports when neither one of us has any drugs," Jesse said. "How did we even get in the car without a couple joints for the road?"

"I thought you had some," Casey said.

"If I had any, we'd be smoking it by now."

"And that's the problem with getting an early start." Casey closed his window halfway. "The early bird doesn't get the worm. He forgets his maps and his stash because he didn't get enough sleep. The worm gets to sleep in."

Jesse wasn't listening. He was looking in the rear-view mirror, eyeing the trooper's brake lights shining bright.

"Oh, shit," Casey looked over his shoulder again. "He's stopping. He's going to come after us."

"Just because you're paranoid doesn't mean they're not out to get you," Jesse said.

"Very funny," Casey kept his eye on the trooper's vehicle.

The brake lights went off and the trooper kept going, much to Jesse's relief. There was no telling what a thorough search of Harley might reveal.

"That's right," Casey said. "Keep moving. Nothing to see here."

Jesse felt invigorated. Nothing makes the heart beat like seeing a police car while on a drug run, even if you haven't scored yet.

It started to rain, an annoying drizzle at first, then hard enough to make deep puddles in the road. The more it rained, the more lost Jesse began to feel.

He was looking for a gas station to get directions when he saw a sign for Boutte, Louisiana. Next to the sign, a man was holding out his thumb for a ride. His clothes were ragged, mainly blue jean. His shoes looked like they might be Converse high tops but they were so battered and worn it was hard to tell. He was short and thin and maybe a mix of black and Creole. His Afro was flattened and matted from the rain and whatever he'd slept in the night before.

"We should pick that guy up," Casey shouted as he pointed. "He might know where the shrooms are."

Jesse pulled over and stopped. Casey got out of the two-door car, flopped the front passenger seat forward, and helped the hitchhiker wedge himself into the back seat. The new passenger smelled like wet dog as he mumbled some kind of thank you in an indiscernible dialect.

"I knew it," Casey said, reaching back to shake the man's hand. "You're Cajun, aren't you? Say something in Cajun."

The disheveled man, who looked to be in his mid-thirties, held out his hand and said, *"Laissez les bons temps rouler."*

"Yes," Casey said so loudly it made the man jump in his seat. "Let the good times roll. I know that one."

The three men laughed together as Jesse got back on the road and shifted through four gears and up to highway speed. Harley still ran like a top, despite its battered appearance.

"We're looking for magic mushrooms and Bayou Lafourche," Casey said, wasting no time, getting to the point.

"I can take you there."

"To the bayou or to the mushrooms?"

"Both."

"No, you're kidding. You really know where the shrooms are?"

"Ya, mon," he said, sounding a little too Caribbean.

"What's your name?" Jesse asked.

"Name Gabriel."

"Nice to meet you, Gabriel. I'm Jesse. You'll have to forgive me, here, but I've done some hitchhiking myself and I'd hate to think you'd let us drive you all the way to your house just because you say that's where the mushrooms are."

Gabriel laughed in a way that made him seem charmingly believable. "No, no. I wouldn't do that. But the best mushroom fields do happen to be right near my house."

"How far from here?" Jesse asked.

"Not far, maybe half an hour, maybe a little more."

"What do you know about magic mushrooms?" Casey asked.

"I know the cows eat the mushroom spores and their body heat germinates the spores and they shit them out and their manure fertilizes them," the hitchhiker said. "After that, all it takes is heat and moisture. We've got both today. They don't need sunlight."

Casey looked at Jesse in triumph at having found the right man for the job.

"That's good enough for me," Jesse said. "How do you know the psychedelic mushrooms that are safe from the poisonous ones that can kill you?"

"The good ones have little purple rings around the stem," Casey interrupted.

"I was asking Gabriel."

"Yes," Gabriel said. "Only eat ones with the purple. You be fine."

The hitchhiker pointed out a road sign that said turn right for Raceland, Louisiana. "Okay, turn left. We don't go to Raceland. This is Highway One. Turn left and it runs by Bayou Lafourche. On the west of the bayou is Highway One and on the east is Highway Three o' Eight. The bayou is in the middle."

"Man, this is some of the flattest country I've ever seen," Jesse said as he made the turn. "I thought Indiana was flat. This place doesn't even have a bump in the road."

Jesse kept driving into the rain, past low-slung houses and shanties with wooden docks along some kind of canal.

"What kind of traffic goes down that waterway?" Casey asked.

Gabriel leaned forward between the seats. "Shrimp boats and tourist riverboats and pirogues."

"What's a pirogue?" Casey shifted into interview mode.

"It's a small boat with a flat bottom so you can push-pole it through the shallow swamp," Gabriel made the motion. "It's a Cajun thing."

"What is a Cajun, anyway?" Casey asked.

"It's a mix of French Creoles who came down from Canada, Indians, blacks, and some English," Gabriel said. "My momma says I've got a little of all of them in me."

"Looks like you might have had a rough night last night," Jesse said.

"It was a Fais do-do," Gabriel said. "An all night party. I guess you can tell I haven't been to bed yet."

"Don't worry about it," Casey said. "You look fine. We've all been there."

"What do you do for a living?" Jesse asked.

"There it is," Gabriel pointed as a waterway came into

view alongside the road. "Allow me to introduce you to Bayou Lafourche. It's more than one hundred miles long from the Mississippi River to the Gulf of Mexico. It be Main Street for Cajun country. Here you find real Cajun cooking and the Zydeco music. Do you know Zydeco?"

"Oh, yeah," Jesse said. "I play in a band. We've got a fiddle player."

"Do you have an accordion?" Gabriel asked.

"Not yet."

"So, come down here and find you one," Gabriel said. "Zydeco is Cajun folk music. It's like country music only with an accordion."

"I can't believe we found Bayou Lafourche," Casey said.

"Gabriel found it for us," Jesse said. "If it hadn't been for him, we would have driven right past it."

Jesse was driving through a part of the waterway that was nearly overgrown with Chinese Tallow, Bald Cypress, and Willow trees when Gabriel said, "The bayou is so far south it makes New Orleans look like a northern city."

"Most of what I know about the bayou comes from the Hank Williams song, 'Jambalaya,'" Jesse said.

"Goodbye Joe, me gotta go, me oh my oh," Gabriel sang. "Me gotta push-pole the pirogue down the bayou."

"That's the one," Jesse said.

"Hey Jambalaya, crawfish pie, filé gumbo," Gabriel continued singing. Jesse joined in on the chorus and they sounded pretty good together as they finished the song. After a little instant harmony, Jesse felt he could trust Gabriel.

Casey turned around in his seat to ask Gabriel a direct question. "This is where the Voodoo comes from, right?"

"Ah, yes, the bayou has all the Voodoo you can imagine," Gabriel's eyes widened in Jesse's rear mirror. "Some of it can haunt you." He thrust his open hands into the front seat. "Some can protect you, even from yourself. It is the magic of the spirit world." He clasped his hands together as if in prayer. "There is much magic here. Today, you will find much more than you are looking for."

"What makes you say that?" Casey asked.

"I don't know why I say it," Gabriel said. "I just know it be true. Feel it in my bones."

"So what about the magic mushrooms?" Casey asked, taking the talk back to the quest at hand. "How much farther? We've been driving almost fifty miles now."

"Not much farther. See, here is Lockport. Next is Larose, where the Intracoastal Waterway intersects Bayou Lafourche. Between Lockport and Larose, that is where we go."

"You mean that's where you live," Jesse said.

"Yes, yes," Gabriel laughed his disarming laugh. "I do live there but that is where you will find the best mushrooms. You will see. I show you."

A few miles past Lockport, the road left the bayou and meandered through a stretch of ranch land. Gabriel motioned for them to stop. Jesse parked Harley off the side of the road in front of a never-ending field. The three of them got out to stretch. The rain had stopped. Across the road was a long, white, cattle fence, four feet high.

"See that fence," Gabriel said. "Climb it and walk a ways, and you find all the mushrooms you can carry."

"Aren't you coming with us?" Jesse asked.

"No, I don't need any. They're all for you. I had too much of everything last night. I need sleep. Thanks, you two, for the ride. Happy times. You have good hunting."

With that, Gabriel began walking down the road. Casey got two paper grocery bags out of the car. He and Jesse crossed the road to climb the fence. Looking around to see if the coast was clear, Jesse realized Gabriel wasn't on the road. He wasn't on the side of the road or walking into a field. He was nowhere in sight.

Casey scanned the area from the top of the fence. "I don't see where he could have gone."

"He's the mystery man," Jesse said. "Come on. Let's get over this fence and hope he wasn't suckering us for a ride all the way to his house."

They walked into the field far enough so as not to be seen from the road. A few cows grazed in the distance. Jesse felt his feet sinking in the sandy soil. The land was relentlessly flat. They crossed a dry creek bed with some shrub trees and began walking into fields of grass. Jesse smelled the piles of manure before he saw them. None had any mushrooms.

The search went on without luck for nearly an hour. The sun came out from behind the clouds. It got hot and steamy in a hurry. Jesse was feeling discouraged. The heat made him wonder why he hadn't thought to bring any water. Everything looked the same. He could tell from Casey's slumped shoulders that his friend was also losing hope in the hunt. He was about to give up the search when he decided it was time to take a leak. There were scattered bushes nearby but he didn't bother to hide behind one since no one was around. He relieved himself in the open field and marveled at the yellow arc of his urine stream glowing in the sun.

The miracle began.

There, at the very end of his shining relief, was a mostly-dry pile of cow manure, covered in magic mushrooms. They looked like a colony of tiny aliens atop the cow pie. He changed his trajectory to avoid pissing on the treasure.

"Casey," he yelled as he shook himself off and zipped up. "You'd better come see this right away. We have mushrooms, lots of them. I was taking a leak and there they were. Like a pot of gold at the end of a rainbow."

By the time Casey arrived, Jesse had already picked his first mushroom out of the manure. It had the purplish ring around the stem.

"That's the real deal," Casey howled as he hopped up and down in a victory dance.

Jesse took a few steps to the right and looked down. "Here's another one with even more."

Suddenly, they were surrounded by a sea of magic mushrooms. Where once had been only sand and dry brush, there was now nothing but piles of cow manure, covered with magic mushrooms. They picked quickly but carefully, so as not to damage their sacred harvest. In minutes, they had half a grocery bag of what looked to be the finest magic mushrooms in all the land. They were big, some of them six inches long and three inches wide.

"Should we try one out?" Casey asked.

"Absolutely," Jesse said as he stuffed a four-inch mushroom into his mouth and began chewing with a grimace.

Casey stifled his own gag reflex. "You're not even going to wash it first?"

"With what?"

Once Jesse finished swallowing the mushroom, Casey wiped one off on his shirt and made a sweeping sign of the cross as he sang, "My father plays dominos better than your father plays dominos, I got a bloody nose, amen."

Jesse laughed at the incantation as Casey popped the entire mushroom into his mouth and winced at the fungal taste.

"Actually, the cow shit gives them a little flavor," Jesse said. "They don't taste that good on their own. They taste like, I don't know, like worms I guess."

"How would you know what worms taste like?"

"I don't. The shrooms just don't taste that good. That's all I'm saying. Maybe they'd be better if you cooked them or put them in a salad with some vinegar and oil and salt."

They kept picking and chatting about their amazing good fortune until their backs and legs were aching, and both grocery bags were filled to overflowing. The sun was in full force and they were sweating profusely.

Jesse felt a subtle body rush sneak up his spine like two cups of strong coffee. It made the hair on the back of his neck stand up. He started twitching his nose as his hands and feet began to tingle. He was breathing more deeply. His hair felt like it belonged to someone else. Euphoric feelings of physical freedom, like walking on clouds, washed over him. Then, the clouds turned into pillows of sexual pleasure, floating in release from the bonds of everyday reality. Arousal surged from the inside out, combined with paisley imagery, undulating, from the outside in. He was stuck in the middle of a world with no beginning and no ending. It became increasingly difficult to remember where he was or how he fit into the scheme of things. He had fallen down the rabbit hole in *Alice In Wonderland*. The world shifted from "knock, knock" to "who's there?" Nothing felt familiar, although even little things became exceptionally enjoyable. Taking a deep breath felt as athletic as doing a back flip. Turning around sent the entire planet spinning. Being able to fly seemed a distinct possibility.

He wandered aimlessly as the visual hallucinations and color changes and otherworldly perspectives began to change everything. It didn't take long for a disorienting paranoia to descend. He turned to Casey and realized his friend was as far out as he was.

The two men hugged each other to get some kind of a grip on reality.

"Hang on tight, my brother," Jesse said. "We have lift off."

"I'm hanging on," Casey said. "I'm hanging on like Sloopy. This is doable. We've been here before."

"It's not as radical as some of the acid we've done."

"Hang on Sloopy," Casey started singing.

"Sloopy hang on," Jesse joined in.

They sang as well as they could remember half the lyrics. They did *not* panic. Jesse and Casey had been tripping since 1968. They were cosmic cowboys. They'd taken a few radical rides on Owsley LSD from the San Francisco area. Even so, they were having trouble staying in the saddle.

The shrooms were potent.

"Breathe deep," Jesse said. "Don't fight the feeling. Let it take you where it will. It's like a rip tide. If you swim against the current it'll drown you."

"I hear you, brother," Casey said. "I'm breathing deep and this shit's taking me places I've never been. It feels like floating on a river in the sky."

"Hang on, Sloopy," Jesse hugged Casey again. "I think we're in the rapids."

The Paranoia came and went, alternating with euphoria. Casey and Jesse began dancing around in wide circles with their arms spread out like wings. The mind-boggling experience was huge fun even though it was more than a little scary. It was a roller coaster ride without a track.

Losing your mind always has its ups and downs.

Every time Jesse had tripped on acid or anything else in the past, he got to a place where he knew no one could possibly save him. The trick, he had found, was in not looking to be rescued.

Casey wandered off and found a dead bull by a shallow, dry creek bed. It looked like it had died of thirst on the spot. He pulled hard on one horn and the head detached from the body. Jesse had to choke back a puke reflex as the head came off with a sickening, flesh-ripping, tendon-snapping, bone-cracking sound. Jesse watched in amazement as Casey became spellbound by the mystical energy of the skull he now held in his hand. The bull hadn't looked decomposed enough for the head to come off that easily.

"Talk about grabbing the bull by the horns," Jesse said.

The detached head mesmerized him. It seemed to be looking into his soul, like it had found new life once liberated from the body of the bull.

The horns were clean and nearly two feet wide. The eye sockets were empty. The nose and broad, flat head still had hunks of hair and flesh hanging on the bone. All the teeth were still imbedded in the upper jaw but the lower jaw had somehow remained with the body. There was no dripping blood. The skull was dry as the sand and appeared to be floating in thin air.

It looked like Casey was about to be devoured by a cannibal zombie bull, raging in revenge at all the meat eaters in the world.

"This is the spirit of Bayou Lafourche," Casey proclaimed as he shook the skull and began picking off some of the larger chunks of flesh and hair. "He will protect us from evil."

Jesse began backing away. "Are you out of your mind? You better drop that thing. I can't believe you're even touching it. It's freaking me out. It looks like the devil himself has come out to play."

Casey laughed at Jesse's squeamishness and began dancing while holding the skull over his head and chanting nonsensically.

The sight took Jesse out of his paranoid nausea and made him start laughing. The mushroom visions turned the skull into a clown balloon. It looked like Casey might float away at any moment. The horror became comical.

Jesse laughed so hard that Casey couldn't help but start laughing too. They couldn't stop. There was a hysterical spirit in the air. They both ended up on their knees in the dirt, trying to catch their breath.

The skull was not laughing with them from its place in the sand.

When they finally got over the laughing jag, they looked at each other and realized the world was nothing like it had been forty-five minutes earlier. The sky was broiling and the earth was rolling like the sea. Jesse was so disoriented he could barely distinguish fantasy from reality. He looked Casey in the eye and it seemed for a moment like his friend was about to panic. Then everything seemed hysterically funny again and he was back in the dirt, laughing until his stomach hurt. Casey was laughing right along with him.

Jesse was first to recover from the laughing jag. "By the way, I'm tripping my brains out. I'm not sure how much higher we can get or how much longer this is going to last. We'd better get back to the car while we still can. Why don't you ask your freaky cow skull friend how much more weird this trip is going to get?"

Casey grabbed the skull by both horns and began doing the twist. He looked like a cross between a drunken matador and one of those guys losing the race at the running of the bulls in Pamplona. Jesse grabbed Casey by the arm to try and stop him from dancing. "Put that thing down. I'm getting a bad feeling out here all of a sudden. A feeling like it's way past time to head for home."

Casey set the skull down. "There, I set it down. See, it's not evil. It won't hurt you. We *will* be taking this home with us, for sure. It's too cool. It's the perfect memento for our bayou trip. More than that, it's got a power all its own. Remember, Gabriel said we'd find more than we were looking for."

"I don't want that mess in my car."

Casey picked up the skull. "Don't worry; I've got an old

towel in the car. We can wrap it up. Come on. Let's go. I'll carry the skull, you get the shrooms."

Jesse could see Casey wasn't going to be talked out of it. He picked up the two grocery bags filled with magic mushrooms like a reluctant carryout boy and began walking back to where he thought the fence might be located.

Walking a straight line proved impossible. Jesse was floating through a world of mystic visions and breathing patterns of color and light in the hot, humid sunshine. He realized how thirsty he was. It occurred to him that he had more than $3,000 of illegal drugs in the bags he carried. It seemed a journey of epic proportion, but Jesse eventually found the white fence they had jumped two hours earlier. He could see Harley parked along the road about a quarter mile away. It was comforting to see something familiar, although even the dull-red Beetle seemed to be hovering several feet off the ground.

Casey slid the skull under the fence and climbed over. As Jesse pushed the bags under the fence, he realized that the contraband could land both him and Casey in jail for a long, long time. As soon as his feet hit the ground on the other side of the fence, Jesse's worst fears were realized. Some kind of police car was coming toward them on the road in the distance. It approached at a high rate of speed. In his altered state, it was impossible for Jesse to tell if the lights on top were flashing or not.

"Let's get out of here," Casey said.

"No, no, we can't run. He already sees us." Jesse said, feeling eerily calm inside. "Just act like we're on our way home from the grocery store."

"What about the skull?" Casey looked like he was getting ready to run.

"He won't see it. Here, have a cigarette. I'll light it for you."

"Oh, shit. We're going to get busted," Casey said as he

fumbled with the cigarette. "Here we are, tripping our brains out and we're going to jail. I'm going to get kicked out of law school. I'll be a failure. My family will disown me. Shit, shit, shit."

Jesse lit Casey's cigarette. "Nobody's going to jail. We're fine. Here we are, stopped for a smoke break. What could be more innocent?"

The police car whizzed by without so much as looking their way. He didn't even slow down to check the abandoned car on the side of the road. Once he was far enough down the road, Casey and Jesse collapsed in a pile of relief alongside the fence.

"Oh, man, I can't take all this," Casey said.

"Okay," Jessie said. "Here's the plan. We walk to the car without all this baggage. Then we get in the car, turn around and come back to get our stuff."

"Good plan," Casey said. "Let's get out of here before that cop comes back. I can't believe he didn't stop to check us out. One look in the bags and we'd be in handcuffs."

"He's probably late for lunch. Or maybe he's headed back to the station for shift change."

Casey pointed down at the skull. "No, I'll tell you what just happened. The Voodoo cow skull just saved our ass."

"What makes you think it's Voodoo?"

"It's Voodoo from the bayou," Casey said. "I can feel it. Look at it. It's staring back at us, like it knows more than we do. It's exactly what the mystery man, Gabriel, said we were going to find."

Jesse looked at the skull and understood what Casey was saying. The skull looked like it was trying to communicate some kind of message. The empty eye sockets and nose bones seemed to be snarling out a warning.

"What's it trying to say?" Jesse asked.

"I don't know but it doesn't look good." Casey bent down to take a closer look at the skull.

"You're the one who wants to bring it home," Jesse said.

Casey picked up the skull by both horns. "Let me tell you something about this skull. We didn't find it."

"What do you mean?" Jesse asked as he stared at Casey and the skull.

"It found us."

CHAPTER TWO

FRITZEL'S

The band had a one-bedroom apartment on Esplanade Avenue on the east side of the French Quarter. Esplanade was lined with tall trees and historic, Creole mansions. The band's apartment building was not one of those mansions. It was a modern-ugly brick building near the Mississippi River and the old U.S. Mint.

The other three members of the band were singing and working on vocal arrangements when Jesse walked in and put his two grocery bags of contraband on the narrow kitchen counter. "You're not going to believe what I got at the grocery store."

"Steaks for a week?" Butch guessed. He was the band's lead guitar player and Jesse's main songwriting partner.

"Better than that," Jesse said.

Tim, the band's fiddle and slide guitar player, had a guess of his own. "Two twelve packs of cold Coors beer?"

Dale, the band's lead vocalist and self-proclaimed "best looking guy in the band," didn't say a word. The look in Jesse's eyes said he was delivering something much stronger than beer.

"Is that what it looks like?" Butch asked, peering into one of the bags.

Jesse picked out a large mushroom and held it up for the band to see. "These came right out of cow pies on the bayou today, gentlemen. Casey and I picked them fresh this morning for your tripping pleasure. Be careful, I ate one about four hours ago and I'm just now able to carry on a conversation. The drive back to New Orleans was a killer. We had to stop every ten minutes. This shit will freak you out."

"Looks like they've still got manure all over them," Tim said.

"Let's try them out right now." Dale reached for the bag.

"No, no, we better wait." Jesse held back Dale's arm. "Believe me, these things will kick your ass. We better wait until we get set up and tuned up at Fritzel's."

"That's only an hour away," Butch said. "It's Sunday. We play 6 p.m. to midnight."

The Fritzel's gig had been a salvation for the band, known as The Divebomberz. It was six nights a week at $120 per night, plus tips, for the whole band. Before Fritzel's, the band had been so broke they spent their last $10 at the grocery store on red beans and rice. The band played on a small bandstand at the back of the club. A door to the right of the bandstand led to an open-air brick patio outside. It was in this private garden that the band gathered for its highly anticipated mushroom ceremony.

Butch had tuned up his Epiphone acoustic guitar with the Barcus Berry pickup and small Fender amp. Tim had his fiddle rigged with a similar pickup and a Marshall amp. Jesse's bass guitar ran through a small Peavey amp. The band used one of Jesse's harmonicas as a pitch pipe for tuning.

Dale was always in tune and always in costume. While the rest of the band wore blue jeans and t-shirts, Dale was in a blue, silk, flowered jump suit with sleeves as wide as his bellbottom pants.

"I believe I'll have two to start," Dale said.

Jesse handed him one. "These shrooms are strong. Start with one and see how you feel in a half hour."

"I'll start with half and see how I feel in an hour," Butch said.

"Me too," Tim said.

"I think I'll have one more just to be sociable," Jesse said.

The band ate the mushrooms and took the stage to kick off the performance with "Jambalaya" and "Hey Good Lookin" by Hank Williams. The club filled up fast for a Sunday. The crowd was singing along by the time The Divebomberz got to "Will the Circle Be Unbroken" and "Sweet Home Alabama." The band sounded great, hitting all the changes and accents perfectly, singing four-part harmony better than ever.

The magic mushrooms began kicking in about halfway through the set. Slowly but surely, the psychedelics started turning the music into something you could taste and touch and see. Rainbows began pouring out of the small but powerful speakers.

"Let's hear it for my band," Dutch shouted between songs as he rang a ship's bell near the front cash register. "First one to the register gets a free Heineken." Dutch ran his bar like a carnival barker. He was a barrel-chested, grey-haired brawler from Holland who loved to shout. He wore a ship captain's hat to emphasize his authority and hide his bald spot.

Dolly, the vivaciously plump waitress, struggled through the growing crowd to bring the band a round of frosty mugs filled with Heineken beer from the tap.

The more the shrooms elevated and intoxicated, the better the band played. The better they played, the more they cranked the volume. The louder the music, the more wild the scene became. The music created a magical loop that spiraled upward into a zany crescendo. Jesse felt like he was riding on top of a freight train. Tim's fiddle was dancing wildly with Butch's guitar. Dale's tambourine turned the euphoria into a gypsy caravan on steroids.

Fritzel's was packed with people by the last song of the set, "Daybreak and Dixie," a bluegrass classic that the band transformed into hard rock. The crowd was on its feet as the band took off like a jet airplane. The entire room, including Dutch, was getting a contact high. The music became a tunnel from the real world to a realm of fantasy and pleasure. Jesse was watching his dream come true. His bass guitar and songs and band were rocking the Bourbon Street crowd into a fever pitch. Six months earlier, he could not have imagined such a scene. Now, he was a major part of making it happen. He looked at each of his fellow band members and saw them being equally swept away by the moment.

The set ended to thunderous applause as the band retired in a full sweat to the back patio garden.

Dale took off his shirt and began drying himself off with a bar towel. "Oh, man, we sound better than ever. And I am officially tripping like a mad dog."

"I need about four beers to get back down to Earth." Tim sat down hard at one of the chairs around a glass-topped table.

Jesse passed him a thick, smoking joint of marijuana.

Tim took a massive hit and passed it on to Butch.

Butch held up his hands. "No way. I'm high enough already. I'm not even sure how I'm playing my guitar. It feels like it's playing itself."

"You sound fantastic," Jesse said. "We all do. The crowd is going wild. It's like they're getting high with us."

"We are," Casey said as he burst into the band's meeting like a magician coming through a curtain. "I've been passing out shrooms since before you got started."

He was carrying the perfectly cleaned cow skull. "Here it is boys. This is the Voodoo spirit of the bayou, from me to my good friend, Jesse. I spent the last few hours cleaning it with bleach and a brush."

The band instinctively took a collective step backward. The

skull was ominous and glowing white in the low light. The bones below where the nose used to be formed a sinister, hollow scowl. On either side of the broad, flat skull, an evil, empty, eye socket glared fiercely, knowingly. The skull presented as a spiritual force of nature.

Dale was the first to recover from the shock of the skull. "What's his name? It looks like he's mad about something."

Jesse leaned in close to his mushroom-hunting, Law School friend. "Jesus, Casey. What are you doing bringing that thing in here?"

"Don't tell me you don't love it," Casey said to the band.

Then he addressed the skull, "This is your new band, Voodoo cow skull. You're going to help them write hit songs and make it to the top of the charts."

"Is he our agent?" Tim asked.

"He's more than that," Casey said. "He's your ticket to spiritual enlightenment."

"I think I'm having enough enlightenment for one night," Butch said.

Casey put the skull down and took a hit on the joint. "How about those shrooms? The mystery man led us right to them. By the way, where are they? I need some more. I passed all mine out to the crowd."

"You did what?" Jesse asked.

"Don't worry, I'm giving them away. I'm not selling anything."

Jesse turned to look at the band and then returned his focus to Casey. "Are you out of your mind?"

"No wonder people are getting so crazy," Butch said.

"Come on, this is going to be a night to remember," Casey said. "What do we care? They were free."

"The Voodoo cow skull says pass them out," Dale said.

"Might as well share the wealth," Tim agreed.

Jesse put his hands on his hips. "You're going to cause a riot."

Casey held his hand out for more shrooms. "Perfect. Let's blow this scene into some front-page news."

The band looked at each other and then at the skull. A unanimous decision was reached without a word being spoken. It was as though the skull had dared them to add fuel to the psychedelic fire.

Jesse relented and gave Casey a large bag of shrooms. Casey left quickly, without saying thank you, to distribute them to the crowd. The band took an extended break trying to get their bearings for the next set. The cow skull hung out, sitting on the table like another member of the band. Tim was the first to ask it a question. "What song should we start the next set with?"

Jesse was surprised to find himself actually waiting for the skull to answer.

"He says come out swinging with 'The Orange Blossom Special,'" Tim said.

The band was still laughing when Dutch came back to the patio. "What's going on back here? It smells like one of your pot breaks that take too long. You've got a packed house out there. It's more than packed. It's getting dangerous. I've never seen it like this. People are lined up on Bourbon Street to get in. I don't know what's going on, but it's time to go out there and knock them dead."

Once Dutch left, each member of the band picked another magic mushroom and held it up for a toast. "Here's to knocking them dead and living to tell the tale," Jesse said.

"I'll eat to that," Dale said.

"God help us all," Butch said, chewing on another mushroom as the band went back into the bar to take the stage.

The club only sat fifty people at small tables, but it had a long wooden bar that stretched the entire length of the shotgun-style building. The header over the bar was covered with hundreds of neckties; a visual gag from Dutch about how many people had "tied one on" in his establishment. Beneath his gruff exterior, Dutch was a good-hearted jokester. Sight gags based on American sayings were his favorites. The tip jar near the cash register was always propped up to "tip" at an angle.

The band had to remove people from their playing area to begin the second set. The small bandstand was a two-level riser, slightly higher on the back. Butch and Tim were set up behind Jesse and Dale. The crowd from the street was surging into the club, pushing people forward and onto the first level of the bandstand.

Somebody outside yelled, "Mushrooms at Fritzel's!" Evidently, Casey had been spreading the word, as well as the magic mushrooms.

Jesse could tell that the night was going to get even crazier than it had already become. People were screaming with their hands in the air. Their eyes were wild and the band wasn't even playing yet.

Tim hit the first note on his fiddle and the roar of approval from the crowd almost drowned him out. The band turned up its volume as "The Orange Blossom Special" went from blue grass to rock and roll and back again. Butch's guitar was blasting a Chuck Berry rhythm under the screaming fiddle while Jesse thumped his bass hard on the one and the five of every chord. Dale had a tambourine in one hand and a shaker in the other, sounding a lot like the drummer Jesse knew the band would have to find. The musical frenzy ignited a primal response from the drug and alcohol crazed fans. They raised their arms and cheered in unison. People were standing on chairs to get a better look at the band. Jesse was overwhelmed by the crowd's enthusiasm.

He could see the crush of people trying to wedge their way into the club. The music was the only force keeping the band from getting overrun. People in back were yelling and pushing to get closer to the action. Women were climbing up on the bar to dance. A few big guys near the front were linking arms to hold back the crowd. Drunks were chugging pitchers of beer. Dolly had trouble maintaining her balance on the slippery floor and fell down with a full tray of Tequila shots splashing all over.

The room seemed to be rotating like a merry-go-round gone wild. Two delirious young women tackled Dale to the floor. He pushed them off and got back up, shaking his tambourine, without missing more than two or three measures. The temperature in the room rose to sauna bath levels. Dutch had called in his backup bartender, who was in a full sweat by the time he fought his way through the crowd and into position behind the bar. The backup waitress never did make it in. The crowd was tight as a rugby scrum. More than a hundred and fifty people had crammed into the club.

Three songs into the second set, Jesse had to stop playing momentarily to puke into a cup. The room was spinning. So was his stomach. Nothing seemed real anymore, not even his own vomit. Butch saw him do it and had to do the same. The music never faltered. The club became dangerously overcrowded. Jesse could see Dutch was having a hard time selling drinks. Customers at the bar were packed so tightly they couldn't move their arms. It was a crush of humanity.

Across the street from Fritzel's, Murphy Campo and his Jazz Saints were playing to an empty house. Next door, Johnny Horn and his Jazz Giants had a roomful of nothing but chairs. The neighboring club owners were not happy with the hippie happening at Fritzel's.

It had been Johnny Horn who sat Jesse down three weeks earlier in the back patio to impart the facts of life about the music business. "Here's the way it is," the older trumpet player said in his raspy, cigarette voice. "We're all whores in this business. What you've got to decide is whether you're a cheap whore or an expensive whore."

That important lesson was on Jesse's mind as the crowd grew ever more wild and crazy. He was feeling expensive.

Near the end of the extra-long set, between songs, Jesse heard what sounded like someone speaking through a bullhorn. The garbled sound was coming from Bourbon Street, behind what could only be described as a mob scene. Whoever it was, he was beginning to make the crowd settle down. Eventually, Jesse could hear what was being said through the bullhorn.

"This is the New Orleans Police Department. You are in violation of the city noise ordinance. Your decibel levels are too high. You must stop playing immediately."

It was obvious the police could no more gain access to the bar than anyone else. But they had a bullhorn, and they were warning anyone who could hear them that further police action was imminent. The band looked at Jesse for a heads up on what to do.

Jesse said to Butch, "Never argue with a man with a microphone." He was referring to himself, not the bullhorn operator.

"Don't do it, Jesse," Butch warned.

"This is the New Orleans Police," the man with the bullhorn said again. "You are in violation of the city noise ordinance. We will start making arrests if you don't stop playing and clear this area."

The crowd booed loudly. So loudly they drowned out the bullhorn.

Jesse quieted them down. His microphone was louder than

the bullhorn. "Okay, everybody quiet down. I need to talk to the police. Please, be quiet so the police can hear what I have to say."

A hush fell over the crowd. Even the bullhorn operator seemed curious and ready to listen.

"Thank you, ladies and gentlemen, for your cooperation. I have something to say to the New Orleans Police Department. Are you ready to hear it?"

"Yea!" everybody in the crowd screamed.

"I said are you ready to hear it?"

"Yea!" everybody screamed again, as if it was possible to get any louder.

A small voice inside Jesse's head told him not to proceed. He paid it no heed. A darker force was driving him. A force that told him he had the hottest band in the world and that the rules no longer applied to him or anybody he knew.

"All right, then. Here's what I have to say to the New Orleans Police Department." He made the crowd wait a full ten seconds before he shouted into the microphone.

"Fuck you, pigs. Fuck the New Orleans Police. Go back to your pigsty. We're having a private party here. Go fuck yourselves."

Pandemonium erupted. The cheer from the crowd sounded like some football star had just scored the winning touchdown as time ran out in the game.

The band kicked into "Little Liza Jane," and the party rocked on as though the evil police had finally met their match and been defeated forever. The bullhorn operator didn't try to compete with the rock and roll hysteria. The band played on with all the wild determination of a herd of horses that just broke through the gate. Jesse saw Dale looking at him with profound admiration. Butch, on the other hand, looked at him like he knew the episode would not end well. Tim kept playing fiddle like he was welcoming the Devil to New Orleans.

Victory was short lived. Eleven minutes to be exact.

As the band was bringing their extended version of "Liza Jane" to a frenzied conclusion, the lights went out like a knockout punch. The music stopped like Death itself changed the channel. A shocked silence pierced the room for a brief moment until it was replaced by a collective howl of disapproval from the disoriented crowd. Shouts of confusion from the crowd turned into screams of panic. The total lack of light disoriented those who were already hallucinating. The sudden darkness left the crowd with nowhere to turn. Desperate souls pushed and punched and shoved and clawed for whatever exit they could find. All Jesse could see in the sudden blackness was the cow skull from the bayou, flashing on and off in the darkest corner of his brain like a subconscious neon sign. He thought he heard it say something, but when he listened again, there was nothing.

The band put down their instruments as best they could in the darkness and groped their way back to the patio garden. Butch lit his lighter. Even in his frightened state, he had to chuckle at the jack-o-lantern faces gathered around. "Looks like we really fucked up this time. Nice work, Jesse. Way to be diplomatic with the cops. Who's ready to go to jail?"

Jesse hung his head. "I'll go. I'm the one who got crazy on the microphone."

"I say we climb the wall and get out of here," Dale said.

Tim sat down cautiously. "Let's just stay back here and hope they don't arrest us."

Dutch walked in, carrying a lantern that was bright enough to light up the entire patio. "Time to pack up your gear and get out of here. I can't have horseshit like this going on in my club.

I don't know what you did to make the crowd so crazy but that thing with the police was more than wrong. I might get shut down for good. So guess what. You're fired."

Dutch turned around and walked out, leaving the band in the dark. Nobody lit a lighter. Darkness was appropriate for the moment. It took a few minutes before their eyes gradually adjusted to the starlight of the patio and the lights from adjoining buildings. Fritzel's was the only club to have its plug pulled.

Butch fumbled for a chair and sat down. "Feels like it's time for a band meeting, but I think I'm too high to concentrate."

"Let's not do anything until the lights come back on," Tim said. "Maybe the police won't come looking for us."

The police never did enter the club to arrest anyone. They had an extremely tolerant attitude toward musicians. In three months at Fritzel's, the band had been busted four times outside the club for smoking marijuana. Each time, the officers simply confiscated the weed and let them go. Musicians were expected to be eccentric and creative. The cops gave them room to move and license to explore. After all, it was the musicians of New Orleans who gave Jazz to the world. They called it Jazz because the girls in the brothels where the bands played wore jasmine perfume.

Knowing the *laissez-faire* attitude of the police, Jesse had been emboldened on the microphone. What he hadn't counted on was the political clout of the nearby club owners who were losing customers to the psychedelic party next door.

When the lights came back on at Fritzel's, about an hour later, The Divebomberz piled most of their gear into the van parked outside on the street. It took longer than usual since they were too disoriented to organize much of anything. They couldn't get everything into the vehicle, and ended up dragging their instruments and microphone stands out to Bourbon Street like a squad of wounded soldiers after a brutal firefight.

Dutch was nowhere to be found. The club looked like a tornado had touched down. Tables and chairs were broken and turned over, shattered glass and spilled booze covered the floor. The window over the front door was smashed. Garments had been left behind. A blond wig was pinned to the ground by a chair with only three legs. Two Mardi Gras posters had been ripped off the wall and stomped to death at the entrance.

Dutch wasn't about to deal with what had happened to his beloved speakeasy. He left the mess for Dolly and the backup bartender to clean.

The Divebomberz retired to the private patio of a friend to drink the night away and lick their wounds. Nobody took any more mushrooms. By sunrise, it was beginning to dawn on Jesse that his band had lost their only source of income.

CHAPTER THREE

SAUCE PIQUANTE

It was hard for Jesse to admit to himself that his showboating had caused so much trouble for the band. He tried to blame the police, the neighboring club owners and even Dutch.

Dale finally had to sit him down for a little talk. "You have nobody to blame but yourself. You know you can be your own worst enemy. You want so much to be the center of attention that you'll do almost anything to get there."

Jesse had to smile at the irony of the situation. "Odd that you, the lead singer, would be talking to me about needing to be the center of attention."

"I might be the lead singer but you're the one who leads us into all kinds of illegal activity."

"It wasn't me who called the cops." Jesse tried to defend himself.

"No, but it was you who got half of Bourbon Street tripping their brains out and then told the cops to fuck off."

Jesse finally had to hang his head in shame. He'd been getting into trouble to get attention since his class clown days in school. He knew Dale was right. "What do you think I should do?"

Dale was ready for that question. "You should come with me and we'll go apologize to Dutch."

Jesse looked up hopefully. "Do you think he'll hire us back?"

"That's not the point," Dale said. "The point is we owe him an apology."

Dutch was waiting behind the bar when Jesse and Dale walked in and took a seat on two stools. He continued washing shot glasses and glared at Jesse as if daring him to speak.

"I'm sorry," Jesse said.

Dutch kept washing. "Sorry for what?"

"Sorry for being such an idiot."

Dutch pressed him. "Being such an idiot about what?"

Jesse lowered his forehead almost to the bar and then looked up. "First of all, for bringing drugs into your club. I can promise you that will never happen again."

"What makes you think you'll have the chance?"

"And second, for being disrespectful to the police."

"That's it?"

"And for disrespecting you and your club. You deserve better. You've always treated us right."

Dutch looked at Dale. "And what have you got to say for yourself?"

Dale wasn't about to join Jesse in the groveling. "I'd like to order two Heinekens, unless they're still on the house."

Dutch turned to fill two frosty mugs and banged them down on the bar. "They're still on the house."

Dale took a big swig of beer and set the mug down on the bar. "Actually, Dutch, I need to join Jesse in apologizing to you. We let things get way out of hand and we're all sorry. We never meant to disrespect you or get you in trouble with the law. You've always been good to us."

Dutch filled up a third mug of beer for himself and drank half of it before setting it down next to Jesse and Dale's mugs. "All I really want to know is what the Hell happened? I've never seen my bar so crowded and out of control."

Jesse decided it was time to come clean. "What happened

was we got a bunch of psychedelic mushrooms and passed them out to the crowd. I was tripping my brains out when I got stupid on the microphone with the cops."

Dutch took another long drink of beer. "Well, that does explain it. I know drugs can turn people into wild animals. So, I tell you this. I will accept your apology if you promise nothing like this will ever happen again."

"Deal," Jesse said as the three men raised their mugs to clink them together.

The band was back onstage at Fritzel's four days after the police pulled the plug. No city action was ever taken against Dutch or his club. He didn't even get a noise ordinance ticket.

The band played on at Fritzel's for the next four months, six nights a week. The schedule was grueling but they continued to pack the club every night. They were making good money, including tips and free drinks. Bourbon Street became a blur, but Jesse got to know the French Quarter and all its characters quite well.

One night, he thought he saw the mystery man from the bayou in front of Fritzel's. He went out to check, but whoever it was had left.

Jesse searched the street for a few minutes. The hair on the back of his neck stood up. He could smell the mystery man getting out of the rain and into his car. He remembered how disoriented he felt when Gabriel disappeared from the side of the road. Jesse knew something big was about to happen.

Back inside the club, he found Dale and Tim talking to a stocky, longhaired man with a thick, Cajun accent. The man looked Caucasian but he sounded like a Jamaican from Brooklyn.

"I hear you're looking for a drummer," the man said, reaching out to Jesse for a handshake. "I'm Rene."

Jesse shook his hand and smiled.

"He's got a big P.A.," Dale said.

Jesse opened his arms wide. "A drummer with a sound system? Are you kidding me? You are the answer to our prayers. I've been looking for you for months. You're hired. When can you start?"

"Right now. You got any drums?"

Dale jumped up from his chair. "We sure do. We've got bongos and an extra microphone. We'll mike you up."

"Great," Rene said. "I've been listening for a set and a half now. I love what you guys are doing. It's like Zydeco only more rock."

Butch came in from the back patio to join them at the table. "What's going on?"

"Nothing much," Dale said. "We just hired the best drummer in the bayou. People call him Bam Bam."

Rene held his hands in the air, palms up. "Please, call me Rene."

Butch looked at Jesse and Dale in disbelief and then introduced himself to Rene. "So, you're the best drummer in the bayou?"

"No, I never said that. But I have been listening to you guys. You got something special going on. I'd love to be a part of it."

"We're thinking of miking him up on my bongos for the next set," Dale said.

Butch took a long swig on his Heineken, and set it back down on the table. "Why not? Let's give it a shot. We can't get out of this place without a drummer. Let's see how it feels."

It took only two verses and one chorus of the first song for Jesse to realize the band had found their drummer. Rene didn't follow the beat; he pushed it. His timing was great. He wasn't busy. He didn't play too many notes. Even on bongos, he kept it simple and gave the band the extra drive it needed.

By the time the first set with Rene was done, The Divebomberz had become a five-piece band.

Jesse felt his prayers had been answered. The band needed a drummer. He knew they couldn't progress without the rocking beat of a kick drum with a snare and a high hat and toms and cymbals.

They needed to evolve musically. The four-man singing group was in constant danger of slipping into a barbershop quartet rut. A drummer would spread things out and give the instrumentation more room to develop. They could become more electric and less acoustic.

A drummer brings the beat, and the beat is the heart of a lot more than rock and roll. It makes hips move and moneymakers shake and shoulders shimmy. It's the Bristol Stomp and the Boogaloo and the Twist and the Locomotion all rolled into one.

Rene brought the jungle beat. He could be primitive and even brutal, or he could sound distant messages from hollow logs filled with jazz and classical roots.

Jesse knew the band needed to get out of Fritzel's. The club was too small and they'd been there every night for way too long.

The drunks on Bourbon Street had become more than tedious. Every night, somebody knew somebody who was going to make the band rock stars. Tales get taller with each drink. Lies get larger. People make promises they can't keep just so they can talk to the band. The Divebomberz had gotten quite good and tight as a musical unit, playing more than six hours a night. It was one long rehearsal. The vocals got better, the starts and stops more crisp and the fiddle and guitar leads more intricately interwoven. The set list of songs got longer and more diversified.

More importantly, they were still getting along as friends

and having fun working together. They were united by their common determination to succeed in the music industry. But after nearly a year, Bourbon Street had lost its luster. The glamour was gone. The famous street began to feel like the gutter. By 3 a.m., it smelled more like the sewer. Amateur drunks piss on the sidewalk and puke a lot.

Jesse knew he needed to get the band playing at Tipitina's or Judah P's or The Fais Do-Do. The larger, uptown clubs required a drummer.

Rene came along at the perfect time.

The band was ready to graduate from the Bourbon Street School of Entertainment and find a way to get their songs on the radio.

Rene took the band to new heights right away.

The first time he played a full drum kit with The Divebomberz was a party at his parents' three-bedroom, ranch-style home in Raceland, on Bayou Lafourche.

The large living room was packed with a Cajun crowd as the band did its first sound check on Rene's monster P.A. He had towers of main speakers, five monitor speakers and six microphones for his drums, all running through a 16-channel Peavey board with Crown power amps.

After a few horrifying rounds of feedback screech, the band kicked off with their standard opener, "Jambalaya."

The sound was so strong it nearly knocked people off the couches. Little children covered their ears. Adults spilled their drinks on the carpeted floor. Jesse signaled the band to stop.

"Too much?" he whispered into the mike.

"Too much," everybody yelled back, waiving hands at the band like that would somehow turn the volume down.

Rene spoke into his microphone. "Okay, sorry everybody. Let's turn everything way down and only use the vocal mikes."

"Do you have any brushes?" Tim asked Rene.

"Don't get carried away. I'm not some kind of jazz drummer here."

The band was still loud after the major turndown on volume but they sounded powerful and complete and wonderful. Dale nodded his head to Jesse in wide-eyed approval as the band rocked on. Butch and Tim were obviously enjoying the ride as well.

"This is the biggest thrill I've had with my pants on," Butch said after the first song.

"Sounds like we've been playing together for years," Tim said.

Jesse recalled one night of humiliation at a big club on Magazine Street. A few hecklers had booed them for not having a drummer or a big enough sound. Let them boo us now, he thought. We won't even hear them.

The Divebomberz played twenty songs in a row that first night with Rene. There were some rough edges but they sounded pretty darn good. By the time they finished, a crowd had gathered on the front lawn, cheering the band on and listening through the open windows.

"Looks like we're going to be bigger and better than ever," Dale said as three people tried to hand him a drink after the impromptu show.

Rene's father was beaming with pride. "You boys are going to be huge, Look at all the people outside. You attracted quite a crowd. The house isn't big enough to hold them all. They're still out there, hollering for more."

Butch took off his guitar and settled down in a cushioned chair with a beer. "Amazing. It finally feels right."

Tim came over to give Butch a triumphant hug. "All we needed was an ass-kicking, Cajun drummer named Bam Bam."

Jesse was unstrapping his bass guitar when he thought he heard a voice. At first, he couldn't understand it. The sound was far away, but it kept getting closer. He looked around the room to see where it might be coming from. He listened more closely. It was the deep voice of an African man, sounding ominous. The more it resonated, the more Jesse realized the voice was coming from inside his own head.

"Welcome to my world," the voice said.

"What was that?" Jesse asked out loud.

"What was what?" Butch responded.

Jesse sat down next to Butch so no one else could hear. "I wasn't talking to you. It's something I heard."

Butch looked at him like he was joking.

"No, really, I just heard a voice say 'welcome to my world.'"

"Are you eating shrooms again?"

Jesse shook his head "no" as he put his hands over his ears. He looked up at the ceiling and then back at Butch. "This voice came from someplace outside my head, but it's not something I'm hearing with my ears. And I think I know who it is. Or what it is."

"What is it?" Butch played along.

"It's the Voodoo cow skull. The one you met the night the lights went out at Fritzel's."

"I wouldn't say I met anybody," Butch said. "I saw a cow skull. A dead cow's skull. And may I emphasize the word 'dead'?"

"I'm telling you it said to me quite clearly, in this deep, rumbling voice, 'welcome to my world.'"

"I never heard the skull talk. What makes you think it was the skull?"

Jesse took his hands off his ears. "I get the same feeling from the voice I do from the skull."

Dale came over to join them. "What are you two rock stars talking about?"

"Jesse says the cow skull is talking to him."

Dale clapped his hands together. "I knew it. That skull is nothing but Voodoo from the bayou. What did it say?"

Jesse gave Butch the evil eye for divulging his secret voice. "It said, 'Welcome to my world.'"

Dale thought about the statement. "Welcome to my world? What does that mean? Is it a good thing or a bad thing? I wonder if the skull is talking about us finally getting our drummer? Did you make a deal with the Devil?"

"Apparently I have," Jesse said as Tim and Rene joined the group meeting.

"You have what?" Tim asked.

"Made a deal with the devil to get Rene as our drummer," Jesse said.

"Hey, man," Rene protested. "We don't need no devil for this deal. I think we sounded great. What about you guys? Come on, now, how'd I do?"

Dale threw his arms around Rene. "You make us sound like a big time band."

Butch joined in on the hug. "I'll second that emotion."

The congratulations and backslapping went around as each member of the new and improved Divebomberz made toast after toast. Nobody seemed at all concerned about the voice inside Jesse's head. Eventually, even Jesse stopped thinking about it.

The conversation evolved into a group embrace that ended with the band in a huddle, humming a long, Buddhist "Om." Jesse started it as low as his voice would go. Everybody joined hands and slowly raised the pitch. As the pitch elevated, they raised their hands and threw them in the air as they shouted in celebration.

After the chant, they looked at each other in solemn silence as if to acknowledge the significance of the moment. There would be no turning back. It was time to fasten the safety belts.

Less than three weeks after their first rehearsal as a full band at Rene's parents' home, the five members of The Divebomberz were getting ready to take the stage in front of five thousand screaming fans at the Sauce Piquante Festival in Raceland, Louisiana. They had only rehearsed five times since the party at Rene's house. It was tough finding a place to rehearse as a full band. Five rehearsals wasn't much time to work in a drummer. Jesse was more than nervous. He was coming to grips with his first real bout of stage fright. He couldn't believe the huge crowd. It made his intestinal tract queasy. His underarms smelled like panic.

Butch scanned the sea of sweaty bodies glistening in the August, afternoon sun. "These people don't know how to pace themselves. It's not even five o'clock. They're so loaded they won't make it to sunset."

Dale was pacing around the back of the stage. "Look at that crowd. That's a lot of people. They're sweating as much as we are, and I'll bet they're not close to being nervous. I'll get us a round of beer. We need to stay hydrated. We need to jack up our levels. Tim, you better roll us a rock-concert joint."

Tim put down his fiddle next to his slide guitar and got out some papers and pot. "I always wanted to play to a crowd like this, but I never felt this sick to my stomach in my dreams. I'm actually freaking out. I just hope the sound guys get our levels right."

The Divebomberz was the third of four bands scheduled for

the day. Rene's father had secured the late booking when one of the previously scheduled bands had to cancel. He had also taken over keeping the band's financial records, saying they needed a more business-like approach.

Three soundmen were scurrying onstage to set up Rene's drums and adjust amps and microphones for the rest of the band. Adjusting sound from one band to the next is always a hit and miss process.

Jesse grabbed a cold beer from Dale. "Thanks, man. It's good to be with you on this momentous occasion."

Dale stopped pacing. "We've come a long way from our little singing trio in the basement of Mother's Tavern in Fort Wayne, Indiana."

"A long way, indeed," Jesse said as he threw his arms around Dale. "You know I love you, my brother."

"And I love you. None of this would have happened without you."

"And you," Jesse backed out of the hug. "Looks like there won't be time for a sound check. They'll have to get our levels on the fly. What about the crowd? You think we're going to go over? We're not exactly the Zydeco they're used to."

Rene joined them for a little encouragement. "Relax. These are my people. They're going to love us. We'll give them something different, something that rocks a little harder than they're used to. Look at them. They're ready for us. They won't even know what hit them."

Jesse and Dale laughed with Rene as Tim and Butch joined in to fire up a joint. The band was standing behind a wall of speakers. Tim fired up the number he had just rolled. "Hit it fast. No one will notice. This whole festival's going up in smoke."

A haze hovered above the crowd. Beyond the sea of people, Jesse could see carnival rides rising above the craft booth flags and colorful, animal signs of the food vendors. The smell of spicy Cajun recipes for gumbo, red beans and rice, wild game, chicken, sausage, alligator, and turtle wafted through the air. Layers of flavor combined with the wood smoke and bacon aroma coming from the hog boucherie. The pungent smell of marijuana smoke mixed into the atmosphere like one more pepper in the gumbo pot.

Jesse pointed to the side of the stage. "Look down there. Amy's selling Divebomberz t-shirts as fast as she can count the money."

Amy was Jesse's girlfriend who'd recently come down from Indiana to live with him. She had arrived in a TR6 sport car, which she and Jesse traded in for what became the band van. Amy had become somewhat of a patron saint for the band. She even designed and silk-screened the band t-shirts.

Amy looked up at the band and waved happily and held up fistfuls of cash when she saw them looking down at her. She was a long-legged girl with thin ankles and an ass that would not quit under any circumstances. She was small breasted and square shouldered with an aristocratic neck and a face that looked like a cross between Cher and Katherine Hepburn.

Jesse held his hands out to her. "That woman is a marvel."

Butch waved. "That woman is wanting you to put a ring on her finger."

"That might not be such a terrible thing," Dale said.

Jesse turned back to the band. "No need to be in such a rush, boys."

The crowd was getting restless. They started chanting, "We want The Divebomberz. We want The Divebomberz."

"How do they even know who we are?" Tim asked. "We're not on any of the promotional material."

Butch pointed at the crowd. "It's the t-shirts. Look, I see at least a dozen people wearing them already."

Jesse shielded his eyes to assess the crowd. "I'm beginning to see how this business works."

"It's all about the merchandise," Dale said.

Rene clapped his hands. "Time to go, boys. Right now, we are the merchandise. Let's start this show off with a group 'Om' at the lead microphone. That'll show them we mean business."

Jesse didn't like Rene taking such a leadership role, but he had to admit it was a great idea. The band walked out, single file, and formed a huddle around the lead microphone as the crowd roared its approval. Once the "Om" began, the audience immediately fell into a curious silence.

The "Om" grew louder and higher pitched, erupting into a shouting cheer from the band that was quickly buried by thunderous applause from the delighted audience. By the time the cheering began to subside, the band was on their instruments and blasting off with "Sweet Home Alabama" by Lynyrd Skynyrd. A wave of energy from the crowd nearly swept the five musicians off their feet. It was inspirational. Jesse had never felt the physical and emotional rush of such a large crowd. It took his breath away.

On one hand, the crowd was an intimidating life force. It was a huge, growling beast, ready and able to devour the stage and everybody on it.

On the other hand, Jesse realized the mass of humanity in front of him was that same beast, begging to be fed. He felt like a lion tamer performing in the circus. The music was both his whip and red meat treat. His bass sounded massive through the arena sound system. It felt like he was moving the entire crowd with his own heartbeat.

Rene's kick drum was in perfect sync with the bass. Powerful enough to thump the audience in the chest and let them know this band meant business. Playing for a crowd this big had been a dream for Jesse and the rest of the band. Now that the moment was upon them, it almost didn't feel real. It was like being washed over by a tidal wave. People were waving their arms in the air like they were witnessing the second coming of the Messiah.

These people aren't being judgmental, Jesse realized. They're cheering us on. All they want to do is party. He wished his father could see him now. He'd see that practicing law wasn't the only way for a lawyer's son to make a living.

Tim was playing slide on a steel guitar for the opening song. The man was a natural born musician. At twenty years old, he was the youngest member of the band. He could play anything. And he did it with no fingers on his left hand. He had been a promising guitar player until the age of eighteen when he cut off all four fingers on his left hand in a power saw accident. At first, everybody thought his musical career was over. But the horrible injury didn't stop him. It didn't even slow him down.

He started playing steel guitar with a slide doing all the work for his missing fingers. Then, he took up the fiddle. He had to play it backwards, bowing with his damaged left hand and fingering the strings with his right.

Today, his face was filled with triumph as he felt his musical rebirth coming of age. He and Butch were weaving rhythms and leads with their electric guitars like they were tying the crowd to the whipping post. Jesse watched Dale singing and dancing like he'd been a rock star his entire life. He took to the big crowd like a pro surfer to a wave. At one point, Dale leaped into the air and landed into a double spin move with athleticism Jesse didn't know he had. When he got to the famous line in the "Sweet Home Alabama" song, "A southern man don't need him around, anyhow," the Cajun cheers were louder than the music. Dale took a solo bow. The band was rocking so steady by the end of the song that they kept playing it straight through for a second time. The crowd cheered them on and went wild as they finally ended with a crunching, full-band stop.

By the third song of the set, people started scrambling onto the stage in their excitement. There was no security to stop them. One woman in a long skirt and tank top wrapped her arms and legs around Dale, who couldn't shake her. Two skinny boys with no shirts tried to take Butch's guitar out of his hands. The band was being overwhelmed.

That's when The Divebomberz met The Wheelers, the toughest motorcycle gang on Bayou Lafourche. They were so tough they were the *only* biker gang on the bayou, ruling hundreds of miles of two-lane highway.

Five Wheelers, with flaming-wheel "colors" on their black leather vests, took it upon themselves to restore order to the event. Overzealous fans went flying off the stage like they'd been shot out of cannons. The Wheelers were tossing people like dwarves. There were a few bruises and a little bloodshed but, all in all, it was an effective sweep of the stage. The crowd cheered every time somebody went airborne, and they groaned in appreciation each time they caught a flying person on their outstretched arms, then bounced them up and down like they'd landed on a human trampoline.

One of the biggest Wheelers grabbed the girl off Dale by her ankles and swung her offstage. Her skirt came over her head, revealing polka dot panties. She could only guess why the men were cheering. She was flying blind.

The stage was four feet above the ground. It looked like she would be seriously injured until the crowd caught her on a cushion of outstretched arms. Amazed at their collective capacity, people passed the girl around like she was a boat on the water. Many others who were forcibly flung were also caught in the safety net of hands over heads. Except for one poor guy, who got thrown hard and low. He bowled over several rows of people like pins at a bowling alley.

Once the crowd realized it could support human bodies and pass them around overhead, the games began. People started climbing onstage just to get tossed onto the crowd. The Wheelers were only too happy to oblige.

Minor injuries notwithstanding, it was a great moment, a historic moment, although no one appreciated it at the time. The Divebomberz, The Wheelers, and the Raceland crowd had brought the mosh pits of New York punk rock to the outdoor concerts of the bayou.

The band played on behind the protective screen of the motorcycle gang. For the next few songs, the crowd seemed as interested in passing bodies as in cheering on the band. Even so, the energy level continued to increase, particularly when Tim pulled out his fiddle and the band kicked into its electric bluegrass numbers.

By the ninth song of a fourteen-song set, The Divebomberz needed a water break. The afternoon sun and intense energy of the big crowd had dehydrated them. They were soaked through their jeans in sweat.

Dale had his hands on his knees. "Man, I thought we were in better shape than this. Since when do we have to take a break in the middle of a set?"

Butch took a breath from guzzling water out of a half-gallon jug. "Since our first show on a big stage in ninety degree heat and ninety percent humidity."

Tim pointed to the audience. "Look out there. Even the crowd is beat. Nobody's getting passed around anymore."

The muscleman longhair in charge of The Wheelers came over to join the band. "I'm Dupre, You guys are great; best band we've heard in a long time. Hope you don't mind the protection."

Jesse stepped up to introduce himself and the members of the band. "You saved our show, Dupre. We can't thank you enough."

"Mind if me and the boys get some of that good water?"

Dale handed him a jug of water. "Come on, step right up. We've got water and beer and some outrageous smoke."

The Wheelers were happy to be invited into the band's inner sanctum. The combination of sweat, booze, and marijuana smoke smelled like a Rastafarian recording studio after an all night session in Kingston with no air conditioning. They were brothers in arms, temporary survivors of a life and death struggle against the outdated rules of the world. Their unspoken bond was strong. As musicians and bikers, they were swashbuckling rebels who made a lot of noise, broke more laws than they obeyed and looked as much like pirates as possible.

The crowd cheered restlessly as they watched the band and the bikers taking a water and smoke break together onstage.

Dupre handed back the water jug. "Okay, time to get back to work. It's show time."

"Let's kick some ass," Rene said as he bounced onto the stool behind his drum kit.

Jesse was taking a last guzzle on a pitcher of ice water when he heard the Voodoo voice speak to him for the second time.

"Drink deep, boy. You got to keep running."

The band was kicking off the next song before Jesse could fully comprehend what had been said to him. It sounded like the voice was being beamed into his head by the sweltering rays of the fading August sun. It had been weeks since he first heard it. This time it wasn't sarcastic. It was stern. Hearing the voice a second time assured him he really had heard it the first time. He had begun to think he only imagined it. In a way, he was relieved to hear the voice again, although it still filled him with foreboding.

Jesse associated the voice with the bayou cow skull. He and his girlfriend, Amy, had tried to get the skull to talk on many occasions. It was hanging on a brick wall in their third floor apartment on Tchoupitoulas Street. It wouldn't talk, no matter what they did. Jesse could tell that Amy was beginning to worry about his mental health.

Jesse knew the entire band was as skeptical about the voice as Amy. Except for Dale, the lead singer, who said on more than one occasion that he believed the voice was real. He was certain the cow skull was a Voodoo spirit sent to guide the band through the perilous waters of the music business. "This thing has come back from the dead. Spirits don't come back from the dead for no good reason. They've always got a purpose."

As the band rocked hard through the rest of its set at the Raceland festival, Jesse couldn't wait to tell everybody he'd heard the rock and roll Voodoo voice speak again. Now, they would have to believe him.

Or would they? He was still the only one hearing the voice. The band might think he was crazier than ever. Why would they believe him the second time if they hadn't believed him the first time? He decided to keep the second episode of the voice to himself.

The crowd screamed for an encore at the end of the set. The band was ready to give them one but the promoter hustled them offstage to make way for the headline act, a legendary but still regional Zydeco band.

In what seemed like an instant, The Divebomberz went from being stars of the show to being part of the audience. It was an ego-crushing experience; like watching a good-looking stranger stealing your woman.

Jesse learned that it takes an accordion to bring out the best in a Cajun crowd. A fiddle is fine, but Cajun music is Zydeco. And Zydeco is all about the accordion.

Jesse thought about the mystery man from the bayou telling him to come to the bayou to get an accordion player. Then he wondered if Gabriel was somehow connected to the Voodoo voice.

Jesse looked over both his shoulders, scanning the crowd, half expecting to see Gabriel hovering over the crowd like a Voodoo angel.

The man was nowhere to be seen.

Once the show was over, The Divebomberz packed their gear into Rene's pickup truck and Jesse's van. Amy threw six empty boxes into the van.

Dale held the van door open for her. "What's with the empty boxes?"

Amy was out of breath. "We sold out of t-shirts. All we've got left is empty boxes. That's a hundred and three shirts sold and two given away to Rene's parents for setting up the gig. At ten bucks a shirt, we took in more than a thousand dollars."

Butch was surprised by the sales. "That's more than the seven hundred fifty we made for the gig."

"Don't feel bad," Amy said. "It was the band that sold the shirts, not me. All it means is you made $1,750 for the gig, minus about two fifty in costs for the shirts. So, the band made fifteen hundred in one day."

Dale held both hands over his head. "That's a record, for sure."

Butch gave him an overhead hand slap. "Too bad we can't do that every day."

Tim joined in on the hand smacking. "Who says we can't?"

Jesse was doing the math in his head. "What say we split the seven fifty at one fifty per man and put the rest in the bank for expenses?"

As the band was agreeing to the deal and dividing up the money, The Wheelers thundered up on their motorcycles and stopped to say goodbye. They covered the band in dust and exhaust fumes.

Dupre shouted loud enough to be heard. "Where you guys playing next?"

"We'll be in Gretna and Thibodaux and then at the Safari Club in about a month," Rene yelled back.

"See you there." Dupre waved and kicked his motorcycle into gear.

With that, thirty-three custom Harleys rumbled off and thundered down the road with enough ground-shaking power to ripple the bayou waters.

CHAPTER FOUR

CARMEN

Jesse decided not to tell even Amy about hearing the voice for the second time. She was busy looking for a teaching job. He didn't want to trouble her. He felt superstition beginning to take control of his mind. Maybe there was a Voodoo doll somewhere with his name on it?

Was it even Voodoo he was encountering? He knew nothing about Voodoo, but there were many in New Orleans who claimed to be expert on the subject. They had shops on Bourbon Street that sold herbs and charms and amulets for healing or protection. They told fortunes for a fee. Most of them were con artists. One woman seemed to be the real deal. She was a tall, Creole woman of French descent who called herself Carmen. Months earlier, Jesse had been introduced to her by Ruthie the duck lady.

Ruthie was a French Quarter character: an older, white woman who constantly roamed the streets with one or two ducks on a string. She looked like a bag lady in the beat-up, plaid housecoat she always wore. She was either crazy or pretending to be. It didn't matter. She knew The Quarter as well or better than anyone.

Ruthie brought Carmen to hear the band at Fritzel's. Jesse paid attention. He was instinctively attracted to the woman with the aristocratic bearing. She held her chin up in a way that seemed more curious than snobby. She had red hair tied up in a bun on top of her head. Red lipstick made her fair skin look pale. Her blue eyes shined confidently, as though they could see through all pretense. Her prominent but graceful nose twitched occasionally as though she was experiencing the world through a dog's highly elevated sense of smell.

Dutch, ever the gracious club owner, welcomed Ruthie and Carmen to Fritzel's and brought them glasses of his best red wine. His bow to the local celebrities was so low and reverent his head nearly touched the floor.

Carmen was an accomplished flirt. "Thank you so much, Dutch. You know I love you." He smiled broadly. The legends of The French Quarter knew each other well.

Dutch returned to tend his bar. Ruthie listened with pleasure as Jesse and Carmen became acquainted quickly and joyfully. They were eager to learn what they could about each other. Carmen was as interested in rock and roll as Jesse was in Voodoo. Their attraction was vaguely sexual at first, but morphed quickly into something far more intimate. Early in the conversation, Carmen put her hand up to Jesse's flowing, white-boy Afro. "May I touch your hair?"

Jesse took her hand and guided it to the curls dangling down his chest. At the same time he put his other hand around her neck and touched the hair on the back of her head. "Only if I can touch yours."

As they touched each other's hair, Carmen took a deep breath. "You will need my help someday soon. Come to me for guidance and I will give it to you freely."

It sounded like more than a ploy to get him to buy trinkets. She sounded like destiny calling. They didn't spend as much time together on their first meeting as either one of them would have liked. Jesse had a set to play and Carmen had to get back to her shop.

Jesse hadn't seen Carmen since their first meeting but he had often thought of her. Now that he needed to know more about Voodoo, she was the only one to consult.

He walked cautiously into Madame Carmen's House of Voodoo, a small shop one block off Bourbon Street on Saint Ann Street. The place smelled like incense and lavender candles and patchouli oil. The walls were packed with masks and rattles and bracelets and beads and tarot cards and jewelry and Voodoo dolls with more accessories than Barbie.

An antique cash register rested quite officially on top of a glass jewelry case. No one seemed to be tending shop.

"Hello," he called out.

A rustling behind the beaded curtain in back caught his attention just in time to see Carmen come gliding out to greet him. She was dressed in a red silk blouse and wearing more makeup than he remembered. Her lashes were so long that when she closed her eyes it looked like curtains dropping on a stage.

She offered her hand. "Hello, hello, I've been expecting you."

Jesse kissed her hand self-consciously. "Do you even remember me?"

"Yes, yes, your name is Jesse and you used to play at Fritzel's but now your band is too big for The Quarter."

"How do you know that?"

"I am a Voodoo queen, a direct descendant of Marie Laveau. I know everything."

"Come on," Jesse said.

"Actually, Ruthie the duck lady keeps me posted."

Jesse laughed at her honesty. "That's more like it. So, who is this Marie Laveau you're talking about?"

"Oh, you have so much to learn. Come in back with me."

"What about customers?"

Carmen turned around to smile at him. "Not to worry. Did you not notice how the old floor creaks?"

She led him back into her lair.

Jesse expected to see a crystal ball on a table, but he was ushered into a large office, packed with books and charts and a modern typewriter and telephone. There were two wooden chairs, one on either side of a massive, hand-carved, mahogany desk.

Carmen sat in the large chair. "Come, sit with me. Don't worry, I'm not charging you. I remember my promise. I made it not so long ago. This is not about money. This is about you and me. So, how can I help you?"

Jesse took his seat obediently. "Let me get right to it. I need to learn about Voodoo. What is it? What can it do? Where does it come from?"

Carmen reached across the desk and held his hands in hers. She closed her eyes and said nothing. Her hands were rough but not callused. Jesse could smell her lavender hand soap along with hints of jasmine perfume and peppermint body oil. Her fragrance was fresh and exotic.

"I feel you," she said after a pause of at least one full minute. "You have a dark reason for asking these questions. Let me shed light on your questions and then we'll talk about why you ask them."

Jesse nodded resolutely. He was completely taken with this woman and her amazing memory, not to mention her intuition.

She smiled in a way that let Jesse know she enjoyed his attitude. "Let me think where to begin on your Voodoo education." She closed her eyes again for a long moment. "All right, how about this? Marie Laveau brought Voodoo to New Orleans after the terrible times of the Civil War. She was the daughter of a free Creole woman and a white man who happened to be the fifth mayor of New Orleans. She was a charismatic who became a political force. Her brand of Voodoo got big fast, as though it had a mind of its own. By eighteen seventy-four, crowds of ten thousand blacks and whites came to watch the blazing fires of her healing rituals on the shores of Lake Pontchartrain, just north of the city."

"Blacks and whites?" Jesse asked.

"Voodoo was bringing the races together a hundred years before Motown started doing it with soul music."

"So, what is Voodoo?" Jesse asked.

"Voodoo is the way we open the gate between the spirit world and the material world of humans. We invite spirits down to possess or protect or even to punish earthly souls."

"Wow," was all Jesse could muster as he and Carmen let go of each other's hands.

"Wow, indeed," Carmen said. "Now, what's really on your mind?"

Jesse poured out his story of the mystery man and the magic mushrooms and the Voodoo cow skull from the bayou and the mysterious voice. Carmen listened carefully and nodded occasionally. She laughed when he told about the image of the skull in his mind the night the lights went out at Fritzel's.

"Yes, we heard about the police pulling your plug," she said. "That probably had more to do with cops being paid by rival club owners. There wasn't anything Voodoo about it."

Jesse rubbed his fingers against his temples. "But why would I see the cow skull flashing in my mind when I closed my eyes?"

"I cannot answer that at this point."

Carmen reached behind her and pulled out a large volume from the bookshelf. "I'm looking into the mystical powers of psilocybin mushrooms." She put on reading glasses and looked sternly over them at Jesse. "You do know you are playing with fire?"

Jesse let his fingers slide down the side of his face and wove them together as a resting place for his chin. "I hadn't thought about it like that."

"I'm not talking about just the mushrooms. I'm talking about the music as well. Music plays a powerful roll in Voodoo. It connects us to the spirit world. I'm sure you've noticed how a song can take you back in time?"

Carmen let the question sink in. "Music transcends time. Music is powerful magic. It flows through time."

"Like an old song makes you feel young again?" Jesse asked.

"It breaks through the illusion of time. Time is an invention of the material mind to make sure everything doesn't happen all at once."

Jesse laughed. What she was saying made sense although he wasn't sure why.

She went on. "Music is more than memory. And it does more than make people sing and dance and fall in love."

"That sounds like enough."

Carmen smiled at him again. "Music connects people to each other. But more than that, it liberates our self from the bondage of the five senses and connects us to the oneness of the universe. You can call it God or Jesus or Buddha or whatever you want. The oneness is hidden from us by the material world. The power of music helps lift the veil off the world of the senses. In a way, the magic mushrooms do the same thing."

"I definitely understand that."

"Yes, I am sure you do. But you might not understand why or how this voice you hear is coming to you. I say you are playing with fire because you have added the power of hallucination to the power of music and Voodoo. It is like throwing gasoline and oil onto a bonfire."

Jesse thought the Voodoo priestess was making more sense than anybody he'd ever met. Carmen pulled out more books and charts and continued reading, alternately shaking her head up and down or side to side.

Finally, Jesse couldn't take it anymore. "What I need to know, is the voice real or is it some kind of hallucination?"

Carmen looked over the top of her reading glasses, more sternly this time. "Oh, it's real all right. Nothing happens by accident on Bayou Lafourche, or anywhere else for that matter."

"So, why me? Why am I the only one hearing this voice?"

Carmen sighed deeply. "You are a fortunate man. The spirit is here to guide you. Do not be afraid of it. I do not know why the voice has chosen you. Or why you have chosen to hear the voice."

"What do you mean, I chose to hear *it*?"

"The spirit world is always there. It is all around us. People are blinded to it. We think it does not exist if we can't see it or hear it."

"But I did hear it."

Carmen waved her hands at him. "Not with your ears. The only sound the spirit makes is inside your soul."

Jesse leaned forward and raised his eyebrows. "Is this spirit coming back from the dead?"

"Ah," she said. "The world of the living and the world of the dead are the same world. The spirit will teach you that."

"Is the voice coming from the cow skull?"

Carmen thought about the question for a moment. "I'm not sure. But I would guess the voice and the skull are the same thing coming to you on different levels so you might better understand."

"Better understand what?"

"Better understand what you must do with your music."

"What do you mean?" Jesse asked.

"I can say no more. I do not know. You must learn for yourself."

He sat quietly for a long moment, pondering all she had said. Carmen smiled big enough to show her perfect teeth as she saw him struggling with the notion that he might have a duty to the music, instead of the other way around.

Jesse smiled back and changed the topic. "What does the voice mean when it says, 'You got to keep running'?"

"What does that mean to you?"

Jesse thought about the underground railroad and how people had to keep moving to avoid capture. "It sounds like I'm a runaway slave."

"Remember this. Words, and signs in general have no intrinsic meaning. They do not mean the same thing to every person. The value is in the interpretation, not in the words themselves."

"I don't feel like a runaway slave."

Carmen looked over the top of her glasses again, this time with a discernible twinkle in her eye. "We are all running away from many things and we are all slaves to many masters."

"I'm not afraid of anything or anybody." Jesse realized it wasn't true even before he was finished saying it.

Carmen threw her hands over her head. "You are whistling through the graveyard."

"What is that supposed to mean?"

Carmen sighed again. "You are pretending to be unafraid. That is a fool's game. You cannot be brave until you admit your fears and face them."

"What are my fears?"

"Ah," she said. "I see we are making progress."

Jesse had to marvel at how skillful she was with her game of mirrors.

"So what should I do now?" he asked.

"First, you must learn the way of Voodoo. It will help you understand and appreciate what the voice is trying to teach you."

"Where do we start?"

"I will take you to the grave of Marie Laveau in the St. Louis Cemetery here in the city. It must be only you and me. We will see if the voice of Voodoo speaks to you there. I will conduct a ceremony to welcome the spirit of Marie. Then, you will see where it takes you."

Jesse's tone turned suspicious. "This is starting to sound like a haunted tour."

Carmen waved her hand like she was shooing away a fly. She became stern. "You must do it with me."

Jesse leaned in toward her. "I wouldn't do it without you."

Carmen smiled at Jesse. "Fine. Then I will tell you one more thing. One more thing you must remember about the voice you hear."

"What?"

The room became eerily still as the space between them filled with the smell of a lavender candle, cleanly snuffed at the wick by an invisible pinch.

Finally, she lowered her voice and looked him in the eye. "Remember this. You do not have to do everything the voice tells you to do."

Voodoo wasn't the only strange thing happening in Jesse's life.

The Gay scene in New Orleans was second only to the Castro District of San Francisco. Men from all over the country flocked to New Orleans to flee the homosexual repression that darkened North America in the 1970's. They came out of the closet with a vengeance once they hit New Orleans and realized the coast was clear. Labor Day became their special celebration.

Hundreds of cross dressers, transsexuals and liberated gay men and women frolicked down the streets for an event known as The Southern Decadence Parade. The revelers did their best to insure the event lived up to its name. Even in the city of parades, this march of crimes was a mocking and a shocking to the stocking.

Devils in orange-flame capes wore overgrown horns on their heads. Queens with giant crowns had flowing, topless gowns with long, golden gloves. The peacock-feathered man was naked except for a red jock strap. His bare ass was as red as his jock from getting spanked by anyone who felt the urge.

All five members of The Divebomberz entered the parade, led by Dale in his bright blue jump suit and tambourine. After two Hurricane rum drinks at Pat O'Brien's Bar, it didn't matter if you were gay or straight. The Decadence Parade was a giant, irresistible conga line. Jesse marveled at the brass bands, dancing troupes, clowns of all kinds, and Cadillac convertibles overflowing with bearded men in lingerie. The customary and mandatory parade beads were tossed to the crowds of horny, gay men shouting from balconies and flaunting their newfound sexual freedom. The streets were flooded with testosterone. Police and city officials were remarkably tolerant of what always turned out to be a peaceful demonstration. It was Mardi Gras with a gay twist.

Rene came up from the bayou for the occasion. Jesse and Amy joined the street party as well. They did circle dances with Butch and Tim until they were dizzy. Dale danced from one provocative embrace to the next. Everybody was loaded to the gills on booze and whatever drugs they could get their hands on.

It took several hours and quite a few miles, but The Divebomberz party, including Dale, eventually became exhausted and spun out of the parade. They walked through Jackson Square to kick back in the French Market at Café Du Monde with beignets and chicory coffee. And water, lots of water.

Everybody was still in a festive spirit when Rene asked Dale, during a lull in the conversation, "What's it like to be gay?"

His question hit Jesse like a bucket of cold water. It wasn't a question he had asked Dale, even though they'd been friends for years. Jesse looked around the table. Nobody gasped out loud but they all turned to see how Dale would react.

"I mean is it always this much fun?" Rene tried to cover as he shifted uncomfortably in his chair.

Jesse looked at the faces turned toward Dale and saw genuine curiosity. Looking back to Dale, he realized the one gay member of The Divebomberz was about to address the issue head-on. Dale looked like his emotional levee was about to fail as the table paused in anticipation. He took a deep breath before continuing. His strong chin and dancing eyes became serious.

"No. Now that you ask, it has not always been fun. In fact, it was a living hell growing up. My family is evangelical Christian from Missouri. To them, homosexuality is a crime against nature and a sin against God. So, even though I always knew I was born gay, they refused to accept me or even try to understand how I could be the way I am. My father took the dolls away when I was five years old. He wouldn't talk to me after that. Having a gay son was a huge threat to his masculinity. My mother didn't give up so easily. She tried everything from counseling to baptism. That blew up in our faces when the preacher kicked me out of church at the age of thirteen for trying to hold hands with another boy. He said I couldn't be a Christian if I was gay."

"That must have been terrible," Amy said.

"It was worse than that," Dale said, tears beginning to well up in his eyes. "I learned to sing in that church. I loved the songs. I knew them by heart. I knew I loved God and Jesus too. The day that preacher told me Jesus had no love for me or my kind was the worst day of my life.

"No, I take it back. The worst day of my life was when my own mother kicked me out of the house at age sixteen. The two of us were sitting at the kitchen table. I was asking her about love and telling her I was in love with a boy at school. She couldn't handle it. Next thing I knew she was showing me the door. She said she was tired of trying to teach a child who would not listen."

"What did you say?" Butch asked.

Dale was losing the battle to keep from crying. A tear rolled down his cheek and into his mustache. He put his head in his hands to hide his face and sobbed, "All I could say was 'goodbye, Momma, I love you.' She wouldn't even look at me as I packed my suitcase and headed out the door."

Jesse and Amy put their hands on Dale's back. Nobody could say a word.

"I'm sorry," Dale said as he uncovered his face with a sniffle and wiped away his tears to regain his composure. "I didn't mean to spoil the party."

"You're not spoiling the party," Butch said. "If it hadn't been for your mother kicking you out, we never would have met you."

"I guess that's right, isn't it?" Dale said, wiping his face with a paper napkin. "But anyway, I don't need to cry about it. I'm in a great band now and we're going to show the world what we can do. I'm going to show my mother how wrong she is."

That led to a cheer and a clinking of coffee cups.

Rene couldn't help himself. He had to ask one more pointed question. "Do you ever see your family?"

Dale took another deep breath and looked at the sky. "No. I don't see them. I write my mother once a month to tell her how great everything is going. She doesn't write back but I hope and pray that one day she will."

Butch changed the topic by saying to Jesse, "Remember when it was just you and me and Dale down here, singing for tips at clubs and trying to sound like Crosby, Stills, and Nash?"

"Oh, yeah," Jesse said. "And Dale got us that paying gig at The Outpost."

"I didn't realize you three played down here before you got together with Tim," Rene said.

"They came back to Indiana to get me because they were short handed," Tim said, holding up his left hand with no fingers.

Everybody groaned and laughed, even Dale.

"Let me tell you about The Outpost," Jesse said.

Amy pushed him on the shoulder. "I know you will whether we want you to or not."

"Go ahead," Dale said. "Rene and Tim need to know their band heritage."

Jesse, as always, was pleased to have a story-telling opportunity. He started this one out like he was scaring young campers around a fire. He lowered his voice to begin. "Okay. Here it is. The Outpost was a leather-levi, gay-motorcycle, no-girls-allowed club. I think it was on Ursulines Avenue, just off Royal Street. There were pictures of naked cowboys on the wall, wearing nothing but hats and boots and six guns on their hips. We set up our little sound system in this club filled with nothing but guys who were definitely checking us out. It was on the second floor so we had some lifting to do."

"A couple big old grisly girls helped us load in as I recall," Dale said.

"Yes, they did," Jesse said. "So, we start playing and everything is going great. They're cheering the music and dancing with each other, and we think we've found ourselves what might be a steady gig. Then, we see them stand some guy up on the bar and pull down his pants and underpants so he can't move his legs. They tie his hands behind his back with his shirt and start hitting him with little whips and pouring drinks on him."

"And he's loving it," Dale said.

"I'll never forget that moment," Butch said. "We were playing 'All Along the Watchtower' by Bob Dylan. The more stuff they did to him the faster we played that song."

"And then they started to—"

Amy put her hand over Jesse's mouth. "Stop right there."

Butch stepped up to finish the story. "We cut that song so short. We packed up faster than a pit crew at the Indianapolis Five Hundred. We left in a hurry and never even asked to get paid."

"I got us a hundred dollar set up fee if you remember," Dale said.

Rene didn't say a word.

"That's right, you did," Jesse said. "But enough of that. Let's go somewhere and get a real drink. I've had enough coffee and water for one day."

Tim stood up and stretched. "We'd better be careful. We could end up getting sober."

"I've got a great idea," Dale said as they got up to pay the bill. "Let's hit Tortilla Flats for tacos and Sangria."

"Sounds like a plan," Butch said.

"What's Sangria?" Rene asked.

Jesse threw his arm around the drummer. "You're about to find out."

CHAPTER FIVE

PUBLIC TELEVISION

Shortly after the Sauce Piquante Festival on the bayou, The Divebomberz got a booking agent who found them gigs at bars and fraternity parties from New Orleans to Baton Rouge. His name was Ron and he took fifteen percent commission off the top. What did he care if the band wasn't right for the job? He got paid, no matter what. One Monday morning, Jesse and Butch paid Ron a visit at his small, cluttered office on the second floor of a rundown building on North Rampart Street, near Louis Armstrong Park. They banged on the frosted glass door. Ron pretended not to be there.

Jesse shouted through the glass. "Come on, Ron. We know you're in there. We need to talk. You owe us money. We need to get paid."

A chair squawked back from its desk and a grumbling shadow shuffled to the door and opened it a crack. Ron was a middle-aged former musician who was mostly gray in hair and skin color. He didn't like being disturbed, especially when he knew his visitors were not making a friendly call. When he saw it was Jesse and Butch, he opened the door wide and pretended to be happy to see them.

Butch was all business. "Don't act like you don't know why we're here."

Ron smiled as if being forced to at gunpoint. "Why, if it isn't The Divebomberz in the flesh and blood. Come in, come in."

Butch was in no mood to accept phony hospitality. "We don't need to come in. We want what you owe us and we need to know why you sent us to the slaughter at that heavy metal bar across the river in Gretna."

Jesse wasn't about to be left out of this house call. "Those speed freaks didn't want to hear a country rock band. They booed Tim so bad on the fiddle he had to put it down and play slide guitar all night."

"You knew we wouldn't go over," Butch said.

Ron motioned for them to come on in. "Relax, I've got your money."

"Getting paid to be humiliated is not our idea of you being a good agent, Ron," Jesse said. "It was a full house before we started. By the third song, half the crowd gave us the finger and walked out. The rest of them stayed to get drunk and heckle us all night."

Ron raised his right index finger to make a point. He took a breath and opened his mouth to speak. No words came out. He cleared his throat and waited for Butch or Jesse to speak. They each took one step closer to their agent.

Ron backed up two steps. "Okay. I'm sorry. I really am. A band backed out on a gig. I needed to fill it. I knew I shouldn't have sent you guys but I thought maybe things would work out. You guys can rock."

Butch followed Ron into his office. "We asked you what kind of club it was. You lied to us."

"No, I didn't know the club was that heavy metal. Clubs change, you know. Anyway, I can make it up to you. New Orleans Public Television is looking for a band to play for its annual outdoor fundraiser. You'll get more exposure than the mayor."

Butch stopped in his tracks. "What does it pay?"

"I thought it wasn't all about the money with you guys?"

"What does it pay?" Jesse persisted.

"It's a freebie, of course. That's the point of a fundraiser. Everybody donates their time for a good cause."

Butch moved closer to Ron. "When is it?"

"Well, that's the thing," Ron said. "It's this Sunday."

Jesse moved in on the conversation. "Six days from now. Sounds like we weren't your first choice. Or did you just forget to tell us?"

"Come on now, I was going to call you today. I swear. I just found out about it last night. They had a band back out and they need somebody fast. You guys are right on time."

"What if we already have a gig?" Butch asked.

Ron sat down and put his feet up on the desk. "I happen to know you don't. And what's more. This might be the best job I ever got you. Television is the wave of the rock and roll future."

"I like it," Jesse said, looking to Butch for approval.

Butch backed up to a respectful distance from Ron and his desk. "How long do they want us to play?"

Ron put his feet down and began rummaging through several piles of paper on his desk like he might find the answer to the question somewhere in the mess. He fumbled around until he finally held up a flyer for the event. "It's a four-hour gig but you only play for an hour of that time. The rest of the time they're pitching for donations. They've got big names doing the pitch. Like Al Hirt and Pete Fountain."

"Whoa," Butch said. "It doesn't get any bigger than that. We'll do it. And tell Al and Pete they can feel free to sit in with us. If they actually show up."

"Oh, they'll show up. Public television is getting to be a big deal. Just make sure you guys show up at the Fairgrounds and get set up by noon for sound check."

Butch watched Ron count out the money he owed them and held his hand out to receive it. "We'll be there. How many other bands are there?"

"Just you guys."

Butch took the money and counted it. "No shit? It's just us and a bunch of New Orleans big shots? Sounds like we got ourselves a deal, Ron. And have I told you lately how much we love you?"

"That's more like it," Ron said.

Jesse took the money from Butch and counted it himself. "So, what else you got for us?"

"I'm still working on the Riverboat gig. It's pretty much a done deal and it means a six-hundred-dollar boat ride for you guys once a month."

"That sounds great, Ron," Jesse said. "But once a month won't keep us alive. We need to work more. Our next gig is The Safari Club on the bayou but that's two weeks away."

"Book yourself some more jobs. I'm just an agent. I'm not your manager. I don't have an exclusive on you."

Butch shook Ron's hand as he prepared to walk out of the office. "You got that right."

The Divebomberz had a band party at Jesse and Amy's loft apartment to watch themselves on television for the first time. It was the first Wednesday after the Sunday performance.

Jesse could tell that Amy was totally impressed to see her boys on television. She was the first to comment. "Look at all that hair. You're all blowing in the wind like some Bob Dylan song."

Dale was dancing to the television. "It was a windy day. Beats a wind machine any day."

Tim was paying critical attention to the small screen. "We had a couple microphone stands blow over."

"The crowd was huge," Butch said.

Rene chimed in, "They loved us."

The band and Amy were sitting around the wooden skid on the floor that served as the main table in the apartment. Besides a few unmatched chairs, the only other furniture was an old porch swing that hung on chains from the rafters. The small antenna television sat on a fruit crate in front of two, tall, leaded glass windows. The walls were exposed brick.

Tim's eyes were glued to the set. "We must have played 'Little Liza Jane' for twenty minutes. That was the longest sing-a-long I ever played."

Amy could barely contain her excitement. "Look at you guys. You look like rock stars. And, oh, here's Bam Bam on a close up."

Everybody cheered.

"Now they know why we call you Bam Bam," Butch said. "You're beating those skins to death."

"Man, I need a haircut," Rene said. "My hair is all over my face. And please don't call me Bam Bam. I never should have told you guys that nickname."

Dale fluffed up his long, curly locks. "We can't be hiding the second best looking man in the band behind his hair."

Butch had to jump in on that one. "So, you're finally admitting I'm the best looking guy in the band?"

"Look," Dale shouted at an extended close up of himself. "I think we can plainly see who's number one. That cameraman fell in love with me."

"Not as much as you fell in love with him," Jesse said.

Jesse was amazed by how photogenic the band looked on television. Maybe they weren't big time musicians yet, but they sure looked the part.

The moment was transformational for Jesse. He would never think of the band the same way again. The television image went straight to his head. It was like looking into a magical mirror that turned the ordinary into the extraordinary. While his confidence took several giant steps forward, it didn't take him to the land of overblown egos. He was still too broke for that. The Divebomberz had sounded big and polished for the public television benefit. The sound team had a great mix. The band was starting and stopping on a dime. They were singing great and playing with precision and determination. It had been exciting to perform for the big crowd with all kinds of cameras pointed at them and filming. The stage looked like a movie set. The lights were blinding. They were six feet above a sea of people. Celebrities like Aaron Neville and Pete Fountain socialized with them like equals. Al Hirt never showed up and Pete Fountain gracefully declined an invitation to sit in with The Divebomberz. Even so, the public television gig was at least as entertaining for Jesse and the band as it was for the people watching them.

And now, it was even more fun watching himself on television. Suddenly Jesse's dream of making it in the music business seemed more than possible. It felt inevitable. The band was young and thin and handsome. The cameras loved them all. They complimented each other. They had the look of a seasoned, professional band, not five guys who happened to get up on stage together. What tied them together was their long, curly, brown hair. They looked like a shampoo commercial, right down to their facial hair. Jesse, Rene, and Tim had full beards and mustaches. Butch and Dale had mustaches and sideburns. They looked like hippie brothers.

It was more than "the look" that unified them. They actually moved like a unit, although there was nothing choreographed about their performance. They moved together with the music, like they were riding the same musical horse.

Jesse maybe jumped around a little too much on bass.

"You've got to tone it down a notch," Amy said. "Bass players are supposed to be grounded."

Jesse could see her point was well taken. "I can't help it. I get excited."

Butch sprang to his defense. "Don't listen to her, Jesse. She's just jealous."

Everybody looked at Amy to see how she would react. The television program had just concluded.

"Actually, I am a little jealous. You guys look great on television."

Amy knew exactly what to say to a rock band watching themselves for the first time on the small screen.

"I propose a toast," she said, lifting her can of beer. "To The Divebomberz, the best band to hit New Orleans and the bayou in a long, long time."

Amy was the only non-band member present for the televiewing event. She could hang with the guys. She smoked and drank like a guy but she cooked like a housemother. Besides handling the t-shirt enterprise, she hauled gear and set up lights. She did everything for the band except run sound. She was everything he wanted in a woman. She was smart and sexy. She was a wonderful cook and she had a green thumb. Everything she planted flourished and bloomed. She would be a wonderful wife. Jesse had thought all that through. Problem was, he didn't want a wife at this point. He was too busy chasing the rock and roll dragon.

As the band members were toasting each other and firing up another joint, the telephone rang. Jesse answered it and motioned excitedly for everyone to tone it down. He talked for several minutes and then hung up slowly for dramatic effect.

"You'll never guess who that was," he said.

Nobody guessed. They were holding their breath.

"That was Pete Dryer. He wants to talk about managing us."

Nobody reacted. They looked at each other with puzzled faces.

"Who's Pete Dryer?" Tim finally asked.

Jesse got their undivided attention by standing in front of the television. "Who's Pete Dryer? He's the guy we've been trying to get for months. I got him to come hear us one night at Fritzel's. He's worked with the Neville Brothers and The Meters. He wants to put us in the studio and make a record. He's talking about starting a Jazz Festival in New Orleans."

"Oh, that Pete Dryer," Tim said.

Rene laughed. "Oh, Pete, our old buddy."

"Oh, for Pete's sake," Butch said.

Jesse waved his arms to regain their attention. "Cut it out guys. This is a big deal. A guy like Pete is exactly what we need."

"What do we need a manager for?" Dale asked. "Looks like we're doing quite well on our own."

Jesse waited until he had everybody's attention. "We need a manager to help us get in a studio to make a demo tape. It's all about the tape. Clubs want to hear it, agents want to hear it, and, most importantly, record companies want to hear it. It's all about getting a recording contract. We can't do that without a tape and we can't get a tape made without a manager."

"Why not?" Tim asked.

"Because we don't have the money," Butch said. "A good manager would have the connections to get us in the studio."

"So, how do we know this Pete guy can do that?" Rene asked.

"We don't know what he can do," Dale said. "But, right now, he's the only one calling."

CHAPTER SIX

THE SAFARI CLUB

The Safari Club was a sprawling music hall with a thatched roof, tiki torches and fake lion heads on the walls. It stood two stories tall and all alone along the bayou in the flatlands between Thibodaux and Raceland. A wide, wooden porch, designed to look like a boat dock, surrounded the club. The thatch was ornamental. A shingle roof beneath the decorative topping kept the rain out and represented half-hearted efforts to bring the old storage facility up to public safety standards.

The Divebomberz were on the way to their gig at the Safari Club when Dupre and The Wheelers intercepted them 10 miles from the club, providing a thundering escort down the bayou. Long hair, black leather, fringe, and colorful headbands fluttered like freak flags in the high-speed breeze. Boots, chains, saddlebags, skull-and-cross-bone mirrors, and spiked crash bars turned every chopper into an ominous instrument of road domination.

Each Wheeler rode solo. There was no woman riding on back of any bike. The Wheelers were always ready for a fight. They were a combat unit, daring anyone to even think about challenging their highway supremacy throughout the bayou. They looked like a post apocalyptic death gang on wheels.

Motorcycles swarmed around The Divebomberz' two vehicles and swerved between the band van and Rene's truck at reckless speeds and angles. Wheelies were pulled at eighty miles per hour. Weapons were brandished like they were holding up a stagecoach. Shots may have been fired into the air but no one could have heard them over the revved up motorcycle engines.

Jesse drove on, happy to have such an outrageous welcoming committee. The overpowering roar of the motorcycles was so invasive that he could barely hear himself shout, "Nobody better mess with us. We've got The Wheelers on our side."

"Let's hope they stay on our side," Butch yelled back at Jesse. The wild escort continued for miles until the impromptu caravan rumbled to a stop in a thick cloud of dust in the vast, gravel parking lot of the Safari Club.

The Wheelers were in full party mode as the band stepped out to greet them.

"You boys ready to get down?" Dupre asked as he gave Tim a big bear hug.

Dale climbed out the side door of the van. "We were born to get down, all the way down and then down some more."

The Divebomberz and the Wheelers embraced each other like long lost brothers. The motorcycle gang had been following the band since their first meeting at the Raceland Festival. Joints were fired up and passed around as the bikers began helping the band haul amps, speakers, and drums into the club.

The celebratory atmosphere was interrupted by what sounded like shouting and trouble from inside the club. Rene came out with two Wheelers, who were marching a bartender out of the club like he was being taken hostage.

A tall, thin Wheeler named Donald explained the situation. "This asshole says the bar's not open for business."

"Bring him over here, Don," Dupre said. "I'm sure he doesn't really mean it."

The bartender looked terrified by the time he was face to face with Dupre. Donald let him go with a mean shove.

The head Wheeler grabbed the bartender by the shoulders to steady him. "You don't really mean the bar's not open yet, do you?"

The bartender looked around like he was hoping to be rescued. The Wheelers crowded in more closely.

Dupre got into the bartender's face. "I want you to think about it real hard. Don't answer until you're real sure you know exactly what you want to say."

The bartender took a deep breath and eventually spoke up like a military recruit in boot camp as he exhaled. "What I meant to say was the bar is now open for business and the first round is on the house."

"My man," Dupre shouted as a mighty cheer erupted. "Come on boys," he said as he led the crew into the club. "The first one's free and don't forget to tip the living shit out of your bartender."

And so the party began. The band set up and did a sound check. The parking lot started filling up by 7 p.m. There was a five-dollar cover charge. The club should have started turning people away by 8 p.m. There were already at least three hundred fifty people in a space fire coded for two hundred twenty-five.

Jesse could see the front box office from his position on the stage. They were still selling tickets as fast as they could count the money.

The Wheeler women were looking tough and sexy. They arrived as singles or in pairs. They wore short skirts or tight jeans with tops that showed plenty of skin and cleavage. Hairdos, make up, nails, and jewelry were completely dolled up for the special occasion. Tim made the mistake of talking to one of the bayou beauties. A Wheeler named Big Ben quickly stepped in to introduce the woman as his date for the night. Tim wisely deferred to the massive biker. Big Ben was Dupre's right hand man, his second in command.

Tim looked at Butch. "Oh, I get it. The single girls are here for the Wheelers. I should have known."

"Me too," Butch said. "I won't be making that mistake."

Jesse came over to talk to Tim and Butch. "Looks like this is some kind of major event. I don't think we're this popular down here yet."

As he spoke, he noticed Amy trying to get in the front door. Dupre was holding court at the entrance and giving her the kind of trouble that could only be called sexual harassment.

Jesse fought his way through the crowd to step between Dupre and Amy.

Dupre was not happy to have Jesse interrupt his game. "You know this woman? She says she's with you but I say she's with me."

Amy looked terrified as Jesse and Dupre stared each other down for a long moment. Anyone nearby quieted down immediately. The tension was spellbinding . . .

Jesse shrugged his shoulders. "Actually, I never saw her before in my entire life."

Dupre waited a couple beats then burst out laughing. Jesse cracked up too as he and Dupre gave each other a brotherly chest bump. Everybody relaxed and joined in the laughter. The street theater between bikers and musicians never failed to entertain.

"What was that about?" Amy asked as she began breathing normally when Jesse walked her inside to the bandstand.

Jesse put his arm around her. "Sorry about that. Dupre was just playing. He knows who you are. He's just a little loaded, that's all. You've got to know how to handle him. He's basically a good guy until you piss him off."

"Let's not do that," she said as she squeezed Jesse's arm tightly.

Rene's new girlfriend, Polly, arrived at the Safari Club about 8 p.m. with three gorgeous female friends to see Rene and his band. They didn't have too much trouble from the Wheelers at the door. Polly and company knew how to handle Cajun whistles and catcalls. They whistled right back, made an obscene gesture or two and kept pushing their way into the overcrowded club.

"You guys got it going on tonight," Polly said to Rene as she finally made it to the bandstand. "We had to park way back in the lot, and there's cars backed up all down the highway."

Rene gave her a kiss on the lips. "You have any trouble at the door, baby?"

"Nothing but the usual thieves and murderers," Polly said.

"Did they make you pay?"

"What, pay for our sins?"

"No, pay to get in."

"Of course not. Me and my girls are always with the band."

"Got that right," Rene said.

Dale came through the crowd with a tray of beer and shots of whiskey for the band. "Man, it's packed in here and they're still selling tickets. The bartenders and waitresses are so busy I had to take matters into my own hands."

Rene overheard the comment from where he sat, beginning to tune his drums. "I heard this is the Wheelers' big anniversary party. Something about riding and ruling the bayou for twenty years."

Butch responded to Rene. "Dupre said he wants to introduce the band and say a few things before we get started."

Tim was finished tuning up his fiddle and slide guitar. "We better get going pretty fast. The natives are getting restless."

People were crowding the bandstand, yelling for the music to start.

Dupre muscled his way to the bandstand and gave Amy a friendly hug. "Sorry about that, girl. You're lucky you've got a big strong musician to protect you."

Amy played along but she gave Jesse a look like, "Get this guy off me."

"Okay, Dupre," Jesse said. "We're ready to go on. The microphone is all yours. You want to say a few things to the party before you introduce us?"

"Damn straight."

The crowd erupted in a mighty cheer as Dupre took the stage with the band. The bandstand was two feet higher than the dance floor. He quieted the crowd, holding out his arms to welcome them, and began speaking with all the panache of a drunken television evangelist.

"Good evening and thank you all for coming out tonight. As most of you know, this is the twentieth anniversary party for the greatest motorcycle club in the country."

The crowd began cheering and stomping so hard it sounded to Jesse like the floor might cave in.

Dupre continued. "We've got some special treats and surprises for you tonight, but before I get into that, could we please have a wild Wheeler shout out for all the beautiful ladies here tonight."

The Wheelers started throwing girls in the air to celebrate. The women didn't seem to mind. They liked being part of the show, and they didn't try to keep their skirts from blowing up on the way down.

"All right, all right, boys. Let's not hurt anybody out there. We're pretty crowded already and there's bound to be more on the way. So let's be careful."

The crowd settled somewhat.

"We want to dedicate this evening to our dearly departed founder, Sonny Daniel. As you know, we lost Sonny about this time last year. He is and will be dearly missed. Could we have a moment of silence for Sonny."

The party went to church in an instant. Not a sound was made for a full twenty seconds.

Dupre brought them back by speaking solemnly at first and then raising his excitement level like a ring announcer at a boxing match. "Sonny never heard this band. But he would've loved them. So let me introduce to you, The Wheelers' favorite band, our personal friends, the band of the future, the hottest band on the bayou, The Divebomberz!"

The band kicked off in perfect time with "Bayou Jubilee," a song by The Nitty Gritty Dirt Band about a Cajun party. The Safari Club swung into high gear. Everybody started dancing. The old warehouse was swinging on its pylon foundation. The wooden floor was bouncing up and down. The rafters seemed to be straining to hold the place together. The band sounded better than ever. All the bodies in the room absorbed rough edges of the sound like water bags, leaving rich, dense tones to permeate the high-ceiling room.

As the first set went on, Jesse had a vague feeling of uneasiness descend upon him. The club was getting so full it felt like it might explode. People were getting crazy high, snorting and smoking and popping whatever they could get their hands on. But that wasn't it. He'd seen crazy crowds before. Tonight was different. It felt like something bad was going to happen. He'd learned to trust his intuition when paranoia peaked its ugly little face over the counter. It usually meant some kind of police intervention was about to happen.

Halfway through the set, the crowd was in full swing. Three women were putting on an extremely suggestive show in the middle of the dance floor. They ripped off their skirts and blouses to reveal matching, silver thongs and pasties. Each of them had obviously spent some serious time on the stripper's pole. They moved in unison like naughty cheerleaders. Then, they wrapped their limbs around each other to perform ballet moves that looked like sexual flowers unfolding in bloom.

The crowd gathered around them too tightly. Their dance area became smaller and smaller until they were swallowed up by the mob. Party people kept pouring into the already packed club. Jesse felt his temperature rising. Sweat from his forehead was getting in his eyes. His hands were so wet he had trouble keeping his fingers on the strings of his bass. He was having trouble breathing. There were no windows to open. The large dance floor became a human gridlock. Dancers had no room to make their moves. There was no place for anyone to go. Jesse could see people struggling to even turn around.

The Safari Club had only two exits, the front door and a smaller, single door out the back that didn't even have an exit sign over it. Despite the growing safety hazard, the crowd continued to cheer as the band played an extra long first set.

At the end of the set, even the band had nowhere to go. The area around the stage was so packed with people there was no way to escape.

Dupre managed to get to the microphone. "All right, everybody. We've obviously got way too many people in this building. I'm calling on all Wheelers to begin directing people to the exits. Anyone on my right will leave through the back door. Don't get in a hurry. Everyone's going to be fine. Anybody to my left, go out the way you came in. Don't worry, we'll get you all back in due time."

As Dupre spoke, Jesse heard a familiar but impossible noise outside. It was the rumble and roar of motorcycles, lots of them. But how could that be? All the Wheelers were inside.

One of the Wheelers yelled the bad news from the front door. "It's the Gypsies!"

The sounding of that alarm turned what had been the beginnings of an orderly exit into a stampede for the doors. All at once, Jesse realized he was trapped in the middle of a gang war. He found Amy and grabbed her arm to get her out of harm's way. There was nowhere to go. Each exit jammed up with so many people that almost no one could get out, not even the big and strong. As a few Wheelers managed to squeeze out the doors, they found the Gypsies had disabled many of their motorcycles by pulling sparkplugs and flattening tires. They were riding circles around the club and kicking up what seemed a storm from the Dust Bowl in the 1930's.

Until that moment, no one knew how big the Gypsies had become. There were at least seventy-five of them, riding crazy and screaming like wild Indians surrounding a wagon train in an old West movie. Rumors had been spreading about a gang rising up to challenge the Wheelers over drug dealing territories. Nobody thought it would come to violence this quickly. Cocaine had become too profitable in the bayou for any one group to hold a monopoly forever. Nothing beats a shrimp boat and ten thousand miles of unsupervised waterways for smuggling drugs into the mainland.

Jesse watched in horror as the party scene inside the Safari Club turned into an insane mob panic. He unstrapped his bass guitar as people began climbing onstage, desperately looking for a way out of the club.

Dupre had to fight to maintain control of the microphone. "Settle down, people. Everybody's going to be fine. Let's keep the exit orderly."

Shouting and screaming from the crowd drowned out the powerful sound system amplifying his voice.

Big Ben was one of the first Wheelers to fight his way out the back door. He ran to the parking lot and tackled the first Gypsy biker he could get his hands on. He couldn't see what he was trying to tackle because of the dust. He dove for the spot right behind the motorcycle headlight and made crunching contact. The two bikers went down kicking and punching each other. The unoccupied Gypsy motorcycle kept rolling toward the club and knocked over a tiki torch filled with fuel. A twenty-foot section of the back porch caught fire instantly. Flames spread up the side of the building. The motorcycle leaked its own gas into the fire and exploded like a bomb.

People trapped inside heard the explosion, smelling smoke as the fire spread to the thatch and quickly set the entire roof ablaze. The temperature elevated quickly in the already overheated building. Horrified guests began pushing and shoving each other . . .

Outside, the Gypsies were shooting up the sky with handguns and shotguns. The explosion, the gunfire, the smoke and heat created full-blown panic among the trapped patrons. People were piling up at the front door and the back door. They tried to climb over each other in futile attempts to escape.

Dale looked at Tim, the terrible conclusion in his eyes. "Looks like this is it, my brother."

Tim grabbed Dale by the shoulders to restore confidence. "No, no. No way. We're going to get out of this somehow."

Jesse disengaged from the danger as a power inside his head began fighting for his attention. He could see Tim and Dale asking for direction, but he was unable to respond. There was so much screaming in the club that he didn't hear the Voodoo voice at first. He knew it was talking to him. He could feel it but he couldn't hear it. His spine was tingling. His vision became blurry. He was falling into a trance. He covered his ears and closed his eyes and took a deep breath.

Instantly, the voice was all he heard. It was calming and reassuring. It spoke to Jesse slowly and evenly, repeating itself for emphasis. "Break down the wall. Break down the wall."

It took only a moment for Jesse to realize the voice was giving him the only practical advice that might save hundreds of lives. He called his band to action by waving one arm in a circular motion over his head.

"Come on, Tim. Come on Rene. Help me knock out this wall behind the stage."

Rene was already coughing badly. "What are you talking about? We can't do that."

"There's no other way out," Jesse said as he pushed his way to the wall behind the stage. Rene and Tim followed him and they started kicking the wall together.

Butch and Dale joined in and the five members of The Divebomberz began kicking the wooden wall with all their might. It didn't give an inch. The drywall inside was on two-by-four studs with thick plywood and siding on the outside. Smoke was getting thicker by the second. Jesse could hear his bandmates choking. They were running out of air. The screaming panic of the trapped crowd sounded like all the evil from Hell.

Jesse knew it was time to organize his troops. "Come on guys. Get in sync. On four, ready? One, two, three, four."

The band kicked together on four. Their collective impact felt superhuman.

The wall didn't budge an inch.

Dupre and another Wheeler joined the kicking. Everybody was screaming out the four count and kicking as one. It felt like the wall was giving way a little.

Jesse's right foot was getting sore by the tenth kick. He changed over to kicking with his left foot and yelled at the others to alternate their kicking feet. Smoke was beginning to overwhelm the crowd. Jesse put his head between his legs to keep from fainting. Standing up, he could see people falling to the floor. The roof was nothing but flames. Escape began to look more and more impossible. Jesse hoped the Voodoo voice was a spirit he could trust with his life.

A few more Wheelers and crowd members joined the desperate break out attempt. "One, two, three, four," they yelled together and kicked on the four count.

Jesse couldn't hear the wood cracking but he could see the wall beginning to break out. On the fifteenth kick, a crack in the wall could be seen about eight feet up. The band kept kicking until a four-foot section of the wall began to give way. One more mighty, collective kick and a small section of wall fell down and out and onto the porch outside.

The blaze was roaring as flames engulfed the rafters. Smoke and dust poured into the club from the new opening in the wall. People stampeded over the bandstand, attempting to get out through the hole, crushing instruments and amplifiers underfoot. The hole wasn't wide enough. Another human logjam prevented escape.

Amy was pushed to the floor and started getting buried by bodies. She disappeared except for one arm, waving wildly. Jesse grabbed her hand and felt his way down her arm until he could get a firm grip under her armpit. He yelled at Dupre for help. The biker pushed people aside as Jesse pulled her up and back on her feet. She came up choking and bruised but far from defeated.

Her face was so blackened that her teeth looked extra white as she shouted at Jesse, "I couldn't get up. They wouldn't let me up."

Jesse kept his arm around Amy as he yelled at his crew. "Let's go. We need another hole. We need another hole."

The band sprang back into action and kicked out another section of the wall, and then another. Each section came down easier than the last. Once the band knew they could do it with their synchronized kicks, they became a Rock and Roll, kung fu wrecking ball.

One, two, three, four! Ten people kicked on the four count with a collective and concentrated force far greater than their number. Never had the power of four-four timing been so well demonstrated and utilized. The room full of trapped people took notice and began kicking their own holes in the wall on the other side of the hall. Coughing people poured out into the parking lot like rats leaving a sinking ship.

The building was totally engulfed in flames by the time the last stragglers stumbled out to safety. The Safari Club went up in a blaze so tall and bright it looked like a towering-inferno rocket ship blasting off into the full moon night. Giant sparks shot up into the blackness to dance with the stars. The fire was so hot it melted cars and motorcycles that couldn't be moved in time. Jesse saw people standing way back from the intense heat, staring at the fire as though hypnotized by the miracle of their escape and survival.

The Gypsies were long gone. They had left when the fire started. It wasn't part of their plan to incinerate five hundred people. At least the disaster postponed all-out gang warfare.

Miraculously, no one died in the blaze, although thirty-eight people ended up going to the hospital. They had suffered smoke inhalation, burn injuries, and broken bones. Fifteen people were in serious to critical condition from being nearly crushed to death. The Gypsy biker that Big Ben tackled was taken away on a stretcher by ambulance. He was expected to live.

Big Ben was black as a coal miner. He had a broken right hand. His beard and hair and eyebrows had been burned off. He looked like a cancer victim. The injuries hadn't stopped him from pulling people out the back door.

The reluctant bartender, who helped get the party started hours earlier, was one of the last persons carried out of the club. A woman with half her hair burned off told Jesse the bartender had hooked up a hose to his water faucet and was spraying down an escape hole in the wall until a flaming beam fell and knocked him unconscious. Two women with no shoes and badly burned arms and backs dragged him out of the building just before what was left of the wall collapsed behind them.

Fire trucks from surrounding communities arrived, mostly too late to do anything but watch the biggest bonfire anyone had ever seen.

Dupre was limping badly. He had broken his foot kicking the wall. He refused medical help. He was too busy rounding up Wheelers to charge out into the night in search of Gypsies.

The band was covered in soot and coughing up smoke and ash as they stood near the bayou, watching The Safari Club burn. Flames shot into the sky a hundred fifty feet. The heat was so intense they had to back further away from the conflagration.

Jesse held Amy close. He had nearly lost her. The smell of smoke in her hair made him want to take care of her forever. He was beginning to realize what a great team they made. Slowly, but surely, her happiness was becoming as important to him as his own.

She tried to wipe the soot from her eyes. "You saved me. You and Dupree."

"Hey, you saved a few folks yourself."

"I wouldn't have been any good to anyone if you two hadn't

gotten me off that floor. I have never been so terrified in my life. They weren't going to let me up. I couldn't move. I was being buried alive. Remind me to thank that big goon, Dupre."

Butch embraced Jesse. "I can't believe we made it out alive. Great call on breaking down the wall, Jesse. We were all goners until you made that move."

"We did it together," Jesse said.

Dale coughed out a cloud of smoke. "We'll probably be the first rock and roll band to win the Medal of Honor."

Nobody laughed.

Rene had Polly on his arm. "How much did we make at the door?"

"My guess is the cash went up in flames along with the door and the floor and everything else about the Safari Club," Butch said.

Dale passed around a large bottle of water. "They'll be talking about this night forever."

Staring into the blaze, Jesse felt the spirit behind the voice. He could have sworn he saw the giant features of a man wearing a horned buffalo hood. laughing. He wondered why the voice would be laughing.

Butch shook Jesse by the shoulder to bring him out of his reverie. "What made you think we could break down the wall?"

Jesse wasn't about to reveal the source of his inspiration. He'd learned to keep quiet about the voice. At least now he knew the voice was on his side.

He tried to shake the soot and ashes out of his hair. "Pure desperation."

They had been too busy evacuating the crowd to save their equipment from the supernatural force of the conflagration.

The only gear they managed to salvage was Butch's guitar and Tim's fiddle. The drums and all the amps and microphones and cables and speakers and monitors and the soundboard—lost.

Butch wondered aloud about the gear they'd lost. "I don't know how we're ever going to replace everything."

As they sat along the bayou and watched the fire burn madly into the night, Tim was the only one to speak. He recited a line the band all recognized. "Smoke on the water, and fire in the sky."

Somehow, the band, as only a band can do, came together in perfect time to chant, like Buddhist monks, the Deep Purple guitar riff for the hit song, "Smoke on the Water."

> Dun, dunn, da
> Dun, dunn, da da
> Dun, dunn, da
> Dunn, da da

CHAPTER SEVEN

THE SEA SHELL

Three days after the fire, the band met at Jesse and Amy's apartment. Butch was first to state what had been troubling everybody since the fire. "We can't go on without our gear and I don't see any way we can afford to replace it."

Dale stood up to give a pep talk like a football coach whose team is trailing by thirty points at halftime. "We're going to get jobs as waiters. We can make good money and put half of what we make into an equipment fund."

"I didn't come to New Orleans to be a waiter," Tim said.

Rene cut the conversation short. "Hold on. No need for all this. I already talked to my father and he said he'll help us get a loan to buy new gear."

Jesse did not like the idea of the band becoming more dependent on Rene and his family. "Getting a loan sounds well and good until you remember we have to pay it back with interest."

The comment caused a thoughtful silence among the band until Rene responded defiantly. "You got a better idea?"

Jesse held his hands up and shrugged his shoulders to admit he didn't have a better idea. He hated being backed into a corner, especially by a drummer who was trying to be the leader of the band.

Rene's father helped arrange a loan to replace the musical gear lost in the fire. The loan provided a major equipment upgrade, but the band was now completely dependent on the financial backing of Rene's family. Jesse may have saved the band from the fire but Rene put them back in the frying pan.

Jesse tried to look on the bright side. The new microphones were better, the drums were bigger, the mixing board got a few more channels and the P.A. got so big it couldn't fit in Jesse's van and Rene's truck. The band would need a U-Haul trailer to haul the new gear. They would also have to come up with seven hundred and fifty dollars a month to pay on the equipment loan. Jesse didn't think about the monthly payment when he was in the music store in New Orleans, picking out a better sound system than he ever dreamed of having.

Rene tried to make nice. "What do you say, Jesse? Are we having fun now, or what?"

Jesse was realizing how grateful he should be. "Your father's being great about all this. I don't know what we would have done without him."

"We would have thought of something," Rene said. "This is a band of destiny."

Jesse gave Rene a big hug. "Yes, it is, my brother. And it's all built on the drums and bass."

"You got that right."

News of the fire at the Safari Club made headlines in the New Orleans Times-Picayune Newspaper. The story focused on the many fire code violations that contributed to the tragedy. The band's life-saving heroics got no ink. Even so, word spread quickly among music lovers about the band that saved its crowd from a terrible fire in the middle of a war between two motorcycle clubs.

The band's agent was now able to book them three or four nights a week, making at least three hundred a night and sometimes as much as seven fifty. On a good week they could make three grand, which sounded great until fifteen hundred was deducted for travel, meals and lodging, loan payment, and trailer charges. That meant take home pay of three hundred a man before taxes, which nobody was about to pay. On a bad week, there was no take home pay. On a worse week, they went in the hole.

Jesse knew the band was lucky to find steady work in an era when Disco Music had nearly wiped out live performances by flesh and blood musicians. Even so, the money got even better when they started playing Mississippi Gulf Coast towns like Lakeshore, Long Beach, and Gulfport. Beach clubs still wanted live bands.

The Divebomberz were working hard and partying harder. It wasn't exactly naked showgirls falling out of hotel windows, but women came out of the woodwork to be with the band. They were ready for anything. Beach parties occasionally turned into naked fire-jumping contests. The band found itself on the front lines of the sexual revolution. There were casualties. Jesse did his best to be faithful to Amy, but sometimes his best wasn't good enough. The women were aggressive and completely entranced by rock musicians.

Amy was not pleased about Jesse being gone for more than a week at a time, suspecting the worst from the wicked excesses of the road. She had taken a job teaching high school art so she was stuck at home during the week. One Friday night, she made a surprise visit to a bar on the beach in Gulfport called The Sea Shell.

Her timing could not have been worse for Jesse. Amy caught him after the first set, on break, outside the club, on the beach, with a flirtatious and curvaceous young woman who was in the process of stripping down for a skinny dip.

"Hey, you! Asshole!" Amy screamed at Jesse over the roar of the surf and a fierce wind.

A storm was blowing in fast and hard. The National Weather Service had issued hurricane warnings. The gale force disaster was nothing compared to what Amy was about to unleash on Jesse.

"Hey, I wasn't going in with her," Jesse said as the young woman began trying to dress herself. The wind blew her shirt into Amy's face. Jesse stepped between Amy and the bare-breasted girl.

Amy threw the woman's shirt to the sand and glared at Jesse. "Don't tell me you're defending this little whore."

"Watch your mouth, bitch," the girl said as she jumped around Jesse, grabbed her shirt and pushed Amy to the sand on her butt.

Jesse bent down to help but he was way too slow. Amy had already regained her footing, launched into the girl and plowed her into the surf like a defensive end sacking a quarterback.

The mostly naked girl was not ready for the sudden attack. Her legs went out from under her as Amy took her down into two feet of choppy water and held her head underwater. All Jesse could see of the girl was kicking feet and flailing arms. Amy wasn't letting her up for air.

"Amy, let her go," Jesse shouted as he ran into the surf. "I don't even know her name. Nothing was going on. She just got drunk and dared me to go swimming in the storm."

Amy didn't even look at him as she kept both hands on the girl's head. The flailing was getting weaker by the moment.

Jesse had to tackle Amy into the water to keep the girl from drowning.

Once the sputtering and choking girl got to her feet, she fled the scene as fast as her legs would take her. She grabbed her shorts, sandals, and shirt and ran down the beach in her wet panties and into the darkness, still coughing up salt water and gasping for air.

Amy pointed her finger at Jesse as they squared off in waist deep water. "You're the one I should be holding underwater."

"Well, you managed to get us both soaking wet. Come on, let's get inside the Sea Shell. This storm is about to hit."

"You go on back to your precious band. If you think I'm going back into that low rent joint with a bunch of raging drunks, you've got another thing coming. And who names a club The Sea Shell?"

Jesse ignored the sarcastic question. "It's a hurricane party. They're just having fun. You need to come with me. You're all wet. It's not safe out here."

"I'm not going anywhere with you," Amy said. "You're the one who's not safe. One week, you almost burn me up in a fire, and now you want to drown me in a hurricane. Why should I be with you? All you care about is yourself. You don't care about me. You asked me to marry you before I even came down here. Now, you won't even talk about getting married or even setting a wedding date. I traded in my TR6 so your band could have a van. I loved that car. I took a job teaching school so we could keep our apartment. I do the band t-shirts for free. I follow you around like some kind of groupie. And what do I get? I get to meet your new groupie."

Jesse winced and shook his head. "She's not my groupie."

Amy's tone amplified to hysterical anger. "What do you call it, then? She's getting naked with you on the beach."

"I wasn't getting naked."

"One more minute and you would have been."

She started to cry as she waded out of the waves, pounding the water for emphasis. "You'd rather be a rock star than be with me."

Jesse tried to grab her but she wouldn't let him. She slipped out of his grasp. She wasn't crying anymore. The rain was starting to come down hard enough to hurt.

"Come on, Amy. We've got to go inside. I've got two more sets to play."

Amy walked away from him. "You go on. I'm going home."

Jesse followed her. "Don't go, Amy. I'm glad you came. Honest, I am. I need you to stay. We'll have fun. You need to stay. You can't drive home in this storm."

Amy stopped and turned on him. "What you need, Jesse, is a good shot of reality. If you think I'm going to wait around forever, waiting for you to grow up, you've got another thing coming. I should have known all along you would never marry me."

Jesse backed up a step. "Wait a minute. I love you. I really do. Don't forget that."

"You don't love anybody but yourself," Amy said as she poked him in the chest with her right index finger.

Jesse didn't know what to say. On some level she was right but, deep down, he knew she was wrong. "I love you more than anything. I'll prove it to you. Let's get married right now. Right here in the middle of the hurricane."

Amy's mouth dropped open like she couldn't believe anyone would say something so thoughtless and insensitive. "You really know how to make a girl feel special, Jesse."

She stomped away through the sand and past the club and into the parking lot. He started to follow her, then thought better of it when he saw her start running toward Harley, Jesse's rusty Volkswagen. Amy had been reduced to driving the little wreck of a car when Jesse had the van on the road. He heard her grind Harley into reverse and grind it again into first gear. She shifted into the night until all he could see was two taillights fading away in the driving rain.

He watched until the lights disappeared. The stinging rain didn't faze him. Watching Amy leave felt like the best part of his heart was being ripped out of his body. Amy deserved better, he realized. She would be crying all the way back to New Orleans and it was his fault. She'd come to help him celebrate on the beach and all he'd done was show her what a selfish fool he really was. She was right. One minute more and he would have been naked.

"Take a good look," Jesse heard the voice say. It sounded like it was coming from the eye of the approaching hurricane.

"Take a good look at what?" Jesse screamed into the rain, never expecting the voice to answer him.

"Take a good look at what you're throwing away," the voice said.

"I'm not throwing anything away," Jesse shouted. "She's the one who's running away."

Jesse listened for a further response. This was the first time the voice had actually answered one of his questions. They were in dialogue with one another. He wondered if he was making progress or slipping into deeper trouble.

"What should I do?" he cried into the wind and rain. "Should I go after her?"

No answer.

He stared down the deserted, rain-swept road for some time, hoping Amy might return. After a few minutes, the rain began to feel like a waterfall. He became dejected, and decided to seek shelter in the Sea Shell.

"What happened to you?" Dale asked as Jesse stumbled into the bar like a wet dog.

"Amy caught me on the beach with Janet. We were just about to go skinny-dipping. Why didn't you tell me she was here?"

"We had no idea where you were or what you were doing," Dale said. "Who's Janet?"

"She's that babe who was dancing so crazy right in front of you."

"Oh, shit, Amy caught you with her. Were you naked?" Dale asked.

"No, but she was, almost."

"Oh, no. Where's Amy now?"

"On her way back to New Orleans, I guess."

"What's up, Jesse?" Butch asked as he joined the conversation. "Why you all wet?"

"Amy just caught him skinny dipping with that crazy, hot, drunk babe who was dancing wild," Dale said. "Now Amy's driving back to New Orleans by herself."

Butch shook his head and looked at Jesse. "That's terrible. Way to go, Jesse. Way to break her little heart."

Jesse tried to defend himself. "She's the one breaking my heart. She shows up unannounced and then leaves in a huff before letting me explain."

Butch wasn't having any of it. "What were you going to tell her? You were on lifeguard duty?"

It's time to go on," Tim said. "The club owner is getting nervous. He wants us back onstage before the storm hits. He doesn't want to lose his crowd."

Jesse was wringing out salt water from his shirt. "What, so we can all die together?"

Dale tried to smooth things over. "Nobody's going to die. It's a hurricane party."

"It's not a hurricane party," Jesse said. "It's a hurricane."

Rene noticed Jesse's drenched clothing. "You better get some dry clothes on."

"I'll change in the van," Jesse said as he headed for the door. "You guys stall for a minute. I'll be right back."

The band and the crowd were ready to go by the time Jesse came back and joined them onstage.

Dale handed him a bar towel. "Man, you're as wet as you were before."

Jesse was breathing hard from running through the storm. "You can't believe it out there. It's really getting scary."

Rene kicked off the next set on his drums. Jesse was on bass, Butch on guitar and Tim on fiddle. Dale was singing lead. The first song was a souped-up version of "Robbin' Banks" by the Holy Modal Rounders. The band sounded smooth and powerful. The crowd had never heard the song before, but they were soon singing along with the chorus, "Lord I love robbin' banks."

As the set progressed, Jesse couldn't get Amy off his mind. He was worried about her driving in the storm, all wet and angry and sad.

The raucous crowd brought him back to the performance. No one drinks like the crowd at a hurricane party on the beach. People were dancing all over the club and not necessarily with each other. Anyone with a glass or a bottle in her hand seemed to be putting an individual twist on the proverbial rain dance. A window facing the beach blew out like someone fired a shotgun. People screamed and laughed at the same time, like they were inviting the storm to come in and join the party. Real danger was pounding on the door but everybody was too drunk to answer it.

Everybody, that is, except Butch and Jesse. Each of them was still sober enough to realize it might be time to stop the party and find shelter away from the beach.

"Does this place even have a basement?" Butch leaned over to ask Jesse as repairs were being made to the window.

Nick, the club owner, had two guys nailing up plywood on all the front windows, which were on the beach side. The massive oak bar was on the other side of the club, the side nearest the road. In between the bandstand and the bar, the crowd kept getting larger and more packed as new people piled into The Sea Shell to get out of the storm.

All the other clubs on the beach had closed. Kicked out patrons who didn't want to stop partying found the lights of The Sea Shell most inviting. Jesse could see that no one was concerned about the powerful danger of the oncoming storm. Everybody was dancing and cheering.

The band kept playing with no break between sets. The crowd was rowdy and demanding.

Jesse wasn't surprised when the power went out. He knew it would only be a matter of time. Everything went pitch black. The only sound coming from the bandstand was the muffled sound of Rene hitting drums with no working microphones.

Jesse had a Voodoo-cow-skull vision like the night at Fritzel's when the lights went out. Once again, the skull flashed like a neon warning sign coming up from out of his subconscious mind. He expected the voice to come back to him since the band seemed, once again, in imminent danger.

The voice said nothing. The only warning it had given him all night was about losing Amy.

Before Jesse had time to wonder how to deal with the storm in the darkness, the power came back on as if by a miracle.

Nick jumped onstage to make an announcement. "Okay, people. We're the only ones on the entire shore who have power. That's because I'm the only club owner around with the foresight to buy a generator."

The crowd cheered wildly as they surged toward the stage like Nick was some kind of new messiah.

"And, as you all know, my band is invincible."

The crowd began stomping its collective feet. Jesse realized most of them had heard about "the Safari Club miracle," as it was now referenced.

Nick pulled out five-hundred-dollar bills and ceremoniously handed them to Dale. "That's hazardous duty pay for the band. And for all of you," he said, pausing for dramatic effect, "next round is on the house."

The crowd stormed the bar.

The Divebomberz kicked back into high gear with an original song, appropriately titled, "Hurricane on the Bayou." The band and the cheering crowd became one, riding out the storm in a fever pitch of rock and roll, tequila courage. Jesse was so exhausted he felt like falling down. He looked around and saw his fellow band members feeling the same way, grinning and bearing it. The only breaks they had were more like pauses to drink shots of tequila provided by members of the audience.

Torrential rain and thunder barrages could be heard even over the intense volume of the band. Jesse couldn't see the magnificent lightning show because the windows were boarded. The club began to feel like a ship that had submerged.

Jesse got the crowd going with a sing-a-long version of "Yellow Submarine." Every voice in the club was screaming the lyrics in joyful unison. It didn't matter that the band didn't know the chords to the song. Rene knew the drum beat and the mob choir did the rest. Try as he might, Jesse couldn't get Amy out of his mind. "Yellow Submarine" was one of her favorite songs. He hoped she made it home safely. What if she'd finally had enough of him and the band? Could he live without her?

Was his life going to come down to a choice between Amy and the band?

In his current state of fatigue and intoxication, Jesse realized for the first time that Amy would be the wise choice. He also realized she would never force that decision on him.

The party raged on until 4 a.m. when the storm began to ease up. The band had been playing encores for two hours. The bar was down to its last bottle of tequila. The place smelled like the inside of an alcoholic's mouth. Marijuana and cigarette smoke filled the room. It was hard to take a breath without choking. Jesse knew the dance floor was slimy from the way the dancers were slipping and falling all over each other. From the stage, he could smell the funk of spilled beer, sweat-soaked clothing, and cigarette butts. The hurricane humidity was a hundred percent. Too many dancing bodies in such a small place turned the windowless room into a steam bath. Men and women greased each other up with sweaty, topless embraces. Jesse saw several couples shamelessly making love on tables and chairs at the edge of the club.

The hurricane party was about to go full orgy when the storm finally began to die down. Jesse could feel the pressure falling. In a break between songs, Dale announced that the rain and thunder had stopped. The announcement took the wind out of everybody's sails. People stopped dancing and hugged each other.

Butch took off his guitar, set it down and stepped up to the microphone. "On behalf of the flight crew and the captain, we would like to thank each and every one of you for flying with The Divebomberz tonight. We did experience some turbulence and we thank you all for your patience. Please keep your seatbelts fastened as we taxi toward the gate. We hope you enjoy the rest of your trip, wherever your final destination might be."

The highly intoxicated crowd screamed for more. A chant

went up for "One more song." They didn't stop even when the band started packing up instruments, wrapping cords and beginning the tedious process of breaking down the gear. The band was done, fried, spent, and wasted. They couldn't have continued playing even if they'd wanted to try.

The real work of loading equipment into vehicles was about to begin. Jesse knew they'd need a bit of a break and some sobering up before taking on that task. He also knew better than to let a bunch of drunks try to help.

People hung around the club, basking in the afterglow of the storm-survival party. A dazed woman in a topless bikini opened up the door to the beach. The first rays of dawn stabbed through the smoky bar, like crusading sabers come to decapitate the heathens. The band staggered out of the club and onto the sand to watch the sunrise. The world outside was shockingly bright as the sun illuminated the debris-strewn beach. A thirty-five-foot sailboat was wrecked and lying on its side not twenty feet from the club. The side of the club was smattered with debris.

The sunrise was so bright it made Jesse moan and cover his eyes. It took some time to adjust to daylight after a night in the party tomb.

Dale stripped naked and waded into the waves. "Come on in," he called back. "The water's really warm."

Nobody made a move to join him.

Dale dove in anyway.

Jesse had a two-fold epiphany as he watched the sun rise in its orange glory through the broken cloud horizon. One, he had to get back to Amy and make things right. And, two, he had to get to Carmen to get to the bottom of his Voodoo voice.

Amy wasn't home when Jesse finally made it back to their New

Orleans apartment at 3 p.m. the day after the hurricane party. The band had slept most of the morning on the beach. He'd tried to call from the pay phone in the bar but there had been no answer. He looked around the apartment. There was no note from Amy. The place felt empty. His life was taking a terrible wrong turn. Amy had become the voice of his better angels. One whisper from her could get him back on track. Holding her hand and listening to her laugh made him happy. Could she be gone for good?

He checked the closet. Her clothes were hanging neatly on her side. He checked the dresser. Her socks and underwear were there. He checked the bathroom. Her make up and hair products and even her toothbrush were there. These were good signs. Maybe she was giving him a dose of his own medicine by making him wonder where she was and what she was doing?

All he could see in his mind's eye was Amy's taillights disappearing in the rain. He kept hearing the voice say, "Take a good look at what you're throwing away."

Jesse felt an unfamiliar emotion rising in his heart. At first, he couldn't identify it. He had never felt it before. It was the fear of losing someone you love. Before he knew what was happening, he had gone from being a heart-breaker to having his own heart broken.

It was a jolting, unwelcome shift of conscience.

He never should have let her drive off alone in the rain. He had done something wrong and there was nothing he could do to make it right. His powers of self-forgiveness had always been truly awesome. Since when did guilt have a seat at his table?

He laid down on what served as their bed, a double mattress on the floor of the tiny bedroom. Two rectangular windows with a view of the Mississippi docks were at floor level. He looked down Tchoupitoulas Street, hoping to see Harley headed his way. No such luck. He was too tired to get up and go looking for her. The last thing he did before falling asleep was smell the delicious aroma of Amy's herbal shampoo on her pillow. She really did deserve much better than he'd been giving her. At the very least, she should know how much he needed her in his life.

He fell asleep.

His dreams were troubled. He was lost in the French Quarter, looking for something but unable to remember what it was. He was staring into the windows of antique shops on Royal Street, and asking strangers for directions. People kept saying they couldn't help him if he didn't know what he was trying to find.

Ruthie the duck lady appeared in her trademark housecoat. She had one duck along on a string. "You're not looking for some thing. You're looking for some one."

"Yes, yes, you're right," Jesse said. "Who is it? Do you know?"

Ruthie smiled her inscrutable smile, a cross between Mona Lisa and Yoko Ono. "You've already found her."

"Where is she? Who is she?"

"She's calling right now."

A shrill ringing from the telephone awakened him. It was Amy and she sounded like she'd been drinking. He looked at the clock. It was 10:30 p.m. He'd slept the day away. Amy was slurring her words ever so slightly. "Sorry to wake you up after your big night. Did your naked little friend come back after I left?"

"Not after you nearly drowned her."

"It's you I should have drowned."

"Come on, Amy, don't be like that. Why don't you come home so we can talk?"

"I think you'd better come see me. I don't think I should be driving."

Jesse thought about her demand for a moment. "Where are you?"

"I'm at Tortilla Flats."

He heard her giggling, like she was having fun with somebody at the bar. "I'll be right there. Don't go anywhere."

Tortilla Flats had been the band hang out since their arrival in New Orleans. It was near the old U.S. Mint and close to the railroad tracks along the Mississippi River. Jesse drove the band van, still full of equipment, and got to the bar in a hurry. Amy was gone. The bartender said she had just left.

Jesse slapped both hands on the bar. Then he turned on the bartender. "I told her not to go anywhere."

"Don't look at me, man." The bartender held up his hands in a mock surrender.

Jesse ran outside and headed for the river. He knew that's where she would go. She loved the river walk. Sure enough, he caught a glimpse of her white shirt in the darkness. He took off after her. Amy was crossing the tracks and on her way to the riverfront docks when Jesse caught up with her.

He tried hard to hide the fact that he was out of breath. "Where do you think you're going?"

"I'm going to catch a slow boat to China," she said.

"Not on my watch, you're not." He realized she wasn't about to let him swoop her into his arms and kiss her. "Let's get married June sixteenth."

"What makes you think I still want to marry you?"

Jesse looked her in the eyes and slowly moved his hands to her shoulders. "I need you to know I still want you to be my wife. I know I haven't acted much like it lately, but it's true. I love you with all my heart."

Amy escaped his grasp, turned away and made him follow her up the concrete stairs to the river walk. Once they were both looking at the Mississippi River, shining like neon in the moonlight, she turned to him and lowered her voice. "Jesse, this band thing seems to be making you crazier and crazier. You're trying so hard to be . . . I don't know what. It's like you're trying too hard. And this voice you keep claiming to hear has me worried."

"The voice saved us all from the Safari Club fire."

"You saved us at the Safari. It was you who got us all kicking down the walls. There was no voice. You don't need the voice. You've got it all. The voice is just you talking to yourself."

Jesse stared at the river, wondering if she could be right. "I wish you were right about that."

"I am right about that. And, now that you mention it, I'm glad you don't talk about it much anymore. It scares me when you talk about Voodoo."

"Why's that?"

"I don't know. It makes me think you might be delusional in this quest for, I don't know, rock and roll stardom I guess."

"I'll always be delusional, whether I make it in the music business or not. You know it's true. I suffer from delusions of adequacy."

She couldn't help but laugh. "That's pretty good."

"Tell me I'm not delusional about us," he said, taking her by the hand.

She had tears in her eyes when she looked at him. "You know I had a terrible day without you."

Jesse squeezed her hand as they walked together. "I'm sorry, baby. I need to make you happy and I haven't been doing a very good job of it lately."

Amy stopped walking and turned to him. "You don't want a marriage. You want the security of having a partner, but you don't want the responsibility. You want a place to come home to, off the road."

Jesse returned her gaze. "I want you to be happy. Listen to

me. That's really all I want. I want you to be happy, happy with me."

His eyes were brimming with tears. So were hers.

He kissed a tear off her cheek as it began rolling down. "We've been having fun down here, haven't we? I mean, it beats teaching school in Indiana, right?"

"So, now I'm teaching school in New Orleans."

They began walking again. "I thought you loved it down here."

She took a deep breath and sighed. "I do love it down here. And I do love you. I will follow you anywhere. As long as there's no other woman involved."

"There could never be anyone but you. I'm not sure I realized it until I came home today and you weren't there. I felt empty and sad and worried and even guilty."

"That doesn't sound like the Jesse I know."

"The Jesse you know . . . needs you more than you know and more than maybe I even know."

Another tear began rolling down Amy's cheek. He tried to kiss it away but she wouldn't let him.

"Behold, the mighty Mississippi," Jesse said, desperately attempting a conversational arabesque. "They're not making one inch of this back in Indiana."

Amy let him off the hook. "It has been fun here. Where else would I get to work on Mardi Gras floats?"

"That's what I'm talking about."

"Do you mean it about June sixteenth?"

Jesse paused for emphasis before answering. "Absolutely. I didn't realize you felt I was putting you off. No, I'm ready. I never met a girl like you. I'm not going to let you get away. You're my one and only."

CHAPTER EIGHT

THE VOODOO VOICE

Jesse met Carmen at The St. Louis Cemetery in New Orleans at 11:45 p.m. on a Tuesday night. She was nothing but a shadow in the darkness. The humid air smelled like molding mummies.

"It's good to see you are right on time," Carmen said. "I knew you would be."

"What's with the smell?" Jesse asked.

Carmen twitched her nose and tilted her head slightly to the right. "Your nose is playing tricks on you. You see all the tombs above ground and you think you smell them. There is no smell here. You will see as we enter the graveyard. Your nose will adjust to the lack of smell as your eyes adjust to the lack of light."

"You're all dressed up," Jesse said. Carmen was wearing a long black dress with an embroidered, purple shawl draped over her shoulders. The red hair on top of her head was wrapped in a burgundy scarf. The colors of her garments were barely distinguishable in the midnight.

"I've come to visit my patron saint, Marie Laveau, the Voodoo queen," she said as she began to lead him slowly into the cemetery.

Jesse followed closely without saying a word. He didn't want to be left behind. The graves looked like a sea of small, stone houses, topped with crosses and statues. Some were larger than others, but each tomb had a front door that didn't open. Names and dates and messages were carved into the ornamental walls of the burial vaults. He strained to read the words and numbers. They were indiscernible in the moonless night. It crossed his mind that every structure represented a soul who lived and died thinking she was the center of the universe. He wondered what they were all doing now.

Carmen floated effortlessly into the incomprehensible maze of death traps. Was this how she made her living, charging for graveyard tours? Or was she genuinely trying to help Jesse understand the voice inside his head?

The October night air became chilly. Jesse began to wish he had a shawl of his own. He was wearing jeans and a long-sleeved, tie-died, t-shirt with Bob Marley on the front.

"Am I underdressed for the event?" he asked.

Carmen stopped and turned slowly to face him. With one finger over her mouth she advised him silently to keep his mouth shut. He thought he saw a hint of a smile behind her finger. Jesse could barely see her. There was very little light in the graveyard, only a glimmer reflected in the clouds from the lights of the surrounding city. He couldn't imagine how she was finding her way. She had been right about the smell, or lack thereof. The only scent he was occasionally catching was the mild potpourri of Desiree's body oils and lotions, mainly lavender and jasmine.

She turned and continued walking, more slowly now. Jesse's eyes were playing tricks on him. He kept seeing movement between the crypts. "Shadows," he told himself. "It's only shadows." He thought about that for a moment and then had to wonder how there could be shadows when there was no light.

Carmen stopped walking without warning. She turned and put her face close to his, holding his head in her hands.

She turned his head to the left and whispered in his right ear. "There it is. We have arrived. This is the tomb of Marie Laveau, the queen mother of Voodoo. Come, kneel with me."

Jesse got down on both knees as if in prayer. There were vases of flowers and bunches of dried herbs and what seemed to be quite an assortment of dolls placed around the crypt. It looked like somebody famous had recently died.

Carmen began murmuring a soft, prayer-chant as she constructed her own small shrine at the base of the tomb. He couldn't see everything she was using to build her tiny altar, but part of it was a doll with long, curly hair that looked a lot like his own.

A shiver of fear went down the full length of his spine.

Carmen noticed him looking over his shoulder. "I thought you weren't afraid of anything."

Jesse took the deepest breath he could take and held it as long as he could. He finally whispered in a long, slow exhale, "You're sure you know what you're doing?"

Carmen didn't respond to him. Instead, she began speaking to the carved stone on the wall in front of her, "Oh, my saint, my Marie, my Mother Laveau, I come to you tonight with a seeker of Voodoo truth. The gift he offers is his inquisitive soul. The risk he will take is whatever voyage you send him on or whatever task you require him to complete."

Jesse could feel the power of the Voodoo voice rising up his spine as Carmen continued her chant. The thought of the voice kept his courage up in the darkness, even though it didn't speak to him. His heart was pounding. He closed his eyes and listened for what seemed like quite a long time, straining with all his might to hear the voice again.

Instead of the voice, he heard Carmen begin a soft moan, as though she were being whisked away in a trance. That would not do, he thought as his fears returned like ghosts in a haunted house. If she was going anywhere, he wanted to go with her. Being left alone in front of this crypt, lost in the darkness with who knew how many haunted spirits, was the last thing he wanted.

Should he grab her arm to bring her back to reality? No, that would definitely not do. He decided to keep his eyes closed and hope the voice would give him guidance.

Carmen's moans turned to groans and then to deep-space silence. He found himself floating momentarily. Then he was back on solid ground and being swept down a cobblestone street by a crowd of people on the move. It was night and the only light came from torches. He wasn't in the graveyard anymore. He was walking on a city street. There were no neon signs, no traffic signals, and no streetlights of any kind. Jesse had somehow arrived in a place, or a time, before electricity. He was still in New Orleans. That much he knew from the Victorian architecture and the oppressive humidity. But it was no longer the twentieth century.

A man on a tall, white horse knocked him off balance and nearly to his knees. Before he had time to yell at the rude rider, Jesse had to dodge a two-horse carriage. It was all he could do to keep from getting run down. He felt the spin of the large wooden wheel as it whirled by his nose.

Everybody seemed to be in a hurry. Children were running, mothers with babes in their arms were trotting along the road. White men with pistols and knives on their belts were striding alongside black men with canes and top hats. They all seemed to be drinking whiskey from the same flask. A celebratory mood was in the night air.

"Where are we going?" Jesse asked two teenaged boys.

"We're going to see Marie Laveau," the tall boy said. "Everyone knows that. What are you, drunk? She's doing

Voodoo tonight. Keep walking, you'll see her giant fire on Lake Pontchartrain."

Jesse stepped up his pace to keep up with the hurrying flow of pedestrian traffic. He looked around, hoping to see Carmen or anyone who looked the least bit familiar. The street became more and more crowded as he approached what seemed to be a major event. He knew he was getting close when he heard the drums, many drums, pounding out an ominous marching beat. He heard voices singing. It wasn't a choir. It was a crowd of people, singing a beautiful song of togetherness. It was a melody at once mournful and uplifting. It was a slave chant that sounded like the beginnings of gospel music. Jesse was deeply moved. He felt like a runaway slave, terrified by evil in pursuit, yet joyful at the prospect of freedom. His feet of clay were on the road to salvation. Nothing could stop him now. He remembered what the Voodoo voice had said, "Drink deeply. You got to keep running."

A fire in the distance was shooting flames and sparks high into the sky. Now, he was running toward the blaze. Everyone was running. As he pushed his way into the gathered crowd, the scene felt more like a public lynching than any kind of spiritual revival. The stage looked like a hanging scaffold. Armed guards surrounded the performance area. The tall, wooden platform was far enough away from the massive bonfire to keep from catching fire itself, but anyone onstage would certainly feel the heat. The blaze was in front of the ceremonial platform. People surged all around like moths to the flame.

Jesse felt someone take him by the hand. It was the mystery man from the bayou, known to Jesse as Gabriel. He was smiling broadly and reassuringly.

Jesse was surprised to see him. He held out his arms for a hug. "Hey man, how'd you get here?"

"Gabriel embraced him. "Same as you, We're in the Voodoo dream."

"Are we here for good or do we go back?"

Gabriel backed out of the hug and gave Jesse a reassuring pat on the shoulder. "Do not worry, my friend. Your mind will find its way home."

Jesse did not find that comment completely reassuring. "I knew you were different when you disappeared on the highway by the magic mushroom field."

"Didn't I say you'd find all the Voodoo you wanted?"

"I do remember that. I've been wanting to thank you."

"You are quite welcome, I am sure," Gabriel said as he escorted Jesse to a perfect viewing position, no more than ten yards from the stage.

Before Jesse could say another word, the master of ceremonies walked onstage like he owned it. The crowd roared its approval. He was dressed like a witch doctor, with a spear, ankle bells and feathers, a belt that looked like it belonged to a boxing champion, a horned buffalo hood and a flowing cape. The ceremonial leader was the vision Jesse had seen in the flames at the Safari Club. The leader did not speak. When he raised the spear over his head, dancers appeared on the stage, jumped down and began gyrating around the fire to a new, more sensual, drumbeat. They wore native Indian costume and threw bags into the fire that exploded into colorful fireballs. The drumbeat rose to fever tempo. The dancers were athletic and even acrobatic. The crowd chanted and clapped hands in unison until the witch doctor took center stage and, once again, held the spear over his head. The drums stopped immediately as the dancers exited behind the stage. The crowd fell silent. Everybody knew the master of ceremonies was about to speak.

Jesse wondered how the man would possibly be heard over the fire and across the vast crowd.

Jesse turned to speak to Gabriel, but saw only Carmen by his side. She squeezed his hand and looked at him lovingly. Her eyes seemed out of focus. She murmured softly and incoherently.

Jesse started moaning himself when he heard the master of ceremonies begin speaking.

It was the Voodoo voice. *His* Voodoo voice.

The voice boomed into the night, loud enough for all to hear. Jesse was so surprised to recognize the voice that he forgot to listen to what it was saying. All he heard was one name spoken, "Marie Laveau."

The crowd gasped collectively as the Voodoo queen appeared. She was dressed like Carmen, but the scarf wrapped around her head was bright red and her dress was many colored.

People immediately fell to their knees.

"No, no, my children," Marie said with a voice nearly as powerful as the witch doctor. "Rise up, rise up. Tonight we rise together. Tonight we heal each other. Tonight we begin the holiday that will last forever. Tonight we bring the Voodoo spirit down to heal every single one of us from all that ails us. The spirit will make the blind to see. It will make the crippled walk. It will free our minds from the sadness of this world in which we toil and weep. It will free our hearts and souls to rise up and be one with the Voodoo world."

An explosion in the fire sent up a massive fireball to provide a terrific exclamation to her prophecy. The crowd roared its approval and began stomping feet and clapping hands in unison. As Marie Laveau continued her ritual, Jesse saw the witch doctor with the Voodoo voice standing on the ground near the edge of the stage. They made eye contact from thirty feet away. Jesse felt irresistibly drawn to the man. He decided to approach him. It was now or never. This was the moment of truth. He would never forgive himself if he didn't at least try to make contact.

Carmen tried to stop him but he dragged her along by the hand until he was face to face with the man, or spirit, who had so perplexed and inspired his soul. She let go of his hand.

The witch doctor opened his arms wide as if to take Jesse into his embrace. His eyes were wildly animalistic. His laugh sounded like a lion's roar.

He felt his heart melting as he leaped forward to embrace the Voodoo voice. Instead of making human contact, he slammed into the marble tombstone of Marie Laveau's crypt and knocked himself unconscious.

He must have been out for a long while. When he came to consciousness, he had a sinking feeling he was back in the graveyard. Everything was dark. There was no fire.

Carmen was cradling his head in her lap. "You had a powerful vision, yes?"

"Oh, my head," Jesse said as he sat up and felt for injury.

She put her arm around him for support. Her nose twitched slightly as though she was conducting a forensic, pheromone investigation. "You are fine. You have a big bump on your forehead and a little blood, but you're going to be fine."

Jesse put his head on her shoulder. "I met the voice. He is the real deal. He is Marie Laveau's witch doctor."

"What did he say to you?"

"He didn't say anything. He opened his arms to me and welcomed me into his world. When I tried to join him, something got in the way. Looks like the tombstone must have stopped me."

Carmen lifted his head gently off her shoulder. "It wasn't the marble that stopped you. You ran into a wall of your own making."

Jesse rubbed his aching head. "What do you mean?"

"The material world creates the illusion that each one of us is at the center of everything. The problem with being in the center is that everything and everyone around you creates a prison that separates you from what you really are."

"So what am I, really?"

"You are part of everything and everything is part of you."

Jesse and Carmen got to their feet as she continued her explanation. "Think of your eyes. Everywhere you turn, your eyes bring the world to you. It is only natural to feel you are the center. But the eyes are the great deceivers."

"I've heard that said."

"Think about it, Jesse. What you see is not what you get. If something moves too fast, you don't see it. If something moves too slowly, you don't see it. If something is too small, you don't see it. If something is too big . . ."

"I don't see it."

Carmen smiled patiently. "And you can't see the Voodoo."

"I just saw it," Jesse said.

"No, you dreamed it."

"It felt so real."

"Now, think of your brain," she said. "Like your eyes, your brain tricks you into thinking the world revolves around you. But it does not."

Jesse looked at her in epiphany and said, "Like the sun doesn't revolve around the Earth."

"Exactly," Carmen said.

"So, how does the Voodoo world fit into the real world?"

"They are two sides of the same coin."

"What are we supposed to do with the coin, besides flip it?" Jesse asked.

"We don't have to do anything with it, other than be at peace with knowing there is more to reality than the material side."

"You're making me dizzy."

Carmen put her arm around him to steady his balance. "Come with me. You're dizzy because you banged your head. We'll get some ice on you and clean up that cut. It doesn't look too deep."

As Jesse followed her through the graveyard, he was no longer afraid. His encounter with the voice had chased the evil out of his mind, at least for the time being.

He was filled with questions. "What can we do with the Voodoo?"

"We can break out of our self-centered prisons. It sounds to me like you did it tonight, for a short time anyway. And then something got in your way to keep you here. Something you can't let go, something that holds you in your jail cell."

Jesse shook his head from side to side. "I was ready to let go and be one with the Voodoo voice."

"Apparently not," Carmen said. "But you made big progress tonight. Do you at least believe the voice is on your side?"

"Yes, that much is clear. I've known that since the fire at the Safari Club. But I still don't see what the voice has to do with music. You said the voice would teach me what to do with my music."

"First of all," Carmen said. "It is not *your* music. You do not own it. Nor does it own you. Music is not something you can hold in your hand. Music is the escape route." "It is one of the best ways out of self. Music connects us all. It sets us free."

"So what's keeping me from being one with the voice?"

"This is something you will have to learn on your own. I can only tell you this. You are missing the whole point of making music."

"What is the point?"

"The point is to give it away, not sell it for profit. We only keep what we have by giving it away."

"How can I keep something if I give it away?"

"Remember," Carmen said. "Music is not a thing. It is not something you can hold in your hand. Music is a force of nature. It has much in common with Voodoo. In fact, music and Voodoo are the same thing. They join the spiritual and material worlds together."

Jesse nodded. "I know what you mean. I've felt it before. I've lost myself in the music."

"Yes, and in this regard, music and love have much in common. They are part of the same river, the river that flows through all of us. Most people dam up the river with their selfishness, trying to keep all they can get. What we need to do with music and love and Voodoo is give it away and let the river run through us so we can all be part of the flow."

"I think I know what you're saying," Jesse said as he followed her closely. He had never thought of music and love as being part of the same thing. And he had never thought of Voodoo as anything but dark and mysterious and evil. "But I still don't get how you can only keep something by giving it away."

"Think about music. Playing music is giving it away. Once you perform a song, it's gone. Maybe it lives on in the heart of the listener. For the musician, every note played is given away. For the lover, being loved is not nearly as important as giving her love away."

Jesse thought long and hard as he and Carmen walked through the burial vaults and crypts.

Carmen led him out the main entrance of the graveyard. "Think of it this way. Music is the laughter of the universe."

"What is it laughing at?"

"You," Carmen said with a beaming smile. "It is laughing at you . . . and at me . . . at anyone who thinks she is the center of the world."

CHAPTER NINE

THE PRISON OF SELF

Jesse held both hands on the bars of the holding cell in the New Orleans city jail. At least the handcuffs had been removed. His wrists were sore. He was thirsty. It had been less than a week since he and Carmen had talked about the prison of self at Marie Laveau's tomb. Now, he was in a jail cell for real. Looking through the bars, he could see police and prisoners going through their motions in front of several officers who sat behind a tall desk. No one was there on his behalf. No one cared that he was feeling highly claustrophobic, being caged like an animal.

He sat down and then reclined on a splintered, wooden bench. No point getting in a hurry. Casey knew enough about the law to get him out eventually.

Jesse had been locked up for four hours. It felt like four weeks. The lyrics to Johnny Cash songs were starting to make sense. He might as well have been stuck in Folsum Prison.

He kept thinking about the line from the Jerry Jeff Walker song, "Mr. Bojangles," "Met him in a cell in New Orleans I was, down and out."

Humming the songs actually helped him ease the pain of his predicament. Carmen was right. Music is one of the escape routes out of the prison of self. Then again, once the song was over, he was still stuck in the same, stinking rat hole of a holding cell. After the first few hours of staring at the walls, he was losing his battle to escape either his prison of self or the prison itself. He felt like a fool. It was Amy's birthday and he'd gotten himself thrown in jail. Now, she was out there, hopefully with Casey, getting the cash to buy his freedom.

It was almost impossible to believe that the entire episode was over nothing more than a traffic accident. Jesse had been driving Harley at a reasonable speed down a narrow street in the Irish Channel neighborhood of New Orleans when a middle-aged woman with a carload of kids crashed into him. No one seemed to be hurt but the woman got out of her car and began screaming at him like he'd done something horribly wrong. She yelled at him as she ran toward him shaking her fist in the air. "What you doing, going the wrong way down a one way street?"

"You're the one who blew the stop sign," Jesse said.

"I don't have no stop sign."

Jesse looked around the intersection. "I don't see a stop sign facing me."

"That's because you're going the wrong way," she said, holding her arms out wide in disbelief. "The stop sign is on the other side of the street, facing drivers who are driving the right way. And look at that sign right there."

Jesse turned and saw the one-way sign, clearly indicating he had been going the wrong way. The accident had been completely his fault.

Once the shame sunk in, all he could do was hang his head and apologize. "Oh, shit. I'm sorry."

"No shit, Sherlock," she said. "You could have killed me and my kids."

Jesse continued to apologize as he and the woman went back to her car to check on the children. Only one of the four kids was crying and even he was already getting over it.

"Here's the drug-crazed hippie who tried to kill us all," she said to the kids.

Sorry as he was, Jesse couldn't let that comment stand. "Come on. I haven't even had a drink. And I'm not on drugs."

The woman calmed down as one of her children waved shyly to Jesse. "I've got to stay here with the children. You find a phone and call the police."

"Do we really need to do that?"

"Yes, we really need to do that," she said. "Look at my car. It's totaled. I need a police report so my insurance company will pay for this mess. I can tell by looking at you and your sorry little car that you got no insurance."

The ashamed look on Jesse's face told the woman she was correct in her assessment. She adjusted her polka-dotted, drawstring dress in self-righteous indignation and motioned him to get about calling the police.

Jesse found a neighbor to let him use the phone. He called Casey first and gave his friend a five-minute head start before he called the police. Even so, the cops arrived on the accident scene a couple minutes before Casey. Jesse avoided them until he could speak to his legal counsel in training.

Casey assessed the scene and saw that Jesse had been in the wrong. "We've got a problem. You've got an Indiana driver's license."

Jesse shrugged his shoulders as he pulled out his driver's license from his wallet. "So, what? It's valid."

"So they take you to jail until the ticket is paid in full if you've got an out-of-state driver's license," Casey said.

"I don't have any money."

Casey couldn't help but laugh at the forlorn look on Jesse's face. "Like I said. We've got a problem."

"You mean *I've* got a problem."

A uniformed New Orleans police officer came up to ask

Jesse for his license just as Casey was telling him not to say anything to the police. The police officer overheard Casey and took off his reflector sunglasses to squint in disapproval. "What are you? Some kind of second year law student?"

Casey smiled and held up his hands at chest level. "Actually, that's exactly what I am, officer. My friend, here, is from Indiana. He's not familiar with the streets of New Orleans."

The cop wasn't having any of it. He put his sunglasses back on. "Looks like your Indiana friend here is going to jail if he can't pay his ticket for driving the wrong way down a one-way street. So, maybe you'd like to go to jail with him for interfering with a police investigation."

Casey wisely elected to remain silent as the officer told Jesse to put his hands behind his back so he could be cuffed. The awesome power of the police state became suddenly apparent to him. He felt vulnerable and exposed with his arms pinned behind his back. The cuffs were so tight they cut into his wrists. Getting into the back of the squad car was painful, awkward and humiliating. It smelled like wino piss.

"Could you please loosen the cuffs a little?"

The officer looked at Casey and chuckled before returning his attention to Jesse. "We'll take them off once we get you into a comfy, little jail cell."

Jesse looked at Casey helplessly through the window as he rolled away in the back of the squad car. "I'll call Amy," Casey mouthed as he held his hand up to his ear like he was using a phone.

So now Jesse lay on the bench in jail, wondering again how long it would take Amy to come up with a hundred and fifteen dollars to pay the ticket. He knew she had less than a hundred in her checking account. She'd just finished paying the rent. Amy was never shy about telling him just how broke they were.

This is a perfect opportunity to practice your patience,

Jesse told himself over and over. He closed his eyes and tried to imagine being on the beach, listening to the surf, swaying in his hammock. It didn't work. For one thing, closing his eyes couldn't block out the clanging noises and rotting smells of the jail. For another, patience wasn't even a word in his emotional vocabulary. He stood up and began pacing back and forth. Anger began welling up in his mind. *How could anyone put me, The Great One, in a cage like an animal?* It didn't help that he immediately recognized such thoughts as laughably delusional. Self-righteous indignation had always been one of his favorite emotions. It always felt good to feel better than the rest of the world. The problem was, he knew it wasn't true. He stopped pacing and tried to calm himself with deep breathing and meditation. It didn't come close to working.

Just when Jesse thought things couldn't get worse, a cop opened the cell door and shoved in a man wearing a devil costume. The man was slurring his words unintelligibly. He sounded like he thought he was making a collect call to his second ex-wife. The only words Jesse could make out were "honey" and "sorry." Jesse didn't need to be a crime-solving detective to know the devil himself was going to puke all over the tiny cell.

The man fell to his knees and began sobbing uncontrollably as he realized where he was. It took a good five minutes, but the sobs eventually turned to gagging noises. Jesse sat on the bench and pulled his legs up underneath him. He knew there was little chance he could completely avoid the splatter. The man in the devil costume started choking. It sounded like a cough at first. Then it sounded like he had something stuck in his throat. Jesse was about to begin the Heimlich maneuver when the man lurched to his feet, turned around and lunged to the cell door.

The drunk ripped off his devil mask. His body banged and clanged into the metal door as he blew lunch through the bars in one of the most impressive displays of projectile vomiting Jesse had ever seen. The man collapsed slowly and thumped his chin on each and every horizontal bar on the way to the floor.

The holding area filled with angry shouting as police rushed to the scene of the slime. One cop slipped and fell backwards, flat into the puke. He tried to get up in a hurry and only succeeded in falling down a second time.

"Shit, shit, shit," the soiled officer complained as he finally regained his footing. "This puke's all over my gun and everything."

Jesse buried his head in his knees so no one could see him laughing.

Another officer yelled at Jesse as he came in to help drag the puking devil out of the cell. "You think that's funny, long hair? I'll show you what's funny."

Jesse looked up to see the officer raising his nightstick.

He put his head down and waited for the blow to fall. It never came. The cop must have thought better of beating him in front of so many witnesses. Jesse felt him walking away to help with the cleanup.

The vomit smelled like rum and rotting garbage. Jesse knew from personal experience that the man had been drinking too many rum Hurricanes at Pat Obrien's Bar in The French Quarter. The vomit created a toxic, nauseous stench when mixed with the pungent smells of cleaning fluids. Maintenance people mopped the floor, wiped down the bars, and then set up a drying fan that mainly blew the entire aftermath back into the cell. It was a stomach turner.

The irony and symbolism of the situation was not lost on Jesse. The devil costume was no surprise. New Orleans was a never-ending Halloween party. Temptation and sin were like trick-or-treat. The putrid smell was also no surprise. It reminded him of Bourbon Street at 3 a.m. What did come as a surprise was the realization that escaping the prison of self and getting one's self out of prison might be the two sides of the existential coin Madame Desiree loved to flip.

It didn't matter. Spiritually or materially, Jesse was unable to transcend his circumstance.

He sat back down on the wooden bench to breath through his mouth and to feel sorry for himself. It wasn't his fault he was from Indiana. It wasn't his fault he couldn't afford insurance. It wasn't his fault the one-way streets in New Orleans made no sense. What was his fault was a rising and increasingly urgent need to urinate. Talk about the prison of self. His own body now had an escape attempt in progress.

At least he had somebody to talk to now. The voice of his own bodily fluids was one talkative companion. It went from, "Let's just piss in the corner," to "Let's bang on the bars and demand a trip to the toilet," to "You can't hold me forever. I know my rights."

In fact, there seemed to be several voices inside his head, each fighting for airtime like squabbling news anchors. His father's voice was retelling the story of how his one night in jail as a scared kid had made him want to become an attorney. His ninth grade history teacher was talking about how many important leaders had formulated grand plans while in prison. Amy's voice was scolding him for being an irresponsible driver.

How could he be one with anything when he couldn't even be one within himself?

The voice he kept listening for, the Voodoo voice, was not to be heard. It would have been louder than all the others combined. Louder and more clearly not manufactured by his thoughts. Where was the guidance when he needed it most? And why, now that he could see the voice in his mind's eye, could he not make contact with it by his own force of will?

Eventually, the only voice he could hear was nature calling. Jesse stood up and did a little dance to keep from wetting himself. As he did, a confinement officer came to open the cell door and said, "You're free to go."

"Free to go to the toilet?"

"Free to go wherever you want. Somebody paid your ticket. She's down the hall to the right. There's a public toilet between here and there."

Jesse took the papers the officer handed him, ran down the hall and ducked into the restroom before Amy saw him. Nothing ever felt so good as that painfully delayed urination. Once he got started, he felt the powerful satisfaction of sweet relief. He washed his face, ran wet fingers through his matted hair to dry his hands and flare up his bushy hair, and went out to greet Amy with open arms.

She let him hug her briefly, but backed off quickly to hold him at arm's length. "You smell worse than the jail. What did you get into?"

One week later, Jesse was in New Orleans traffic court with Casey, trying to get back the money Amy paid on the ticket. Turned out, the fine she paid was technically a bond. The city was giving him an opportunity to be guilty until proven innocent.

The courtroom was packed. At least fifty cases were scheduled for the morning. Casey gave Jesse advice as he waited for his name to be called. "Get up there and look that judge in the eye. Tell him you're sorry but you're from Indiana and the roads are different up there."

Jesse's name was called before he had time to get himself emotionally prepared to be his own attorney. He went before the judge, who was sitting high above the rest of the courtroom behind an ornate desk.

The judge looked down and talked to Jesse like he was a horse about to be ridden. "This is a driving the wrong way ticket. What have you got to say for yourself?"

Jesse tried to be polite. "Good morning, your honor. Thank you for giving me the opportunity to be heard."

The judge smiled slightly. "Go on, then, be heard."

"I'm from Indiana, sir, and I'm not familiar with the traffic patterns or street signs of New Orleans."

"Are you saying you were not going the wrong way down a one-way street?"

"No, I'm not saying that. I'm saying . . ."

"What you're trying to say is you are guilty as charged. Once you say that, there's really nothing left to say."

"Well, excuse me, your honor, but I was hoping to plead guilty with an explanation and, hopefully, have some leniency shown."

A ripple of chuckles swept through the courtroom. The judge laughed aloud. "Ignorance of the law is no excuse and certainly no reason for leniency."

"Then, let me say, your honor, that my finances are extremely limited."

"It is obvious that you can't afford a haircut," the judge said. "What do you do for a living, if anything?"

"Actually, your honor, I'm a musician." Jesse could see the judge beginning to soften. "I played Bourbon Street for more than a year."

The judge sat up straight in his chair. "What clubs do you play?"

"Most all of them, sir. Papa John's, Judah P's, Jimmy's, Johnny's and, most recently, Fritzel's."

"Well, why didn't you say so in the first place?"

The courtroom erupted in the first laughter the place had heard in a long while. The judge was restating an obvious truth. Musicians get special treatment in New Orleans.

The judge put his head down and began writing. "I'll tell you what I'll do for the Bourbon Street musician. I'm going to find you guilty and waive your fines and costs."

"What does that mean?" Jesse asked.

"It means you can get your money back if you take this piece of paper to the clerk's office on the way out the building."

"Thank you so much, your honor," Jesse said as the bailiff handed him his copy of the court order.

"You are quite welcome. Just don't let me see you in here again. Things might not go so well."

By the time Jesse got his money back from the clerk, Casey was beside himself with glee. "Did you see what you just did? You turned a grumpy old judge into your personal buddy in one minute flat. I'm glad I let you go up there by yourself. I couldn't have done that. You see what I've been saying? You're going to make a great trial lawyer someday."

"I think it was being a musician that saved the day, Casey, not being a natural-born lawyer."

On October 20, 1977, Lynyrd Skynyrd's plane went down near Gillsburg, Mississippi. The Divebomberz gathered the next day in grief and disbelief around the television set at Jesse and Amy's apartment. They groaned when Walter Cronkite mispronounced the famous band's name.

Dale stood up and yelled at the television. "Come on, Walter. Get it together."

"Looks like the generation gap just got a little bigger," Butch said.

Jesse motioned for everyone to be quiet. "We need to hear this."

The crash killed bandleaders Ronnie Van Zant and Steve Gaines, as well as four others. The rest of the band and crew survived.

Rene threw his hands in the air. "That's it for them. Ronnie was the heart and soul of that band."

Tim tried to offer some comic relief. "That's what would happen to us if I died. The Divebomberz would be history."

Jesse was still stunned by the terrible news. His heroes had literally just gone down in flames. He was unable to engage in the conversation.

Dale looked at Tim. "No. That's not what would happen. We'd miss you but we would find another fiddle player."

Nobody laughed. The band was fresh out of glib remarks. The pain was settling in. The Lynyrd Skynyrd plane crash was almost beyond belief, even though they were watching the news report on television.

Rene finally broke the silence. "Let's not fly, guys. Even when we make it big."

Dale began singing softly. "So, bye, bye, Miss American Pie."

The band joined in to sing about the day the music died. They ended the song on the chorus about good old boys, the whiskey and rye, and "this will be the day that I die."

Once the singing died down, Jesse decided to lighten the mood. "Hey, I've got an idea."

"What's that?" Rene asked.

"Let's carry on where Lynyrd Skynyrd left off."

"I'll drink to that," Butch said as the band members and Amy raised beer cans in a toast.

Tim began the toast while still seated. "Here's to Lynyrd Skynyrd. They were one helluva band."

Jesse stood up to finish the toast. "And here's to The Divebomberz. May we never go down in flames."

CHAPTER TEN

THE TRUCE

About a week after the Lynyrd Skynyrd plane crash, Casey arrived a little out of breath at Jesse and Amy's apartment. "We've got a problem."

Jesse waited for his friend to catch his breath. "Who's we?"

Casey sat down and gathered himself. "The Divebomberz. Remember Gypsy, the guy who sold us mushrooms until we found our own fields?"

"I never met the guy," Jesse said. Amy pulled up a chair and sat down next to Casey.

Casey sounded urgent as he tried to jog Jesse's memory. "You did but you didn't know it. I brought him to Fritzel's one night. You had a couple drinks with him."

"So, what's the problem?"

Casey lowered his voice and actually looked over his shoulder in a paranoid way before saying, "Gypsy is head of the Gypsies, the motorcycle gang."

Jesse and Amy waited for him to continue. Amy stood up and clung to Jesse's arm.

"The Gypsies are planning to ambush the Wheelers at your show at the Raceland Music Hall."

It took Jesse several beats to fully register the bad news. "Like they did at the Safari Club?"

Casey got up and began pacing. "Worse than that. The Safari Club was just a warning shot across the bow. Nobody was supposed to get hurt. There wasn't supposed to be a fire. But things have changed dramatically since then. At least six guys from each gang have been killed. You know about the shootouts."

Jesse grabbed Amy and hugged her tight. "Who told you about the ambush? Certainly not Gypsy."

"No, it was one of his dealers."

"Why would a dealer talk to you?" Amy asked.

Casey looked at Jesse as he answered. "He said he was afraid some of my friends in the band might get hurt."

Jesse took a deep breath and let it out slowly before he began asking careful questions. "Where were you when he told you this?"

Casey hesitated, unwilling to disclose the location.

Jesse and Amy waited him out.

"Okay," Casey relented. "It was at the law school."

Jesse continued his cross-examination. "What's a Gypsy drug dealer doing at the law school?"

Casey hesitated a full thirty seconds before he answered. "He's a law student, third year."

Amy leaped to her feet and pointed at Jesse. "That's how you can pay for law school. Dealing drugs. Why didn't we think of this sooner? You know you're going to need your law license so you can defend all your criminal friends in court."

Jesse ignored her sarcasm and bore down on Casey. "Is this guy part of Gypsy's gang?"

"Yeah," Casey said. "And the way he told me about the ambush made me think he expected me to tell you and get back to him."

Amy got back into the questioning. "Why do you say that?"

Casey pulled a piece of notepaper out of his back pocket. "He gave me his phone number."

Jesse and Amy looked at each other without saying a word, as though questions and answers could be more efficiently communicated in silence. Amy always looked her most beautiful, Jesse thought, when she was reading his mind. Her eyes narrowed. She stuck out her chin like getting stubborn would be part of any plan.

Amy began thinking out loud. "Maybe the Gypsies want some kind of truce with the Wheelers?"

Jesse saw her point but he returned to the main issue. "So, now you're mediating a turf war between two drug-dealing motorcycle gangs."

Casey cocked his head like a dog trying to understand his master's command. "Maybe that's the problem."

"What do you mean?" Jesse asked.

"Maybe the problem is neither club has a distinct territory. We might be able to carve out a geographic settlement. You know, Gypsies south of Bayou Lafourche, Wheelers north."

"We?" Jesse asked.

Casey sat down and pulled his chair close to Jesse. "You know. You and me. It could be the first negotiation of our future law firm."

Amy sat down and pulled her chair into the decreasing space of the conversation. "What future law firm? And what about me? Am I part of this or what?"

Casey hugged her. "You're part of the firm. You know that."

Amy hugged him back. "Thank you, Casey. But don't you think this getting in the middle of a gang war might be a little dangerous?"

Jesse looked at the two of them, his best friend from childhood and the woman he might be spending the rest of his life with. "It sounds to me like we might get shot if we don't get involved in some kind of truce. I'll tell you what. It's time for a band meeting. Everybody needs to know what kind of a jam we're in. And we need Dupre to come to the meeting for a chat on behalf of the Wheelers."

The Divebomberz had an afternoon meeting at Tortilla Flats, before the dinner crowd arrived. Rene came up from the bayou to New Orleans for the session. He was the first to address the dilemma. "We can't just cancel the Raceland show. We've got a ton of people coming. And, besides that, the Wheelers come to all our shows."

"I don't like getting in the middle of this gang thing," Butch said. "Maybe we should call the police or the FBI or something."

Dale grabbed Butch by the shoulder. "That would be the fastest way to die. We'd have both sides of the war coming to get us and paying the police to help."

Tim spoke up. "I say we negotiate us some peace. Dupre's coming soon, isn't he? Let's see how he wants to play it."

Ten minutes later, Dupre and Big Ben walked into the club like gunslingers from the Wild West. The afternoon was hot and humid, but the two bikers were wearing long coats. The few drinkers at the bar left in a hurry.

Dupre seemed to be in a good mood, considering the circumstances. "Good afternoon gentlemen. Don't make any sudden moves. You're completely surrounded."

"Hey, we're on your side," Jesse said.

Dupre laughed at his own joke. "Bartender. Bring us another round of whatever these guys are having and bring two extra glasses. And while you're at it, see what the boys outside are drinking."

"I'm all over it," the bartender said as he looked around nervously at his suddenly empty bar.

Dupre took off his coat and adjusted the sawed-off shotgun and Uzi submachine gun hanging under his arms from straps crossed over his shoulders and chest.

Dale jumped out of his chair and moved two steps away from Dupre. "Oh, my God. Is all that really necessary?"

"Yes, it's necessary. It's called survival of the fittest." Dupre said. "Check the restrooms, Ben, just in case. And make sure the bartender doesn't use the phone."

He turned to address the band. "Sorry for all the drama, but in case you haven't heard, there's a war going on."

Jesse tried to regain his composure. His heart was still pounding at the sight of automatic weapons. "We know all about it, Dupre. It's terrible. We've been feelin' for all The Wheelers. So thanks for coming. It looks like we might be in a position to help. But let's be clear about one thing. We're on your side. Always have been, always will be."

"Let's drink to that," Dupre said as he raised his glass of beer. "Let's toast to the peace talks of Tortilla Flats."

Jesse was relieved to hear the word, "peace," come out of Dupre's mouth.

Dupre returned to the topic at hand. "Now, what's this I hear about you boys talking to the Gypsies?"

Jesse looked at his fellow band members and realized he was the only one who could respond to the question. "One of my friends got tipped off that The Gypsies are going to ambush you guys at the Raceland Music Hall."

Dupre drained his beer mug in one chug and contorted his face in anger. "Those bastards. That's New Year's Eve. They know we'll all be there with our women."

Jesse tried to calm him down before he went over the edge. "No, wait. We think the tip off might be just a signal that they want to talk."

Dupre refilled his mug and chugged it, faster than the last one. He belched and wiped his mouth on his bare arm. "That's a funny way to say hello. Who's this friend of yours?"

The band members listened intently as Jesse explained how he and Casey had become involved with the Gypsies in the magic mushroom underground. As the conversation continued, Casey walked in under escort from Big Ben.

Jesse jumped up to greet his friend. "Casey, you're right on time. We were just talking about you."

Casey didn't look happy. "Yeah? I couldn't hear you from the parking lot. These guys about gave me a wedgie during the frisk."

Dupre looked Casey up and down. "Anybody with you?"

"No," Casey answered. "Hi guys," he said to the band.

Tim and Dale and Rene and Butch each responded with a sullen "hello," instead of their usual, warm embrace. Nobody looked too pleased about what increasingly felt like a hostage situation.

Casey took charge of the situation as he grabbed a chair and sat down facing Dupre. "Hey, Dupre, I'm Casey. You know me. I'm Jesse's good friend from way back. You and I have partied at a couple of the shows."

Dupre stared hard at Casey, raised an eyebrow at Jesse in disbelief, then looked back to Casey without saying a word.

Casey continued, amazingly undaunted for a guy who'd just been closely and roughly searched. "I'm pretty sure The Gypsies are ready to call a truce. They've had enough. The war is crazy. Nobody's going to win it. Too many have died. I was sorry to hear Junior got shot up pretty bad in Thibodaux last weekend."

Dupre dropped his head as if in prayer. "Yeah, he got careless, riding solo on a run. They came up from behind and shot him in the back. It's a miracle but it looks like he's going to walk out of the hospital on his own two feet in a couple days."

Butch spoke up. "That's good news. We heard they killed him."

"Junior's a tough boy. He laid the bike down when he heard the first shot. Four riders with handguns and only one bullet hit him. He broke his right leg in a couple places and he's got some awful road rash, but he's going to make it. The bullet missed his spine."

"This needs to stop," Jesse said.

"Yes, it does," Dupre said with a heavy sigh. "I'm getting tired of seeing my boys shot up. I used to love gangster movies, especially the shootouts. It's not so much fun in real life. Besides, it's bad for business. Nobody can go anywhere."

"I'm pretty sure the other side feels the same way," Casey said. "This shit needs to end. There's enough cocaine and heroin coming up the bayou for everybody to get rich."

Dupre looked at Casey incredulously. "What are you? Some kind of spokesman for the Gypsies?"

"Think of it this way," Casey said. "I'm the lawyer for the Gypsies and Jesse's your lawyer."

Everybody laughed, even Dupre.

"Get this man a drink," Dupre yelled at the bartender. "He's delusional."

Casey didn't let up. "Okay, I'm not a lawyer yet and Jesse hasn't even gone to law school. That doesn't mean we can't negotiate a truce. We can start right here. And don't forget one very important fact."

"What's that?" Dupre asked, clearly amazed by Casey's chutzpah.

"We're free," Casey nearly shouted. "Neither one of us is charging any fees."

"We'll all drink to that," Dale said, raising his beer mug.

Rene was the first to rise to his feet. "Let's get us a truce. Without it, we won't be able to play anywhere."

The mood at Tortilla Flats brightened considerably as even Dupre and Big Ben joined in the toast. Before the end of the meeting, Casey and Jesse and Dupre had hammered out a proposal for a territorial split between the two motorcycle clubs that could end the war. It was a crooked line, but basically the Gypsies got the east bayou and the Wheelers got the west. The city of New Orleans was not part of the deal because it had long been under the control of a much larger criminal enterprise.

Within the week, both sides had agreed to the truce and the war was over, at least temporarily. There had been a lot of back and forth and even some give and take. In the end, it was the perfect settlement. Neither side was particularly happy with the result but each side reluctantly agreed to live with it for a while to see how the artificial boundaries held up under pressure.

A week after the truce, Casey came over to Amy and Jesse's apartment for a victory celebration. "Jesse, our first case together was a huge success. We saved a lot of lives and made sure the band can play anywhere it wants. What do you think about practicing law now?"

Jesse gave Casey a big hug. "I have to admit, it was fun playing lawyer, even more fun than traffic court. I'll never forget the look on Dupre's face right after he shook Gypsy's hand to finally seal the deal."

Amy was curious. "What did he look like?"

"He looked like he couldn't believe Casey and I had actually pulled it off."

"No, I mean what does Gypsy look like?"

Casey fielded the question. "He looks like his name. He looks like a gypsy. He's got a goatee and long hair with a bandana around his head. He's not as muscular as Dupre but he looks super strong. He's tall, got to be at least six foot three. And thin, or more like sinewy. The most striking part about him, though, is his eyes."

Jesse added to the description. "His eyes are so bright blue they look right through you. He knows it too. He uses his stare like a weapon."

Amy shook her head in admiration. "I'm amazed you got Dupre and Gypsy into the same room."

Casey looked at Jesse. "That took some doing. You haven't told her the story?"

"I didn't want her to worry," Jesse said.

Amy punched him on the arm. "Thanks so much, Jesse. So, tell the story now. How'd you get those two guys into the same room?"

Jesse took a deep breath, pleased as ever to have a story to tell. "It wasn't a room at all. It was Jackson Square, down by the river in the center of New Orleans. Gypsy came in from St. Ann Street and Dupre came in from the opposite side of the square on St. Peter Street. They each walked to the statue of Andrew Jackson in the center."

Casey couldn't help but join in. "Plenty of people around, it was high noon, like the shootout at the O.K. Corral. Each guy could see the other one coming and see that he was alone and unarmed."

Jesse continued. "Funny thing was, they both walked with a limp, and they were trying hard not to show it. Dupre broke his foot at the Safari Club fire."

"And Gypsy got shot in the hip about a month ago," Casey said.

Amy looked at both of them like they were out of their minds. "So, where were you two?"

"I was walking right behind Dupre and Casey was right behind Gypsy."

Amy covered her eyes with her hands. "Oh, my God. It sounds like a duel. You could have been killed. Go on. What happened next?"

Jesse made her wait for it. "It was the coolest thing you ever saw. The two toughest dudes on the bayou coming face-to-face to shake hands over the deal they'd worked out with me and Casey. And then the shocker. Dupre actually smiled when they shook hands. He smiled and said to Gypsy, 'Good to see you again, man.'"

"Turns out they'd done some dealing with each other back in high school, before the gangs got started." Casey said. "Gypsy actually laughed when they shook hands."

"What did he say?" Amy asked, bouncing up and down on her chair.

Casey chuckled at her eagerness. "Gypsy said, 'Looks like we're going to be partners again.' Then Dupre said, 'It's a little late to be talking about being partners. All we're trying to do here is not kill each other.'"

Amy wanted more. She stopped bouncing. "So what happened next?"

Jesse picked up the story. "They shook hands again and turned around and walked away. It was like something out of an old movie, neither one of them looked back. Casey and I stayed behind at the statue, looking up at St. Louis Cathedral like we'd just witnessed a miracle."

"I almost thought they were going to hug each other," Casey said.

Amy looked at Jesse and Casey in wide-eyed wonder. "That is so cool. That is so cool I can't stand it."

Casey returned to the legal theme of the tale. "I wonder

what real lawyers would have charged them for negotiating the truce?"

"A fortune and then some," Jesse said.

Amy looked at him with eyebrows raised. "Maybe we ought to think a little more about practicing law."

Casey and Jesse looked at each other. Jesse knew what she meant by using the term we.

He looked at Amy like she had just crossed some kind of imaginary line in the relationship sand. "Maybe we should think a little more about booking the band."

CHAPTER ELEVEN

PETE

Pete invited the Divebomberz to spend a couple days at his ranch house along the Tchefuncte River, north of New Orleans, across Lake Pontchartrain. He had first contacted the band after their public television performance. His invitation was a big deal to Jesse. Pete said he was interested in managing the band and was talking about putting them in the studio to make a record. He offered his house for two days of rehearsal and a chance for him to get to know the band.

So they headed across the 23-mile, Lake Pontchartrain causeway. Tim rode with Rene in his truck while Dale, Butch, and Jesse crowded into the band van with most of the equipment. Each vehicle was filled with marijuana smoke as they traveled, side by side, down the two northbound lanes of the sea level bridge. With water stretching out on either side, it felt like they were in a boat race. Jesse and Rene jockeyed for position and nearly collided several times as they came closer and closer to each other in the center of the road. Jesse was a thrill seeker in his own right but Rene was flat-out reckless. Jesse found himself backing down again and again. He didn't like being the chicken.

Butch was relieved to see Jesse exercising uncharacteristic restraint. "Good man. No need to get us all killed."

Jesse's spirits were high. The band was finally going to make a recording of their music. What little he knew about the music business told him it was all about getting a recording contract. To do that, they would have to make a demo tape.

Dale leaned forward and put his hand to his ear. "I hear destiny calling from across the lake. Listen, can you hear it? It's calling our name."

Butch pretended to listen. "I hear it calling my name but I don't hear your name, Jesse."

Dale laughed. "Jesse doesn't have to listen. He's got his own voice. Isn't that right, Jesse? You've got the Voodoo voice. Where's it been lately?"

Jesse decided to be candid for a change. "I haven't heard the voice since I met him in the graveyard a hundred years ago."

Butch and Dale looked at each other in shocked surprise. Jesse hadn't shared anything about his Voodoo connection in quite some time. Nobody said anything more for several miles. Jesse knew they were waiting for more so he finally told the story of his trip to the graveyard with Carmen. Butch and Dale were spellbound as he told about his Voodoo vision and meeting the African man behind the voice at Marie Laveau's healing fire.

"And you say there was no electricity?" Butch asked.

Jesse realized his account was difficult to believe. "Look, I don't know if it was a dream or a spell or a trance or what it was. All I can tell you is, it felt as real as this. And it was in a time before electricity. The only light was from the fire."

Butch responded slowly and carefully. "Jesse, I'm seriously starting to worry about you. Maybe you've been hitting the magic mushrooms a little heavy."

Dale didn't share Butch's concern. "Far out. We've got Voodoo on our side and we're on the road to meet our new manager."

"He's not our manager yet," Butch said. "I like Pete fine, but from what I've heard, he's mainly a real estate agent who thinks he can start some kind of music festival in New Orleans. I don't think he knows anything about managing a band."

"He doesn't have to know anything if he's ready to pay for our recording time," Jesse said.

"But what does he want in return?" Dale asked.

Butch thought about the question for a minute. "I guess we find out soon enough."

Dale turned to Jesse. "Is this witch doctor voice you've been hearing connected to the bayou cow skull?"

Jesse was pleased to have Dale asking intelligent questions. "Carmen seems to think the skull and the voice are the same thing, trying to get through to me by sight and sound."

Butch reluctantly got on board the inquiry. "So what is this Voodoo thing trying to tell you?"

Jesse thought for a minute as he drove across the lake. "It's telling me that music has the same kind of power as Voodoo. It connects the spirit world to the material world."

"Sounds like you're talking about God." Butch said.

Dale jumped in on one of his favorite topics. "God is bigger than Voodoo. God might use Voodoo or rock and roll or whatever to get his point across, but God is bigger than all of our spiritual and material worlds."

Jesse did not want to get Dale going. "God's a pretty big word. I don't know what God is. I don't think anybody knows. The people who claim to know God are the ones that scare me."

"I don't claim to know God," Dale said. "But I do claim to feel the presence of God in all that is good in the world."

Butch intervened. "Okay, okay. I don't want to have a big theological debate here. I'm just wondering how this voice Jesse claims to hear is going to affect the future of The Divebomberz."

"I don't know if the voice has anything to do with us heading to Pete's ranch," Jesse said. "But I'll tell you this. It was the voice who saved us in the Safari fire."

"You saved us there," Dale said.

Jesse took his right hand off the steering wheel and pointed his index finger upward to make his point. "It was the voice who told me to kick the walls down. Before I heard the voice, I was pretty sure we were all going to die."

"Why didn't you tell us that before?" Dale asked.

"I know you all think I'm crazy about this voice thing so I just stopped talking about it."

Butch was shocked by the revelation about the voice at the Safari fire. His mouth was open long before he began speaking. "Don't worry about us thinking you're crazy. We knew you were crazy long before you started hearing the voice. The thing about the voice is this. I'd believe it a lot more if I heard it myself. It doesn't make sense that it would only speak to you."

Meanwhile, Rene's truck and trailer had fallen into line behind the band van. He and Tim were having their own discussion about the band's current and future course of action.

"I think it's a good idea to get a manager," Rene said. "We need somebody besides Jesse running the band."

Tim looked at Rene in surprise. "Do you really think Jesse runs the band?"

"He's the one who brought you to New Orleans, isn't he? He's the one who does the booking. He's the one who decides what songs go on the set list."

"He's the one who wanted you in the band," Tim said.

Rene looked hurt. "Was it just him?"

"No, we all wanted a drummer. And we all think you're perfect for the band. But that's the point. Jesse doesn't try to run the band. We all run the band. Butch is probably the closest thing we have to a musical leader."

Rene drummed his fingers on the steering wheel. "No, I'm not trying to get into a power struggle with Jesse. All I'm saying is it would be a good thing to get a manager. What do you know about this Pete guy?"

Tim responded thoughtfully. "I don't think he's ever managed a band before."

"So why are we going to his house in the country?"

"For one thing, we need a place to rehearse. Your drums have made our sound too big to rehearse in anybody's apartment."

Rene did a drum roll on the steering wheel. "You got that right."

Tim continued. "That's why we got burned, rehearsing outdoors, giving a free concert to all those kids at the Race Street Park."

Tim was referring to the band rehearsing at a city park pavilion and giving a free concert to kids and grownups who streamed in from everywhere within hearing distance. There was a huge turnout since The Divebomberz could be heard eight blocks in any direction.

Unfortunately, someone saw the band loading all the equipment into the van after the performance. That same someone saw the van get parked nearby in front of Jesse and Amy's apartment, which was only two blocks from the park. The next morning, Jesse awoke to find his driver's side window shattered and all the band's new gear stolen. Everything the band had purchased on borrowed money after the Safari fire was gone. In a sickening flash, Jesse realized how stupid he'd been to show all the poor kids in the neighborhood where the valuables were stored. The thieves had left the back door and the sliding side door of the van wide open.

Jesse discovered the devastating loss just six hours before the band's debut booking on the riverboat. At first, he thought there was no way the band could do the gig. Amy found him sitting dejectedly on the curb beside the burglarized vehicle. Once he showed her the loss, Amy swung into action. "Don't even think about feeling sorry for yourself and missing that job on the riverboat. Let's get on the phone and call the guys. We've got to beg, borrow, or steal instruments in a hurry."

After a mad scramble to rent and borrow equipment, The Divebomberz covered the gig. The band was set up in front of the paddlewheel that powered the boat. The only thing between the band and the churning water was a glass wall. It was tough playing on strange instruments, through a makeshift sound system. Nobody on the riverboat seemed to notice. The big wheel kept on turning.

There was no insurance to cover the loss. The Divebomberz had to borrow money from Rene's father again to buy its second round of gear in less than two months. They'd gone wild upgrading equipment after the Safari Club fire. This time they were more frugal. Even so, it gave them one more bill to pay each month.

"I can't believe Jesse got all our gear stolen," Rene said as he continued driving across the lake to Pete's house.

Tim stopped rolling the joint he was preparing. "That wasn't Jesse's fault and you know it. What is it? You've got a problem with Jesse?"

Rene was on shaky ground. "No. No. All I'm saying is we need to be more careful. With our gear and our career."

Tim fired up the number and passed it to Rene. "Are you worried about Pete?"

Rene took a huge hit and passed the joint back to Tim. "It's all about making a record. That's what this business is all about. If Pete's ready to help us do that, I'm all for him. Plus, I hear he's got connections with Allen Touissant."

"Who's that?"

Rene looked at Tim like he couldn't believe what he had just heard. "Who's that? Allen Touissant is the biggest thing in New Orleans. He owns Sea Saint studios. He worked with

Fats Domino and Dr. John and the Neville Brothers. They had a string of hits in the sixties. I can't believe you haven't heard of him."

"Sounds like we need Touissant to manage us, not Pete," Tim said.

"We can't just walk in and talk to Allen Touissant."

"Why not?"

Rene pounded out a beat on the steering wheel to emphasize his point. "We need to record a few songs first so we can take him our demo tape."

"What happens if he likes us?" Tim asked.

"I don't really know. I'm not a music manager. I'm just a drummer. A drummer who knows we need to make a record and that's about all I know."

Tim and Rene rode on in silence as they followed the band van across the lake and wound their way into the giant trees along the Tchefuncte River. Swampland Oaks and Seneca and Butternut trees combined with all kinds of pines to create a lush canopy that nearly blotted out the sun.

"Are there alligators here?" Tim asked.

"Lots of them," Rene teased. "Be careful when you get out of the truck."

"Come on, man," Tim said. "Don't joke about that stuff. You know it freaks me out."

As the truck and the van were pulling up in front of Pete's sprawling ranch house, Tim heard the voice for the first time. There was no mistaking it. The voice was just as Jesse had described it, deep and booming and African.

"This man is a slave owner," the voice said as Pete walked out of the house.

Jesse noticed Tim remaining in the truck. "Come on, Tim. What's the holdup?"

Tim got out of the truck and grabbed Jesse by the shoulders

to whisper in his ear. "I just heard the voice. I know it's the same one you've been hearing. I just heard it. It sounds exactly like you said."

Tim's eyes were so wide Jesse knew he had to settle him down somehow. It was obvious Tim wasn't playing with him. He looked like Jesse had felt when he first heard the voice, like he'd just seen a ghost. Or heard one.

Jesse hugged him tightly. It was a great relief to have someone confirm he wasn't out of his mind for hearing a Voodoo voice in his head. "What did it say?"

Before Tim could answer, Pete walked up to greet the band. He was wearing a light blue suit with no tie. It was early afternoon. Pete was obviously done with real estate for the day. He didn't look anything like Jesse had imagined. Pete was only twenty-nine years old. Jesse had expected him to be an Italian man in his fifties with slick black hair. Pete was five foot nine with blonde hair and a fair complexion.

"Welcome, Divebomberz, to my humble abode," Pete grinned as he shook hands all around. His teeth were big and white and perfect. It seemed he had forgotten all about the beautiful woman standing behind him. Then he remembered his manners. "This is Darlene," he said, introducing a slightly taller brunette. She looked elegant, even in jeans and a work shirt. She was a person quite used to having her picture taken.

Pete hugged her. "She's my number one ranch hand."

Darlene quickly demonstrated her southern belle charm. She shook hands warmly with each member of the band. The diamond ring on her left hand was hugely noticeable.

"So good to meet y'all," she said. "Pete's told me so much about you. I feel like I already know y'all."

"Welcome to the ranch," she said to Dale. "We thought we'd take a walk down to the river to start things off right."

She turned to Butch. "A little walk will be good after your drive, won't it?"

"We love to explore new territory," Butch said as he shook her hand.

"And you must be Jesse," she said. "I wish I could get my hair to curl up so pretty as yours."

Before Jesse could comment or wonder how many more times she could say "y'all," Darlene pivoted to Tim, who was still staring off into space.

"So, you must be Tim, the fiddle player. I can't wait to hear y'all play right here in our party den. We've got all the furniture moved over so y'all can set up."

Tim snapped out of his daydream and remembered his manners. "Thank you for having us. It's nice to get out of the city."

Pete must have been waiting for Darlene to complete her introduction. Once he felt she had properly welcomed each band member, he organized the party. "All right then. Come with me and discover the magic that is the Tchefuncte River."

Jesse felt like he was walking into a jungle as the band followed Pete and Darlene down a grassy, two-track road into what seemed an impenetrable array of trees, shrubs, and undergrowth. A cacophony of sounds from insects and birds and frogs and things that crawl gave the hike a forbidden forest feel. The mosquitoes were big and bad.

Darlene handed Dale a can of bug repellant. "Here, spray this on everybody. The bad news is you're really going to need it. The good news is, it works."

Tim was watching the ground closely. "Does it keep the snakes away?"

Rene couldn't resist the opportunity to play with him. "It's pretty good on snakes. But it doesn't work at all on the alligators."

Tim looked at Pete with the paranoia all northern boys feel when they get close to the swamp.

Pete laughed at the look on Tim's face. "Don't worry about the gators. They're down here all right. But they don't bother humans. The only time you'll see one is when they're trying to get away and hide."

"I'd rather not see one at all," Butch said.

The road turned into a path that wound its way to a sand bank on the edge of a brownish green stream running through large rocks and fallen trees.

Pete pointed out the sights. "This is the swimming hole. See that round place down there? It's almost five feet deep. You guys can take a quick dip if you're so inclined."

Butch couldn't stop looking at the water. "Is this the Tchefuncte?"

Pete was only too happy to continue his tour guide duties. "No, this is a branch of the main river. The main river's that way to the west. It's big enough we can waterski on it. I've got a boat docked in Covington. That's a town about three miles from here. There's a couple big clubs you guys could play."

Dale took off his shirt and headed for the swimming spot. "I don't know about you guys. But I'm going for a dip. This is too good to pass up."

Darlene made her exit. "I'll let you boys have fun. I'm going back to the house to make us snacks."

"I'll be along in a minute," Pete said as she left. He seemed a little uneasy as he described the acreage of his ranch. He became even more nervous as the band began stripping down to take a dip.

He made his exit. "I'm not swimming for now. You guys go ahead. I'll go back to the house and help Darlene. You can find your way back, right?"

"Are you sure it's okay if we take a swim?" Jesse asked.

Pete waved as he was leaving. "You are more than fine. That's what it's there for."

The band said goodbye and eased their way into the deep part of the stream. The cool current was soothing as they formed a circle facing each other.

Jesse looked at Tim. "Tell them what you heard."

Tim looked at each member of the band. "I heard the voice."

"Bullshit," Butch said.

Dale slapped the water. "Jesse put you up to this."

"What did it say?" Rene asked.

They all spoke at once as they splashed water Tim's way. It didn't take long to see he wasn't joking around. Tim wasn't laughing. He was serious.

"What did it say?" Rene repeated.

Tim paused to formulate his thoughts. "It spoke to me as we were driving up to Pete's house."

Rene moved in closer to Tim. "Wait a minute. I was right in the truck with you. I didn't hear anything."

Tim started getting more confident in his description. "It's not like that. It's not out loud. It's inside your head and it sounds exactly like Jesse said it sounds."

"How's that?" Dale asked.

Tim answered him. "You know. It's a deep, loud, black man's voice."

"What did it say?" Rene persisted.

Tim looked around again and then over his shoulder as if to make sure no one could be listening. "It said, 'This man is a slave owner.'"

Nobody spoke as Tim's words sank in.

Dale sank down to his neck in the water. "I don't like the sounds of that at all. I'm not saying I don't believe you, Tim. Hell, I believed Jesse all along. But now, this whole thing is feeling a little spooky. Like this whole swimming hole thing could be some kind of a trap. Don't you think it's strange they would walk us down here and leave right away?"

"They're just getting ready for company, Dale," Butch said, beginning to sink into the water himself. "Besides, they could see we don't have bathing suits. I'm sure they didn't feel like getting naked with us right off the bat. So listen. We don't know what this voice is or what it means by the things it says. It's not an evil thing is it, Jesse?"

"Not at all. Like I told you, it saved our lives at the Safari Club."

"What's this about the Safari Club?" Rene asked.

"That's right," Butch said. "You weren't in the van on the way here when Jesse told us about the voice at the Safari Club."

Now Tim was curious as well. "What are you talking about?"

Jesse repeated his story to Rene and Tim. "The voice told me to kick the walls down. That's how I got the idea that saved us. It was the voice. And the voice is definitely on our side. Now that Tim has heard it too, maybe you'll all stop giving me so much shit about it."

Rene was incredulous. "So is it telling us to stay away from Pete?"

Jesse thought about it for a minute. "I don't know for sure. But it tells me we'd better be careful about him."

The band walked back to Pete's house and set up for what turned out to be a productive, three-hour rehearsal. Jesse's senses were tingling from the drive and the swim and the new development with the voice. The song to learn for the day was "Big Old Jet Airliner," by Steve Miller. It was a song Rene wanted to add to the set list. Jesse opposed the tune on the grounds it was too "pop" but agreed to see how it sounded in rehearsal. By the third time through the song, it was obviously going to be part of the show. Tim started out playing on the slide guitar, but the song kicked into overdrive when he switched to fiddle.

Pete applauded wildly. "Wish you could play fiddle and slide guitar at the same time. You guys are playing that song better than Steve Miller's band ever did."

Pete turned out to be a great cheerleader as the band rocked on for two sets without a break. He clapped his hands and stomped his feet at the end of every song, and made comments to each member of the band about how great he sounded.

It seemed to Jesse as if Pete was auditioning to be band manager.

Darlene kept the cold beer coming. Tim kept rolling joints. As the band was passing around a joint before the third set, Pete brought out a mirror tray filled with long, thick lines of cocaine. "Here's a special treat for y'all. I was going to wait until after dinner but now seems like the perfect time."

Jesse was pleased to see the expensive drugs come out. "My man. I knew we liked you right from the start."

"Tim took the straw from Pete and started in on the first line. He had to pull up, choking. Each line was thick enough and long enough to be four lines.

Pete patted Tim on the back. "Just don't cough on the tray. Now, go on. Finish your line. There are sober people in Japan."

Tim had to gather himself before hunkering down to finish what was left of the six-inch line. Jesse snorted his line with as little fanfare as possible. Cocaine was something he did when somebody else was paying for it. He didn't want to let on like it was any big deal.

Once they were good and cranked up, the band was more than primed to roar through a thunderous and glorious third set. The cocaine took Jesse to new levels of emotional euphoria and lightning-quick creativity. He had not yet learned that the rosy glow of early cocaine use would eventually turn into paranoid impotence and soul-sucking addiction.

Pete and Darlene were more than enough of an audience. Jesse was having big fun being high and playing with the band. Everything sounded tight and massive. Jesse felt like they were rocking the planet itself. The sun set through the trees and turned the rehearsal space golden as the angular rays flooded through the windows. The music sounded as brilliant as the light appeared.

Jesse had forgotten, for the moment, the ominous comment Tim had heard from the Voodoo voice.

Darlene was happy to be part of the moment. "Pete told me y'all were good but I wasn't ready for this. Y'all sound like a big time band."

Pete was quick to correct her. "They are a big time band. Come on, gentlemen, let's do one more line and take a little stroll to the pasture before dinner. If we leave Darlene alone, she'll have a masterpiece meal ready by the time we get back. Isn't that right, Darlene?"

Darlene flashed a runway pose with one hand on her hip and one hand waving. "That's right dahlin'. Don't get lost now, you hear?"

Walking in the darkening evening, Pete talked a mile a minute about a strategy for the recording studio. "I think we need two original songs and two cover songs. I've got a studio and a producer picked out. I'll pay for it with no strings attached. I don't need you to sign any contracts. Let's just see where this goes. What do you say?"

His plans aroused Butch's curiosity. "Why would we want to record covers of other people's songs?"

"I'd like them to hear you on songs they're familiar with," Pete said.

"Who we talking about?" Rene asked.

Pete slowed down his sales pitch. "Record companies. The goal is to get you a recording contract."

"What about Allen Toussaint right here in New Orleans?" Tim asked.

Pete put his hand on Tim's shoulder. "He's a producer, not a record company. But it's odd you should mention Toussaint. I've got an amazing opportunity for you guys that involves him in a round about way."

"We're all ears," Dale said.

"Okay. Here it is. You can be the opening act for the hottest night Tipitina's Nightclub has ever had. It's on December twenty-third and guess who else is playing?"

"Allen Toussaint?" Jesse guessed.

Pete smiled at the obvious guess. "No. It's three of his best songwriters and piano players ever; Professor Longhair, Dr. John, and Aaron Neville."

Rene got so excited he got in front of Pete and stopped him in his tracks. "Are you shittin' me? All three of them on one stage? That's incredible."

Dale joined Rene to block Pete's forward progress. "How did you pull it off?"

Pete began his explanation as he gently pushed his way between Dale and Rene. "It's not exactly my gig. Toussaint's doing it because Dr. John is coming home from L.A. for Christmas. I've been talking to Allen a lot lately, mainly about this Jazz Festival idea for New Orleans. He got to telling me about this gig he was setting up at Tipitina's."

Jesse knew Tipitinas as the hottest club in town. So far, he had been unable to get a booking there. It was a New Orleans insiders' joint.

Pete walked on with the entire band now in tow. "I told him I had the perfect band to get the crowd going for his big show. Your rehearsal this evening convinced me I was right."

Butch caught up to walk next to Pete. "Are we talking about *the* Dr. John, the guy who wrote 'Right Place Wrong Time'?"

"Yes sir, the man himself," Pete said. "He's as big as it gets and he's native New Orleans. He's bringing the Voodoo to rock and roll."

Dale was a huge fan of Dr. John. "Holy shit. Will we get to play with him?"

"Right now, you're the warm up band. But who knows what might happen? There's talk about a jam at the end of the night."

"Sign us up," Butch said.

"What's this about Dr. John bringing Voodoo to rock and roll?" Tim asked.

Pete stopped to gather the band around him in a huddle. "Dr. John is all about Voodoo rhythms and chants. He hangs out with some priestess named Carmen in The French Quarter. Professor Longhair taught him to play at a very young age. The boy was a natural born musician but he was wild and running with the wrong people. By nineteen sixty-eight, he had his first record out and titled the album, Gris Gris.

"*Gris Gris* is a Voodoo amulet that protects you from evil," Rene explained.

Jesse was shocked at the mention of his friend, Carmen, but he tried to hide it. "How much does the Tipitina's gig pay?"

Pete clearly enjoyed having the band hanging on his every word. He paused before answering. "Well, that's the thing. It only pays four hundred but this gig is a tremendous opportunity for the band."

"Do you guys know who Professor Longhair is?" Rene asked.

"Not really," Butch answered for the four Indiana boys in the band.

Rene quickly explained. "Professor Longhair put the funk

in New Orleans music. He put the rumba and the mambo and the calypso and the African-Cuban beats into jazz and rhythm and blues."

"Yeah, I've heard of him," Tim said. "He wrote that song everybody sings, 'Go to the Mardi Gras.'"

Pete clapped his hands. "I'm happy to hear somebody knows about Professor Longhair."

"How old is this professor guy?" Dale asked.

Pete continued his impromptu seminar on New Orleans music. "He's in his sixties. His career stalled in the fifties. He was a janitor and a big gambler for most of the sixties, but he's back now, bigger than ever. He had a huge influence on The Meters."

"We've heard The Meters around town," Butch said. "Great, great band."

"The Meters brought second line grooves to New Orleans music," Pete said.

"What does second line mean?" Tim asked.

"It comes from the Mardi Gras parades," Pete said. "The people with the main parade are the first line. Behind them are all the second liners, dancing and singing in off beat styles. Second line drumming plays off the marching beat. It's syncopated. The strong beats get weak and vice versa."

Rene jumped in. "Think about the song, 'Iko Iko.' It's that bump, da bump, da bump, bump bump thing. I throw it in all the time."

Pete shot Rene a look of admiration. "By the way, you guys should add 'Iko Iko' to your show before the Tipitina's gig."

"What about this Aaron Neville?" Butch asked. "I know he's part of the Neville Brothers, but what else?"

Pete broke the band out of its huddle and began walking back to the house as he continued talking like a guest lecturer at a college class. He went from how Neville has Indian blood in him to how Native American culture is a big part of the crazy New Orleans mix. "You've seen Wild Tchoupitoulas, the guys with the big, feathered headdresses and all the dancers?"

Dale began bouncing on the balls of his feet. "Oh yeah. We love those guys. And I remember Neville's hit song, 'Tell It Like It Is.' I can't believe we'll be on the stage with New Orleans musical royalty. Count us in, right guys?"

Everybody agreed to do the show. It was a no brainer. More importantly, Jesse came away from the conversation realizing Pete knew a thing or two about New Orleans music.

They returned to Pete's house for a jambalaya feast prepared by Darlene. The food was spicy-hot and filled with seafood and sausage. The wine was red and expensive and from all around the world. They drank many bottles. Pete talked about New Orleans politics and organized crime. "It's like all the riverboat gamblers and musicians and hustlers rolled down the Mississippi River and ended up here. That's what the city is, the end of the line for all the dreamers and schemers of North America."

"Some people call it the asshole of the Mississippi," Dale said.

"We don't appreciate that reference," Pete said.

The band peppered him with questions. He managed to be the center of the show while still keeping his guests involved in the conversation. He was the perfect host. He and Darlene were a good team at making their guests feel right at home.

By the end of the meal, Jesse and the band felt like they had found their manager.

It was going on 11 p.m. by the time they retired from the dinner table and settled into comfortable chairs in the den by the fireplace. Darlene brought out a tray of cigars and Port wine. Pete brought out the mirror tray with a half-ounce pile of Peruvian marching powder.

"The hits just keep on coming," Dale said as the band hunkered down to put a serious edge on the night.

"That's a lot of cocaine," Tim said.

Pete did the first line himself without missing a beat. "There's more where that came from. And I do need to talk to you about your connection with The Wheelers. My guy gets his stuff from them, I'm pretty sure. I was thinking we could cut out the middle man."

"We can make that happen," Jesse said as he snorted his line.

Butch seemed distracted as he took the straw from Jesse. "We can't afford this stuff."

Pete began pouring glasses of Port. "That's going to change with any luck at all."

Darlene breezed in to do a line. "You boys want a fire in here?"

Rene looked at her like she was the last woman on Earth. "No thanks. We're lit up enough already."

The party raged on until the cocaine ran out. Jesse was surprised to find himself seriously wanting more. He had snorted his share of cocaine, but it had never done much for him before. He used to say the best thing about cocaine was playing with the mirrors and rolled up bills and chopping up the product with razor blades. But something clicked in his mind that first night at Pete's. Some cocaine switch inside his head turned on. He began to see what all the fuss was about. He wanted more in a way he had never wanted more before.

The party broke up about 4 a.m. Jesse and Tim were sharing a room. Jesse told Tim about wanting more cocaine. Tim seemed to understand Jesse's dilemma. The two of them were lying in twin beds. Sleep was clearly not going to happen for some time. The cocaine was still coursing through their veins and keeping them awake. They ended up talking about the voice and Voodoo.

"You know. I've always felt like a spiritual guy, but I never felt like I do now," Tim said.

"What do you mean?" Jesse asked.

"I mean I almost feel like someone's watching me."

Jesse thought about that for a minute. "I know. I do think it's watching over us. I just don't understand why it won't answer questions."

"What questions have you been asking?"

Jesse sighed deeply. "Oh, you know, the usual ones. Like where should the band be going and what should we be doing to get there."

"We're never going to know," Tim said. "Probably the voice doesn't even know."

Jesse sat up on the edge of his bed and looked at Tim. "I'll tell you what. It makes me feel a whole lot better that you heard it too. At least you know I'm not crazy now."

"I never thought you were. I just wonder why the other guys can't hear it."

Jesse had been developing his own theory on that topic. "Maybe the Voodoo connection is there for everybody but people can only hear it when they get tuned in for one reason or another."

Tim and Jesse talked until the first light of dawn began to shine. It felt like they were about to make a great spiritual breakthrough for a while and then the whole thing faded back into mystery and confusion.

They fell silent for quite a while and were trying to get to sleep when Tim said, "Maybe this is what that voice meant when it said, 'This man is a slave owner.'"

Jesse knew Tim was talking about the cocaine, which was still keeping them uncomfortably awake. Instead of responding directly to the drug issue, Jesse used a line of wisdom from Carmen. "We are all running away from many things and we are all slaves to many masters."

CHAPTER TWELVE

TIPITINA'S

Jesse walked into Tipitina's on the night of the big show and was surprised to run into Carmen in full party regalia. She was dressed for the evening in a purple-velvet Nehru jacket that came down to the mid-thigh of her lime-green, silk slacks. Her red hair was tied on top of her head with a golden ribbon. She wore no hat or turban. Her necklace was clasped in front with golden snakes that looked like they were making love. Her high-heeled shoes were as golden as the snakes and shimmering like glitter on a mirror.

Jesse looked her up and down and let out a low wolf whistle before asking the question he'd been wanting to ask for some time. "Why didn't you tell me you know Dr. John?"

Carmen smiled broadly and spun around for Jesse to get the full view of her outfit for the evening. "I'm not a namedropper."

It was 7 p.m. and The Divebomberz were setting up for the show along with musicians and soundmen for Dr. John, Professor Longhair, and Aaron Neville. Carmen was a guest of honor. She was holding court like she owned the place.

Jesse remembered his manners. "You look fabulous."

Carmen held out her hand for Jesse to kiss it. "That's more like it. If you want, I'll introduce you to Dr. John when he gets here. You two have a lot in common."

"I would love that," Jesse said as he escorted her to the bar and asked if he could buy her a drink.

The longhaired bartender came around the bar to give Carmen a big hug. "No one but me will be buying this bayou queen a drink. Let's see, what'll it be? Let me guess. Oh, I know. The lady will have her fabulous rum potion."

"Thank you, Jackson," she said with a Cheshire smile. "You know what I like. This is my friend, Jesse."

"You playing tonight?" Jackson asked Jesse.

"I'm with The Divebomberz."

"Right on, man. You got some heavyweight company tonight. This place is going to be on fire."

Dale heard the comment as he walked up to the bar. "Let's hope it doesn't go up in flames like the Safari Club."

"Was that you guys?" Jackson asked.

Dale was only too happy to enlighten anyone within hearing distance. "Oh, yeah, that was The Divebomberz at the Safari fire. If it hadn't been for Jesse here, the band and five hundred people would've died in that fire."

Jackson reached over the bar to shake Dale's hand. "Well, well. It is, indeed, a pleasure to meet you. We've heard all about The Divebomberz. Wow, it's going to be a wild night."

"Somebody must have been watching out for you at the Safari Club," Carmen said with a wink that only Jesse caught.

"Madame Carmen, I presume," Dale said, bowing in introduction. "I'm in Jesse's band, or he's in mine, we're not sure which. It is a great pleasure to meet you. Jesse's told us so many good things about you."

Carmen reached out for Dale. He kissed her hand with a flourish that was not lost on the Voodoo priestess. She pretended to nearly faint from excitement. "Oh, my. I see we have an experienced gentleman here."

Tim and Rene and Butch joined the conversation at the bar. Carmen greeted each one like an old friend. "Don't forget, I was a fan of The Divebomberz back when you were playing Fritzel's."

"Jackson," she said, turning to the bartender, "Could we get a round of Heinekens for my band?"

"On the house," Jackson said.

Carmen beamed at the band. "See, I even remember what you drink."

Looking around the club, Jesse could see it wasn't big enough to hold what was bound to be a massive turnout for the show. Tipitina's was a two-story, wood-frame house along the main curve of the Mississippi River where Napolean Avenue runs into Tchoupitoulas Street. The club had only recently been opened by a group of music lovers known as The Fabulous Fo'teen. They founded it as a tribute to Professor Longhair and a place for him to play out his later years.

"How many people will this place hold?" Jesse wondered out loud.

"We'll be dancing across Tchoupitoulas Street and across the tracks and down to the river tonight," Carmen said as she took a mighty swig from her rum and coke double with a thick slice of lime and a dash of coconut.

"We got a ten dollar cover charge," Jackson said. "That'll keep out some of the riff raff. Probably get about three hundred and fifty people in here if the fire Marshall don't show."

As he was talking, Jesse saw the mystery man from the bayou walk in the door with Ruthie the duck lady. Somehow, on some level he didn't understand, it made perfect sense that Ruthie, the mystery man, and Carmen would all be in the same place at the same time. Ruthie was obviously much more than the quack she pretended to be. She had introduced Jesse to Carmen, who had explained the Voodoo of the mystery man, and now the mystery man was bringing Ruthie to Tipitina's.

The straight line of Jesse's mind became a circle. His knees went so weak he almost fell to the floor. In a flash, he realized the truth about the universe. We manufacture our own reality, he thought. These three people are all part of the same thing. We find people to teach us what we know we need to learn. We are all part of each other's learning curve. This epiphany nearly blinded him as he saw the light for the first time. He had accidentally stumbled onto what the Buddhists call "the nature of mind." His heightened state of consciousness didn't last long. He forgot most of the inspirational moment the instant he began to speak.

He ran over to greet the man from the bayou. "Hey man. Long time no see. Remember me?"

The mystery man answered with a question that let Jesse know he remembered their first meeting. "You going to sing 'Jambalaya' tonight?"

"Every night," Dale interjected as introductions were made all around.

Ruthie wasn't wearing her housecoat. She was in costume as some kind of fairy tale princess. She had no ducks in tow. She greeted Carmen like a long lost sister. "You look like the Voodoo queen."

Carmen hugged Ruthie and the mystery man at the same time. "We only serve the Voodoo queen, and I am quite sure she will be here in spirit tonight."

"How do you know Ruthie the duck lady?" Jesse asked the mystery man.

The man looked at Jesse and winked. "Everybody knows Ruthie."

Carmen took Ruthie by the hand. "Where's Professor Longhair?"

"He's staying sober for the most part," Ruthie said. "He and Dr. John are over at Aaron Neville's house for dinner."

Carmen laughed and drank the rest of her drink. "Imagine that gumbo."

As the band was excusing itself to complete their set up, Jesse took the mystery man aside. "Don't leave without getting with me. I think we've got some catching up to do."

The man gave Jesse a thumbs-up sign. "I'll be around. I'm not going anywhere. This is the place to be."

"Oh, and by the way," Jesse added. "Thanks for showing us the mushroom field. It paid off in a big way."

"Did you find the Voodoo or did the Voodoo find you?"

"I'm still working on that. I'm beginning to think it might be a little of both."

The club was packed to the rafters. The crowd was already going crazy by the time The Divebomberz played a couple rocked up Hank Williams tunes. Jesse couldn't believe he was actually onstage at Tipitina's and being cheered by the local crowd. After a few more songs, the band began sounding more full and musical than ever. Somehow, they had vaulted up to another level of musicality. Jesse couldn't put his finger on what was happening. It felt like the band was levitating. He looked at Butch and he could tell Butch was feeling it too.

When he turned around to check it out with Rene, he saw a black, bald-headed man playing along on one of the three pianos set up for the evening. It was Professor Longhair. The nickname originated in his younger days, when he still had hair.

The Professor was such a sympathetic player you barely noticed he was there, filling in the perfect spaces and driving home one musical point after another. He gave The Divebomberz a new and improved sound. Jesse had never experienced anything similar. Everything that had been rocking was now rolling as well.

The crowd didn't notice "Fess" until he took a lead on a hard rock version of "Foggy Mountain Breakdown," a bluegrass standard generally reserved for banjo. Tim was playing fiddle on the break until Professor Longhair took over with a choppy syncopation of right hand triplets that turned the whole song inside out. The light man illuminated the Professor in the middle of his virtuosity. The crowd cheered so loudly it felt like the room might explode. Everybody knew the night was going to be as wild a ride as the one the Professor just took on his piano.

After playing for a few more songs, the legendary music man waved happily and left the stage for the band to finish their set. The crowd begged him not to go. Jesse would never again be musically satisfied until he found a keyboard player of his own. Professor Longhair had shown him the missing ingredient.

The band strutted through the rest of their high-energy set. The crowd was with them all the way. For the last song, they rocked the club with a rousing, sing-a-long version of "Big Old Jet Airliner." The Steve Miller song they had learned at Pete's house on the river came in handy as a set closer. Jesse had to admit to himself that he had been wrong in not wanting the song on the playlist. People were screaming for more and stomping their feet on the wooden floor. Butch and Jesse put down their instruments and walked off the stage to let the crowd know the set was over. A commotion of people began moving through the crowd toward the stage. Once the group reached the lights, out stepped Dr. John himself. It was like Hollywood Jesus jumping out of a birthday cake. The crowd recoiled in amazement as he climbed onstage and took control of the event on the lead microphone.

"What did you expect?" he shouted as the crowd recovered and roared its approval. "This is Santa Claus Dr. John and I'm back home in New Orleans for Christmas."

The crowd cheered and surged forward. Bouncers took positions in front of the stage to protect Dr. John. The club was dangerously overcrowded and many more were still trying to get in. People were lined up outside the door and around the corner for two blocks down Tchoupitoulas Street.

Dr. John tried to settle them down. "Hey now. Don't nobody get hurt now. Settle down with me. We've got things to do tonight. I thought I'd come by to play with my main man, Professor Longhair. Y'all good with that?"

The crowd response was deafening. It rocked the old house like a boat on the water. People stopped crowding forward in a noticeable response to Dr. John's request to think about each other's safety.

"Oh, and let's not forget my other main man, Aaron Neville."

Somehow, the crowd got even louder.

"So, how about a big hand for The Divebombers? I see they got you going."

The crowd let the band know they had held their own at the epicenter of New Orleans music. Their applause made Jesse feel the power of music deep in his bones. The vibration in the room felt like it could heal all wounds and bring harmony to every corner of the world.

Dr. John left them cheering and went backstage as the soundmen set up for the main show. Pete motioned for the band to join him at the rear of the stage. "Gentlemen, I'd like you to meet Allen Toussaint. Allen, meet The Divebomberz."

"Oh, wow, what an honor," Butch said as he shook Toussaint's hand. Jesse shook his hand without saying anything. For once, he was at a loss for words.

Toussaint bowed slightly, like a southern gentleman. "The

honor is mine. You guys sounded great. I love your sound. The crowd loved you. And you must be doing something very right if you've got Professor Longhair sitting in with you."

Jesse related instantly. "I know, I couldn't believe he did that. I felt him playing before I heard a single note."

Toussaint acknowledged the phenomenon with a nod of his head and turned the conversation to the music business. "Pete tells me he's going to put you guys into the recording studio. I'll be ready to hear what you can do, especially with your originals. Who knows? We might be working together someday soon."

As Butch was saying how much the band would love to work with Toussaint, Carmen interrupted. "Gentlemen, I've got some people here who want to meet you."

Jesse turned to see Dr. John, Professor Longhair, and Aaron Neville stepping out of the backstage shadows to congratulate the band on their set. Jesse was speechless. It felt like he had arrived, in a way, but it also felt surreal.

"I can't believe this is happening," Dale said.

Tim reached out to shake Professor Longhair's hand. "You sounded great, Professor. Thanks for playing with us."

The Professor was all grins and good times. "My pleasure, gentlemen. I don't think I've ever played bluegrass like that before. I had fun but I couldn't help but think it might sound even better at a slower tempo."

"Hallelujah," Rene said. "I've been telling them that for months."

Butch was star-struck. "I can't believe I'm meeting three of my all time heroes at the same time. This is like being backstage at the Grammys."

A waiter stepped in with a tray of drinks. All present took whatever cocktail they could grab.

Aaron Neville spoke from experience. "I can guarantee you. This is a lot more fun than the Grammys."

The Professor agreed. "It's more real, for sure. This crowd is over the top tonight."

Dr. John proposed a toast.

Everybody raised his glass and waited.

"A toast to Tipitina's and to Professor Longhair, the man who taught us all, that when it comes to music, and everything else, the only way to keep what you have is to give it away."

The musicians clinked glasses and drank together. Jesse could see they were energized by each other. He could feel the magic of the crowd eagerly awaiting their music. Jesse realized he'd heard the message of Dr. John's toast before, from Carmen.

The best thing about the backstage moment for Jesse was the realization that The Divebomberz had been invited to join a brotherhood of the highest order.

Aaron Neville took the stage first. It didn't take him long to swoon the room with sweet soul. He had a drummer with a kit quite a bit smaller than Rene's. Neville's bass player and guitar player laid down a rhythm that was completely in the pocket. The Divebomberz listened and learned. There were such powerful emotions coming out of Neville and his band. They were not driving as hard as a rock band. They were more sensual and even sexual. Neville was turning the crowd on to the sweet mysteries of musical magic.

Before people knew what hit them, Dr. John and Professor Longhair were easing themselves into the band, along with several horn players and backup singers. It was a gradual buildup that couldn't have been planned any better than it evolved. The musical train started chooglin' on down the line.

Neville started smooth, Longhair made it funky and Dr. John pushed the whole thing into show band mode. The train kept picking up speed, blowing by small town stops on its way to rocking-soul city.

Just when the crowd felt they couldn't take it anymore, the band backed it down for a ballad by Neville. He sang "Tell It Like Is" better than Jesse had ever heard it. One overhead spotlight bathed him in light like he was standing beneath a street lamp. It was a breathless moment.

Once the song was over, it took people a few seconds to collect themselves and begin applauding. The applause was as soft as the singing at first. Then, it grew into an ovation befitting the legendary talent who had just given their souls a tune up. Neville stood up and took a gracious bow. Then he sat down and did a complete mood shift with a surprise version of "I'm Walking" by Fats Domino. Jesse couldn't believe Neville's emotional range. Professor Longhair jumped on the New Orleans beat and sang a verse. Then Dr. John did the same. The horn section hit the roof as the saxophone wailed an inspirational solo. Jesse looked out at the crowd. They looked like they were witnessing the rapture.

From there, the three piano men took off into a blues-jazz instrumental. The Professor rolled out a beat motif. Neville pounced on it and turned it over to Dr. John, who ran with it. The legendary musicians were playing a three-way game of pitch and catch with rhythms and melodies. The drummer and the bass player and the horns were in perfect sync. It was a blend of musical styles and genres. It was musical gumbo.

Jesse took mental notes on performance dynamics and how to take an audience on an emotional roller coaster ride.

"These guys are putting on a clinic," Butch yelled in Jesse's ear.

Jesse agreed. "Oh, yeah. We've got to start doing this kind of stuff. Passing the ball around, I mean."

Jesse saw Amy trying to work her way backstage. He fought through the fans and hugged her back into the shadows. She was crying tears of joy. "I never thought I'd be part of anything like this. It's like a gospel revival and a blues review and a jazz fest all rolled into one. You guys sounded great, by the way." Jesse kissed her and held her at arm's length to look in her eyes. "When did you get here?"

"I was waving at you during your set but I couldn't get close enough to get your attention. Everybody else was waving too."

Jesse tried to introduce Amy to Toussaint but the music was too loud. Toussaint smiled at her and settled back to being swept away by the magic. The great New Orleans song master looked like he'd seen it all but hadn't seen anything like this.

Jesse was amazed and more than a little intimidated by the bass player on stage. He was a thin, black man, at least fifty years old, with extra long fingers and bent-over posture. He was respectfully caressing a beat-up, electric, Fender bass. The instrument looked like it had been played for years, up and down the Mississippi River from Chicago to St. Louis to Memphis to New Orleans. He wasn't playing anything all that technically difficult, but he was smooth and powerful at the same time. The man understood how long to hold a note. Starting on the seventh fret of his four string bass, he could run down the major scale to a bottom-of-the-well, open E note that lasted two full measures. He was so locked into the bass drum that the two sounded like one. When he ran up the neck for a thrill fill, he changed the entire feel of the song. He drove the musical vehicle like Bootsy Collins pushed James Brown's band in the early 1970's. His bass playing laid the foundation for the rest of the band. He seemed to know exactly what the piano players were going to do. The few times he got fooled he simply dropped out for a couple of measures and even that sounded cool.

Jesse had a sinking feeling he would never be as commanding a talent as the player he was watching and admiring.

Tipitina's was too packed with people for anybody to really dance. Still, the music made them fluid. The crowd became one as they moved together like an ocean in a storm. There was more room to dance behind the stage. Carmen swayed and swirled herself into what looked like a Voodoo trance. She was being transported to another world.

Jesse peered out at the crowd and saw Ruthie and the mystery man in the front row, apparently headed for the same strange land as Carmen. Ruthie had her arms stretched out in front of her as if to welcome the music with a warm embrace.

The collaborative super band didn't take a break all night. Musicians would drop out for a song or two but the band never stopped. Songs didn't end; they morphed into the next tune.

Near the end of the night, Dr. John led a version of "Right Place Wrong Time" that seemed to make every person in the club feel like part of the band. The song changed through blues, jazz, pop, and boogie-woogie until it finally landed in a zone so funkadelic that even George Clinton would have been knocked out.

The band kept soaring to new heights and then climbing even higher. By the time Professor Longhair did "Go to the Mardi Gras," the delirious crowd nearly drowned out the band with their sing-along.

People were standing on the bar and hanging from the rafters and riding on each other's shoulders to get a better look at the show. The lights changed colors on the sweating musicians and their gleaming instruments. They looked like mad scientists experimenting in the laboratory.

Professor Longhair took over for a version of "Got My Mojo Workin'" that pretty much set the place on fire with sexual energy. It was hard to get a drink. People started buying booze by the bottle and passing it around. It was the same for marijuana. The smoke was so thick you didn't have to take a hit to get high.

Just when the crowd thought no one could get any higher, Dr. John called up The Divebomberz for a grand finale of "Iko, Iko." People sang along like there might not be a tomorrow and, even if there was, it wouldn't matter because tonight was so much fun. The two drummers played off each other like jungle brothers. Three piano players shot off like fireworks streaking into the night. The singers started sounding like horns and the horns started sounding like singers.

Butch and Tim managed to plug their instruments in and play along. Jesse was happy banging a tambourine and being onstage with the greatest bass player he had ever encountered. The song went on for a good half hour and nobody missed a beat or a riff. All the musicians were in the zone. It was musical revelation, one that anyone present would talk about for the rest of her life.

It was after 3 a.m. by the time the performance finally ended. The crowd screamed for more until the stage lights went down and the house lights came up. It took another hour for people to leave.

Once the club shut down and the crowd was gone, the musicians hung out, basking in the afterglow and beginning to pack up gear. Pete was everybody's best friend with the cocaine station he'd set up inside a backstage maintenance closet.

Amy went home when she realized she couldn't stay up as long as people who were powered by jet fuel.

Jesse got his moment with the mystery man. "What's your name, anyway?"

"I told you, name Gabriel."

Jesse slapped his head in embarrassment. "Oh, yeah, that's right. I forgot."

Gabriel smiled at Jesse forgivingly. "You forgot my name but you didn't forget me."

"Why is that?" Jesse asked.

"Because I brought you to the Voodoo."

"So did I," Carmen said, suddenly appearing with Dr. John in tow. "Tell my friend, Jesse, about the voice, good Doctor."

Dr. John started off with a question. "You been hearing it? That's a good thing."

"How long have you been hearing it?" Jesse asked.

"Since I was about seventeen, I guess."

Jesse did not want to miss his chance to learn more about the voice. "Are we all hearing the same voice or does everybody hear a different one?"

Dr. John laughed a little and then got serious. "The voice connects us all. Each of us hears our own version of the voice. It's telling us to pay attention to the side of life many people do not believe exists, the spirit world. Be careful, though. Sometimes your head makes up things the voice never said. That's when you get in trouble."

Jesse heard the voice laughing inside his head. "I hear it laughing right now. Do you hear it?"

Tim joined in. "I've heard the voice too, but I don't hear it now."

Dr. John listened for a moment. "I don't hear it now. It's not like the voice is a person, saying the same thing to everyone at the same time. It's much more personal. Be thankful when you hear it."

Jesse looked at Dr. John. "Why would the voice be laughing right now?"

Dr. John looked Jesse right in the eye. "That's for you to

decide. Just remember, you learn from your interpretation. You might think the voice is laughing at you for being foolish or you might think the voice is laughing because we all just put on the greatest show of our lives. If you think it's laughing at you, you might want to wonder what's making you feel insecure."

"I'll go with the greatest show on earth," Jesse said.

Dr. John seemed to understand what Jesse was really feeling. "How'd you like my bass player?"

"That might be why the voice is laughing at me," Jesse admitted.

"Why? Because you're not as good as him?"

"No, because I'll never be as good as him no matter how long and hard I try."

Dr. John put his arm around Jesse. "Now, now. Don't go down that road. You'll never be him, that's for sure. You be you and don't worry about anybody else. I watched you play. You got good chops. And I hear you write songs. My bass man never did that. You're going to be fine. How do you think I feel playing with Fess?"

Tim spoke up. "Yeah, I wondered about that. It must have been strange, playing with the man who taught you how to play."

Dr. John did a little spin move with his arms out for balance. "You got to be you. Everybody else is taken."

Carmen threw her arms around Dr. John. "That is why I love this man so much. He tells it like it is."

Dr. John kept his eye on Tim and Jesse. "Music's not a competition. It's a group effort. And by the way," he said to Tim. "You got it going on that fiddle."

"Thank you, man. That's a big compliment coming from you."

"Hey, we're all just helping people over the river," Dr. John said.

"What do you mean?" Jesse asked.

"I mean to tell you what I've learned from the voice of Voodoo," Dr. John said.

They waited, expectantly, for him to complete the thought.

"I've learned that music can transport people across the river of confusion."

Dale joined the conversation. "Oh, yeah, the river of confusion. What a great song title."

"You got that right," Dr. John said.

"What about the river?" Jesse asked. "Why is it even there?"

Dr. John took a deep, thoughtful breath before answering. "The river runs between the spiritual and material worlds. The river runs through each one of us and connects us all if we let it. Most people don't know about the river. They damn it up all the time with their selfishness. They end up with a hole in their soul and they try to fill it with booze or drugs or sex. That shit doesn't work. Believe me, I've tried it all. The only thing that fills the hole is letting the river run through you."

Carmen looked at Jesse. "Does any of this sound familiar?"

"It's really starting to make sense," Jesse said.

"What's it like making it in the music business?" Dale asked, not realizing he was changing the course of a deep conversation.

Dr. John didn't mind being interviewed by a fellow musician. "It's about the music, not the business. The people who survive in this game are the ones who make music for the sake of making music. Just remember, don't sign anything until you find someone you can trust."

"Will the voice help me know who to trust?" Jesse asked.

"I do hope so, my friend. I've learned to trust it over the years. But I still get fooled. Sometimes because the voice doesn't talk to me and sometimes . . . because I don't listen."

CHAPTER THIRTEEN

RACELAND MUSIC HALL

The New Year's Eve party at the Raceland Music Hall got off to a fast start. The Wheelers thundered into town on their Harleys. Their girlfriends arrived in separate vehicles. All the survivors from the Safari fire and most of their friends came. Half the bayou showed up.

The music hall was a two-story, corner tavern with a long history for live music. They called it a hall because the building had been gutted to make room for a large stage and dance floor. People came to dance their hearts out and party without inhibition.

Most importantly, there was no trouble with the Gypsies. The truce had been holding up for more than a month. Peace had been restored on the bayou. Hopes were high that everyone would have a prosperous New Year. The Wheelers posted a watch of armed guards in a one-block perimeter around the club, just in case.

The Divebomberz played better than ever after their Tipitina's inspiration with Dr. John and Professor Longhair and Aaron Neville. Rene slowed down the tempo on a few songs. Jesse became more deliberate on the bass. Tim and Butch started giving each other more room for solos, and Dale varied the levels on his singing for a more dynamic style.

The band played two sets of foot stomping music. The crowd was having so much fun that nobody seemed to notice the midnight hour approaching. Amy got Jesse's attention by pointing to her watch.

"All right, everybody," Jesse said. "I don't know if anybody's noticed, but it's going to be a New Year in two minutes."

"That's right," Dale said as the crowd began cheering in anticipation. "It's time to make your resolutions and get ready to kiss the lover of your dreams like there will be no tomorrow."

Jesse's favorite part of any New Year's gig was just before midnight. It always felt like a rocket ship was about to lift off the launch pad at Cape Canaveral. He and the band got the entire crowd involved in the countdown. Amy came onstage with Jesse, Terry with Butch, Loretta with Tim, and Polly with Rene. The only band member without a partner onstage was Dale.

Everybody cheered and kissed each other as midnight arrived. Then, they joined arms and sang along to "Auld Lang Syne." It was a traditional celebration, but Jesse had a feeling the night was going to be filled with surprises. The back of his neck was tingling like the Voodoo voice was trying to get through to him.

"You want to know what my new year's resolution is?" Dupre asked Dale once the kissing and the singing were over and the band had taken a break.

Dale did not want to know but he played along. "Why, yes I do."

"I'm resolving to not shoot anybody," Dupre said.

"I'd have to say that's a good resolution," Dale said.

"First year I've ever had to make it."

"What if the truce doesn't hold up?"

"Then I'll have to break my resolution," Dupre said, laughing like a spook show host and patting the .45 handgun holstered under his left arm.

Dale put his hands against the sides of his face. "Oh, I hope it doesn't come to that."

"It won't. Business is better than ever all around. By the way, who is this Pete guy who claims to be your manager? He's buying some serious quantity lately."

"How much?"

"Last week he paid cash for two kilos."

"That's a lot of cocaine."

"No shit," Dupre said. "Don't look now but I think your good old boy is in it up to his eyeballs."

"He's not selling it to us," Dale said. "We can't afford it."

"Well, here's a little something to get you through the night," Dupre said as he slipped an eight ball of coke into Dale's palm. "I've got one for everybody in the band. Spread the word."

People were dancing to taped music through the P.A. while the band was on break. Tim and Loretta were doing a crazy waltz-polka when Dale whispered the cocaine news to Tim, who quickly directed their dance steps to meet with Dupre for the surreptitious drug pass.

Tim and Loretta were already in high spirits. The night was the zenith of a whirlwind courtship that saw Loretta moving in after the first month. Their duplex apartment on Annunciation Street in New Orleans had become a hangout for musicians and Indiana refugees. They played bluegrass and folk music on the wide front steps of their house while the neighborhood kids danced on the sidewalk below like they were dancing for tips on Bourbon Street. Loretta was a black-haired, buxom beauty with a broad smile. She was shy, but she had a big laugh and a twisted sense of humor. She read and collected back issues of an offbeat comic book called "Amputee Love." She and Tim made a great couple. They balanced each other well. Her dark side brought out his bright side.

Tonight they were ready to party until dawn with the band and all their friends.

Terry and Butch took the next pass from Dupre. They had settled in quite nicely together in their garden street apartment, head over heals in love. Butch and Jesse had recently written a song about Terry, entitled "I Want to Believe."

Butch wanted to believe in love. He wanted to believe a man and woman could actually be happy together. His parents had not succeeded. His alcoholic father had mistreated and eventually left his mother. Butch did not have a mean bone in his body. He could be shy, socially, but he was never shy with Terry. He was as energized with her as he was playing guitar.

Rene and Polly were next. They were in their full glory. Raceland was their hometown, and all their friends were there to hear Rene with his up-and-coming band. Rene took a behind-the-back drug pass from Dupre like they were playing basketball for the Harlem Globetrotters.

As soon as Dupre made the pass to Jesse, Amy dragged her fiancé outside as fast as she could and shook a finger in his face. "I don't like what happens to you when you do that shit," she scolded. "You go off in your own little world and forget about me. It's like I'm not even here."

Jesse hung his head. "C'mon, Amy. It's New Year's Eve. It's time to party."

She grabbed him with both hands by his shoulders and got her face up close to his. "If you want me to stay, you won't be snorting that cocaine I saw Dupre hand you."

Jesse hated being given an ultimatum. Part of him wanted to tell Amy to go on home and leave him alone. But he didn't want her to go. He loved her and he loved the way she could tell him to his face what he needed to hear. He remembered how bad he felt the night she left him in the rain outside the Sea Shell. He decided to lie to her.

"Okay, I won't do any. Come on, let's go back inside. We've got another two sets to play. The natives are getting restless."

He kissed her and took her by the hand, back into the club. Amy followed him with a deep sigh. She realized she couldn't control him

Butch had a line of cocaine set up for everybody in the band on the back of his amp. By the time they started playing, they were practically goose-stepping to the jolting rush of the drug. The crowd was right there with them. The Hall seemed to be floating about a foot above its foundation.

Nobody knew that Dupre was outside, getting busted in the parking lot. Federal agents snuck up on him, cuffed him and whisked him off in an unmarked car so quickly that none of the Wheelers knew what was happening. Dupre's girlfriend only saw the tail end of the federal arrest. He wasn't holding any drugs when they nabbed him. He had given the last of his stash away only moments before his arrest.

It took some time for the Wheelers to realize it was a federal arrest. Dupre's girlfriend mentioned she had seen DEA logos on jackets and hats. Big Ben was stomping around the parking lot behind the club in a full-blown rage. "This has to be Gypsy, ratting us out."

No one dared contradict him or even suggest that more facts were needed to properly assess the situation. The Wheelers quickly assembled to plan a swift retaliation against The Gypsies. Word of the arrest spread quickly through the party. A paranoid chill replaced the rowdy atmosphere. Most people in the crowd were holding some kind of illegal drugs or firearms. Who knew when the agents might come back to make more arrests?

The party came to a screeching halt. People scattered like frightened animals, stashing drugs and guns in the hall and slowly walking away from the club without getting into their cars or onto their bikes. Nobody felt sober enough to be on the road with federal agents prowling the area.

The band packed it up for the night, hiding their marijuana and cocaine in instrument cases. Butch asked if anybody had seen Pete all night.

Jesse shook his head. "He told me he was definitely coming. As far as I know, he never showed."

"Big surprise," Butch said.

"What do you mean?"

Butch took a deep breath before continuing. "You know how you can tell if someone's a drug addict?"

"How?" Jesse played straight man.

"He's not around."

Jesse groaned in agreement. "Let's just hope he didn't have anything to do with Dupre's arrest."

CHAPTER FOURTEEN

METRO GNOME

The week after New Year's, thanks to Pete, the band found itself in a professional recording studio in New Orleans. The place was awe-inspiring. The control room had a twenty-four channel mixing board surrounded by amplifiers and sound processing machines with blinking lights, a two-inch, reel-to-reel tape machine, monitor speakers and more electronic gear than anyone in the band had ever seen. Looking through the glass wall in front of the control room, they could see into a large performance area with a piano and at least ten microphones on stands with cords coiled like snakes on the floor. Off to the side of the main staging area were soundproof booths for drums and vocals. Once again, Pete was missing in action.

A pale-faced, thirty-year-old hippie in blue jeans and a Grateful Dead T-shirt rose from behind the board to greet the band. "Welcome, Divebomberz. I'm Jonathan, your chief engineer. I own the place, or maybe I should say it owns me."

An impeccably dressed man Jesse knew he'd met somewhere also introduced himself. "I'm Drew. I'll be producing your session for Pete. He can't be here but he told me to make sure we get a hit record tonight."

Butch restated the obvious. "Pete's not here a lot more than he is here."

Dale stopped gawking at the studio. "Where is Pete? We're starting to get worried about him."

Drew spoke up in Pete's defense. "Nothing to worry about. He's off on some real estate deal."

Jesse had met with Pete regarding Dupre's arrest at the Raceland Music Hall. Pete did not look good, like he hadn't slept in days. But he convinced Jesse he hadn't gotten himself into legal trouble and that working with the feds was the last thing on his mind. He was mainly concerned that his new and improved supply line for cocaine would dry up. Or worse, that Dupre would inform on him. He said Dupre's arrest had more to do with murder charges than drug dealing. The newspaper had reported charges for both murder and dealing. Too many people had been dying for the authorities not to take some action. The truce had cooled things down for a short time, but nobody expected it to last.

Rene didn't seem to care where Pete was. He was all business with the studio engineer. "Where do you want me to set up my drums?"

Jonathan led Rene to a small room with a door that opened onto the main performance area. "Let's put the drummer in the drum booth. We'll run a click track through his headphones."

"What's a click track?" Rene asked.

Jonathan did a double take to make sure Rene wasn't kidding. "It's a metronome so you can keep the band exactly on time."

Rene would not enter the drum booth. "I'm the one who keeps the band on time. I hate metronomes. They keep speeding up and slowing down."

Drew wasn't sure if Rene was kidding. He decided to exercise his producer prerogative. "Let's mike him up and see how it goes. We don't have to do anything you don't want to do, Rene."

Jonathan helped direct the set up. "We'll put the bass, guitar and fiddle in the main room. You guys set up however it makes you feel comfortable."

"Wait a minute," Rene said. "You mean I'm not going to be able to see them when we play?"

Jonathan tried to be reassuring. "There's a window in the booth. You'll be able to see everybody just fine."

Rene put his hands over his face in obvious disagreement. "It doesn't look like it to me. Come on, guys, don't let them put me in that room with their metronome."

The band couldn't help but laugh. Rene sounded like he was being sent to Siberia.

Rene wasn't about to walk into the drum booth. "It's not funny. I don't like small spaces. My drums need room to sound out."

Butch came over to put his hand on Rene's shoulder. "Your drums are going to be miked up. We'll all hear them in our headphones. Just try it. If it doesn't work we'll put you in the grown-up room."

Watching Rene go into the drum booth like a reluctant racehorse into a stable stall, Jesse realized he wasn't the only musician in the band who had bouts of self-doubt.

As Jonathan and Drew began having discussions with Rene about how to mike a drum kit, Jesse shouted out to the entire studio. "We're all egomaniacs suffering from inferiority complexes!"

Everybody in the studio stopped dead in his tracks upon hearing the pronouncement. Jesse did not elaborate, which was unusual for him. Nobody commented on the statement. They considered it for a full ten seconds, and then got back to work. The thoughtful moment had a calming effect on the session.

It took forever to get a drum sound that made both Drew and Jonathan happy. They argued about where to place the microphones, how many to use and what effects to use on each one.

Drew tried to use his producer title to pull rank on Jonathan and put reverb on the high hat and phase shifting on the snare. Jonathan wasn't having anyone tell him how to be an engineer in his own studio, and he didn't want the recording to sound like "disco from hell." Between the producer and the engineer, it took way too much time to get the guitar tone, the fiddle tone, the bass tone, the slide guitar tone and the vocal tone. Two and a half hours after entering the studio, the band still hadn't played a note together.

Butch took Jesse aside for a two-man huddle. "This can't be right."

Jesse was as bothered as Butch by the delay but he hadn't been in recording studios enough to know what was normal and what was not. "We'll just have to see how it turns out."

At the three-hour mark, Jonathan finally asked the band to perform as a unit. Drew stopped them before the first verse was over. Jonathan looked at Drew like he wanted to shoot him. "They've got to keep playing if I'm going to get my levels."

The band was having trouble with the mix in their headphones. Half an hour later, they started playing again. This time they made it through the entire first song, "Hurricane on the Bayou," written by Jesse and Butch and most famously performed at the hurricane party at The Sea Shell.

Drew got excited about the performance. "Love, love, love the song. We might want to end on a vocal chorus instead of the instrumental thing. Come on in for a listen."

The band came into the boardroom, expecting to hear a polished, radio-ready recording. What they heard made nobody happy. Jesse wanted more bass, Rene wanted more drums,

Butch wanted more guitar, Tim wanted more fiddle and Dale wanted more vocal.

Jonathan let them have their say. "Okay, guys. You see what's happening here. Everybody wants more of himself. That's quite common. Don't worry, we'll get the mix eventually. Right now, we want to make sure we're getting everything down."

"Tell you what," Drew said. "Let's everybody come up to the board and grab the fader switch that controls the volume level on your instrument. Come on up, there's room."

"This is a bad idea," Jonathan said.

Drew was not about to be denied. "No, come on. Let's try it. I'm the producer and I've done this before and I know it will work."

Once the band crowded up to the mixing board, Jonathan reluctantly hit the play button to roll tape. By the end of the song, each musician had his own level turned up so loud that the recording sounded like an electrical explosion in a fireworks factory.

"See what I told you," Jonathan said.

Drew smiled triumphantly. "No. See what I told you. Now, we know what will not work. Too many producers spoil the broth."

The band had to agree with his assessment as they went back out and prepared to play again. They also agreed that Drew's idea of ending the song on a vocal chorus was a good idea.

At that point, Jesse remembered where he'd met Drew. Late, late one night, on the tail end of a mushroom trip, Jesse was sitting on a bench, alone, in Jackson Square. Drew sat down next to him, looking for sexual action. When Jesse said he wasn't interested, Drew adroitly turned the conversation into what a great musical producer he was and how he could help Jesse and his band. Jesse had realized Drew was too much of a self-promoter to be the real deal. Now, in the studio for the first time, he got a sinking feeling that the session in progress might not turn out as well as everyone hoped.

Rene sat down next to Jonathan. "How about turning that click track off in my head? It's driving me crazy."

"Okay," Jonathan said. "Click track is off. Let's try another take."

"You've got a better one in you, gentlemen," Drew encouraged.

Four hours later the band was totally exhausted and burned out. They had recorded three original songs and the Steve Miller tune. Their first studio experience had been more than uncomfortable.

Jesse took off his headphones, too tired to care.

CHAPTER FIFTEEN

ROD'S

The band retired to Rod's, an all-night breakfast joint in the French Quarter. Almost all the customers were very tall shemales dressed in harlotry. The "girls" were rowdy as all night can get. They paraded and sang and danced and shouted across the room at each other, mostly good-natured and pretend bitchy. Theatric behavior was tolerated and even encouraged at Rod's. There was only one rule. It was written in red lipstick on a white poster board near the front door.

"No Food Fights."

The bacon and coffee air was filled with catcalls and lewd remarks when the band arrived and took their place in line to order. A man dressed as a playboy bunny called out to the band in a deep, booming voice. "Hey cute boys, come on over and talk to me."

A tall man wearing mesh stockings flirted in a voice that sounded almost like a woman. "Ooh, real men."

"You boys must know how lonely a girl can get," a drag queen called out.

Dale took the lead as he always did when the going got gay and the gay got going. "Good morning ladies. I know you're all big fans of The Divebomberz."

The girls did their best high-pitched imitations of teeny-boppers at a Beatles concert. Jesse couldn't help but laugh as he covered his ears.

"Are there any women here?" Rene asked Dale in a whisper. It was Rene's first time at Rod's. The rest of the band had been regulars since their days at Fritzel's.

"The ones with Adam's apples in their necks are guys," Dale explained discreetly. "But sometimes you can't tell because they have operations to shave the Adam's apple down."

Rene headed for the door. "Oh, man. This is all too much. I got to get my Cajun ass out of here."

Dale grabbed him by the arm. "No, no, no. You need to broaden your horizons, if you'll pardon the pun."

Dale pushed Rene into the line in front of him. "Besides, it's the best all night food in the French Quarter."

Rod was at the grill, cooking up grits, biscuits and gravy and three-egg omelets. He wore a white skullcap, blue jeans and a black t-shirt with a pack of Camels rolled up in his right sleeve. A lighted smoke always dangled from his lips, which explained the occasional ash garnish on an egg dish. "Adds to the flavor. Part of my recipe."

Rod was a sailor from Russia who jumped ship years ago and defected to America. He waited tables in the French Quarter until he saved enough money from tips to open his own restaurant. He liked to make a big deal out of the band's arrival. "Ladies and gentleladies," he shouted. "As you can see, we have celebrity company, The Divebomberz, live and in person. They are my personal favorite band. Keep your hands off them if you can."

Everybody laughed and cheered. Anybody who came into Rod's was likely to be announced, even if Rod had no idea who they were.

Rod was fifty-two years old but insisted he was forty-two. He was bald but he never showed it. When he wasn't wearing the cap, he was wearing a wig. He had a butch look with the t-shirt and the smokes, but the eye makeup and rouge gave him away as a person of cosmopolitan proclivity. Every single soul who entered his restaurant was treated with dignity and kindness. Rod had found his place in the world to make a stand. He loved people, rich or poor, gay or straight. It wasn't uncommon for him to give away a breakfast to someone in need.

Actually, he didn't give it away. He took the money out of his tip jar, which was a gallon-sized pickle jar. It was always stuffed with bills. Rod never made anybody feel like they were getting a handout. "Pay me double next time or I'll feel like you don't love me."

The Divebomberz began giving Rod their breakfast orders. He took his own orders and always had a friendly word with each customer. Servers delivered steaming plates of food to long wooden tables once the diners had taken their communal seats. Rod was as much an artist as a cook. Plates of food were well-balanced marvels of composition and color. For finishing touches, he added flowered carrots, cucumber ribbons, or radish fans.

The man relished his place in the world. "I'm a feeder of the people. I fill their bellies and I fill their souls." Even the rowdiest of guests settled down once she'd had her moment with Rod and been served a gourmet breakfast.

When it came Jesse's turn to order, Rod lowered his voice and said, "Ruthie the duck lady was in yesterday. She said Madame Carmen is looking for you."

Jesse leaned in close over the counter. "I'm looking for her too. Things have been getting weird lately."

Rod left his grill untended for a moment to get close enough to whisper to Jesse. "Tell me about it. The feds were in two days ago. Your name came up."

"Oh, great," Jesse said. "What did they want to know?"

"They wanted to know about you and some guy named Dupre. I told them I knew you to be a fine young man but I had never met Dupre. What's up with the feds?"

"Dupre's gang, the Wheelers, kind of adopted the band. They follow us around. Dupre got arrested at our New Year's gig in Raceland."

"For what?"

"Murder and dealing narcotics."

Rod took a deep drag on his cigarette and exhaled thoughtfully as he returned to his grill. "Oh, my, how perfectly charming. By all means, do invite him to Rod's."

"He's innocent," Jesse said.

Rod sounded deeply distracted as he flipped the potatoes and onions. "We all are, my boy. We all are. But I digress. What are you having this fine morning?"

"What else?"

"Rod's cheese and hot pepper omelet with homemade corned beef hash and a side of fresh fruit?"

"I do believe that would make the world go away," Jesse said.

"I'm afraid the world is here to stay, my boy. But, anyway, *Bon Appetit*."

Jesse took his seat with the band. He didn't share Rod's message and warning. They were already in full discussion regarding the recording session.

Butch was in a playful mood. "That producer at the studio was trying hard to impress. Looked like he might be interested in you, Dale."

Dale almost choked on his water. "Not my type. All he seemed to do was piss off Jonathan. Now, that guy, I love."

Rene was still feeling uncomfortable. "I hated his drum booth almost as much as I hated his click track. I didn't feel like myself all night. I think this record is going to suck, big time."

Butch tried to bring Tim into the conversation. "What about you, Tim? You've been pretty quiet all night."

Tim stretched his arms out on the table. "I know man. I've been tripping my brains out. I'm sorry. I did a hit of LSD just before we started."

Jesse was surprised. "You could have fooled me. You played your ass off. It didn't sound like you were high."

"It did to me," Tim said. "The whole thing was too far out. I had to really concentrate to stay with the song. Hope it doesn't sound too bad. Wish I hadn't done the acid. It pretty much ruined the night. Except for I feel pretty good now that I'm coming down a little."

Dale gave him a pat on the back. "Trust me. Everybody's studio experience got ruined tonight."

Five beautiful plates of breakfast arrived simultaneously. They smelled and tasted better than anything at Brennan's.

Jesse savored his corned beef special. "I've got a feeling this breakfast is going to be the best part of our recording session."

CHAPTER SIXTEEN

THE WARNING

Jesse took Tim to see Carmen the day after Rod's warning about the feds. She was helping a customer at the cash register so Tim had time to take a good look at her shop. He wandered to the back wall where the Voodoo dolls were displayed. "This place is far out. I've got to get a Gris-gris. I could use a little Voodoo thing around my neck for protection."

Carmen was finishing with her customer when she heard Tim's comment. "Come here to Madame Carmen. I've got something special for each one of you, my Jesse and my Timothy. How about our night at Tipitina's? Was it the best ever? And Tim, that fiddle of yours will take you places you never dreamed, if you can stay out of trouble."

Jesse gave Carmen a big hug. "Are we in trouble? Ruthie the duck lady told Rod we needed to come see you."

Carmen backed out of the hug and got serious right away. "Yes, you are in trouble and, yes, you need to see me. Here, special Gris-gris for each of you. No charge. These are on the house. A gift from your number one Voodoo fan."

Jesse and Tim studied the cloth-covered amulets that were filled with what felt like beads and sawdust. They smelled of lavender and mint. Carmen helped each man put on her gift. "There, around your neck. Tuck it under your shirt. No one needs to know but you. Now come with me. We must speak in private."

Jesse and Tim followed her through the beaded curtains and into her office. She sat them down in the chairs on either side of her desk and leaned over them like a stern teacher addressing two misbehaving students.

"Who is this Pete man?" she demanded. "And who is this Dupre?"

Jesse began to explain but she cut him off. "I know *who* they are. But do you know *what* they are? Do you realize the black magic they are throwing on you?"

Jesse said nothing. It hurt him to think of his friend Dupre as a negative influence. He had always thought of Dupre as a protector of the band, not somebody who would bring trouble to them.

Tim spoke up shyly. "The voice told me that Pete is a slave owner."

Carmen looked at Tim in surprise. "So the voice has come to you?"

Before Tim could answer, she turned to Jesse. "I see why you brought him along."

Jesse got to the point. "Rod said federal investigators have been asking questions about the band."

Carmen's nose began its inquisitive twitching. "Yes, I can taste your fear. You know the danger you're in, although you have yet to admit it. That's because you've put yourself in the middle of a major drug-dealing operation. Dupre's connections are now Columbian and Pete is part of a pipeline that will soon connect to New York City. Dupre is in jail and he will talk eventually. Pete is snorting so much of his inventory he'll kill himself soon."

"How do you know all this?" Jesse asked.

Carmen was not quite ready to reveal her sources. She offered a limited explanation. "The eyes of Voodoo are everywhere.

There are spirits who take human form and there are spirits who take no shape at all."

"We're not selling drugs," Tim said, looking at Jesse for backup.

Carmen's nose twitched again. "When you hang out with drug dealers, you are a drug dealer. Jesse helped negotiate the truce between the motorcycle gangs that turned the bayou into a cocaine highway. Dupre was arrested at your New Year's performance. Do you not realize they are watching you? Pete still has no idea what he's getting himself into."

"How can Pete not know?" Jesse asked.

"He knows the players. He doesn't know how big they are becoming. Soon, he'll be needing trucks for the deliveries they have in mind."

Jesse felt confused. "Why do they need Pete?"

"Pete is a link in the chain, a link with a respectable business cover. He has friends in banking and mortgage who can launder larger sums of money."

"Have you talked to Pete?" Jesse asked.

Carmen took a deep breath and tried to calm herself down. "I don't need to talk to Pete. The spirit world is abuzz with all this. The darkness is spreading like cancer through our lands. Your band is being used. Deliveries and payments are made when dealers meet at your shows."

Jesse was feeling sick to his stomach. He had looked the other way too many times. "Is that why Dupre was arrested at our New Year's Eve show at Raceland Music Hall?"

"They knew he'd be there," Carmen said.

"We pretty much know what the bikers are up to." Tim said.

Carmen stood up tall and spread her arms wide to make her point. "You have surrounded yourselves with greed and violence and narcotics. It's soiling your souls. Can't you smell it? You can't wash it off. The only thing to do is run from it. You will be killed or jailed for a long time if you do not immediately extricate yourselves from the middle of this growing criminal enterprise."

Jesse knew, instinctively, that everything she said was true. Amy had been telling him the same thing since Dupre's arrest.

"The killing between the Wheelers and the Gypsies is about to begin again, worse than ever," she said.

"Is the voice telling you all this?" Jesse asked.

Carmen placed her hand on Jesse's shoulder. "The Voodoo has shown me I need to intervene on your behalf. But that is not where I get my information. My main source is the man you call the mystery man. He is with the Gypsies. They are preparing for war because they know the Wheelers will blame them for Dupre's arrest. Also, Ruthie the duck lady knows a federal agent who told her that informants have infiltrated each gang. Every meeting they have is being recorded and has been for some time. The evidence against them is piling up so high they have to store it in a warehouse. The feds arrested Dupre to confront him with the evidence and see how loud he'll sing."

"What should we do?" Tim asked.

"You must take your music out of this region. You must leave New Orleans and Bayou Lafourche." Carmen spoke with such conviction that neither Tim nor Jesse considered challenging her conclusion. They knew she was right.

"Where should we go?" Jesse asked.

Carmen looked at them both for a long pause to make sure she had their undivided attention. "An opportunity will soon arise to show you which way to go."

Jesse and Tim looked at each other. They knew what they had to do. As they stood up to leave, Carmen said, "Wait. Before you go. You must understand what is really going on here. This isn't about motorcycle gangs and drug dealers. This is about light versus darkness. You have been traveling down a road of darkness. The darkness of the soul seeks riches and fame and pleasure. This road leads only to sorrow and betrayal. Each of you must change your course to seek the light within, the light which connects us all."

"What's going to happen to us?" Tim asked. "If you can see the future, I'd like to know how this is all going to turn out. I don't know what's light and what's dark. I just want to know what's going to happen."

Carmen had to chuckle at his desperation. "The darkness makes you selfish. It makes you think fame and fortune are all you need to be happy and satisfied."

"What about the light?" Jesse asked.

"The light shows us the path out of self centeredness," Carmen explained. "It will show you that trying to be famous is much less important than making music to bring peace and joy to the world."

Tim held his hands up over his shoulders. "I've always felt that way."

Jesse raised his head. "I'm trying to get there."

Carmen bent down to kiss Jesse on the forehead. "Jesse, you still have no idea where you're going. You know I love you but you must also know that I understand the struggle going on inside your soul."

Jesse didn't comment. He knew she was talking about the band and marriage to Amy and his fear that he would end up being an attorney in Indiana at his father's firm.

"So, where should we be going?" Tim asked.

Carmen kissed Tim on the forehead so as not to show favoritism. "I've told you all I know. I've told you all you need to know. But I will tell you one more thing."

"What's that?" Tim asked.

"A powerful force is coming to the band from our night at Tipitina's. You will be pleased once it gets here."

"What is it?" Jesse asked.

"I cannot say. To predict the future is to interfere. Contrary to popular opinion, my Voodoo has nothing to do with fortune telling."

CHAPTER SEVENTEEN

RICK

Less than two weeks after Tim and Jesse's warning from Carmen, The Divebomberz were scheduled to play Johnny's Cimarron, a huge club in Shreveport, Louisiana, three hundred miles northwest of New Orleans. Jesse was amazed at the rapid turn of events. He hadn't seen any way out of New Orleans until the door to their exit opened like a magic stone gate to a secret, mountain passage.

Rene's parents had moved north and realized the clubs in that region would love the band's country-rock sound. Rene's father booked the job in Shreveport, which paid eighteen hundred for Wednesday through Saturday. The band would be filling in for another group that had to cancel.

Jesse was beginning to see that many of their opportunities happened because someone else couldn't make it. Even more amazing than the miracle booking was that The Divebomberz became a six-man band shortly after New Year's Eve.

Jesse answered the phone one morning and heard a man with a smooth New Orleans drawl speaking softly. "Hey, man. It's Rick. Madame Carmen says you need me playing keyboard for your band."

Jesse immediately wondered if Rick was the powerful force Carmen had predicted would come to them from Tipitina's. It shocked him that a keyboard player would come into his life so soon after he first realized he needed one. He entertained the notion he had dreamed him up, but that's not what happened. Rick did appear as if by magic. He had seen Professor Longhair sitting in with the band at Tipitina's and realized how much The Divebomberz needed a keyboard player. He got Jesse's phone number that night from Pete and called Jesse after the holidays.

Jesse was cautious at first. "How do you know Carmen?"

The man chuckled at Jesse's reaction and introduced himself. "Sorry for calling out of the blue like this. Like I said, my name is Rick. I've been playing around New Orleans most of my life. Sooner or later, we all get to know Madame Carmen and Ruthie the duck lady."

"You say that like they're one and the same person," Jesse said.

"They may well be. The two of them have serious Voodoo connections. Dr. John introduced me."

Jesse was stunned. "You're a friend of Dr. John's?"

Rick paused long enough for Jesse to think he might be telling the truth. "We know each other pretty well. I love the cat. He's helped me out a lot. But I learned most of what I know from Professor Longhair."

That was all Jesse needed to hear. "That's way good enough for me. Can you come to the Fae Do Do Club on Magazine Street on Saturday around noon? That's tomorrow. We're trying to get a rehearsal in the afternoon before our gig at nine."

"I'll bring my organ down if you'll help me get it off the truck."

Jesse had to laugh, thinking Rick was joking. "How big is it?"

Rick was serious. "It's a Hammond B-3 with a Leslie. It's big and it's heavy."

Jesse had no idea what he was talking about, but he wasn't ready to admit his ignorance. "We'll take care of it. We're used to hauling gear."

Rick didn't arrive at the club until two. He was five-foot-eight with shoulder length blond hair and a goatee to match. He looked and sounded like the rock and roll keyboard star, Edgar Winter. Rick had played with everybody, including the Dixie Cups on their big hit, "Going to the Chapel." He was twenty-eight years old.

"Sorry I'm late, man. I had to borrow this pickup truck and the guy was late."

The band gathered round to behold the B-3. It was five feet long, four feet tall and three feet wide. It was made of beautifully carved wood and looked like it belonged in a cathedral. Jesse thought it was the coolest thing ever, never thinking ahead to what it would be like to haul it from gig to gig. It took four guys to lift the thing out of the truck. Rick had heavy-handled hauling devices that strapped to either end of the organ. Jesse, Rene, Butch, and Tim hoisted it into the club and up on the stage like slaves building an Egyptian pyramid.

Rene wasn't pleased with the possible addition of another musician. "So, what? You just invite somebody to join the band without even telling us?"

Jesse was amazed at what a pain in the ass Rene was becoming. "He just called yesterday. He knows Dr. John and Professor Longhair. I thought you'd be thrilled. I didn't invite him to join the band. He's just sitting in. If you don't like him, we'll send him on his way."

The moment he started playing, Rick became a member of The Divebomberz. He was classically trained but incredibly funky. The B-3 through the Leslie was so rich and full it turned the band's chicken-vegetable soup into Gumbo Ya Ya. The Leslie amp spins around in its cabinet, giving the organ an expansive, well-rounded tone. Rick could make it moan and he could make it scream, like he was making love to a gypsy queen.

The first song the band played with their new keyboard

man was "Jambalaya." The Hank Williams song only has two major chords, C and G. Rick made it sound like Beethoven had gone wild in the bayou with Buckwheat Zydeco. He took a lead and held onto one high note so long it felt like an invasion of the body snatchers. Jesse looked over his shoulder to see Rick with one arm held high over his head as he dragged out the one-note wail. Butch caught it too. Rick was a showman.

When the five-minute jam finally came to a perfect, crunching end, all six members of the new and improved Divebomberz could only stare at each other in amazement. Jesse thought the band sounded better than anything he'd ever heard. Now, he was certain that Rick and his B-3 were exactly what Carmen had predicted.

Rene got off his drum stool and reached over the organ to shake Rick's hand. "Welcome to The Divebomberz."

"Does this mean I'm playing tonight?" Rick asked.

"You're in for an equal share," said Butch.

"How much is that?"

Butch looked at the rest of the band for confirmation. "Fifty bucks. We're only making three hundred tonight but we'll do a lot better, I promise."

The Divebomberz' silent vote was unanimous. Each member shook his head affirmatively and they were, suddenly, a six-man band.

"I don't doubt we'll make more money," Rick said. "This band sounds big-time good. Count me in."

Jesse realized that Rick had no idea he was joining a band that was leaving town to escape a drug war and possible federal arrest. He decided not to mention it. Why spoil the moment?

The new and improved band spent the rest of the afternoon rocking the empty club. During breaks, they had a few beers and joints and got to know each other. Rick told war stories about playing with the music legends of New Orleans and getting addicted to heroin along the way. "I kicked thirteen months ago. Don't worry, I'm never going back to that nightmare."

"Good to hear," Butch said. "We've all done our share of too much cocaine."

Rick was not amused. "Don't bring that shit around me. I don't even want to see it. That's how I got started."

Tim raised his glass of beer. "We're back to booze and pot."

"I'll drink to that," Rick said as the band got back to introducing him to the set list.

The band's first rehearsal impressed the staff at the club. They applauded after every song for the entire session. By 6 p.m., they had called everyone they knew to come hear the new band they had discovered.

That night, The Divebomberz played like demons at the Fae Do Do. Jesse couldn't believe how full they sounded with Rick. It was like playing with Professor Longhair, only even better. Rick was more rock and roll.

The packed club cheered them on like musical history was being made. The crowd kept getting bigger as the hour got later, always a good sign for a band. Rick didn't know half of the songs but it never took him more than a verse and a chorus to find his part. He knew when to fade out and when to come on strong. His dramatic sense of timing gave the band new dynamics.

After the show, the club manager tried to book the band for more money and the first weekend of every month. Jesse had to turn down the offer. The band had to get out of New Orleans.

A few nights after their first performance as a six-piece band, The Divebomberz had a meeting at Dale's apartment in the French Quarter.

"So, who gets to sleep with Dale?" Rene joked about the three hotel rooms booked at the Royal Royce Hotel in Shreveport, Louisiana. The club owner was providing the rooms.

"I'll take that spot," said Butch, who was always very protective when anyone teased Dale about his sexual preference.

"I'm not sure I'm ready for a place named the Royal Royce," Dale said. "It sounds like a whore house in London."

Jesse was quick on his pick. "I'll bunk with Tim. That way Rene and Rick can get to know each other."

Rene hung his head slightly and turned away. Jesse saw he wasn't happy with the roommate selections, nor was he agreeable to Jesse making the decisions. He needed to pay more attention to Rene.

"Okay, then," Jesse said. "I can feel the presence of an unhappy drummer. So how about this? It's me and Rene in the honeymoon suite, Tim and Rick in the Hollywood double, Butch and Dale in the whatever-you-want-to-call-it room."

Rene shrugged his shoulders, somewhat appeased by the new pairings. With the rooming situation resolved, the band retired to its favorite hangout, Tortilla Flats, for a couple rounds of Sangria and the chance to jump a passing train. Jesse was excited to initiate Rick.

The band was starting to get a little loud and loaded when Dale quieted them down. "Listen. Do you hear that?"

Everybody fell silent and listened. The restaurant crowd turned to see what was wrong.

Tim shouted for joy as he jumped up out of his seat. "I hear the train a comin'. I think it's time we took Rick for his first ride."

Rene got up from the table and headed for the door without looking back. "Follow me, men."

"Put us on the tab, Bobby!" Butch yelled as the entire band stampeded out the door and headed for the railroad tracks by the Mississippi River.

Rick tried to finish his sangria and then had to run to keep up. "You guys can't be serious. I've never jumped a train. I don't know how to do it. I can't believe I'm even doing this. People lose their legs playing around trains."

Jesse waited for him to catch up. "Don't worry. We won't let anything bad happen to you."

The band reached the tracks and hid behind a shed as the lead locomotive rumbled past them. It shook the ground with its rolling weight. The headlight was so bright it split the night in two. It smelled like a steel mill and looked like a fire-breathing dragon.

"Why are we hiding?" Rick asked.

Butch peeked around the corner of the shed as lookout. "There's no point letting the engineer know we're going to jump his train."

Jesse watched the engine and the first few cars roll by. "This is perfect. Nice and slow, just how we like it."

Rick was shivering. "I don't like it nice and slow. I don't like it at all."

Jesse led Rick out of the shadows as the band ran for the train. "Follow my lead. Run along next to a ladder, grab it up a few rungs with both hands and then jump onto the lowest rung of the ladder."

Rick ran reluctantly behind Jesse. "What if I fall?"

"Don't let go of the ladder," Dale said as he ran ahead to the next car and swung himself up the side ladder. He made it look easy. Rick ran alongside the train for about twenty yards before he finally got the nerve to grab the ladder of a car that was three cars behind the one Dale was now riding. Rick had trouble finding his footing on the ladder but he was soon sailing along on the side of a moving train.

"What do I do now?" he yelled at Jesse, who was still jogging alongside him.

"Climb the ladder so I can jump on," Jesse said. "And make it quick. There's a bridge up ahead."

"I cannot believe I'm doing this," Rick said as he climbed up the ladder. Jesse jumped on. He urged Rick onward and upward. "Keep going all the way to the top of the car."

The train whistle blew as Rick reached the top of the ladder and threw himself, spread eagled, on top of the train car. He was holding on for dear life as the train rumbled through the French Quarter. Jesse was laughing so hard he could barely stand up. Rick looked like Charlie Chaplin doing slapstick. The train wasn't going more than ten miles an hour. Rick was hanging on like he was on the wing of an airplane in flight.

The city lights were shining bright on the right. The Mississippi River was in her full glory on the left, shimmering reflections from the lights on bridges, docks, warehouses and the Dixie Beer Brewery. The train rumbled west toward Baton Rouge.

Jesse bent down to Rick. "Try to stand up. We're not going that fast. You won't get much of a view hugging the roof of the car. This is a perfect night. You don't want to miss it."

Rick rolled over slowly and sat up carefully, keeping his hands widespread and on the roof. "Where are the other guys?"

"Look," Jesse said as Dale leaped from one car to another in the moonlight. "Here comes Dale."

"Oh, Lord," Rick said. "I am not doing this."

Jesse pointed over Rick's head. "Look behind you. That's Tim, one car behind, and Rene, behind him."

"Where's Butch?" Rick asked, fearing the worst.

Butch popped up on top of the same ladder Rick and Jesse had climbed. "Hey guys," he said as he stood up to take in the shimmering scenery. Looking down at an obviously terrified Rick, he asked, "How's it hanging, hobo?"

Dale jumped onto the car. "This is how we initiate new members. How are you doing?"

Tim and Rene joined them in a minute and, before he knew what was happening, Rick was being helped to his feet by the entire band. Once he stood up and realized he could keep his balance, Rick got his train legs together fairly quickly.

Rene helped Rick steady himself. "I remember when they took me on my first ride. I thought they were crazy. Now, it's one of my most favorite things to do. You'll see. You get used to it."

"Did anybody bring a train ride joint?" Dale asked.

"Way ahead of you, bro," Tim said as he fired up a number.

Rick took a hit and looked like he might be about to smile. "Is this thing going to speed up once we get out of the city?"

Dale took the joint from Rick. "Yeah. But don't worry. It slows down again in Baton Rouge."

Rick looked warily at the faces surrounding him until he saw Butch crack a smile and say, "That's a joke. We'll be getting off in a couple miles, the same way we got on. Then, we'll hit the bars on Magazine Street and bum a ride back to the Quarter. We've done this before. We know the way."

Jesse relaxed as the train took them through the city. His entire life was beginning to feel like one inevitable train ride. Events were coming at him like they had a mind of their own. Rene showed up with all his sound gear, more or less on cue. Rick came out of nowhere as soon as the band realized it needed a keyboard man. Gigs mysteriously materialized in the north when the band needed to get out of town. The Voodoo voice seemed to be guiding and protecting him wherever he went.

Even so, Jesse remained plagued by one of his pet theories:

the little things of today foretell the big things of tomorrow. A girlfriend who forgets a birthday won't be around much longer. Or a dead bird on the porch foreshadows the death of a close friend.

When he first came to New Orleans with Butch and Dale, they were auditioning as a singing trio at a bar on Decatur Street. Back in the corner, an old drunk kept feeding coins into a jukebox. He couldn't get it to play no matter how hard he tried. He'd put a coin in, slam the side of the box with an open hand and curse the machine when it rejected his coin and wouldn't play music. When he started kicking the box, the bartender threw him out of the club. Ever since that sad bit of street theater, Jesse worried that he was the wino and the jukebox was the music business.

The band sounded better than ever with Rick onboard. But there was one thing becoming increasingly wrong. Dale's lead vocal was getting lower and lower as the band grew louder. Butch and Jesse had originally recruited him because he could sing the high notes in a three-part harmony. Now, his falsetto voice couldn't hold up to the full band sound. He had to fall back on his natural, bass-baritone voice. Butch and Tim started singing more lead, which left Dale playing tambourine and other rhythm instruments. The band needed a new lead singer, or no lead singer at all.

Dale was the most flamboyant member of the band, but his costumes and dance moves were starting to stick out like a sore thumb. The band was evolving into a hard-driving force. Nobody was dancing, just bearing down on his instrument. Sure, the Rolling Stones had Mick Jagger with all his prancing and parading, but Dale couldn't sing like Mick. Jesse knew better than to consider a female singer. When a band with a female lead singer makes it, only the female lead singer makes it. His mind was rolling down the tracks between the Mississippi River and the crescent city. Where was the Voodoo voice when he needed it?

Jesse looked around and saw each member of the band drifting into his own reflections. Everyone seemed to snap out of it when it came time to get off the train. Jumping off is always the hardest part.

Rick had even more trouble going down than getting up. The train was picking up speed. He balked at the end of the ladder. "I'm not doing this. I know I'm going to die."

Butch yelled down from the top of the train car. "Come on, Rick. We can't get off until you do."

Dale was just above Rick on the ladder. "Don't just jump. Hang on to the ladder and get your feet under you. Run alongside the train before you let go."

Rick did as he was told, but it took him at least twenty yards before he finally let go of the ladder. He ran a few steps after letting go and then fell down on the rocks and rolled himself away from the train. He cut his right shoulder and bruised his head but he wasn't seriously hurt. The roll was quite athletic. He was standing in no time.

Dale swung down shortly after Rick and gave him a triumphant hug. "Way to go, Ricky. You did it. Nice roll. See, that wasn't so hard, was it?"

Rick was still dusting himself off and checking for injury. "I can't believe I just did that. I can't believe I'm in this crazy-ass band. I can't believe I'm headed for Shreveport to stay in some hotel called The Royal Royce."

CHAPTER EIGHTEEN

JOHNNY'S CIMARRON CLUB

Johnny ran his Cimarron Club in Shreveport like the captain of a ship. He was a walk-the-plank kind of owner, but he worked harder than anyone. He greeted The Divebomberz on the wide sidewalk in front of his club and helped the band unload their gear from the truck, trailer, and van.

Johnny tugged on the brim of his cowboy hat. "I never hired a band without hearing them first. You guys better be good. I spent a ton on promotion for tonight. I got you billed as the hottest band on the bayou."

After the load-in was complete, Johnny said, "Your keyboard player better be extra special good. I think I threw my back getting that beast of an organ out of the trailer."

Rene put his arm around Rick. "He is extra good. We'll do a sound check in a few minutes here that will blow your mind."

Jesse sidled up to Johnny. "The posters look great. How did you get a photo of all six of us? We've only had Rick for two weeks."

Johnny took a good long look at Jesse's wild, frizzy hair. "Your manager or promoter or whatever he is got me the shot. That guy is one hell of a salesman."

Rene stepped forward. "That's my dad. And you're right. He's one great salesman. He's sold everything from car parts to life insurance."

Johnny got down to business quickly. "Okay. Gather round guys, and let me explain the rules of the house."

The band made a tight circle around the club owner. Johnny was pushing fifty years old. His beat up hat looked like it never left his head. He wore faded blue jeans and boots with silver pointed toes. He was five-foot-seven in his boots. He had the build and look of a boxer who lost too many fights. His nose was slightly flattened and crooked. He wore a wide, leather belt with a state of Louisiana buckle. He kept a can of mace in a special holster on each hip. "See these bad boys on my gun belt? This is the way I enforce the first rule of the club. Can you guess what that rule might be?"

Dale was in his usual, let's get acquainted mode. "No naked dancing?"

"That's absolutely correct," Johnny said. "No fighting."

The band laughed. Johnny obviously had a sense of humor underneath his gruff exterior.

"Rule number two is band breaks can never, and I mean never, ever, exceed fifteen minutes. You start at nine, play until ten. Sets are always an hour long. Second set starts at ten fifteen and so on, four sets a night. So, let's see how good your math is. When do you finish playing?"

"One thirty," Butch guessed.

"One forty-five," Johnny corrected. "Last call's at two. If you've got a good crowd going, I expect you to work it until then. I'm a fair guy. If we do great at the door and at the bar, the band gets a bonus."

"What about drinks?" Jesse asked.

Johnny raised his hands like he was being held up by a robber. "Oh, I see I'm dealing with professionals. So, I tell you what. Drinks are on the house until the first one of you falls down or pukes on my stage."

"Fair enough," Jesse said as the band laughed in agreement.

They set up and sound checked in less than an hour. The only soundman they had was Tim, who had the mixing board on the stage next to his fiddle and slide guitar amp. Each member had a set up assignment. Jesse placed the main and monitor speakers and ran the cables. Butch set the amps and instrument cables. Rene set up his drums. Dale set the microphones and ran the cables to the board. Rick set up his Hammond B-3 and the Leslie amplifier, as well as a Fender Rhodes electric piano.

Tim tried to make all the sound levels balance onstage and throughout the dance hall. Not an easy job when you're standing on the stage.

Johnny noticed the band's efficiency and division of labor. "Looks like you guys have done this before."

"Once or twice," Butch said as the band counted in to its traditional opening song, "Jambalaya."

The sheer force of the musical explosion almost blew the cowboy hat off Johnny's head. Tim had the levels cranked way up. It was loud but well balanced. By the middle of the song, Johnny grabbed a waitress and started two-stepping her around the large, empty dance floor. At the end of the song, the band paused and bowed in unison for their small but special audience. Johnny and the waitress clapped and hooted, as did every employee in the place.

"Looks like we've got ourselves a big-time band from New Orleans," Johnny shouted as he came up to shake each member of the band's hand. "I do believe that's the best version of 'Jambalaya' I've ever heard. You do Hank Williams proud."

The band played a couple more songs as Johnny went from corner to corner in the huge room to help Tim get the main speakers dialed into the space. Once the sound check was done, Johnny invited the band to join him for a round of Heinekens.

"I hear you like good German beer. Am I right?"

Rene grabbed his icy mug from the waitress' tray. "Absolutely. It's nice to know my father got the details right."

Johnny waited for everyone to be served. "Okay, gentlemen. Let me tell you about the history of where you are. You might not know it but Shreveport was one of the nation's musical capitals in the nineteen-fifties. There was a radio and television program called Louisiana Hayride. It was huge all over the country. It brought the stars of the day to the world. Hank Williams, Johnny Cash, Bob Wills, and even Elvis Presley, the king himself, got their start right here in Shreveport. I saw it all because I worked there. We broadcast right out of the municipal auditorium here in town. I started out bussing tables and ended up running sound and booking major musical acts. It's how I got my start in show business. And look at me now. I'm about to showcase The Divebomberz."

Johnny knew how to sweet-talk the talent. The band ate it up, peppering him with questions about the old days. Johnny told stories about drinking with Hank Williams and doing pills with a young Elvis Presley.

Johnny's voice became reverently soft. "Hank was the biggest inspiration and the biggest disappointment at the same time. He was always down to earth and friendly. You'd never meet a nicer guy. But one minute he could be singing the sweetest songs in the world, and the very next minute he'd be too drunk to talk to you. I will say I never saw him get too mean. It was a shame the way he went out. Elvis too."

Dale was hanging on Johnny's every word. "Why do so many of the great ones die from booze and drugs?"

Johnny swigged down half a beer. "First of all. It's not just the great ones. Most of my friends are gone already, all because of booze and drugs. As for the great ones, as you call them, you just read about them more because they're famous. In reality, they're just like the rest of us. So watch out, boys, or the boogeyman will get you too."

Johnny sounded like he was telling ghost stories around the campfire. He knew how to spin a yarn. Jesse ate it up. To think he had finally arrived at the same spot Hank and Elvis played.

"I can't believe Elvis just died," Johnny said. "Last August sixteenth to be exact. Man, that was a shocker. I knew Elvis before he got so big he had to go make all those bad movies in Hawaii. He was a good, hard-working kid. None of us figured he'd get into drugs so heavy. I mean we saw him get fat and take up martial arts when he got older, but, hell, that kind of shit happens to all of us."

"Do you think fame turns people to drugs?" Dale asked.

"I'll tell you what," Johnny said, tipping his cowboy hat back slightly. "Fame messes everybody up. Nobody I ever met could handle it. And I saw most of them on the way up and half of them on the way back down. You better hope it doesn't happen to you, fame that is.

"But as for what gets people on drugs, it's the drugs that does it, not the fame or the money. The more drugs you do, the more drugs you do, until it kills you. It's as simple as that. It doesn't matter if you're famous or not."

Tim looked at Johnny like he was the guru from the mountaintop. "Isn't fame what the music business is all about? Getting a big name so you can sell a million records?"

Johnny relished his role as preacher of rock and roll gospel. "It's not about the money. It's about the music. Make music for the people who need to hear it and don't worry about selling records or getting your picture in the magazines."

Jesse was surprised to realize that Johnny and Dr. John and Carmen were all delivering the same message.

After a couple rounds of beer, Johnny decided it was time

to show the band its quarters at the Royal Royce Hotel. They walked the two blocks to the hotel in high spirits.

Johnny turned around to make sure everybody was with him as they passed beneath the granite archway of the old, five-story hotel. "So, listen up. Some of her glory has faded but The Royal Royce Hotel has seen the best of the best. Hell, I remember walking Dolly Parton into this same hotel back before she was big. Well, she was always big, but you know what I mean."

The band walked through the worn-out furniture and beat-down carpeting of the large and deserted lobby. The place smelled musty as a library on a rainy night.

Nobody was at the front desk. Johnny tapped on the counter bell until an older woman came through a squeaky, wooden door to see what was the matter. She looked around at nothing in particular because she was mostly blind. "What can I do for you?"

Johnny was kind. "Hello, Henrietta. It's me. I've got three rooms on the top floor for the band."

She looked ten years younger when she smiled at Johnny. "Oh, hi, Johnny. Yes, of course. We've been expecting you."

The band didn't find out until later that rooms on the top floor were much cheaper. The roof had a tendency to leak in a hard rain.

The elevator did not inspire confidence. It had a sliding door that had to be shut from the inside. Once the door creaked to its close, Jesse got a distinct feeling he might not be getting out. Terrible noises filled the shaft when it lurched to a start. The clangs and screeches sounded like a medieval drawbridge being raised.

Dale looked at Butch with real fear in his eyes. "Is this thing going to make it?"

The elevator only had room for four people. It was Butch,

Johnny, Dale and Jesse in the cramped space with their suitcases stacked on top of each other.

Johnny continued guiding the tour. "The only problem area is between the fourth and fifth floors."

"Problem area?" Dale asked.

Johnny laughed like a bartender at a lame joke. "Just kidding. I've only been stuck a couple times."

Now it was Butch's turn. "That's two times too many. Maybe we should start taking the stairs."

"Not a good idea," Johnny said. "The stairs get a little creaky."

The ride was bumpy until it mercifully jolted to a stop at the fifth floor. Johnny opened the sliding door. The elevator was six inches lower than level with the floor.

"Watch your step," he said, leading the way.

The halls were narrow and covered with purple carpet that looked black in the dim light. Johnny walked them to a window at the end of the hall. "See out there? That's a fire escape that goes almost all the way down."

Butch tried to look out the window. "Almost all the way down?"

"Yeah," Johnny said. "You'd have to hang on to the bottom rung and drop about five feet to the alley. Don't worry, there's never been a fire."

Jesse went to the window and looked up. "It looks like it goes up to the roof."

Johnny nudged Jesse and winked. "All the way to the coolest roof you ever saw. Whatever you do, don't go up and party on the roof."

Tim and Rene and Rick got out of the elevator and joined Johnny and the rest of the band in the hall.

Dale greeted them like a punchdrunk carny. "Enjoy the ride?"

Tim and Rick laughed at the question. Rene looked pale and seemed genuinely shaken by the experience. "That death trap is definitely not up to code."

Johnny shook his finger at Rene. "Don't tell anyone, or you'll be sleeping in the club. So, come on, guys, the rooms are clean and the beds are good."

Each room was comfortably large with one double bed and its own modernized bathroom. Quite nice, actually, except for the fact that everything was purple. Purple drapes, purple carpet, purple bedspreads, purple chairs and even purple shower curtains. No doubt, the purple was meant to hammer home the "royal" theme of the hotel.

Johnny threw open the curtain of a tall, Queen Anne window. "Look at her. There she is, in all her glory . . . downtown Shreveport. Look, right down there is the courthouse and right behind that is the new Parrish jail. Do not end up there."

"Nice view of the jail," Dale said with a wide-eyed, side look at the band.

"We're not troublemakers," Butch said. "But if we did get into trouble, you could help us out, right?"

Johnny put his arm around Butch. "Provided I'm not in jail with you."

The band laughed a little nervously. Jesse wondered what he had gotten into here. The hotel felt like a cross between a haunted house and a nursing home.

"I'm only kidding. I know every cop in this town. You'll be fine as long as you don't kill somebody."

"So far, so good," Tim said.

Johnny prepared to make his exit. "Okay, then. You're in your rooms. Relax. I've got to get back to the club. We're going to have a big night tonight. I can feel it in my bones."

Once Johnny left, they had a field day making fun of their new accommodations. Dale was the first. "You should see our room. It looks like somebody gets murdered in there every night."

Butch was next. "This place is like a purple people eater."

Tim tried to be positive. "The bed feels pretty good. Which side do you like to sleep on, Rick?"

"I'll take the floor if that's okay with you," Rick said.

Rene couldn't get over their host. "What about Johnny? Is he a combination of John Wayne and Ed Sullivan or what?"

"Let's see what kind of crowd he draws tonight," Jesse said.

"And let's get something to eat," Butch said. "I thought I saw a cool, little diner between here and the club."

Johnny's was packed by the time The Divebomberz showed up at 8 p.m. People were lined up on the sidewalk. Johnny had hung posters all over town and done a lot of radio advertising. The crowd inside parted to allow the band access to the stage in the back. Butch asked Jesse a question as they squeezed their way along the bar. "How do these people even know who we are?"

Jesse excused himself through the crowd as he responded to Butch. "They don't need to know us. They love us because we're the hottest band on the bayou."

Butch grabbed his arm. "Since when?"

"Since Johnny said so."

The crowd was rowdy and diverse. Bikers and their babes in leather were partying with college boys and their dates in short skirts. Johnny's bartenders and waitresses were serving drinks at a record-breaking pace. The air was dense with cigarette smoke and the unmistakable aroma of marijuana.

Johnny welcomed the band from behind the bar like they were celebrities. "What do you think of my club now?" he shouted over the pounding, jukebox music. "I'm going to make you guys stars by the end of the week."

He had six frosty mugs of Heineken beer set up at the end of the bar. "Grab them while they're cold. You might as well start a little early. Everybody's ready."

People started chanting, "Divebomberz, Divebomberz," as soon as Rene sat on his stool to fine-tune the drums. He looked at Tim and smiled like a kid who just got his favorite toy for Christmas. "Looks like all we can do is shatter the myth."

Dale was more than ready to rock. "We're going to knock them dead. Look at this place. There must be two hundred and fifty people in here, with more waiting outside. People are standing on chairs in the back. Look at them. They're waving at us."

Even Rick was impressed. "I take back every bad thing I ever said about Shreveport and the Royal Royce. This place is a blast."

Johnny watched to see when the band was ready to start. When Butch gave the sign, the club owner took over the lead microphone to welcome the crowd and introduce the band. He was the consummate professional.

"Good evening, ladies and gentlemen. Welcome to Johnny's Cimarron, the hottest music club in the south."

People cheered mightily. Johnny waited for them to settle down.

"And I'm Johnny."

The crowd screamed their approval. Johnny waited again for them to settle.

"Tonight, we have a special treat for you. We have the band that saved its crowd from the fire at the Safari Club down on the bayou. We have the band that survives hurricanes, the band you'll soon be hearing on the radio. Ladies and gentlemen, we have, right here in Shreveport, Louisiana, all the way from New Orleans, the hottest band on the bayou, The Divebomberz."

The band drowned out the roar of the crowd by kicking off the night with their standard opening song.

The music sounded so good the band looked at each other in wonderment. Yes, it was big and powerful and in tune and unique. But something else was happening. It was the acoustics of the long room with twelve-foot ceilings, packed with people. The music was perfect for the crowd, the crowd was perfect for the room, and the room was perfect for the music. It was the circle of life for rock and roll with a country fiddle and a gospel-soul organ. People actually backed up, at first, from the power coming off the stage. It didn't take long for them to recover and rush the dance floor to get closer to the band. Fortunately, they didn't mob the stage.

Jesse and Dale were on a one-foot riser in front, Butch and Tim on a two-foot riser behind them and Rick and Rene on the three-foot riser in the back. The band stacked up like a tower of power. Dancers took over the floor in front of the band. One group of eight dancers seemed to have some kind of choreography going on. Jesse was delighted. It was the first time he had seen line dancing.

It was square dancing without partners. They moved in unison. Two steps to the front, slide to the right, spin around and take two steps to the left. They kept it going for a couple songs. Then, individual dancers overwhelmed them.

The band kept the tempo cranked until the middle of the set when they slowed things down with "Can't You See" by the Marshall Tucker Band. As the crowd began singing along, Jesse made eye contact with a beautiful Italian woman. She had big eyes with just the right amount of makeup and long, black hair. Jesse smiled at her and she smiled back. It was one of those moments when the rest of the world stands still. Jesse knew he was in trouble right away. He tried to look away but every time he looked back she was right there, waiting for him with a sly smile. She had a wholesome look, but her dress was short, black and low cut. It showed off plenty of fair-skinned cleavage when she bent forward to shimmy.

The band finished off the first set with a couple original songs and a rhythm and blues version of "I've Just Seen A Face." Beatles songs were always crowd pleasers and excellent set closers. When Tim and Dale and Butch and Jesse sang together, they could make a chorus sound almost as big and rich as the fab four. Then again, nobody ever sounded as good as the Beatles, not even The Beatles.

The Divebomberz took a break in the small area behind the stage by the restrooms. It was impossible to make it up to the bar. Johnny had way too many people in the club. He came back to congratulate the band on their set and made sure they had chairs to sit on and a small table. "You guys got it going on. This place is rockin' tonight. Keep up the good work. And remember, fifteen minutes for the break. Looks like you'll be getting a bonus tonight."

Johnny rushed off to try and manage his bar just as the young, Italian woman with Jesse in her sights walked by to go into the ladies room.

Dale saw Jesse following her with his eyes. "Who is that? Not only is she gorgeous but I saw her looking at you, Jesse, like she wants to eat you for dinner."

Rene saw the woman looking at Jesse as she passed. "Maybe you should go in and see if she needs any help, Jesse."

In a short time, a long line formed to get into the women's rest room. They all wanted to talk to the band while they waited.

"Who's that drummer?" one woman asked another, loud enough for all to hear. "I hear he's Cajun."

"He's Cajun cute is what he is," the second woman teased.

Rene loved it. "Now, ladies. You know I can hear you talking. And I'm liking what I hear."

The line into the restroom began to morph into a rush on the band. In a flash of pulchritude, the band members were completely enveloped by the sweet smell of female adoration. Johnny came over to save them after only ten minutes. He could see the scene had become unmanageable. "Time to get back to work."

"See that door in the corner," he said to Tim. "Go through that door after the next set and lock it behind you. There's an office upstairs you can use for breaks. It's the only place for privacy. I'm sorry I didn't think of it sooner."

Jesse was strapping on his bass for the second set when he felt a soft hand on his shoulder. He turned around to find himself looking down into the face of the Italian girl. She was even more striking up close, her touch more captivating than her smile.

"I'm Rose," she said. "Sorry about my crazy friends and the groupie crush. You guys are fantastic. Best band we've had here."

"Thank you Rose," Jesse said. "It's nice to meet you. I'm Jesse. Thanks for coming out tonight."

"I wouldn't miss you for the world," she said as she disappeared into the crowd.

Dale took a couple steps to Jesse and whispered in his ear. "I wouldn't miss you for the world."

The Divebomberz kicked off the second set with the traditional New Orleans song, "Iko, Iko." People got so excited they started jumping up on the bar and chairs and tables to sing along. Johnny and his staff managed to clear the bar but there was nothing they could do about the tables. Three guys fell off one table but the crowd caught them. There was simply no place to fall.

Jesse kept looking for Rose but he couldn't find her in the melee.

The band played on through the end of an hour-and-a-half second set and took a much-needed break. They were exhausted and drenched in sweat from the intensity of the performance. Tim showed them Johnny's door and they took refuge in his upstairs office.

Butch was the first to recognize their situation. "Okay. Does anybody see the problem we are facing?"

Dale shrugged his shoulders. "What? Too many crazy, drunk people?"

"No," Rene said. "That's not what he's talking about. He's talking about we can't get drinks up here."

Tim slapped his head. "Oh, shit. We should have thought about that."

While the band debated what to do, someone started knocking on the window. It startled everyone. How could anyone be able to knock on a second-story window?

Rick moved cautiously to the window. "There's a fire escape. It goes all the way down to the alley. That makes this building more safe than the Royal Royce Hotel. Here, I'll open the window."

Sure enough, Johnny had sent a waitress up the back fire escape with a round of beer and Tequila.

The waitress handed the heavily loaded tray through the window. "Johnny said to tell you this isn't his first rodeo. Enjoy. I'll be back in seven and a half minutes to see if you need anything else. Johnny says remember the fifteen-minute rule. Does anybody need anything before I go back down?"

Rene helped Rick with the drinks. "Tell Johnny thanks. The only other thing we'll be needing is a couple joints if you've got them."

"I'll see what I can do," she said as she closed the window and disappeared down the fire escape.

"How does she get out of the front door of the club and through all those people with those drinks?" Tim asked.

"There must be some kind of back door to the alley," Dale guessed. "This old building is full of surprises."

Butch saw the full potential of the fire escape. "You know, we could use it to go get what we need."

"Let's wait," Dale said. "Let's see if she comes back with any weed."

Rick raised his mug. "We should've asked her to bring up a couple bottles of champagne. Now, that would be delivery to write home about."

Rene took a seat in Johnny's chair behind the desk, which was four inches deep in paperwork. He put his feet up on a corner of the desk. "So, this is what it feels like to be a big-time club owner. Looks like somebody's a little behind in his bookkeeping."

Tim pretended to be taking his picture. "All you need is a cowboy hat and a couple cans of mace."

Butch checked out the scene. "Look behind you, Rene. Isn't that a safe under the back table?"

Dale got excited. "Yes, it is. Look in the desk. Maybe we can find the combination."

"Dale," Butch warned.

"Just kidding," Dale said. "You know I would never do anything like that."

Rene took his feet off the desk. "You know what we need to do? We need to open up our own club. We could be the house band and invite big name acts to come play with us."

"And then we could start our own radio station and open up a record company with a state-of-the-art studio," Butch joked.

The band clowned around in Johnny's office for a few more minutes until they heard knocking on the window again. It was a bartender this time.

"Come on in," the band said in unison.

The bartender opened the window. "I can't come in. I just came up to give you this and to remind you that you're on again in five minutes."

He handed a large joint through the window and left without saying goodbye.

Tim grabbed the joint and lit it up without further adieu. "Unbelievable. This club keeps getting better and better."

The band smoked the joint, which turned out to be incredible weed, and went down to play another set. People were not going home even though it was approaching midnight on a Wednesday night.

Jesse noticed Rose sitting on a barstool not far from the bandstand. She waved and shook her silky hair back over her mostly bare shoulders.

The band kicked off the set with "Satisfaction" by the Rolling Stones. Butch had the Keith Richards lick down perfectly and Dale sounded surprisingly good on the lead vocal. Halfway through the song, Jesse closed his eyes to concentrate on the feel of the song. Instead of floating away on the beat, he got a shocking, bright-white, flashing image of the Voodoo cow skull. He hadn't had such a powerful vision of the skull since the lights went out at Fritzel's on Bourbon Street. When he opened his eyes, the after-image outline of the skull was filled with the eyes of Rose. She was smiling at him like she knew what he had just seen inside his head.

He closed his eyes again and waited. He could feel the Voodoo voice tingling up his spine before he heard it speak in his mind.

"Do not be tempted," the voice said.

It was after three in the morning when the band finished their first night at Johnny's Cimarron. People were drunk and didn't want to leave. Johnny raised his voice firmly. "It's time to go. You don't have to go home, but you have to go somewhere. You can't stay here."

He and his staff eased everyone out of the club. Rene and Tim and Rick said goodnight and went off in a large van, filled with very intoxicated women. Dale disappeared into the night.

Rose was nowhere to be found. Jesse was beginning to think she might have been a vision from the dark side of his Voodoo dreams. But everybody had seen her, not just him.

Johnny gathered up Butch and Jesse. "Let's go get breakfast. I've got a table reserved at my favorite late-night hangout."

Butch was ready to go. "Sounds good to me. I'm starving."

Jesse agreed and Johnny led them out his secret exit. At the end of the bar, there was a walk-in cooler the size of a moving van. The back wall of the cooler was covered in plastic aprons. Behind the aprons was a narrow, metal door that led to the alley behind the club.

Butch followed Johnny through the door. "So this is how she got all those drinks out. Man, you've got secret passages everywhere."

Jesse squeezed out the door and Johnny locked it from the outside.

"Not to mention fire escapes," Johnny said as they took a few steps down the alley and saw the fire escape on their left. "I'll bet you were surprised when the waitress delivered drinks through the second-floor window."

Jesse tried to make out Johnny's face in the darkness. "You know, she scared the crap out of us at first."

Johnny laughed and slapped his knees with both hands. "How about the weed?"

Butch responded. "That was right on time and it was some good shit."

"You can thank my bartender for that," Johnny said. "I don't partake myself."

Jesse couldn't believe it. "Oh, man, you don't know what you're missing."

"I know what I'm missing, all right," Johnny said as he led them down the dark alley. "I'm tired enough as it is. Weed just puts me to sleep."

In less than a block, Johnny stopped and knocked on a door that neither Butch nor Jesse had seen in the dark. "Watch yourself, it's a pretty big step up," Johnny said as a short man in a white server's coat opened the door. They walked into the bustling kitchen of a large Chinese restaurant. The smell of fresh-cut onions brought a tear to Jesse's eye.

Johnny saw Butch and Jesse checking out the kitchen. "Don't worry. They make the best American breakfast around and they're open all night."

An Asian man who looked to be the owner greeted Johnny warmly and seemed pleased to be introduced to his musician guests. After names and handshakes were exchanged, he led them to a circular table with high, plush seats and eight-foot, red curtains all around.

The owner bowed to Johnny. "Nice and private, just for you. Many people are here from your club tonight." Then he bowed to Butch and Jesse, "I know you do not want to be mobbed for autographs."

Butch and Jesse had to laugh at that remark. Signing autographs was not yet part of their job description.

Once they were settled in, Butch leaned over the table. "Looks like you've got this whole town wired, Johnny."

"The alleys of Shreveport are filled with surprises," Johnny said. "Here, check out the menu. The omelettes are fantastic, so is the sausage gravy. I always get the country omelette with the gravy on top."

Once the order was taken, Jesse turned to Johnny and asked, "How'd we do tonight?"

Johnny waited a moment before answering, "You boys broke my bar record. And it was on a Wednesday night. That is exceptional. I was going to wait until the end of the week to tell you, but you earned a three-hundred-dollar bonus tonight."

Jesse was more than pleased. "That was one of the best crowds we've played. You do one great job on promotion."

"You should be our manager," Butch said.

Johnny held up his hand. "Hold on, cowboy. We just had our first date. Let's not be getting married yet. Besides, I heard you have a manager."

"Who told you that?" Butch asked.

"Your drummer's father, Burt, I think his name is."

"Did he say he was the manager?" Jesse asked.

"No, he said you've got somebody in New Orleans, connected with Dr. John, who put you in the studio and is about to make you all big stars."

"Did you believe him?" Butch asked.

Johnny chuckled. "Of course not. I've been in this business too long."

"So why did you hire us?" Jesse asked.

Johnny lowered his voice and got serious. "Truth is, there's a bit of a buzz on you boys. Most of it is good. The Safari Club story put you on the map. People are starting to follow you guys around. But some of it isn't so good."

Jesse knew what he was talking about. "Like what?"

"Like you got yourself in the middle of a biker war and a

drug dealing operation and people are starting to end up in federal prison."

That remark got Jesse going. He told the whole story of the gang truce and having nothing to do with Dupre going to jail. He told him about Pete Dryer and the studio recording that wasn't even good enough to use for promotional purposes. He told him about the cocaine dealing that was turning the bayou into a war zone.

"Sounds like you made the right move coming north," Johnny said as the omelettes arrived.

The three dug into breakfast like starving men and continued talking about the band and the club circuit from Dallas, Texas, to Jacksonville, Mississippi. Johnny said he could help keep the band in steady work.

They finished what turned out to be a belt-loosening meal. Johnny got quiet as he leaned back in his seat to relax.

Butch and Jesse started talking about what it would mean to hit the road and, possibly, leave New Orleans. They talked for some time until their conversation was interrupted by Johnny's cowboy hat falling off his head and onto the table. Johnny had fallen into a deep sleep. The top of his head was bald as an eagle. This came as quite a surprise, since he looked like a longhaired, country boy in his hat.

"Should we wake him up?" Butch asked.

Jesse nudged him awake. Johnny grabbed his hat and put it back on his head. He could tell Butch and Jesse were amused and somewhat embarrassed by his baldness.

Johnny wasn't worried in the slightest. "Relax, boys. I know I'm bald. Now you do too. What can I say? It's a bitch getting old. And, don't forget. It's going to happen to you too."

CHAPTER NINETEEN

ROSE

Johnny's cover charge had gone up to fifteen dollars by Saturday night. The Divebomberz were the toast of the town. The crowds were standing room only, and there was a long line outside the front door. Local musicians and artists had come around on Thursday and Friday to make friends with the band and join the all-night, after-show parties on the roof of the Royal Royce Hotel. The air was crisp but not too cold for drinking whiskey and smoking pot and marveling at the lights of the city. Dawn was always a beautiful surprise to those left standing.

Jesse was not on the rooftop Sunday morning. He had gone home with Rose. The band saw it coming. He and Rose had gotten more and more friendly with each passing night. Butch and Dale tried to talk him out of it, but Jesse was on a mission. Why would he listen to his old friends from Indiana if he wouldn't pay attention to the Voodoo voice? The voice had specifically told him to not be tempted by Rose. He kept reminding himself what Carmen had said about not having to do everything the voice said.

Rose let Jesse drive her home in her car, kissing his ear and neck and rubbing his right leg as he drove. He was in a breathless tunnel of love by the time they made it to her place. She held his hand as she walked him up the stairs to her second floor apartment. In an amazing fluidity of motion, she unlocked the door and led him straight into her bedroom. He kissed Rose at the edge of her bed. Her lips were hot and wet and tasted like trouble.

They left the light on as they began slowly and sensually undressing and caressing each other. She fully aroused him with her fingers and long nails and took him into her mouth. Then, she fell back on the bed, naked and inviting. She looked even more beautiful than Jesse had imagined.

"Come to me, Jesse," she implored. "I need you."

Jesse joined her on the bed and began kissing her all over as she moaned in ecstasy. He closed his eyes and devoured her delicious body. She was moist with desire.

Suddenly, he felt her stiffen in fear. She pushed his head away. He opened his eyes and realized the bedroom light had gone out.

At first, he thought someone had turned off the switch. He sprang out of bed, looking for an intruder. He heard Rose cry, "Jesse, what's wrong?"

When he found no one, he told himself the light bulb must have failed. His hand felt for the switch. It was in the off position. Someone, or something, had turned off the light. He had purposefully left it on because the light had been erotically caressing and bathing her soft, pale skin. He stumbled around the corner, cursing the darkness, again looking for whoever or whatever had flipped the switch. Even in the darkness, he knew no one else was in Rose's apartment. He felt for the switch again and flipped it up.

The light came on in both the bedroom and in Jesse's mind. He turned his head around, slowly and warily, to look back at the bed. He was afraid of what he was about to see. He sensed the Voodoo voice was playing tricks on him.

He saw Amy, naked in the bed and every bit as beautiful as Rose. She was looking right at him and crying softly.

"No," he said as he turned the light back off.

"No, what?" Rose said. "What do you mean, no? What's wrong with the light?"

Jesse turned the light back on and saw Rose again. "I mean, no, I can't do this. I mean, no, I've got to go."

Jesse dressed himself, bolted out the door of Rose's apartment and ran most of the way back to the Royal Royce Hotel. It was a four-mile run. What had just happened? Had the Voodoo voice taken control of his conscience? Had it flipped the light switch? Since when did he pass on an opportunity to pleasure himself? What about seeing Amy in the bed? He had never had such a vision. Previous pangs of guilt, yes; visions of guilt, never. His powers of self-forgiveness had always been truly awesome.

Hearing the voice was one thing. Having the voice take control of a room and what he saw in it was frightening. If it could turn off a light and show him a vision of Amy, what would stop it from stabbing him in his sleep if he did something really wrong?

He had almost run out of the panic by the time he found himself in front of the Royal Royce Hotel. He could hear distant sounds of a party still raging on the roof. As he was heading for the front door, a beer bottle shattered on the sidewalk in front of him. One more step and it would have killed him. The bottle was at least half full. His shoes and pants were soaked with beer. It didn't matter much since the rest of him was already soaked in sweat from the run.

As he jumped out of his skin in shocked surprise at the shattering bottle, a deep realization broke through his fear and confusion. The voice might have turned off the light and shown him Amy in bed. But it wasn't the voice that made him leave the apartment. It was his love for Amy. He felt ashamed for going home with Rose.

He walked in the hotel, got in the elevator, and shut the door behind him. As the creaky old beast hauled itself up to the fifth floor, Jesse realized what Carmen meant when she talked about the connection between love and Voodoo. He could hear her speaking. "They are both part of the same thing, the eternal river that flows through souls and connects us to the spirit life."

Whether it was Voodoo or love that made him faithful, it didn't matter. He stepped up and out of the elevator onto the fifth floor. It felt good, being loyal to Amy, at least in the end. It felt right.

He climbed through the window at the end of the hall and up the rusty fire escape to the roof. Tim and Butch were smoking a joint and looking nervously over the edge of the building.

Jesse walked up and surprised them. "Looking for the beer bottle that almost killed me?"

Butch whirled around. "Jesse, how close was it? We heard it smash on the sidewalk. Thank God you're okay."

"What should we do?" Tim asked.

Jesse had to laugh. The two of them looked so stoned and so horribly guilty. They thought he had been completely drenched by the exploding beer. They didn't realize he was mostly soaked in his own sweat.

"You might start by cleaning up the mess down there," he said. "If word gets out you're throwing beer bottles off the roof, the party up here will be over for sure."

Butch tried to explain. "We didn't throw anything. Tim tripped on that piece of wood you're about to step on."

Tim demonstrated. "I let go of the bottle as I caught myself on this ledge. I was lucky. The ledge is only two feet tall, as you can see. I could have gone over myself."

"Did anybody call the cops?" Butch asked.

Jesse told him no. "It's four in the morning. Your secret is safe with me."

"What about the front desk?" Tim asked.

Jesse had to laugh again. "There is no front desk at the Royal Royce. This place is a ghost hotel, especially at night. But, come on, let's go down and do some clean up. I'll help."

Rene and Dale were entertaining a group of people near the back ledge of the roof. Rick had gone down to his room to sleep on the floor.

"Careful not to drop anything over the edge," Butch said as they headed for the fire escape.

Dale tried to slow them down with a question. "Where you guys going?"

Rene knew what they were doing. "What did you drop?"

Butch kept walking. "Just a beer bottle. No cause for alarm. We're going to clean it up."

"Did you kill anybody?" Dale laughed.

"Not yet," Tim said.

"So, a strange and scary thing happened to me at Rose's apartment tonight," Jesse said as they started picking up glass off the sidewalk.

"We knew that's where you went," Butch said.

Tim joined in Butch's disapproval. "What about Amy?"

"Well, that's just it. Rose and I were getting hot and heavy when the light went out."

Butch tried to correct him. "You mean the light came on."

Jesse realized he had to explain. "No, we were keeping the light on."

"Kinky," Tim said.

Jesse continued. "Anyway, the light went out, mysteriously, and when I turned it back on, it was Amy on the bed instead of Rose."

"What happened to Rose?" Butch asked.

"When I turned the light off and then back on, it was Rose again."

Tim was beginning to understand what the Voodoo voice was doing for Jesse. "The Voodoo turned the light out and changed Rose into Amy?"

"That's how it feels to me," Jesse said.

Butch voiced his feelings. "More like your own guilt did it. And, might I add, I'm glad to see you living up to your vows."

Jesse got defensive. "We're not married yet."

Butch shrugged his shoulders. "You might as well be."

Tim was beginning to process the tale. "Wait a minute. Are you telling me the voice is actually moving things around in your world? That makes it more than a voice. That makes it a force of nature. That makes it something that could get scary."

Jesse pointed his finger at Tim "Exactly. Next thing you know it will be throwing beer bottles off roofs to shatter at my feet and jolt my thought process into a new gear."

"Now, you're getting carried away," Butch said.

Tim had to speak his mind. "The thing about the voice is it makes you feel different after you hear it. It's only spoken to me once, but ever since then, I've felt an almost out-of-body thing, like I'm watching myself from somewhere else."

Jesse ran his hands through his hair. "For me, it's more like somebody else is watching so I'd better be on my best behavior."

CHAPTER TWENTY

DMITRY

The band returned to New Orleans for a few days after their successful first week in Shreveport. They wouldn't have long to regroup. Johnny had them booked on the club circuit along Interstate 20 across northern Louisiana. Towns like Minden, Ruston, and Monroe all had watering holes that were still hiring live bands. So did Vicksburg and Jackson, Mississippi; Hot Springs and Little Rock, Arkansas; Longview and Tyler, Texas; and thousands of towns across the middle of the country. Disco deejays had not completely taken over the heartland.

"You can always find work if you're willing to hit the road," Johnny said. "There's more bars in this country than churches. And, if you're smart, you can play the churches too."

Between playing nearby towns and making regular returns to Johnny's Cimarron as home base, it looked like The Divebomberz could be working steady for the foreseeable future. As Johnny laid the endless road map out in front of them, Jesse saw huge potential for making money. He wasn't thinking what it would be like to play the same songs, over and over, night after night, until all the clubs and all the drunks started to look and sound the same.

Jesse was glad to get back to New Orleans. He needed to touch base with Carmen and Pete and Casey to find out what was going on with the Voodoo voice and the cocaine cartel and the Wheelers and the Gypsies. He wanted to know if Dupre had been able to bond out of jail. He tried to explain to Amy why he wouldn't be seeing her much for the next several months.

She turned her back on him as he was talking and stared out the window. When she turned around to look at him, he could see she was already crying. "Oh, I see. I drop everything and move to New Orleans to be with you so you can hit the road and leave me here alone. Is that what you're telling me?"

Amy was a good, strong woman, but her one weak spot was her terrible fear of abandonment.

Her father had died suddenly when she was only ten years old. She could never forget the day her daddy collapsed in the garden of the new ranch house he had just finished building for the family. Her frantic mother yelled for Amy to call the ambulance. She tried and tried but the phone was busy. It was on a "party line," several residences using the same telephone number. It took Amy fifteen minutes to make the emergency connection. By the time the ambulance arrived an hour later, even a ten-year-old girl could see her daddy was never coming home.

It took years for her to stop blaming herself for her father's death, but she never got over the nagging fear of being left behind. Daddy had been her best friend and her hero.

Jesse wrapped his arms around her and held her close as she tried to stop crying. "Honey, I'm not leaving you. I'll be coming home all the time and you can come hear the band whenever you want. We won't be that far away."

"You're going to have so many groupies you'll forget all about me."

Jesse held her head in his hands and kissed her on her salty lips. "We're getting married June sixteenth, remember?"

Amy kissed him back and stopped crying. "That's right. I forgot. I'm so smart I'm marrying a rock star. What could go wrong with that?"

Jesse stayed positive. "Nothing could go wrong with us. Let's think about today. No more worrying about the future. What say we have a little fun, right now?"

"We've already had more than our share," Amy said, referring to their wake-up lovemaking.

Jesse smiled. "Yes, that was more than fun. But wait, there's more. What say we go down to the docks and jump a ship today?"

Jesse was a bona fide thrill seeker. Besides train hopping, he was an avid water tower climber, parade crasher and traffic dodger. But jumping ship was, by far, his favorite thing to do. Amy loved Jesse's crazy side, even though she did her best to keep him in check. It had taken many tours of the local docks before she learned to appreciate the joys of jumping ship.

Jesse and Amy arranged to meet Tim and Loretta at 4 p.m. to set off on their adventure. It was going to be a couples' kind of thing. Tim had been boarding ships with Jesse for months. Loretta was new to the ship jumping game, and she was more than uneasy about the entire process. "What if we get arrested? Would they put us in a tiny jail on the ship and take us back to their country?"

Tim tried to reassure her. "Nobody's going to get arrested. The sailors are always happy to see us."

Loretta was not convinced. "Isn't it a little dangerous for us to get onboard a ship of horny sailors who haven't been with a woman in months?"

"I've never had a problem before," Amy said.

That wasn't enough for Loretta. "There's always a first time."

The four of them walked across Tchoupitoulas Street at Race Street, crossed the railroad tracks and approached the international docks along the Mississippi River near the Huey

P. Long Bridge. They walked right up to the long gangplank of a Russian freighter. The red, hammer-and-sickle logo was painted on the hull of the ship, fore and aft. Jesse felt strangely drawn to the Russian ship, although it was one of many docked on the river. He felt the presence of the Voodoo voice, although it said nothing. He could feel a tingling coming up his back and neck and into the base of his skull.

There was not a soul around, nobody guarding the docks.

"Stay close," Jesse said as he led the way up the steep, narrow walkway to the ship. The wood plank and rope pathway swayed slightly underfoot.

Loretta followed reluctantly. "This thing is moving every step I take. We're all going to end up in the river."

Amy tried to help. "Go on in front of me, Loretta. It's safe. All the sailors use it. We'll be on deck in no time."

"Does anyone remember there's a cold war going on?" Loretta asked.

Jesse turned around to talk to her. "There's no cold war on the Mississippi River. This ship is a welcome guest in our country. Think of yourself as a goodwill ambassador."

Loretta didn't say anything until the four of them were safely on the deck of what felt like a massive ghost ship. There was no one there to greet them. The three-story loading cranes were unmanned. The decks were cleared and empty of cargo. Even the captain's bridge, high above the deck, seemed deserted.

Loretta turned around to leave. "Okay. This is way too spooky. It feels like a trap. Let's get out of here."

Jesse took her hand. "No way. Let's walk to the bow. We've got this ship to ourselves. The crew is on leave in the city. Maybe we could hijack the whole thing."

"Now, that's exactly the kind of crazy stunt I was afraid you'd pull," Loretta said as she turned again to walk back to the gangplank.

"Come on, Loretta," Amy said as she coaxed Loretta back into following Jesse to the ship's bow. "He's kidding about the hijacking. We've done this before. There's never any trouble."

The four of them had just reached the bow and were looking over the edge at the river when Jesse felt like he was being watched. He turned his head around and, sure enough, a man with binoculars was standing on the top floor of the bridge, looking right at him. The man was talking into a radio. As Jesse was waving to say hello, two men with rifles came running out a steel door at the base of the bridge.

Loretta collapsed at Tim's feet and wet her blue jeans. A dark spot spread around her crotch. "I knew it. We're all gonna die."

Tim and Jesse already had their hands in the air. The men with rifles were running toward them. A third man came out of the steel door and yelled at the other two to stop. They cowered at his Russian command. He spoke in English as he approached his uninvited and frightened guests. "You can put your hands down. Sorry about the rifles. Anyone can see there is no need for violence. Somebody gave the wrong order. But I must ask, what are you doing on my ship?"

"Are you the captain?" Jesse asked.

"Maybe yes, maybe no. Do you not answer my question?"

Jesse talked fast as he lowered his hands. "Oh, sorry. We live right over there on Tchoupitoulas Street. We're musicians. We love ships."

The man smiled approvingly and held out his arm for a handshake as he said, "Musicians from New Orleans. I love the Jazz music. Welcome to my ship."

Amy smiled her sweetest. "Thank you, commander, for your hospitality."

"I am no commander. I am cargo ship captain."

"Pleased to meet you," Loretta said, collecting herself as she stood up. "I thought we were going to get shot for a minute there."

The ship captain looked at her wet jeans but pretended not to notice. "Yes, please excuse my men. They are on watch for thieves."

Tim glanced around. "I don't see anything to steal. It looks like you are empty."

"Yes, we have unloaded," the captain said. "But there are many valuable things below deck. Come with me and I will show you. Will you have drink with me?"

Jesse was pleased and relieved by the invitation. "Absolutely. We'll do our part to end the cold war."

"Ah, that is in newspapers only. It is not in the hearts of the Russian people. And I am sure not in the hearts of Americans."

"I don't know," Amy said. "Too many Americans think communism is a dirty word."

"Do you think my country is communist?" the captain asked. "Do you think China is communist? Come with me and we will have a toast to the myth of communism."

The captain led his four guests into the steel door at the base of the bridge and down several flights of steep, metal stairs. Sailors peeked out of their rooms as the group made its way through narrow halls. There were some catcalls when the women were spotted, but the hecklers quickly ducked back inside their rooms when the captain barked at them. The now-invited guests were deep within the ship and totally disoriented by the time they came to a tall, oval door, ominously marked with a large, red star. Amy gave Jesse a look that said she thought this might be some kind of trouble. Jesse motioned for her to step into the captain's room.

"Here we are," the captain said as he led them into his quarters, compact but roomy as a large, mobile home. The first thing Jesse saw on the wall was a framed photo of Vladimir

Lenin. On the captain's table was a copy of the official state newspaper, the Pravda.

"Oh, my," Loretta said. "It sure looks like communism in here."

The captain laughed as he brought out a bottle of Russian vodka and poured five shots into small water glasses. "Here's to communism, a great idea that never happened."

The five new acquaintances clinked glasses and downed their shots.

The captain softened his tone. "Come, sit with me. This corner table has room for eight people. I sometimes meet my officers here." He poured another round of shots and held up his glass. "And now we drink to American Jazz, yes?"

They clinked glasses again and drank quickly.

Jesse decided to set the record straight. "Actually, we're more rock and roll than jazz."

"Ah, I should have known," the captain said. "You look like rock and roll. Who is your favorite band?"

"The Beatles," Jesse answered without hesitation. No one contradicted him.

The captain agreed. "Of course. We know of Beatles. We can sometimes buy record on black market. Rock and roll is official banned in Soviet Union. The people, they love, but party . . . no."

"That's just wrong," Loretta said a little too loudly. The vodka had loosened her up quickly.

Everybody laughed nervously as the captain poured another round of shots. This one they sipped slowly as they talked for a good long time about what was wrong with their respective countries. Eventually, they all agreed that most of what ailed the citizens of both countries could be blamed on government. The conversation shifted from politics to food to movies and religion and back to politics. If loose lips sink ships then drunken lips keep them afloat. Jesse was having a ball getting blasted in the captain's quarters.

By the time they lifted the glasses for the fifth toast, the captain paused, and then continued in a hushed tone. "Shall we drink to the Voodoo?"

Tim joined in the toast. "By all means. We're in New Orleans, and Jesse knows the Voodoo queen."

The captain downed his shot and looked at Jesse. "Really? I need to talk about the Voodoo."

Jesse was ready to talk Voodoo. "Go ahead. There's no tape recorder in here, is there?"

"No," the captain laughed. "My country too cheap for recording devices. What I want to say is not to be recorded. I should not say. I sound crazy."

"Join the club," Loretta said.

The captain looked around the table at each pair of eyes eagerly awaiting his confession. "Yes, I say it. I am hearing a—what you call—a voice. We dock in the city and, same night in my bed, I hear voice."

"Was it the very deep voice of an African man?" Tim asked.

The captain grabbed Tim's arm. "Yes. Yes. You hear it like me?"

Tim deferred to Jesse. "I've heard it once but Jesse has heard it many times."

Jesse tried to conceal his excitement. This was even more than he suspected from his feelings of premonition upon choosing to board the Russian ship. "What did it say to you?"

The captain looked around his cabin suspiciously before finally answering in a slow whisper, "It says . . . leave ship."

"You mean, like defect?" Amy asked. "Like, run away from your country?"

The captain hung his head. "Yes. To betray Mother Russia."

"What about your wife?" Amy asked.

"I have no wife, no children."

"You should do it," Loretta said, clearly relishing the thickening of the plot. "You can walk right off this boat with us and no one will be the wiser."

"I do have one friend in New Orleans. We write letters. I can go to him. He owns restaurant in city center."

"What's his name?" Jesse asked.

The captain hesitated again, as if he were about to share another secret. Then he answered. "His name is Rod. He is gay."

"We know Rod," Tim and Loretta and Jesse and Amy all howled happily.

"We love Rod," Jesse said. "We eat at his grill all the time when we're in the French Quarter. We don't care if he's gay."

The captain seemed vastly relieved. "That is good to hear. Good you know Rod. I can't believe it. You have been sent to me. Now I say what I never say in my country."

"You can say anything you want," Loretta said as she encouraged him by holding his arm.

The captain paused and looked around the table again. He took a deep breath. "I am gay." He looked at his guests to check their reaction. He was holding his breath.

They let out a cheer for him. It was so loud he had to motion for them to keep it down.

"Don't worry about being gay," Tim said. "Our lead singer is gay. Half the French Quarter is gay."

"It is big problem in my country," the captain said. "In my country, is illegal. Go to jail, or worse."

Loretta was now on a mission. "We're not leaving this ship without you."

They had another round of vodka and talked excitedly about the captain making his escape. He began gathering what belongings he wanted to take with him, and had his new friends put his personal items in their pockets. Tim and Jesse put on several layers of his shirts and jackets. He couldn't be seen leaving with a suitcase in hand.

By the time they left the captain's quarters, it was almost 8 p.m. They were all barely able to walk, both from the Vodka and the excess baggage. Jesse had on three pair of the captain's pants and four of his shirts. Tim also had several layers. Loretta was able to carry a bag of underwear and toiletries between her legs, under her long dress. The five of them were drunk as lords as they stumbled down the swinging gangplank and made their way across the tracks to Amy and Jesse's apartment building. The captain didn't say a word until they were safely inside. At that point, he let out a triumphant shout.

"I did it. I am free man. Thank you for saving me."

"Can somebody else drive the ship back to Russia?" Amy asked as they walked up the three flights of steps to her apartment.

"Oh, yes. I have good friend on board who can take the ship. He will know what is going on. He is cover for me."

Amy got everybody a glass of ice water as they packed the captain's belongings into one of her suitcases. After all the vodka, they needed hydration. The captain seemed like he was in a state of shock as he slowly realized there would be no turning back.

"I can't believe I do it. I leave ship. What I want to do for so many years," he said. "Last year, I was close. This year, you, my new friends, save me."

They gathered together for a group hug as the captain broke down and wept tears of gratitude and relief.

It didn't take long before the five of them piled into the band van and drove to the French Quarter. Jesse parked a block away from Rod's. They were all in a celebratory mood. Rod was at the grill when he saw the captain walk in the door. After a double take and then a triple take, he dropped everything, and ran to embrace his long lost friend. "Look what my favorite band brings me," he howled. "My long lost brother in love, Dmitry!"

The two men hugged and danced and then hugged and danced with anyone in the restaurant who was willing and able. Jesse felt privileged to witness such a touching and joyous reunion. He tasted his own tears before he realized he was crying.

"Oh, my goodness. I'm burning everything," Rod glanced to the kitchen. "Sit, everybody, sit. I'll make us all a special Russian omelette. Come with me, Dmitry, I'll show you the kitchen and your room upstairs. Let me just put this grill on hold for a minute. I can't believe you finally did it."

"I'm not sure I could have done it without my new friends," Dmitry said. "They helped me be brave."

"Smells like you had a little vodka courage going for you as well," Rod said.

As they waited for the late, late breakfast to be served, Amy asked, "So what is it with this voice everybody but me seems to be hearing?"

Loretta put herself in Amy's category. "I haven't heard it."

"I've only heard it once," Tim said.

The three of them looked at Jesse.

"All right," he said. "I'm no expert but it seems to me the voice only comes to you when you are truly seeking."

"What do you mean?" Amy asked.

"It's kind of like they say, when the student is ready the teacher appears," Jesse said.

"Are you saying I'm not ready?" Amy asked.

Jesse realized his untenable position. "No, that is definitely not what I'm saying. You probably don't need any answers right now. The voice seems to be need based, wouldn't you say, Tim?"

"I'm not saying anything," Tim said. "You dug yourself into this hole. I'm dying to see how you dig yourself out."

Amy let him off the hook. "Don't worry about it, Jesse, the only voice I need to hear is yours."

Everybody moaned appreciatively and the table swung back into its good-time spirit. Dmitry rejoined the group as the food arrived on steaming plates, piled high with peppers and sausage and eggs and potatoes. They were all hungry after an evening of drinking on the Russian freighter.

No one noticed Carmen's arrival until she was standing at the edge of the table with a huge grin on her face.

"You must be Captain Dmitry. Welcome to America. We've been waiting a long time to make your acquaintance."

CHAPTER TWENTY-ONE

SLAVE REVOLT

Jesse met his friend in law school, Casey, at Felix's Oyster Bar to get all the latest news. Casey did not disappoint. He told Jesse that Dupre was out of jail and that one of his law professors was working on the case. He said the plan the feds had to make Dupre testify against his club members had not worked since Dupre exercised his constitutional right to remain silent. His attorneys got his bond reduced and Dupre posted bail.

"What about the Wheelers and the Gypsies?" Jesse asked.

"Everybody's laying low," said Casey. "Both gangs have been infiltrated by the feds. It looks like the bayou won't be cocaine alley for long. Anybody with half a brain is leaving the region."

"What about Pete?"

Casey had all the answers. "Pete's in rehab. Somebody told me he actually had a stroke. He got scared and checked himself in. He was deep in the shit."

"He's about as much of a cocaine dealer as he is a band manager," Jesse said.

Casey agreed. "Pete's a real estate agent who got lucky on a couple big sales and thought his roll would never end."

"I knew he wasn't the guy for us when he started not showing up all over the place," Jesse said.

Casey signaled the waiter for another round of Guinness beer. "He couldn't stay out of his own stash."

Jesse clapped his hands and rubbed them together in a washing motion. "Let that be a lesson to all of us who don't have our stash."

"So, I hear you're big stars in Shreveport," Casey said.

"How'd you hear that?"

"I think it was you who told me on the phone."

Jesse vaguely remembered the call. "Oh, yeah. Maybe I exaggerated a little that night."

"It was three in the morning and it sounded like you were knee deep in booze and babes," Casey said.

"I was calling from Johnny's Cimarron. It's a great club. The owner is helping us book gigs up north."

"Speaking of up north," Casey said. "I got a call from your father in Indiana a couple days ago. Said he can't get an answer or leave a message on your home phone. He wants to know why I haven't talked you into law school by now."

"What did you tell him?" Jesse asked.

"I told him you were too busy being a rock star."

"What did he say to that?"

Casey took a long swig of beer. "He asked if you were too busy to call your old man every once in a while."

"Yeah, I need to do that."

"So, what about Amy?" Casey asked. "Is the wedding still on? Your mother would like to know."

"Oh, man," said Jesse. "I really do need to call."

Casey clinked beer bottles with Jesse. "They're worried about you. And frankly, so am I."

"What's to worry about?"

Casey stammered slightly like he always did when he was about to make an important point. "It seems like you're running off down the road without much of a plan. What happened to making a good demo tape and shopping it to record companies?"

"We're going to get to that. Johnny said he might be able to help us. He's been talking to some people."

"Who is this Johnny?" Casey asked.

"You've got to come up and meet him. He's been in the business for decades."

Casey closed in on his main issue. "The music business or the bar business?"

"Wait a minute," Jesse said. "It's sounding like you should be managing the band."

Casey took the bait. "All right. Let's say I am managing the band. First thing I would say is you need to move to a music center like New York or Los Angeles. Shreveport doesn't sound like a step in the right direction. It sounds like the road to hillbilly hell."

Jesse held up his hands and lowered his head. "Hey, man. We had to get out of New Orleans, and Shreveport seems to be opening up a lot of doors for us. The crowds are great."

"What about the voice?" Casey asked. "What's it got to say about your new direction?"

"Funny you should ask. Last I heard from the voice was kind of indirectly, through a Russian ship captain. Did I tell you that story?"

Jesse told him the story of helping Dmitry defect and reunite with his old friend, Rod. He described the captain's quarters in detail and talked about the blast of a Vodka buzz from downing so many shots in such a short time. Jesse made it sound like smuggling the captain's personal effects off the ship was striking a major blow against the Cold War.

Casey was genuinely impressed. "Oh, man. Wish I'd been along for that trip. That's one thing about you, Jesse. One of many things I love about you. Everywhere you go, you find yourself right in the middle of something weird and wonderful.

I used to think this Voodoo voice thing was just too many drugs. I've never heard it myself, but I'm starting to listen for it."

"You'll never hear it through all those legal briefs clogging up your brain."

"Wait a minute," Casey said. "I think I'm hearing it right now."

"What's it saying?"

"I'm getting a message. Yes, I am. Give me a minute. There. There it is."

Jesse set himself up. "What's it saying?"

"It's saying Jesse is completely missing the point."

Jesse was on his way to Carmen's shop in the French Quarter when he ran into Ruthie the duck lady.

Ruthie answered his question before he asked it. "She's not there."

"Who's not where?" Jesse feigned ignorance.

"I know where you're going. She's been looking for you."

Ruthie laughed and fed a few breadcrumbs to her two ducks on a string. Jesse wondered why she always showed up, even in his dreams, whenever he was looking for somebody. And how did she always know who he was looking for?

She smiled and answered his unspoken question. "I'm part of your world and you are part of mine."

"I don't doubt that for a minute, Ruthie. Here we are bumping into each other at the same time on the same street in the same city and on the same planet."

Ruthie lowered her head

Jesse gave her a hug to get back on her good side. "Oh come on, Ruthie. You know I'm only teasing. You know I love you. I miss you. I haven't seen you since the Dr. John concert at Tipitina's."

Ruthie brightened up with a big smile and wide eyes. "Wasn't that a mind-blowing night? Best music I ever heard. People are still talking about it. Your band was good, too."

The mention of his band as an afterthought stung a bit. Jesse decided he had that one coming.

"Ruthie, before you tell me where Carmen is, there is one question I've been wanting to ask."

"Ask away, dahlin'."

"What's with the ducks?"

Ruthie's eyes sparkled with delight. "Funny you should ask. Nobody ever asks. They just assume I'm crazy."

Jesse waited patiently for her to continue.

"You might think I keep the ducks on a string to protect *them*. Actually, it's the ducks keeping *me* on a string. They remind me to watch where I'm walking."

It took a second to sink in, but the thought of Ruthie's "guard ducks" keeping her on a string was hugely funny. It reminded Jesse that most of life is how you look at it.

He laughed so hard he spun himself around. Ruthie had opened up a hole in his reality, a new way of looking at things. As he looked up, the sky and the top of the old, French buildings swirled around in his head like a Monet painting. He felt like he could be leaving the planet. The only thing that kept him grounded was the sound of his own laughter. When he recovered and completed the spin, he found himself staring into the beaming smile of Madame Carmen.

Ruthie the duck lady was holding Carmen's hand.

Jesse blinked his eyes in disbelief. "Where did you come from?"

"I stepped in from the shadows," Carmen said as she and Ruthie had a good chuckle.

Jesse knew something big was about to happen. His world was about to turn upside down. He could feel it in his gut.

"No, seriously," Jesse said, "What's going on?"

"Come with me to my shop," Carmen said without answering his question. "We need to talk."

Jesse took her offered hand and kissed it as if by courtly instinct. His mind slipped into a subtle Jasmine confusion. She took his arm and they headed off for her shop at a stately pace. Ruthie and her ducks didn't follow. Jesse turned around to look for her. She was gone.

Walking with Carmen down Bourbon Street was like walking with the Queen of England. All who saw her coming quickly yielded the right of way. Shopkeepers and bar owners came rushing out to greet her. Even midday drunks tried to straighten up in her presence.

"Hola," she said to those who greeted her, sounding vivaciously and irresistibly cultured. She unlocked the door to her shop and locked it back up after she ushered Jesse inside.

"Whoa," Jesse said. "What's with locking the door?"

Carmen dismissed the question. "Nothing. I simply do not wish to be disturbed. Do you know why I have brought you here today?"

"I thought I came on my own," Jesse said. "Then again, I thought you were Ruthie. Or Ruthie was you. What happened to me when we met today?"

"You are being shown that you are not in control. Everything is not as you perceive it. What you see is not what you get."

"That's fine with me. I don't seem to be doing such a great job as CEO of the universe."

"Why do you think the Russian captain came to you?" Carmen asked as she led him in to her office.

"I thought I found the Russian and helped him escape his ship."

"Jesse. Listen to me very carefully. We bring people into our lives to teach us what we know we need to learn."

"What was it I needed to learn from the captain?" Jesse asked.

"Remember what the voice said to him?"

"Yes, it was telling him to leave the ship."

"So what does that mean to you?" Carmen asked.

"Maybe I have a ship that needs leaving?"

Carmen's eyes lit up like she was surprised Jesse could reach the proper conclusion. "Exactly. Don't take the voice too literally. The ship might be a place or a time or a profession or anything keeping you from what you really need to be doing."

Jesse was feeling in tune with Carmen. "I get what you're saying about creating our own reality. It kind of goes along with my theory that the little things of today foretell the big things of tomorrow."

Carmen smiled patiently. "Take that one step further. We create the little things that lead to the big things."

"Do we create each other?"

"I'm saying we are all part of the same thing. The illusion is that we are separate individuals, fighting with each other for limited material resources."

"So that's why you and Ruthie sometimes seem like the same person?" Jesse asked.

"We are only what you make us out to be."

Jesse thought about that for a moment, and then returned to the issue at hand. "So, why did you bring me here today?"

"Come, sit with me. I've been reading and studying and talking to people about you. Somehow, you are in my life to teach me something I need to know. It's not just you learning from me. We are learning together.

"I need to help you escape this place and time. It's important for you to look at yourself from a different perspective. Do you trust me to do that?"

"Yes."

She handed him a small cup of what looked like black coffee. "Then drink this."

"What is it?"

"Call it love potion number nine."

Jesse drank the offering without further hesitation. He didn't hold his nose, but he did close his eyes. He didn't sip it. He threw it back like a shot of booze. It tasted like licorice and scotch whiskey. It never occurred to him to ask Carmen if she would be drinking with him.

She did not drink her own potion.

Whatever was in the little cup made him immediately relax in his chair. The same dizzying feeling he had felt in the street a half hour earlier, just before he saw Carmen, came over him. He felt lightheaded. The world began to swirl. He put his head between his knees. He lost consciousness.

He awakened to find himself standing around a large fire in the middle of a gang of angry black men who were shouting and armed with machetes and muskets. He was in a jungle that didn't look anything like Louisiana. There were too many palm trees. He had a sinking feeling he was no longer in North America. Was he on an island in the Caribbean Sea? He could smell the salt of an ocean breeze flavoring the dark night air.

It took a few minutes to realize what was going on. The men were speaking a strange language, but Jesse understood every word. He was one of them. They were screaming about cutting off heads and ears and anything that might be attached to the white men who had beaten them and kept them in chains for so many years. He felt his own anger taking control. The group of at least three hundred men was gearing up to go out on a night attack.

Jesse looked at his hands and arms. His skin was dark brown and shining with sweat. He ran the fingers of his left hand through his hair. It was thick and wiry with a receding hairline and a bald spot on the back of his head. He had a black powder pistol in his right hand. The weapon felt comfortable in his grip. He had fired it many times. He knew how to use it, how to load it and how to take it apart for cleaning.

Jesse looked around the fire and saw many faces he knew well. Dupre and Big Ben and Gypsy were there. So were Pete and Tim and the whole band. Casey was at his side. Dmitry was nearby, standing next to Johnny. Dr. John and Professor Longhair and Allen Toussaint and the mystery man from the bayou were all playing drums in ominous beats.

They were all slaves. Jesse got the distinct feeling that he knew, or had known, every single person in the angry, jungle mob.

A hush fell over the gathering as a Voodoo priestess walked into the fire ring and took control of the ceremony. She was thin and had a European face with an aristocratic nose. She was wearing a red, silk, wraparound dress with a tall, feathered hat that looked like a crown. Around her waist was a thick leather belt that carried a long, Spanish cavalry sword. She began by drawing a grid in the dirt with white paint. "This will unlock the material world and serve as a spiritual gateway," she said as she threw down potions, both solid and liquid, and began chanting to summon the spirits for protection in the upcoming battle. She was not the only woman at the fire. Carmen and Ruthie and Amy and Loretta were serving as the priestess' handmaidens. They, too, had become African women. Jesse wanted to go to Amy's side but found he could not make his body follow the emotional desire.

The priestess conducted a call and answer chant that whipped the makeshift army into a frenzy. More people joined the fire as she called to the moon and the stars for strength and courage. She warned the men not to rape the white women, even though their own wives and daughters had been raped. She spread her arms wide to issue the command. "Kill them but do not rape them. The Voodoo gods will not tolerate rape. The white people must pay with their lives for what they have done to us. But we must not sink to their level of sin."

The handmaidens brought forth a two-hundred-pound black hog and tied it with ropes to the trunk of a large tree at the outer edge of the fire circle. They had trouble with the animal as it squealed and squirmed, trying to break free.

All eyes fixated on the sword of the priestess as she slowly drew it from the sheath and held it high to glint in the firelight. She sang a song of sacrifice. "There will be much blood on this night. Let this sacrifice show that it will not be our blood flowing from the battle but the blood of our oppressors, the plantation owners."

The cheer was deafening. The drums pounded out a victorious crescendo.

The priestess pointed the sword at the pig. The crowd quieted suddenly. She leveled the sword, grabbed the handle with both hands and approached the pig. She began wailing a song that seemed to terrify the doomed animal. She moved forward with her sword and slowly but relentlessly plunged it into the front of the beast, through its heart and out the backside. Its horrible squealing stopped with a silence that stunned the gathering.

The night air was completely silent. Even the crackling of the fire and the sounds of insects ceased. Jesse held his breath until he managed to suck in a lungful of damp jungle air.

The pig fell against the tree, eyes wide open in the shock of death.

Two warriors cut the ropes from the tree and hoisted the pig by the sword that killed it. They paraded the bleeding sacrifice around the fire. Men began to moan as they held out their hands to receive the blood and spread it on their weapons and bodies.

The ceremony morphed into well-organized squads of men, who began marching into the jungle on their mission of murder. Jesse was going to battle. He was someone he had never been. His feet and legs were running down a narrow path. He was being swept along by an energy not his own. His squad of men ran for nearly a mile before they came to a clearing with many plantation buildings neatly arranged in a compound.

There was no guard on duty. The owners and their families were sleeping. A gentle breeze was swaying the palms. Everything was peaceful until the slaves used their torches to set all the buildings on fire. The wood frame structures were fully engulfed in flames by the time screaming women and men with weapons came pouring out to defend their homes.

The white people never had a chance.

Jesse raced into the confusion of battle with no fear in his heart. This was the moment he had waited for his entire adult life. His mind whirled into a kaleidoscope of memories of chains and whips and slavery and brutal oppression. He had nothing but murder on his mind. The next thing he knew, he was about to fire his pistol, point blank, into the silver-haired head of a white man. The man was on his knees, begging for mercy. Even though the man's face was contorted in terror, Jesse knew he recognized him from somewhere besides the plantation.

The pleading man's house with the long front porch was in flames behind him. Women and children were screaming. Warriors were shouting. Rifles were exploding.

The white man begged with his hands clasped in front of him, as if in prayer. "Please, please. I have a wife and children. I am a man of God."

Jesse showed no mercy. He pulled the trigger and felt the power of the exploding gunpowder recoiling his arm and shoulder. The shot made a clean hole on the man's forehead and came out the back of his head in a grotesque spray of brains and blood and bone. The man slumped into a pile of lifeless flesh and bones at his feet, a father and husband no more.

Jesse looked down at his victim. Even in death, something about the man seemed so familiar he was sure he must have known him well at some point. It felt good to kill him. The power and finality of revenge surged through his veins. His spine jolted an electrical shock from his buttocks to his brain. His mind was clearer than it had ever been. Decades of torture and depravity had fueled his violence even more than the adrenaline rush that was making him feel superhuman.

He reloaded his pistol with powder and shot. The smell of blood and gunpowder and screaming terror filled his nostrils as he sucked a deep breath of the wicked air into his lungs.

A white man with a sword charged at him, screaming out of the darkness of thick bushes at the edge of the fire. Jesse let him get close enough so he couldn't miss. The pistol exploded with a blinding flash as he pulled the trigger. The man staggered as the shot ripped into his chest and tore through his heart. Blood spurted out twenty feet. A shocked surprise filled the mortally wounded man's eyes as his sword kept swinging forward in a death throw. Jesse stepped aside to avoid the blade. Blood splatter temporarily blinded him. He dropped his weapon to wipe his eyes, first with his fingers and then with his shirt. The complete vulnerability of blindness panicked him until he could see again. He picked up the dead man's sword and plunged it in the ground, as if that would offer protection. Once he could see again, he scooped up his pistol and reloaded it.

Amy ran up to him and grabbed his arm, screaming, "You've got to stop. The killing must stop. The battle is won. The owners are surrendering."

"There will be no surrender," Casey said grimly as he came upon the scene and stepped between Amy and Jesse. He appeared as a massive slave, covered in blood. His face was deeply cut from his right ear to his chin, flesh exposed to the bone. "There will be no surrender," Casey repeated. "There will be no prisoners."

Amy collapsed in grief at Jesse's feet, realizing her plea for compassion would not be heard on this bloodthirsty night.

Dupre and Big Ben appeared as slave warriors, leading four horses they had saved from a barn fire. "No point burning up good animals," Dupre said.

All members of The Divebomberz, now fellow slaves, gathered around Jesse, awaiting combat directives. They looked stunned from the shock of merciless battle. White women and children were being beheaded, their screams abruptly ending.

Carmen walked out of the shadows, holding a finger to her lips as if to request a silence.

Jesse heard the voice behind him. There was no mistaking that deep rumble. It was the Voodoo voice. It was bringing him out of the dream world and back to New Orleans.

"Death to the slave owners," it said. "Death to slavery."

Jesse came back to the so-called real world in Carmen's office. She was standing in front of him, holding her finger to her lips, as she had in the dreamlike vision. Jesse shook his head and rubbed his eyes. He still smelled blood and black powder. It took some time before he could acclimate to his surroundings. His entire body was shaking.

"My God, woman, what have you done to me?" he heard himself shouting. "You've got me killing people in my sleep."

Carmen told him to settle down as she offered him a cold drink. Jesse looked at the water. He was so thirsty his tongue was barely able to move in his mouth. Even so, he pushed the glass away. "No way I'm drinking that. Last time you gave me something to drink I ended up slaughtering human beings in some jungle I've never seen. I'm not a killer. I don't believe in it. How could you do that to me?"

Carmen's voice remained soothing. "Here, drink this. It's only ice water. Look, I'll take a drink. See. No problems."

Jesse took the water and drained the entire drink down his throat in one motion.

"How long have I been out?"

"Only about half an hour."

Drinking the water helped him calm down. "Really. It felt like I was gone for hours."

Carmen was on her knees, close to his face, peering deeply into his eyes. "Where did you go? What did you see?"

"You don't know? You didn't send me there?"

"No, you only go where your mind will take you."

That remark made intuitive sense to Jesse. "So I can't blame you for turning me into a merciless killing machine?"

"No. You can't blame me for anything. You can only thank me. Now tell me everything. Where were you? Who was with you? What happened?"

Jesse told her the story in great detail. It took him longer to tell the story than it had taken to live it in his dream.

"What kind of pistol did you have?" she asked.

"I don't know. It was a black powder pistol. That's all I know. But I knew how to use it really well."

"How do you know it was a black powder pistol?"

"Because I had to load it several times," Jesse said, trembling at the memory. "I was killing people, shooting them at point blank range."

Carmen comforted him with a hand to his forehead. "You killed no one. You were with me the entire time. Look around. You will see no blood."

She got off her knees and took a seat at her desk. "From

everything you say. It sounds like you were at the ceremony of Bois Caiman. The date was August of 1791 and the name of the priestess was Cecile Fatiman. This is the most famous of all Voodoo uprisings. You say the pig was black?"

"Yes, the pig was definitely black."

"That is the Bois Caiman. That black pig sacrifice is legend in all of Voodoo. How did you ever end up there?"

"You tell me."

Carmen stood up and turned around to pull two books off her shelf. "It happened in Haiti. Hundreds of plantation owners were killed. They had created a cruel world. Their slaves outnumbered them, ten to one. The slaves took over. The rebellion led to a free Haiti for generations. Then, the Americans took them over again and ruined everything.

"This is where Voodoo got its bad reputation for black magic and evil. White people had to say Voodoo was bad because it beat them at their own game. That's when white people tried to reduce Voodoo into evil images of sticking pins into dolls. Voodoo is not black magic. Voodoo is a pathway for the soul."

Jesse listened intently but his throat was getting drier by the minute. "I need some more water. This killing people really makes you thirsty."

He was trying to be funny but he was still mainly recoiling in horror from what he had seen and done.

Carmen got him a pitcher of ice water and took a wet cloth to his face. "Look at you, you're a sweaty mess. Come on and stand up. You need to stretch."

"Do I have blood on me?"

Carmen handed him the wet cloth. "No. There's no blood on you. Now, tell me again about this silver haired plantation owner you killed in the dream. The one you thought you recognized."

Jesse thought back. Details remained crystal clear. He could still see the man's face as he was begging for mercy. He could hear his voice as he said he was a man of God. It sounded like it might be Jesse's father talking. The man's praying hands looked like Jesse's own hands. His fingers were long and quite straight for a man his age. Jesse looked at his hands and flashed back to the old man's hands. Then, he could see the man's eyes. Something about looking into his eyes felt like looking in the mirror. Gradually, Jesse was able to see through the silver hair and beard and into the identity of the man he had killed. The realization came into focus. It crept up on his mind and then smacked him right between the eyes with a big stick of understanding.

Jesse nearly fell back into the chair. "Good Lord, that was me I killed. That silver haired guy was a middle-aged me. I shot myself in the face. I felt good about it. How can that be?"

Carmen was bouncing on her toes in excitement. "Oh, this dream has been much better than I expected."

"What do you mean by that?"

She settled down to look closely at Jesse. "Think about what the voice said."

"It said, 'Death to the slave owners.'"

"What else did it say?"

Jesse had to think for a minute. Then it came to him. "It said, 'Death to slavery.'"

"That's it," Carmen said, bouncing up and down again.

"What are you talking about?"

Carmen went back to one of the books on her desk and opened it to a page she knew well. "Don't you see? In the dream, you were both a slave and a slave owner. You killed yourself to escape yourself."

"I don't get it."

"Yes, you do. In this life we are all prisoners of our own self-centeredness. We are both the slave owner and the slave. We give the orders and we take the orders in order to satisfy our selves. It's a vicious cycle of never getting enough of anything to fill the hole in our soul. We have the key to escape but we don't know how to use it."

Jesse was still trying to come to grips with the horrific violence he had so willingly committed. "So how do I end up in the middle of a slave revolt I have never even read about?"

"That, my friend, is the power of Voodoo."

Jesse couldn't resolve the violence of his vision with Carmen's message of escaping self. "So Voodoo will help me kill myself?"

"Don't say it like that. Voodoo is the power that connects you to the spirit world. You are set free once you realize there is more to the world than you at the center of it."

"Why was I so much older in the dream?"

Carmen had to think about that question as she looked through the book in front of her. "Perhaps you realize, deep down, that it will take years before you can get over your big, fat self."

Jesse had to laugh at that reference. "So, I have dreams where I kill my self-centeredness. That's well and good, as long as I keep dreaming. But now I'm awake. And here I am, back at the center of my universe. Can you guess what my selfish mind is thinking?"

"I know what you want. That's too easy. You don't need Voodoo to know that what you want right now is a good, stiff drink."

Jesse stood up. "That is correct. This water is not doing the job."

Carmen looked up from her books. "Escaping the prison of self is a process, not an event. Believe it or not, you are part of my process as much as I am part of yours. I find myself most at peace when I am helping you. You are helping me learn how to escape my self."

Jesse was surprised by Carmen's confession. "I only find moments of peace here and there," he said. "Most times, life is like a traffic jam, driving me crazy."

Carmen looked at him over the top of her reading glasses. "Think of it this way. Life is a spiritual obstacle course, designed to see if you can get over your self."

"I like that."

She closed her book, stood up from the desk and came around to give Jesse a hug. "Good. Let's go to Fritzel's and get that drink. Dutch will be there, running the bar, and he'll be happy to see us. But first, use my phone and call Amy. She'll want to join us."

"How do you know that?"

Carmen looked at him like he was missing a major point. "Think of the dream. She's the one you need. She's the one who will help you get your self under control."

"What about the voice?"

"The voice has been good to you as it has been to me. Our hope to hear the voice has turned into some degree of faith that the voice will guide us. Now, the goal is to evolve the faith into trust."

"Trust in what?"

Carmen laughed at the exasperation in his tone. "Trust that the universe has it all together and that everything will be all right, no matter how much we try to mess it up with our plans and schemes for greatness and glory."

"So, trying to be a rock star might not be the purist of motives?"

Carmen smiled as she quoted Dr. John. "The people who

make it in the music business are the people who make music for the sake of making music."

"I like that. It sounds like Johnny too."

"Johnny from Shreveport?"

Jesse was not surprised Carmen knew about Johnny. "Evidently, he's somebody I've created to teach me what I need to know."

"Very good," Carmen said as she led them out the door of her shop. "Now, tell me more about that drum section around the Voodoo fire with Professor Longhair and Dr. John. I need to hear those drums in my dreams."

CHAPTER TWENTY-TWO

THE BARMUDA TRIANGLE

Jesse booked a four-night stand for the band at The Barmuda Triangle in Minden, Louisiana. The owner was a tough-talking woman named Sheila who shook her blonde hair back over her shoulders as she greeted them.

After a round of introductions, Sheila looked out the long front window of her club. "You boys must have a ton of gear. I see a truck with a U-Haul trailer and a van. You want me and my girls to help with your set up?"

Rene headed out the door to start hauling his drums. "We can handle it on our own."

Rick tried to be cute. "Unless you really want to help. We love seeing women lifting heavy objects."

Sheila shouted out to her waitresses. "Oh, girls. We've got a hot one here. Thinks maybe we've never seen a rock band before."

"Johnny said you had rooms for us?" Jesse tried to steer the conversation back in a more business-like direction.

"Oh, he did, did he? Do you believe everything Johnny says?" Sheila moved closer to Jesse in an overtly flirtatious manner. She grabbed his left arm in both of hers and escorted him to the nearest table.

"Let's all of us have a seat and get acquainted," Sheila said. "Jennifer, why don't you and the girls take a break and join us for a little sit down."

Sheila was in her early fifties and still in great shape. Her jeans were tight and her shirt was loose. She was showing all the cleavage she could muster. It was 2 p.m. but she was already in lipstick and lashes. Her staff wore short shorts and bikini tops. They looked more like dancers in a strip club than working waitresses. Jesse wondered if they'd stumbled onto a tribe of Amazon warriors.

Sheila noticed the band slipping into drool factor four. "You boys look like you haven't seen a woman in months."

Jennifer flattered the band as she brought a round of Heineken beers in frosted mugs to the table. "Sheila, you didn't tell us they were going to be so cute."

Dale turned the tables on Sheila and Jennifer and the other waitresses who joined them. "You are all completely beautiful. If I didn't know better, I'd say we stumbled onto the Sirens of Titan."

"Ooh, strap yourself to the mast, big boy." A lanky, brunette waitress named Sherry sat down on Dale's lap. "I love a man who knows his mythology."

Tim was pleased to grab a beer. "Johnny must have told you we like Heineken."

Sheila helped pass the beer around. "Johnny told us everything. But, help me out here. Which one of you is the gay one?"

The female club owner was wasting no time in checking out the band. She wanted to see who would get offended and who would get defensive. The girls sized up the band and seemed to focus in on Jesse.

Jesse could see he would have to defend himself. "I know. It's the hair. But it's not me. Don't let the big hair fool you. I'm not the gay one. I've only got one gay bone in my body."

Everybody laughed, especially Sheila, who sidled up a little closer to Jesse. "I like sick humor."

Butch took the fall. "You might as well know. It's me. I'm the gay one."

The band laughed so much that the ladies knew it wasn't true.

Dale eased Sherry off his lap and stood up to take a bow. "Let there be no doubt about it, ladies. I am the chosen one."

Sherry stomped her feet in mock displeasure. "I always go for the gay guys."

Rick was still on a roll. "Don't worry, dahlin', there's plenty of me to go around."

Thus began the sparring between staff and band. It was always a little testy at first. The employees usually wanted to let the band know they'd seen plenty of musicians passing through and they weren't all that impressed. The band usually wanted to recruit the staff for drinks and food and help with the set up. This encounter was different for The Divebomberz. They'd never encountered a matriarchal society.

Dale broke the ice nicely with his chivalrous, Prince Charming act. "We are truly pleased to make your acquaintance. We will do our best to help you entertain your guests."

Sheila was impressed. "Perfect. Why can't all men be like you?"

The musicians and the staff had fun getting to know each other over two rounds of drinks. Sheila finally stood up to get down to business. "Let's get back to work. I want these floors mopped and the tables cleaned, top and bottom. Here are the keys to the No Tell Motel, Jesse. You've got two real nice double rooms. I know you need three, but two was all I could get. Once you get set up, I'm sure you'll want to check in and freshen up. Showtime is 8 p.m. Do *not* be late. It's Wednesday and you know what that means at the Barmuda Triangle."

"Ladies night," the waitresses yelled.

Sheila elaborated. "Women get in free. The place will be

packed. It would be anyway. People are talking about your band. You've got a lot of buzz coming out of Shreveport. But ladies' night will make it that much crazier."

"So about the No Tell Motel," Tim asked. "That's not the real name, is it?"

Sheila laughed. "No. That's just what we call it. It's the only one around. Turn left out of the driveway and go half a mile and there it is on the right. The actual name is The Dixie Motel."

Butch couldn't resist an observation. "Like the Civil War never ended."

Sheila took no offense. "Everything is Dixie this and Dixie that. I don't get it. I'm from Ohio."

"Hey, we're from Indiana," Butch said.

Sheila was not surprised. "I know. Johnny gave me the full report. Don't worry, I won't tell anybody that the hottest band in the bayou is actually a bunch of Hoosiers."

The band set up on the large stage at the back of the club. The waitresses stopped working long enough to listen and dance at the sound check. The band played like they had a full house, eager to impress and hitting it hard from the first note. They hadn't jammed in several days so it was fun to get back together.

After the sound check, Rick took Sherry aside. "By the way, why do they call this club the Barmuda Triangle?"

Sherry seemed pleased to be singled out. "Because people come in here and get so loaded they disappear, never to be heard from again."

"Maybe that'll happen to you and me." Rick was shameless.

"I don't think there's any doubt about it." Sherry accepted his proposition.

Jesse found himself being cornered by Sheila's manager, Jennifer, a tall, shapely woman with beautiful brown eyes. Jennifer was Jesse's age and she clearly wanted to do much more than talk. "Tell me about the fire at the Safari Club. I heard you pretty much saved everybody."

Jesse was surprised to see her actually batting her eyelashes. He looked more closely to see if the lashes were real. That turned out to be a mistake. Jennifer moved in close enough to kiss him but stopped just short of putting her lips on his.

Jesse backed up a step and caught his breath. He did not want to find a Rose in every town. "Those can't be your real eyelashes."

Jennifer smiled and did not accept the attempted brush-off. "They're as real as when I put them on this morning."

Jesse couldn't look into her eyes. He didn't want to get sucked into something he knew he shouldn't handle. "Well, they are beautiful and so are you. But I've got to get busy here or the boys will think I'm slacking."

Jennifer let him go, but Jesse could see she was watching him as the band did its sound check. After set up, the band checked in to the hotel. It was no Royal Royce but it was clean enough. Picking rooms and beds was not a simple process. Rick was already complaining that each member should have his own room. Rene and Jesse were not happy about sharing a bed. Dale offered to sleep on the floor but Rick talked him out of that. "The floor is not really an option. I found that out the hard way at the Royal Royce."

Once they got the rooms and beds settled, it was still two hours until show time. Jesse talked the band into taking a drive to check out the countryside and, perhaps, find a restaurant.

The rolling hills of northern Louisiana didn't disappoint. The views were breathtakingly bucolic. Red barns and white farmhouses and green fields with wooden fences highlighted the vistas. Herds of horses and cows grazed in the late afternoon light as the sun buttered the landscape. Oak and Ash and Maple trees cast lengthening shadows across the rocks and grasses of the sloping terrain. A lone, white horse on a hill caught Jesse's attention. He pulled the van off the road and drove up a dirt path to get closer to the horse. He stopped the van and got out. "Come on guys, follow me. I'm going to ride that white stallion."

As the band got out of the van, Butch tried to restrain his friend. "I don't think that's such a great idea, Jesse."

"I'm sure the farmer who owns the horse won't think it's such a good idea either." Rick threw in his vote of caution.

"Nonsense," Jesse said as he started up the hill. "That horse is begging for me to ride it. It's calling my name."

The band looked at each other nervously. Tim called after him. "How does the horse know your name?"

Jesse didn't answer the question, although he realized it was a good one. He kept walking. Seeing that Jesse was not to be deterred, the band followed him up the hill until they were within twenty feet of the horse. The horse did not move or seem the least bit disturbed by their presence. It was much larger than it had appeared from the bottom of the hill.

Dale tried to talk some sense into Jesse. "You're going to need a ladder to get up on that beast."

"All I need is a running start," Jesse said as he took off toward the horse at a full sprint. The band watched in stunned silence and disbelief. Surely, he wouldn't go through with this crazy joke of a stunt.

The horse turned its head around as it heard Jesse coming from the rear. Jesse put his hands on the horse's hindquarters, and attempted to vault up onto its back. It was a pretty good vault but not quite good enough. His head and chest made it onto the horse's back but the rest of him crashed into the proverbial horse's ass.

The impact knocked the wind out of Jesse and spurred the horse into action. He could feel the kick coming as he slid down the backside of the large beast. He managed to land on his feet and hopped backward as far and as fast as he could. The horse kicked back with both legs as Jesse was moving away. One of the hooves caught Jesse squarely in the right thigh with such force that it knocked him down. He could hear the band running forward to distract the horse. The world was spinning slowly. He wasn't sure if he could move. The horse turned around and was now looking down on him. He could feel the animal's hot breath on the back of his neck. He attempted to roll out of harm's way.

The horse could have stomped the life out of him right then and there, but it seemed more puzzled than angry. The band screamed at the horse as they charged and waved their arms. The horse looked at them warily. Jesse started rolling down the hill, realizing the horse had kicked him hard enough to cause serious injury. He could only hope the femur wasn't broken. In a flash of shame, he realized a broken leg was exactly what he deserved for such a foolish, show-off move.

The horse trotted off, and the band came down the hill to Jesse's side.

Tim was the first to reach him. "That's the dumbest thing you've ever done."

Butch and Dale answered in unison and without hesitation. "No, not even close."

"He's done way more stupid things than that, although I can't think of one right at the moment." Butch was laughing until he realized Jesse was actually hurt. "Are you okay?"

Jesse was holding his right thigh in obvious pain. "I was so close to riding off into the sunset. If only its ass wasn't so damn big. I couldn't get over that hump. I think the tail got in my way."

Rene was out of breath from laughing and running to Jesse's side. "It looked like you were trying to have sex with it."

"Can you walk?" Dale asked. "It looked like that kick nailed you pretty hard."

Jesse moaned and held his leg with both hands. "Lucky I was moving away when he got me,"

Rene became concerned. "I don't see any bones sticking out. That's a good sign, right?"

Dale was the first to suggest treatment. "We'd better get you back to the hotel and put some ice on that thigh. You might not be able to play tonight."

"I'll play tonight if I have to sit in a wheelchair."

Jesse limped into the Barmuda, holding his thigh and wincing in pain.

"What happened to you?" Sheila asked.

Jesse sat down in the nearest chair, extending his injured right leg. "One of your local horses kicked me."

Sheila snapped her head around to look Jesse in the eyes. "What were you doing with a horse?"

The band told her the story, each member adding a gory detail of his own.

Sheila got serious. "You're lucky you weren't killed. People die that way. You know that, don't you?"

Dale put his arm around Jesse. "He's been watching too many cowboy movies. You should have seen him, running full speed up the backside of that horse."

Jennifer brought out an ice pack and tied it to Jesse's leg with an elastic strap. She used the opportunity to run her fingers high up his thigh. The move was smooth and playfully sexual. Nobody else saw her do it. She was kneeling in front of Jesse, blocking their view. She dragged her fingernails back down his thigh to adjust the ice. Before Jesse had time to get completely wrapped up in the moment, Jennifer snapped the strap so it stung the back of his leg. Then, she got businesslike. "All right, gentlemen. That ought to do it. Get you a chair onstage, Jesse. You're on in five minutes. We was getting worried about you."

The sting of the snapping strap was still on Jesse's mind as he attempted to ignore Jennifer's terrible grammar. He could overlook almost any character defect, even lying or being overweight. But bad grammar was a serious problem. It was a deal-breaker.

The club was filling up fast with rowdy women and their male companions. Each woman got free admission and her first drink on the house, with all other drinks at half price. The band kicked into the first set with Jesse sitting down. Jennifer brought him two shots of Tequila for the pain. Within ten songs, and two pills of unknown prescription from Jennifer, he was playing on his feet again. A few songs later, the ice pack came off.

The Divebomberz were an instant hit with the ladies' night crowd. The girls had arrived ready to party and blow off some steam. It didn't take much to whip them into fever pitch. When Tim kicked in on the fiddle for a couple rocking bluegrass numbers, the cheers turned to screams of delight. Near the end of the first set, women started dirty dancing. The dance floor quickly became a girls-only area. The men formed a circle around the dancers to cheer them on.

The party went from sixty to a hundred in one second flat when a buxom young woman started waving her bra over her head. Several more ladies followed suit. The band looked at each other and laughed as they cranked it up with fast tempo songs. Rick took a solo on the B-3 organ that sent the club into an orbit all its own. Women were trying to out-dance each other. One girl got totally naked and instantly became the star of the show. Sheila and Jennifer hustled her off to the ladies room.

Jesse knew there would be trouble brewing in the parking lot when he saw Sheila and her girls turning people away at the front door. It was a good thing. She had already sold three hundred and fifty tickets at ten dollars each. The building was fire coded for two hundred fifty-five.

The club got so crowded and pushy that the band had to take its break in the parking lot behind the kitchen.

Rene was in good spirits as the band started passing around a joint. "I'm starting to feel like a rock star."

Tim was more specific. "That naked babe had some serious dance skills."

Dale put his hands on his hips. "Was it the dance moves or the bare ass that really caught your eye?"

"She was so drunk she won't remember a thing tomorrow," Butch said. "Sheila did her a big favor dragging her out of the party."

Rick was thinking money. "Looks like we should start playing for the door. Or at least get a percentage of what they take in on the cover charge."

Dale was on the edge of being alarmed by the crowd. "I've never seen people get this crazy on a Wednesday night."

Butch took a thoughtful hit on the joint. "I think ladies' night at the Barmuda is a bigger deal than anybody thought it would be. It almost feels like some kind of women's movement thing going on."

Sheila broke into the band circle in a little bit of a panic. "Sorry to interrupt. You boys better get back in there and play. These women are fixing to tear my place apart."

"Is it like this every Wednesday night?" Dale asked.

Sheila looked at him like she was surprised he didn't know. "This is our first ladies' night, and it seems like half of Louisiana is ready to come out and get some equal rights."

"What's making them so crazy?" Dale asked.

Sheila had a ready answer. "I think I better rethink the half-priced drinks."

The band went back in and took the stage. Sheila had some pretty tough looking ladies trying to handle the crowd and keep people off the stage. But the party quickly spiraled out of control. The crowd rushed the stage. The band was overwhelmed by a Tsunami of naked flesh and wet undergarments. Somehow, they were able to keep playing. The women were careful not to trash the musicians or their gear. No one wanted the music to stop.

The party came to a screeching halt when police lights began flashing all over the parking lot. Sheila came back in the front door, frantically waving her arms, and signaled the band to stop playing. Something had gone terribly wrong outside. Screaming could be heard once the music stopped. Jesse thought he heard a voice in the parking lot screaming someone had been shot. The band remained onstage as an ambulance arrived and police began clearing the club. The Barmuda was officially a crime scene investigation.

Sheila came back inside, crying and shaken up pretty badly. She climbed onstage to inform the band.

"It's my girl, Jennifer. She got shot. They're not sure if she's going to make it. She got shot in the stomach trying to break up a fight. It was two idiot men fighting over a girl. I can't believe this could happen at the Barmuda. I've been here for twelve years and we've never had any trouble like this."

Jesse was stunned. He couldn't believe the woman who had been flirting with him was now fighting for her life. Sheila began sobbing as Jesse enveloped her in a hug of despair. "Did they catch the shooter?"

"I think so but nobody knows for sure what really happened," Sheila said.

Sherry came onstage. "Did you guys hear the gunshot?"

"We couldn't hear anything in here." Rick put his arms around Sherry like she'd been his wife for ten years. She started crying.

Sheila broke out of Jesse's hug. "I've got to get to the hospital. Sherry, here's the keys. I'm sorry but I need you to stay here and lock up. Guys, I'll come to the hotel as soon as I know what's going on."

They sat down at a table near the bar. The cops had cleared out the place in a hurry. Only Sherry and two other waitresses were left to close down the large, empty hall.

Jesse felt strangely responsible for what had happened. In a way, it felt like his fault. Then he came down to earth and reminded himself that he wasn't the center of the universe and that everything didn't happen because of him.

Sherry brought them a bottle of Tequila and six shot glasses. Nobody in the band said anything as they downed their first shot. Dale broke the silence as he poured out the next round. "No way any of this is our fault. I don't know why we're sitting here feeling guilty."

"It's just being part of a scene where somebody gets killed," Butch said.

Tim downed his second shot. "At least it didn't happen in the club."

Jesse responded softly. "I didn't even hear the shot. But I looked through the window and saw Jennifer get loaded into the ambulance on a gurney. She damn sure didn't deserve anything like that."

Dale hung his head and folded his hands in a praying motion. "Maybe she'll be okay."

Much later that night, after the band had fallen into bed, good and drunk, Jesse was having troubling and frightening dreams. All the traumatic experiences of recent months were fighting with each other on the stage of his overloaded and intoxicated brain. In his dreams, the Gypsys and the Wheelers were killing each other. The ship captain was riding the white horse. The Safari Club was burning. Pete was choking on his own cocaine. The slave uprising on the Haitian plantation was connecting with the tragic ending to ladies' night at the Barmuda Triangle.

Jesse was desperately trying to revive the white-haired plantation owner he had just murdered when he started hearing a loud voice shouting at him.

He awakened to find himself pumping Rene's chest in the double bed they were sharing at the hotel. Rene was yelling at him to stop.

Dale jumped out of his bed and turned on the lights.

Rene pushed hard on Jesse's chest. "Jesus, Jesse, get the Hell off me. What are you trying to do?"

It took some time for Jesse to fully awaken and let go of Rene. Eventually, he got off him and sat on the edge of the bed. He put his head in his hands in a futile attempt to regain control of his mind. Rene and Dale sat down on either side of him, ready to do whatever it might take to bring him back to reality.

Dale rubbed Jesse's back. "You were dreaming, my brother. It's okay. It was just a dream. Everything's going to be fine. We're here together and we're awake. What kind of dream was it?"

Jesse gave Dale a guilty look. "I killed somebody and I was trying to bring him back."

Rene got off the bed and stood up. "Oh, great. You were trying to kill me. That's some heavy shit."

Jesse waved Rene off to let him know nobody was trying to kill him. "No, it wasn't you in the dream. It was somebody I barely recognized. Man, oh man, that tequila put me over the edge last night. How much did we drink?"

Rene groaned. "More than any of us can remember."

Dale stated what all three of them were thinking. "It might be time for us to back off the bottle for a while."

"No shit," Jesse said as he got off the bed and staggered to the bathroom just in time to throw up in the toilet.

Butch and Tim and Rick stormed into the room.

Butch talked directly to Dale. "What's going on? It sounds like people are fighting in here."

Dale was relieved to see the cavalry come to the rescue. "What took you so long? We could all be dead by now."

Rick offered an explanation. "We were out pretty hard. So what is going on?"

"Jesse just had a bad dream," Rene said. "He thought he'd killed somebody and he was on top of me, trying to revive me."

"Serves you right for sleeping with him," Dale said.

Butch chuckled. "He wasn't giving you mouth-to-mouth was he?"

Rene laughed "No. Thank heavens for small favors."

Tim was still waking up. "Oh, man. My head is killing me."

The band was all wide-awake now, and trapped in the middle of a collective hangover.

Sheila met the band the next day at the club. She started crying as soon as she walked in the door. "Jennifer is gone. She didn't even make it to the hospital. By the time I got there, she was already gone."

The band hugged her and mumbled sympathies as they sat down at a round table near the front door.

"I guess you know I've got to shut down for a while. I can't just go on like nothing happened. I've got to shut down for I don't know how long. It's out of respect for Jennifer and for my own sanity. I'm sorry. I can't pay you for the whole week. I can pay you for last night and tonight but I can't pay you Friday and Saturday if I'm not open. I know none of this was your fault. I would ask, though, that you check out of the Dixie by 3 p.m."

Nobody said a word.

Sheila tried to stop crying. "Who would have thought this would happen on my first ladies' night?"

"Did she have any kids?" Butch asked.

Sheila started crying again. "That's the worst of it. She has two little girls. They're eight and five years old. What's going to happen to them? Neither of their fathers has ever been any help at all. Jennifer had to support them herself. She was such a good worker. She was my right hand. Her mother kept the girls when Jennifer worked. I guess grandma will have to be mom now."

Sheila paid them in cash for two nights out of four and said she had to get going to help make funeral arrangements. The band hugged her goodbye. After one day, Jesse felt like he'd known her forever.

They packed up their gear and said goodbye to the day bartender, who was putting up a sign outside the front door that read, "Closed for Jennifer's Funeral."

CHAPTER TWENTY-THREE

MAD DOGS

Jesse arrived home two days early from the cancelled gig. Amy threw her arms around him and hugged with all her might. She had been worrying herself into a nauseous state since Jesse told her on the phone about the murder at the club.

She pulled out of the hug and looked him in the eye . . . "Who kills a woman on ladies' night?"

Jesse took her hands into his own. "A jealous, drunk man with a gun."

Amy took a step backward. "These bars you're playing up north don't sound like classy establishments."

Jesse teased her. "How could you say that about a place named the Barmuda Triangle?"

"No, seriously, Jesse, I'm worried about you. Who's to say it won't be you getting shot next time?"

"You know me. I'm invincible."

Her face turned into a pout. "That is exactly the attitude that has me concerned."

Jesse kissed her to show he could be serious. "To be honest, the whole thing pretty much freaked out the band. We didn't see or hear the shooting. It happened in the parking lot. All we knew was our gig was going great until the cops shut us down. I don't think Sheila is ever going to get over losing Jennifer."

"Who's Sheila and who's Jennifer?"

"Sheila owns the club and Jennifer's the one who got killed. She was Sheila's assistant manager."

"Sounds like you got to know these women pretty well in such a short time."

"Amy, don't be like that."

"Be like what? Be a little jealous when you tell me women are throwing underwear at you?"

"I probably shouldn't have mentioned that on the phone."

"Maybe not," Amy said as she gave him a playful shove.

Jesse went to grab a beer out of the refrigerator. Before he shut the door, Amy was hugging him from behind. "I don't mean to be grumpy. I am so happy to have you home with me. That's all I really want to say."

She led him into the bedroom and pounced on him with all the pent-up energy of a woman who really did miss her man.

"I am the luckiest man on the planet," Jesse said once they collapsed into each other's sweaty embrace after an intense round of premarital bliss.

Amy kissed his chest. "Have you been having any more Voodoo dreams?"

Jesse told her about the incident with Rene.

She slapped him on the shoulder, playfully. "That's what you get for sleeping with another man."

"You should stay at the Dixie Inn. If you think the clubs are tacky, you should see the hotels."

"So, how is playing this circuit ever going to get you anywhere?"

Jesse tried to answer her question. "Bands have to hit the road to keep playing and find their sound. That's why the Beatles had to go to Hamburg. They played every night for a long time and sounded like a great band when they returned to Liverpool."

Amy held his head with both hands so she could get close enough to make her point. "Just because one band out of a million got lucky, doesn't mean it's going to happen for you."

"Are you saying I should give up?"

"No. What I'm saying is playing these roadhouses doesn't seem like it's ever going to pay your bills. How much did you bring home this week?"

"You know we each only took home seventy-five. We didn't get paid for Friday and Saturday because the club was closed. I told you that on the phone. The band has too many bills. We've got two loans to pay on top of everything else."

Amy changed tactics. "All right. I get it. It's not about the money. It's about the music."

"Thank you very much."

She sat down in an old wooden chair that creaked like it might fall apart. "So what happened to that tape Pete paid for? I haven't even heard it."

Jesse took a seat on the swing that hung from the rafters. "You don't want to hear it. It sounded muddy. They got too much reverb on the drum tracks and they can't fix it. They would have to re-record it and Pete has totally dropped out of the picture."

"So, what about the Voodoo voice? Won't it tell you what to do? Maybe we should have another talk with the skull on the wall."

Jesse had not told her about drinking Madame Carmen's potion and going back in dreamtime to a Voodoo slave revolt. And he definitely did not tell her about the incident with Rose and the voice. Amy didn't like violence and she wasn't too crazy about Carmen. The thing about Rose would have been more than a problem.

Jesse decided to go with the "everything's going to be all right" angle. "The voice, if you remember, saved our lives from the fire at the Safari club. It's been telling me all along that everything's going to turn out fine. Look how we found a drummer with a P.A. system. And Rick came along to play keyboard right after the gig at Tipitina's. I'm telling you, everything is happening right on time."

"You always say that."

"That's because it's true. And you know what else is happening right on time?"

"No, what?" Amy pretended to not know what he was going to say.

Jesse got off the swing and went across the room to kiss her softly. "We're going to get married June 16, 1978. It's March 4 right now. When are we going to start making plans?"

March, April and May of 1978 saw The Divebomberz playing so steadily that they were able to pay off one of the two equipment loans and have nearly two grand in the bank for emergencies. Rene's father was running the band checking account. Rene was trying to run the band.

The band's set list became Rene's main bone of contention. He wanted more pop-rock songs and less original songs and country material. Butch and Jesse wanted original material. Tim favored the country and bluegrass numbers. The band had to have a voting system for the set list. It took four of the six members of the band voting for a song to keep it on the list. Rene and Rick got outvoted a lot. The boys from Indiana stuck together. The band's musical identity and direction was in a constant state of flux, yet, somehow, evolving. The sound became tighter and more polished. Original songs like "Going Crazy" and "I Want to Believe" were going over well with the crowds.

Rene's father, Burt, purchased a large home in the woods

near Shreveport with enough porches and gazebos and garages to house the band between gigs. He also hired a welder in the middle of April to help the band build its own trailer. He pulled rank as the band's financial advisor. "We can't keep paying the U-Haul bills. It doesn't make good business sense."

"We'll build it out of steel so nobody will ever be able to steal our gear again," Rene said, looking at Jesse like the previous theft in New Orleans had been his fault.

Tim responded before Jesse could get too pissed off. "We don't need a tank that's too heavy to haul."

Burt was quick to defend his plan. "Don't worry. My guy knows what he's doing. It'll be a great band project."

Three days later, the band had a trailer that looked like an ironclad battleship from the Civil War. Rene and Tim were the only two band members who really helped with the assemblage. Rick refused to participate. Dale did a little spray painting. Butch and Jesse helped carry materials.

Dale offered to paint "The Divebomberz" on the side of the trailer.

Rene shot the idea down. "We don't want anybody to know what's in the trailer."

Jesse was fed up with Rene being bossy. "Nobody could get in this thing if they wanted to."

Tim stepped between Rene and Jesse. "If they see it's a band, they'll break into the truck and the van."

So they painted the trailer olive green like it was property of the U.S. Army. But that wasn't the worst part. Despite having four wheels and good balance, the beast had no aerodynamics. Whenever Rene towed it behind his truck, the trailer seemed to not want to follow.

Rene remained defensive. "It's okay. I can handle it if we put some weight in back of the truck to help the rear wheels keep the trailer in line."

Rick was on Jesse's side regarding the trailer. "We should have bought one from U-Haul."

Rene wheeled around and pointed his finger at Rick. "Easy for you to say. You were no help at all and it was your organ that made us need the damn trailer in the first place."

Butch tried to mediate what was becoming a full-band quarrel. "Now, boys. Look at the bright side. We've got our own trailer and we don't have to rent one anymore."

The trailer's real test came while trying to reach a club near Hot Springs, Arkansas, in a freak spring snowstorm. With two inches of snow and hail on the road, the band had the only vehicles on the highway. Southern drivers don't do snow. The road was slick enough to let the trailer have its way with Rene's truck. It jackknifed him off the road on three occasions. Each time, the band had to muscle the truck and trailer back onto the highway.

Everybody was exhausted by the time they arrived, late afternoon, at the Mad Dog Saloon. The bartender was a thirty-five year old man who looked a little like the posters of Joe Cocker that hung around the huge club. It looked to Jesse like the owner was a big fan of Cocker's tour and record album, "Mad Dogs and Englishmen."

The place smelled clean, not the usual odor of cigarette butts and stale beer. It looked ready for a convention of doctors. There were several levels of seating beneath a tall, timber-frame ceiling. The main room was all wood and brass. The well-stocked bar stretched from one end of the club to the other. On the other side of seating for at least three hundred people, was a theater stage that was four feet above the dance floor. It was the largest and most modern club Jesse had ever seen.

The bartender barely acknowledged the band's entrance. "You guys can go ahead and set up. I doubt if we're going to have any kind of a crowd tonight. Folks won't go out in this storm. We haven't seen anything like it, long as I remember."

Jesse tried to get him to look up from washing glasses in the sink. "Are you the owner?"

The bartender looked up like it was a chore to do so. "Do I look like the owner? No, I am not the owner. I wish. But I talked to her about an hour ago. She said to have you go ahead and set up. Oh yeah, and there's a suite of rooms for you guys, upstairs behind the stage. I'm supposed to show you. So, come on. Follow me."

The accommodations were modern, well kept, and spacious. There was a large common area with a kitchen, three bedrooms with two beds each and two, full baths.

"This is where all the bands stay?" Rene asked.

"That's right," the bartender said. "You're wondering why it's not all trashed out?"

"We weren't going to mention it," Dale said.

The bartender looked straight at Dale. "We stay on top of the cleaning and maintenance. And we charge bands for any damage they do."

Butch jumped in. "You won't have to worry about us. We're nice, respectful Indiana boys."

"That's what Donna says. She's the owner. She's real hands-on. She'll be here soon. Says ya'll come highly recommended from Johnny in Shreveport."

Tim slapped his hands on the kitchen counter. "Man, Johnny does get around."

"Yes, he does," a woman who looked like a slender Dolly Parton said as she burst into the room. "Hello gentlemen, I'm Donna. Welcome to the Mad Dog Saloon. We're pleased to have you here. Sorry about the weather. Don't worry, I'm not a cancelling kind of girl. We'll see what happens. Johnny says I'm going to love you guys. I can't wait."

"How do you know Johnny?" Jesse asked.

"We used to work together at the Louisiana Hayride, the radio and television production company. I'm sure he told you all about it. Sheila at the Barmuda Triangle worked there too. Terrible what happened at her bar. I heard you were playing there when it all went down."

Dale stepped up as the band's main greeter. "We didn't see anything. It happened in the parking lot. We didn't know anything was wrong until we saw the police and ambulance lights through the windows. It was so hard on Sheila. It was her first ladies' night. We know it almost killed her to lose Jennifer. Has she reopened yet?"

Donna hung her head briefly but raised up with no tears in her eyes. "She will. She's a tough girl. You've got to be tough to run a bar in this man's world. She and I are close. I think we're the only two women running clubs in the entire southern United States."

"There's lots of men who say they're running bars when it's actually the women doing all the work," Dale said.

Donna smiled beautifully. "I like you boys already. Okay, let's not be too chit-chatty. Get settled in and set up and we'll see what happens tonight. Anybody on the road when you came in?"

"Not many," Rene said. "Is it still coming down?"

Donna shook her head. "Yes, it is. I was the only car on the highway."

By 8 p.m. the club was still empty, except for one bartender, three waitresses and Donna. She had told most of the staff to stay home. The band was onstage and getting ready to start playing when they realized they were completely out of marijuana.

Tim felt himself in a major crisis. "What are we going to

do? I haven't played straight in I don't know how long. Maybe never."

Rick decided to save the day. "I've got half of a pretty good joint up in the room. I've been saving it, but I'll donate it to the cause."

Dale began heading up to the room. "Let's go get it and fire it up."

They went back to the band apartment and huddled around the last joint like cavemen at a cooking fire. It was good stuff. They smoked it up quickly, went downstairs, and started playing pretty close to on time. They sounded wonderful from start to finish of the first set. Not one customer was in the club. Donna listened to the performance like she was auditioning the band for a record company. She applauded and hollered after every song and even danced with her bartender. After the set she invited the band to join her for a drink at a large round table in the center of the room.

"Johnny wasn't wrong about you boys," she said as she hoisted her whiskey and soda for a toast. "Here's to making a record that sells a million copies."

The band joined her toast with their beer mugs. Jesse wondered what kind of an offer she was making. She must have noticed the curiosity and suspicion in his eyes.

She set her mug down carefully "No, I'm not just another drunk going to make you stars. I'm not even in the record business. But I know people who are and those people need to hear this band."

"We'll all drink to that," Dale said as the band joined her in another clinking of glasses.

They played another set and only two tables of people arrived, looking like refugees coming in from the blizzard. Donna agreed to shut it down for the night.

So Thursday was snowed out. Friday got a little better and,

by Saturday, Donna had a full house. She also had a longhaired visitor from Los Angeles, who wore tea shades and a coat that looked like a cape.

Donna seemed thrilled to introduce him. "I'd like you to meet Tony. He flew in for the weekend. He's with Capitol Records and he likes what he hears."

Tony shook hands all around. "You guys sound tremendous. Donna was right. Best band I've heard in a long while. Do you have a demo tape I can take back with me? I'm in the A & R department."

"What's A & R?" Dale asked, unafraid to show his ignorance.

"A & R stands for artist and repertoire," Tony said as he gave Donna a hug to bring her close. "In the old days, A & R guys brought artists together with their material, or repertoire. Artists and repertoire, A & R, get it? Now, what we mainly do is bring songwriters and performers into the fold. Most artists write their own material these days."

Jesse was mesmerized to be hearing the language of show business he was so eager to understand.

Tony clearly relished the role of big-time record label guy. "So what about that recording, the demo tape?"

"We're working on that," Jesse said. "In fact, we're looking for someone to help us get that done."

"Have you done any recording?" Tony asked.

"We were in the studio a few months ago but what they recorded pretty much sounded like shit," Rene said. "They messed up when they set levels on the drums and they couldn't fix it."

"You guys need to get to L.A. and into a decent studio," Tony said.

The notion excited Butch. "Tell us when and where and we'll be there."

Rene wasn't so sure. "Wait a minute. We don't have the money to relocate to Los Angeles. We just spent most of our reserve building the trailer."

Tony had the solution. "There's always Muscle Shoals. You're not that far west of Memphis, and Muscle Shoals is not that far east of Memphis."

The very mention of the legendary studio in Muscle Shoals, Alabama, had Jesse feeling weak in the knees. It had never crossed his mind that his band could record there. Everybody from the Rolling Stones to Aretha Franklin to Lynyrd Skynyrd had made hit records there.

"Have you ever been there?" Rick asked.

"I was there in 1976 when Bob Seger recorded his 'Night Moves' album. That was one ass-kicking session."

Dale was swooning. "Oh, come on. That is too cool to be true."

Rick was more particular. "How was it? I mean, I know Capitol did that record. But what was it like to work with Seger?"

Tony slammed down a shot of whiskey. "It was completely out of sight. That place has a sound like no other, as you know. I was in the control room for the first mixes. We all knew it was going gold. Seger's got such a voice and, oh my, can that boy write a tune. You guys have original material, right?"

"Were you here for 'Hurricane on the Bayou' and 'I Want to Believe?'" Butch asked.

Tony seemed overjoyed. "I loved that one about the Hurricane. You guys wrote that? Far out. That's all it takes. All I need is an ass-kicking band with great songs. Nothing to it, right?"

"You got that right," Rick said.

Rick had been around more than the rest of The Divebomberz.

He'd even played keyboard with the house band at Muscle Shoals Studio, the Swampers. "If you can get us in, we'll be there tomorrow."

"We might be able to do it," Tony said. "But first, I need a tape so the people with the money can decide if they want to invest in you."

"We'll get you the tape," Dale said.

The rest of the band was completely star struck by Tony and his war stories from the trenches of big time rock and roll. He wasn't even forty years old and he'd already seen it all. At least that's how he liked to tell the tale. Tony hung around all night, partying with the band and Donna and several waitresses. It was obvious he had flown in more for Donna than for the band. About 2 a.m., once the customers cleared out, he and Donna started laying out lines of cocaine on a low counter behind the bar.

As Jesse walked toward the bar, he was looking right at Tony when he heard the Voodoo voice say, "That man is a thief."

Jesse stopped in his tracks. There was no doubting what he had heard. He listened for more but there was nothing. He hadn't heard the voice in such a long time he was beginning to think it had forgotten about him.

The rest of the band passed him by and did their lines, even Rick who swore he'd never touch the stuff again. Eventually, Jesse stepped around the bar and took a long snort of cocaine that jolted him wide-awake. Although the band had tried to take seriously Johnny's warning about hard drugs, there was no effort to abstain once the cocaine opportunity appeared. After all, they were running low on what little marijuana they'd been able to scrounge, and the alcohol they'd been drinking all night needed a kick in the ass.

Jesse looked at Tim to see if he had heard anything from the voice. Tim was too busy with one of the waitresses to be any help at all.

Donna noticed Jesse not being the life of the party. "What's with you, Jesse? You got quiet all of a sudden."

Jesse tried to snap out of it. "Don't mind me. I'm just a little high. Maybe what I need is a shot of tequila to take the edge off."

It was nearly 1 p.m. on Sunday before the band woke up and got around to packing up their gear. They were getting a late start on what would be a long drive back to New Orleans for everybody except Rene. He and the equipment trailer would hang out in Shreveport until the return engagement at Johnny's coming up on Wednesday. Spring had returned and the roads were perfectly dry.

Donna came in to pay them and book a return engagement in August. Tony wasn't with her, but she had his hand-written instructions on how and where to send a demo tape.

"So what did you think about my friend from Los Angeles?" Donna asked. "I told you I had friends in the music business."

"He seems like the real deal," Rene said. "Do you really think he can help us?"

"If Tony can't help you, you can't be helped," Donna said. "And I know he can. He said he would."

Donna left after a short visit and the band finished packing up. Excitement levels were high about their new Los Angeles contact. Everybody was sure they had found the man who could help them get a recording contract with a big record label.

Jesse continued winding up chords without saying a word.

"What's with you, Jesse?" Dale asked. "You're not saying much about the big breakthrough. Don't you think Tony is our guy?"

Jesse didn't say anything. He wasn't about to use the Voodoo voice as a bucket of cold water on the newly raised hopes and dreams of the band. "I'm a little concerned that he didn't come by today to say goodbye."

"You're a little concerned that he wasn't your idea," Rene said.

Rick sided with Rene. "Come on, Jesse. Don't be such a downer."

Jesse shrugged it off and tried to show some enthusiasm for making a tape and getting it to Tony in Los Angeles. But, at this point, it wasn't Tony that had Jesse worried. What concerned Jesse was the alliance between Rick and Rene that made him feel like he was losing control of the band. They had even made comments about how he needed to improve his bass playing and how he maybe shouldn't sing so much. He was beginning to think that every member he added to the band took him a little further away from making the music he wanted to make. When the band started, it was just Jesse and Butch. It was two guitarists, singing original material. Once Dale and Tim got added, Jesse shifted to bass guitar and the band started rocking up bluegrass and country standards. By the time Rene and Rick came onboard, the band was mainly learning popular hit songs because people in clubs want to sing along with songs they already know.

To top things off, the voice of Voodoo seemed to be warning him that every move he needed to make in the music business was going to be a wrong turn. It had warned him that Pete was a slave owner. It had told the ship captain it was time to defect. Now, it was warning him that Tony was a thief.

Jesse drove the band back to New Orleans. He had a lot of time to think. There was no conversation. The boys were asleep. The miles rolled by quickly.

Jesse didn't like slipping into a funk about the future. He tried to talk himself into a more positive frame of mind. Maybe they would get to record at Muscle Shoals for Capitol records.

That would be a dream come true. But the voice sounded quite sure that Tony was a thief. At least it hadn't called him a slave owner. The fact that Tony came to hear them at all was definitely a good sign. Everyone who came to listen loved the band.

Jesse couldn't help but slip into uncertainty and trepidation. He didn't think Capitol Records was going to work out. Tony would forget about the Divebomberz once he got back to L.A., like he would forget about Donna. Tony was in it for Tony. That was plain to see.

Jesse kept driving and listening for the Voodoo voice. There was nothing on his private airwave but his own thoughts. That was a good thing. He was beginning to realize that listening for the voice was as important as actually hearing the voice. Listening for the voice was getting outside of himself. He didn't need to hear anything. All he needed was to get out of the center of everything.

The sun had set by the time the band made it back to New Orleans. They awakened, one by one, as the city lights loomed in the distance. The Crescent City looked like a giant party palace, shimmering in the night.

Nobody talked much. By the time he dropped off each band member at his respective dwelling, all Jesse wanted to do was get home to Amy.

CHAPTER TWENTY-FOUR

RED LIGHT

Jesse and Amy didn't have much time together. He got home late Sunday and she had to be up early Monday to teach school. That left him alone all day with nothing but his guitar to keep him company. That was fine with Jesse. He often said, "Your friends will let you down. Even your family will let you down once in a while. But your guitar will never let you down."

So he made himself a pot of coffee and sat down to play guitar and write himself a song. What the heck, he thought. That's how it all started out. What am I worried about with all the band politics? I don't have to let anything stop me from writing a song.

He decided to write a tune about his game of running red lights. He kept track of how many times he got away with it before getting arrested. He was up to two hundred and forty-five successfully run red lights, and counting.

It took four hours, three pots of coffee, a half pack of cigarettes and three joints before he finally had the song completed. It was a good one. The song practically wrote itself. One verse led to the next. The chorus leaped out of thin air and grabbed him by the throat.

It didn't matter what anybody else thought. He had learned to trust the process of listening for the muse. It was pretty much the same thing as listening for the Voodoo voice. Both the muse and the voice were something you felt more than actually heard. Listening for either one was like letting yourself out of a cage.

The song started on a cool country lick in D. The refrain went to E minor and the chorus started on a good old cowboy C chord. Jesse wrote it for his vocal range. He could sing it well. The tune had a ton of lyrics, but Jesse had them memorized by the time Amy got home from school. He played the song for her.

Late one night at the traffic light
I was waiting for the stop to go
I looked both ways but there
Wasn't nobody coming

So there I was obeying the law
When I began to feel a little foolish
I said the light was red
But man those streets were empty

So I took a deep breath and stepped on the accelerator
Guess I knew they'd catch me sooner or later
Sure enough come a police car right out of nowhere
Wants to see my license
Wants to smell my breath

Well I told the law he was being small
For taking me to the jail
I said that red light
Can't see what I can see

But as you might guess I was in a helluva mess
Because I ran a red light that night

But I must confess I'm gonna
Do it every chance I get

Cause it's so much fun running red lights
Especially in the dark without no headlights
It makes me feel like an urban guerrilla
It's a revolutionary thriller
And a genuine time killer

So remember this song when your chance comes along
To strike a blow against the great computer
Stop wasting gas
In the name of electricity

You might find when you make up your mind
There's a lot of red lights to run
And you better run a few if you're gonna
Get where you're going

Cause that red light can't see what you can see
Go ahead and run it
That red light can't see what you can see
Yeah, yeah, yeah, run it

Amy bounced up and down and clapped enthusiastically as Jesse finished the song with a flourish and held the guitar over his head for emphasis. She hugged him as he set down the guitar. "Do you think the band will play it? It's a little bit of a novelty song."

Jesse winced and shut his eyes as he tilted his head toward the ceiling. "What do you mean by that?"

"Nothing bad," Amy said. "It's just not your standard I love you but you broke my heart so I'm leaving."

He waited for her to continue but she clammed up.

"What? That's all you've got to say? Come on, I can see you've got more."

Amy shrugged her shoulders and lowered her head. "Well, you know how I feel about your red light game."

Jesse took a big breath and puffed out his cheeks as he exhaled. "You don't like it."

Amy looked up at him and tried to be the voice of reason. "It's not that I don't like it. I think it's funny and all. I like the stand up for your human rights bit. But it's going to get you in trouble. We can't afford any more tickets. I've already bailed you out of jail once. I'd rather not do it again."

Jesse thought back to his one-day stay in the New Orleans jail and realized she was right.

Amy kept up the pressure . . . "And another thing. You've been talking about how we all need to escape the prison of self, or whatever you want to call it. Then, you turn around and run red lights like the law doesn't apply to you. Call me crazy, but I think breaking rules for sport is about as self centered as you can get."

"I only run red lights when there's nobody else around. When it's stupid to sit and wait for no reason other than to obey the law. It's not selfish to want to be free. The people of this country had to fight to be free, and now our freedom is vanishing in a terrible web of technology."

"If a red light challenges your sense of freedom, I'll hate to see what having a wife will do."

"You wouldn't tell me to wait for traffic that wasn't there."

The phone rang. It was Butch, right on time. Jesse put the phone on a chair and played him the new song. He sang it soft and slow so his songwriting partner could hear the changes coming and feel how the words fit with the melody.

Amy applauded after she heard the new tune again.

Jesse talked with Butch for a minute, then said goodbye and hung up the phone.

"Well?" Amy asked.

"He loved it," Jesse said.

"He's not mad that he didn't write it with you?"

"That's not how we are," Jesse said.

"What about the rest of the band?" she asked, alluding to the fact that original material was losing out to hit songs on the band's playlist.

"Once Butch learns the guitar part and I get the bass line down, the rest of the band will turn this little song into a monster hit."

"Excuse me, Jesse. It's not a hit until you sell a million copies."

Jesse grabbed her and lifted her off her feet in a huge hug. "Details, details, my beloved. Your future husband just wrote a great song today."

Jesse was jinxed as soon as he wrote the song. The very next night he got a ticket for running a red light in the Garden District. The New Orleans police officer didn't care that Jesse was the only car at the intersection, and that no one had been put in danger. Nor did he care to hear Jesse's new song about running red lights. The officer wrote Jesse a ticket and gave him a stern verbal warning. "Traffic safety applies to all drivers," he said as he shook the ticket in Jesse's face. "You better be a lot more careful. You're going to get cute one night and kill somebody."

Jesse drove away in Harley, scarcely able to believe he had not been able to talk his way out of the citation. It pissed him off that the cop had been so condescending.

Jesse watched in his rear view mirror until the law turned off his emergency flashers and drove away in the opposite direction. Once the police car was out of sight, Jesse crumpled up the traffic ticket, threw it out the passenger window and promptly forgot about it.

CHAPTER TWENTY-FIVE

MACED

Amy came up to hear the band on the Friday of their third booking at Johnny's Cimarron Club in Shreveport, Louisiana. At least thirty motorcycles were angle parked, back tires to the curb, in front of the club. This was the night The Wheelers decided to make a long road trip to catch up with their favorite band.

The club was packed as she worked her way inside during the middle of the second set. The Divebomberz were putting a funky spin on "Sympathy for the Devil" by the Rolling Stones. Dale was doing a great Mick Jagger, alternating between deep, dark warnings and fierce whispers. Jesse and Rene and Butch were laying down a solid, rhythm thunder that sounded like a Mardi Gras parade trying to squeeze down Bourbon Street. Rick was wailing on the Hammond B-3 organ and Tim was fiddling like the devil in the song, laying traps for troubadours who get killed before they reach Bombay. The band sounded like moonshine music from the forbidden swamp.

Amy couldn't believe it was the same band she had seen getting their start at Fritzel's on Bourbon Street. It was a much better band, even, than the one she had seen on public television in New Orleans. Rick and his keyboards, and months on the road, had rounded out the sound and vaulted the band to new levels of musicianship. Her eyes filled with tears of appreciation as she waded through the crowd to get Jesse's attention. The band looked more professional than the last time she had seen them. Their stage movements were more fluid and controlled. They looked more self-confident. Jesse wasn't jumping around anymore.

The Wheelers had the same reaction as Amy. Their favorite band had gotten much better since the last time they heard it. They got as close to the band as they could, and shouted out their appreciation like bloodthirsty fans at a boxing ring.

Jesse was shocked to see Dupre dancing right in front of him, doing a two-step without a partner. Dupre wasn't limping anymore. The Safari fire injury had healed. He waved at Jesse with the sarcastic wit of an inmate who'd just gotten out of federal prison. It was so loud in the club that Jesse had to read his lips when he pointed all eight fingers at himself and said, "I can't believe I'm here."

Rose, the Italian woman, was also dancing right up front. She was doing a hippy shake that caused her short black skirt to ride up dangerously high. She had not given up on Jesse.

Jesse saw Amy making her way through the crowd. He waved the bass at her, and gave her a big smile. This was going to be interesting, he thought, having Rose and Amy in the same spot. Rose turned around to see what Jesse was smiling at. When she saw Amy, Rose turned back to glower at Jesse. Jesse wouldn't meet her stare.

The band finished the second set with a spirited rendition of "Your Cheating Heart" by Hank Williams. They didn't play it like Hank's slow rolling version. They played it like the English punk rock band, the Sex Pistols, hard and fast. The crowd loved it. Country punk had come to town.

Once the band took a break, Dupre came up to give Jesse a big hug before Jesse could put down his bass guitar. The biker crowded Amy out until Jesse took her into his arms for a welcome-to-Shreveport kiss. Rose was standing right next to Amy after the kiss.

Jesse thought he was going to have to introduce the two women until Amy spared him the trouble. "Hi, I'm Amy. Jesse and I are getting married in June."

It was a definite "back off, he's mine" move. Rose looked at Jesse, who smiled to let her know it was true. Rose turned around abruptly and disappeared into the crowd.

"Who was that?" Amy asked. "She didn't look too happy to hear you were getting married."

"She's just another music lover," Jesse said as he hugged Amy to reassure her.

Meanwhile, The Wheelers were taking center stage. Dale reached out to greet Dupre. "It's so good to see you, big daddy. We were worried about you."

Dupre pretended to be offended. "So worried you left town."

Butch came over and shook Dupre's hand. "Dupre, how's it going, man? I see you beat the heat."

Big Ben from the Wheelers joined the reunion. "The heat's been dodged. All is well. And I got to say, you guys sound better than ever. Who is this keyboard player?"

Rick looked up warily at the giant biker. "I'm Rick. You must be Big Ben. I've heard good things about you. I'm the keyboard man, the one with the big organ."

Everybody laughed as The Wheelers and The Divebomberz got down to hand shaking and back slapping. The rest of the crowd gave the band and the motorcycle gang all the room they needed.

Johnny sent over several trays of drinks. As the beer and tequila were arriving, Dupre managed to whisper in Jesse's ear. "I don't want to alarm you, but I'm told our bikes outside have attracted some unwanted attention."

"From the police?" Jesse asked.

"No, some bike club up here," Dupre said. "Don't worry, we won't start anything if they don't."

"That's not very comforting," Jesse said as Amy wrapped her arms around him.

Amy was excited. "The band sounds so hot I can't believe it. And, hello, Dupre. Is that really you? Last time I saw you, you were giving me some serious trouble at the Safari Club."

"Aw, you know I was just foolin' 'round. And don't forget I helped Jesse save you from being buried alive."

"That you did," Amy said as she hugged him carefully. "And I will always thank you for it."

Dupre graciously bowed out of the hug. "Good to see your beautiful face again. We rode all the way up here to Shreveport to hear our favorite band. And I have to agree with you, they sound great. They keep getting better and better. It won't be long before they'll be too big to pay any attention to us little people."

"That will never happen," Tim said as he moved to greet Dupre and Big Ben.

Big Ben opened his arms wide for Tim. "There's the best fiddle player in the world. We all figured you'd of left this bunch of losers by now."

Tim laughed. "Oh, no. Haven't you heard? We're headed for the top."

"The top of what?" Dupre asked.

Tim got close to Dupre. "The top of the Royal Royce Hotel after this joint closes down. I hope you'll come up and party with us."

Dupre was visibly pleased by the invitation. He tilted his head back to laugh and held his arms up to an imaginary heaven. Then he came back to the moment. "Cool. I'll send one of the boys to get us some rooms. We need a place to crash. It's getting a little chilly to camp out."

The band retired to Johnny's upstairs office for what was left of their break. Amy joined them. The Wheelers did not. There were too many of them.

Amy was eager to see the bartender deliver drinks to the second story window. She wanted to see if the stories were true.

Once they were in Johnny's office, Amy addressed the band. "I didn't realize you guys are such a big deal up here. Jesse told me the crowds were good, but these people are absolutely rabid. I see why you have to take your breaks up here. And what's with The Wheelers being here? Did they know I was coming, or what?"

Dale was happy to see Amy. "You seem to attract bikers; bikers and musicians. How was your drive up?"

Amy stretched her arms out to hug Dale. "Much longer than I expected. This place is all the way to Arkansas. I left school a little early. It took more than six hours to get here. I thought I was going to miss you."

As she spoke, a knock on the window startled her. It was the bartender with a round of drinks, including one for Amy.

Butch laughed as she jumped at the sound. "You knew it was coming and it still scared you when it got here."

"I must say," Amy said as drinks were delivered through the upstairs window. "This is something you have to experience to believe."

"So you haven't checked into the Royal Royce yet?" Rene asked.

"No, and all my stuff is in the car," Amy said. "Will it be safe? It's parked around the corner."

Butch reassured her. "Downtown Shreveport is quiet, except for Johnny's. You'll be fine."

After their short break, the band went down to start the third set in a timely fashion. The bar was more crowded than when they had left. Jesse looked out over the heads as they kicked off the set and realized a problem was developing. He saw at least twenty bikers he had never seen before. They weren't with the Wheelers. He could tell by their black leather jackets. He couldn't make out the insignia, but it wasn't a flaming wheel.

There were no problems throughout most of the third set. The place was rocking out in a peaceful manner. Then, the sea seemed to cave in near the center of the room. Jesse could see a hole opening up in the crowd. He knew it was a fight. People were going down.

Amy was sitting at a round table in the center of the room when the violence erupted at the table behind her. It wasn't two men going at it. It was two women, and the fight was ugly from the start. They were kicking and clawing and pulling each other's hair out, drawing blood and screaming loudly enough to be heard over the band.

The Divebomberz stopped playing as they always did when a fight broke out. The two women went down on the floor and disappeared under the table. When one man bent down to break up the fight, another man attacked him. The fight spread like wildfire. Soon, bikers were entering the fray. Jesse could see fists flailing in the air. In an instant, the club turned into a riot zone.

Jesse caught a glimpse of Amy putting her head on the table and trying to cover up with her hands. She was smack dab in the middle of the worst bar brawl he had ever seen.

Johnny vaulted over the main bar like a rodeo clown and did a quick draw on the cans of mace hanging on either side of his belt. His movement was so fluid he didn't even lose his cowboy hat. Jesse watched in awe as Johnny bounced into the center of the fight in what seemed like slow motion and sprayed down the entire area with mace. Women were screaming. Men were shouting and cursing. Tables were overturning. Chairs were flying. Johnny kept spraying until the peppery mist became overwhelming. He alone seemed unaffected by the toxic cloud he was dispensing. People began choking and trying to get out of the contaminated zone as fast as they could.

Jesse threw his bass guitar down and fought his way through the panicking and fleeing people, trying to rescue Amy.

By the time he reached her, Amy was sitting alone at the table with her hands still over her head. Johnny had chased most of the crowd out the front door. Jesse grabbed her by the shoulders. She fought him off until she realized who he was. Jesse screamed at her. "Amy, Amy, we've got to get out of here."

Amy raised her head off the table and gradually realized it was Jesse. "I can't breathe. I can't see. What's going on?"

Jesse was choking up himself. "We've been maced. Let's go."

Dale was right by Jesse's side. They scooped Amy up and whisked her back upstairs and into Johnny's office. The rest of the band came up too. It didn't take long to realize they couldn't stay in the office. They were so covered with mace they had to open the window and walk down the fire escape to air out. By this time, Amy's tears from the mace were mixed with sobbing from the violence she had been close enough to feel in her bones.

She tried to talk. "When you got me from the table. I could see the one girl's legs still under the table. She only had one shoe on and her leg seemed to be twitching. Is she going to be all right?"

Jesse handed her a towel he had grabbed on the way out. "Yeah, she just got knocked out. She's going to be fine."

Amy tried to wipe off her face. "How do you know?"

Jesse looked at Dale. "You know, I don't know. Let me go back in and check. Will you stay here with her, Dale? I'll try to bring back some wet towels to get the mace off her."

"Bring a bunch of towels," Butch said. "We're all contaminated."

The band stayed with Amy while Jesse went back to the front door of the bar to check the damage. Mace hung in the air like poison gas in a trench of war. It hurt his eyes to even look in the door. He noticed the motorcycles had all vanished into the night. The Wheelers weren't ones to hang around and wait for the police to make the scene.

Johnny was helping a woman to her car. The woman was holding one shoe in her hand and looking quite dazed.

"Is that the woman from under the table?" Jesse asked.

Johnny answered without looking up. "Yep, she's going to be fine. Isn't that right, dahlin'?"

The woman nodded and gulped deep breaths of fresh air as she bent down to put her shoe back on. Johnny had to steady her. "You shouldn't be driving just yet. Tell you what. I'll have somebody drive you home."

"Did you call the police?" Jesse asked.

Johnny smiled politely. "Not unless someone gets killed. The only people I'll call will be the cleaning company. I've got to get this place ready for tomorrow night."

Jesse watched in amazement as Johnny arranged for the woman to be driven home in an old Ford pickup truck. The man actually cares, Jesse thought as he ducked into the bar to get an armful of towels.

He found Amy in the alley and walked her to the hotel in silence. Before entering the Royal Royce, she took off her clothes, including her bra and panties, and threw them in a trashcan. Jesse wrapped her in a big towel he'd found behind the bar, and took her up to the room.

Amy wouldn't look at him. "I never want to smell those clothes again."

Jesse hugged her close. "Chances are good you won't."

"You really know how to entertain a girl," Amy said as they reached the room. "The bar fight, the mace, the antique elevator, the purple everything. It couldn't be more heavenly."

She got in the shower without making eye contact. Jesse thought she might not speak to him for the rest of the night. Then he heard her humming a little as she washed the mace out of her hair. He was listening right outside the bathroom door. She must have known he was there.

"Come on in. The water's hot and wonderful."

In that moment, Jesse realized, once again, how much he loved this woman. Deep down, she was tough and resilient. He remembered the day, many months earlier, when he decided to ask Amy to come live with him in New Orleans. He was talking to Casey about what seemed an impossible situation. Amy was in Indiana. Jesse had no money and no way to get to her. The band was living off the tip jar at Fritzel's on Bourbon Street. He'd just spent his last five dollars on breakfast for him and Casey.

Jesse confided in his friend. "She won't come down unless I ask her to marry me. And it's got to be in person. The telephone won't do. That's what she said. I get the feeling she's been talking to my mother."

Casey contemplated the situation for a short time before responding. "You've got to get up there. I've got a little cash set aside. I'll buy your plane ticket."

"I can't let you do that."

"You can't stop me from doing it," Casey said. "I've heard you talking about this girl for too long now. In all the years we've been friends, I've never seen you like this over a woman."

Jesse remembered getting down on one knee for Amy in the family kitchen in Indiana, in front of his mother and father and three sisters. Amy laughed and said "yes" when he proposed. She cried when he stood up to kiss her. He didn't have a ring and she didn't care. His mother served homemade carrot cake. His father took Jesse aside to say he approved of Amy. "I'm glad to see you marrying a good woman. You know, it might be a good time to think about going to law school."

"Not now," Jesse said to his father with no anger or even a sigh of exasperation. "I'm having way too much fun."

All the details of the marriage proposal flashed through his mind as he got in the shower with Amy. He was ready to wash the mace out of his hair.

They stayed naked for the rest of the night. Neither one of them mentioned the terrible bar fight. Violence was the last thing they wanted to talk about . . . Love was busy conquering all. It was dawn when they fell into a blissful slumber in each other's arms.

The next afternoon Amy drove back to New Orleans by herself. Jesse didn't try to talk her out of it. He knew he had lost her support for the band's never-ending road trip. Without Amy cheering him on, he wondered how much longer The Divebomberz could survive the hazardous duty of playing rowdy roadhouses.

"Amy left," Jesse said to Butch as the two of them had lunch at a diner near Johnny's.

Butch finished chewing and swallowed a bite of his burger. "Can you blame her? She could have been seriously hurt last night. It's amazing she wasn't. She was right in the middle of the worst fight I've ever seen. I'm surprised nobody got killed."

"A couple people got hurt. Johnny never called the cops."

Butch gestured toward Jesse with a French fry. "Johnny wouldn't call the cops if he was surrounded by zombies."

Jesse couldn't resist. "He is surrounded by zombies every night."

Butch had to agree. "Drunks, zombies, what's the diff? I

can't believe we're playing tonight. You'd think Johnny would take a day off after a riot like last night."

"Not a chance," Jesse said. "It's Saturday night. He'll raise the cover charge and double the drink prices. People will pay good money to return to the scene of chaos and mayhem."

Saturday night started off slowly at Johnny's Cimarron Club. Word had spread about the Friday night fight. Some folks thought the club would be shut down, but all the regulars knew Johnny's would be open for business as usual. Johnny had a crew working most of the day to clean out the mace and the blood. They mopped the floors and walls and ceilings and tables and chairs. Giant fans and open doors kept the crew from succumbing to the fumes. They had the place smelling like a woman's restroom by opening time.

Johnny hung a large banner under his front sign that said, "No Colors." By 10 p.m., the club was packed as though nothing had happened the night before.

CHAPTER TWENTY-SIX

DALLAS ALICE

Several weeks after the macing, Jesse and Butch were rudely awakened on a Monday morning by the Dallas police banging on the side of the van. It was not quite 7 a.m. when Jesse slid the side door open to see two officers pointing their pistols at his head.

He resisted the urge to slam the door shut in their faces. He had to think fast and be polite. "Good morning, officers. Did we do something wrong?"

"You're parked in a residential neighborhood," the older officer said. "We got a caller says you been here most of the night. People are afraid you might be one of them Charlie Manson types."

Butch poked his head out from under a blanket, causing the two officers to point their weapons at him. He ducked back under the covers like blankets would protect him from bullets.

"Come on Butch," Jesse said. "You can't hide from the law. They can still see you."

Butch uncovered himself and tried to regroup. "Is there any way I can get you to stop pointing those guns at me?"

The police realized there was no need for weapons and holstered their side arms quickly.

Jesse tried to explain. "We're musicians on the road. Our band is The Divebomberz. We're here to see Steven Mory, the attorney who represents bands. We didn't want to pay for a hotel room. This street looked okay. We're sorry if we scared anybody. We'll get out of here right away."

As Jesse spoke, he noticed and remembered they had an open bag of marijuana in plain view on the console between the two front seats. How could they have been so stupid?

Butch realized the situation about the same time as Jesse. He started making small talk with the cops as a diversion. As long as they were looking at him in the side door, they wouldn't look in the front seat to see illegal drugs lying all over the place.

"I hope we haven't upset the neighbors too much," Butch said. "Honest to God, we didn't even think about that. We should have been more considerate. We were just looking for a safe place to crash."

The two officers looked at each other. The younger officer held out his hands as if to say, "Maybe we should let them go." The older officer looked at Butch and said, "Okay, I'll tell you what. If you guys leave here right now, we'll let you go. We won't even give you a ticket."

Butch reached out to shake the officers' hands in thanks. That was all the cover Jesse needed.

"Thank you so much, officers," Jesse said as he got behind the wheel. He swept the marijuana under the driver's seat and put the key in the ignition with one fluid motion. Neither officer saw the sweeping move to hide the drugs. They were too busy shaking Butch's hand.

The younger officer started waving goodbye. "You know, I've heard of you guys. You play Johnny's in Shreveport every now and then, don't you?"

Butch was surprised and flattered by a Dallas cop knowing about the band. "Why, yes we do. How do you know Johnny's?"

"Believe it or not, one of my sisters works there."

"What's her name?" Jesse asked.

"Her name is Alice. She's real cute, about five-eight, blonde, thirty-four years old."

"We know Alice," Butch and Jesse said together.

"She's Johnny's right hand girl," Jesse said. "We love Alice."

"Small world," the older officer said as he started walking away.

The younger officer moved in closer. "Next time you see her. Say her little brother, Bobby, let you off the hook in Dallas."

Jesse put the van in drive. "That will be our great pleasure."

Butch said goodbye to the police as he slid the van door closed. Jesse drove away slowly, scarcely able to believe their good fortune. Butch said nothing until they were out of the neighborhood. "Smooth move on the marijuana."

Jesse wasn't about to take the credit. "No, that was all about you. Way to go, shaking their hands. That gave me all the time I needed."

Butch breathed a huge sigh of relief. "Man, nothing beats waking up with guns pointed at your head."

Jesse pounded on the steering wheel in triumph. "I can't wait to tell Alice about her little brother, Bobby the cop, letting us go in Dallas."

"I don't think we should mention the marijuana to her," Butch said.

"No, absolutely not," Jesse agreed. "But can you believe we left it out in plain view like that?"

Butch reached under the driver's seat to retrieve the marijuana. "Why do you think they call it dope?"

It was May 22, 1978. The band had been playing, non-stop for months. Jesse was keenly aware of the date because he and Amy were getting married on top of a sand dune in Pentwater, Michigan, on June 16, less than a month away.

The band would be driving much too far to play the wedding. The only gigs they had for the Michigan trip were a "Lunch in the Park" show in Indianapolis on June 7 and a private party in Fort Wayne, Indiana, on June 10. Jesse knew that two bookings for a two-thousand-mile road trip was a recipe for rock and roll disaster.

But on this fine, Dallas morning, Jesse was feeling euphoric. "I can't believe that cop is Alice's brother. Butch, I do believe we're two of the luckiest cats on the planet. In fact, I predict we're going to get in to see Steven Mory today and he's going to sign us to a management contract and put us in a fantastic recording studio."

Butch was used to Jesse waxing expansive. "You might be going too far out on a limb with all that. This attorney doesn't know who we are and we don't even have an appointment with him."

Jesse had heard about Atty. Steven Mory from the musicians in Loose Boots, a band they'd met in Shreveport. The bass player made the recommendation to Jesse one night on the roof of the Royal Royce Hotel. "If you want management and a chance to get in the studio and go for a recording contract, Steve Mory is your man. He put us in the studio, a good one, right outside Dallas. He's big and getting bigger. He's about to manage Bob Dylan's next touring band."

That was enough to start Jesse booking the band in a series of cowboy bars on the way to Dallas. He knew the bit about Bob Dylan was probably bullshit. But Loose Boots was a damn good band. If Steve Mory was good enough for them, The Divebomberz would give him a shot.

Five hours after being held at gunpoint by the police, Jesse and

Butch were walking into the well-appointed personal office of Atty. Steven Mory.

"You guys look like rock stars," the attorney said as he shook their hands warmly. He was a charmer, in his mid-thirties, wearing an expensive, three-piece suit with a wide tie. His black hair was straight and fell over his collar. He looked like Prince Valiant from the adventure comic strip. Butch and Jesse had enough hair on their heads and faces for five guys. Jesse's hair was frizzy and wide and three feet long. Butch's blonde hair was halfway down his back. The two of them were beginning to look as wild as their life style. They had managed to shower and change clothes at the home of a musician friend in Dallas. They knew Atty. Mory's telephone number. One miraculous call later, they were invited to his office.

Jesse looked around the wood-paneled room and tried not to seem too impressed. "Thanks for seeing us on such short notice. The guys in Loose Boots say you're really helping them a lot."

"You caught me at a perfect time. I had a court hearing cancel this morning. I've got some time. Sit down, gentlemen. Take a load off. And, yes, I represent Loose Boots. Great band, don't you think?"

Butch sat down carefully in a leather chair. "We love their sound. They're playing a lot of the same clubs we are."

"The important thing is you're working steady," Atty. Mory said. "That says it all. If you can get work in this age of disco, you've got to have what it takes. In fact, I've been following The Divebomberz for a couple months now. My people tell me you've got it going on. Something about a fiddle player and an organ maestro and some great original songs?"

Jesse leaned forward in his chair. "That's us. Psychedelic, bluegrass, rock and roll."

The attorney laughed out loud at the zany description, then buzzed his secretary for three cups of black coffee without asking Butch and Jesse if they wanted any or how they liked it. "Country rock is where it's at. I'd say your band is right in the pocket from what I've heard. By the way, how old are you, Jesse?"

"I'm twenty-eight."

"How about you, Butch?" He was good with names.

"Twenty-five."

The attorney winced. "Man, you guys better get a move on. It's getting late. This is a young man's game. You're already getting a little long in the tooth."

"But we still look good," Butch said.

Atty. Mory laughed. "Yes, you do. Like I said, you look the part. Having the look is a good start. Having the songs and the performance skills is much more important."

Jesse was feeling confident as the secretary arrived and served the coffee. "We've got the original tunes. In fact, we'll prove it to you if you give us a shot in the studio."

Atty. Mory leaned back in his high-backed chair. "I like your attitude."

They talked for quite a while about where the band was playing and how big the crowds were. Atty. Mory was interested in the latest reports from the road. Of course, Johnny's name came up.

"So I hear you've been going over quite well at Johnny's Cimarron Club in Shreveport."

Butch answered. "Between us and the motorcycle gangs, that place is rockin' every night."

"I know it's a rough joint," Atty. Mory said. "Johnny's a character, isn't he? I heard he maced the place down one night and had it open for business the next night."

"We were playing the night of the great macing episode," Jesse said as he wondered how the attorney knew so much about the club. "Do you talk to Johnny?"

The attorney took a sip of coffee. "No, I talk to his main gal, Alice. She's one of my scouts."

Butch and Jesse looked at each other in disbelief. Alice, a woman they barely knew, suddenly seemed at the center of their world. Could it be the same Alice whose brother was a Dallas cop? It had to be.

"What did she say about us?" Butch asked.

"You know it was good. You wouldn't be sitting here if it wasn't pretty damn good."

Jesse wanted details. "But what did she say? Inquiring minds need to know."

Atty. Mory began slowly. "Okay, I don't want to violate any confidences here, and I don't want to make your heads get too big. But she said you're the best band she's ever seen at Johnny's."

Butch nearly spilled his coffee. "Wow. That's quite a compliment, coming from her. She treats us like we're just another band."

"No offense, but you are just another band to her. She's been at Johnny's too long. Don't tell anybody, but I'm thinking of bringing her to Dallas to be part of my organization."

"Then she'll be Dallas Alice," Jesse said.

Butch and Jesse were pleased to see Atty. Mory laugh and recognize the Dallas Alice reference from the song "Willin" by Lowell George of the eclectic rock band, Little Feat. The rock and roll lawyer knew his music.

It was hard for Jesse and Butch to keep from telling Atty. Mory that Alice's younger brother, the Dallas cop, had briefly held them at gunpoint earlier in the day. It wouldn't do to let on they were still sleeping in the band van.

The attorney suddenly had a question. "Who writes the songs?"

"We do," Jesse and Butch said in unison.

He toasted them with his coffee cup. "Good. Looks like I'm talking to the right people. It's all about the copyright."

He leaned forward in his chair and put his elbows on the desk with his fingers interlocked to make a resting shelf for his chin. He looked at Jesse, then at Butch. Then he took a deep breath and let out a long, thoughtful sigh.

"Tell you what. I'm going to take a flyer on you guys and put you in the studio. Let's see how you sound on tape. If it works out, we'll sign a deal. You'll both be key men on the contract, it will be exclusive, all advances will be recoupable and my organization will own the tape. How does that sound?"

Jesse looked at Butch with raised eyebrows, scarcely able to believe what he had just heard. The fact that he didn't understand much of what the attorney had said bothered Jesse, but he liked the part about going to the studio to record.

"It sounds great," Jesse said, trying to hide his excitement and confusion.

"Count me in," Butch said.

Atty. Mory rose from his chair to escort them out of his office. "Perfect. You'll fill out an information form with my assistant so I can get in touch with you to make arrangements for the recording session. Don't worry. We're not signing any contracts at this point. We'll get to know each other a little better before we sign up. So, good . . . any questions?"

Jesse thought about mentioning the wedding tour to Michigan for the sake of scheduling, then thought better of it. No point complicating matters unduly.

He shook the attorney's hand. "No questions. We're looking forward to working with you."

Atty. Mory led them into his assistant's office. "Maurice, these are new clients of ours. Could you please open up a file under the name, The Divebomberz?"

Maurice took over as Atty. Mory left to return to his office.

"Wow," she said as Jesse filled out the client data form. "That was fast. You were in there less an hour. I've never seen a file get opened so fast. He must really like you."

Jesse and Butch rode back to Shreveport on a pink cloud.

Butch was the first to speak. "All these tie-ins with Alice are downright spooky. It's like the Voodoo is connecting the dots for us."

"Alice in Wonderland," Jesse mused aloud.

"What does the Voodoo voice have to say about all this?" Butch asked. "You said this morning that we'd meet with the attorney and he'd put us in the studio. I thought you were crazy. Now, it all happened, just like you said it would. Is there something you're not telling me?"

Jesse kept his eyes on the road. "No, I haven't heard the voice in quite a while. But I do know this. There's no such thing as coincidence. I need to get with Carmen about this Alice thing. It's weird, but it does go along with my two favorite theories."

"Let's see," Butch said. "The little things of today foretell the big things of tomorrow."

"That's one," Jesse said.

"And we find people to teach us what we need to learn."

"Amazing," Jesse said.

"Not so amazing," Butch said. "I've only heard you say them a thousand times."

Jesse didn't respond. It felt like Butch was telling him he repeated himself too much.

Butch realized why Jesse got quiet. "No, no, don't get

offended. I love your theories. I don't see how they apply here. But I love your theories."

Jesse decided to expound. "Think of the cops this morning as all the trouble we've had trying to get a tape made. Then think of Alice as the Voodoo voice, guiding us. Atty. Mory is the guy who will teach us what we need to know. I'm telling you, today is telling us we're going to land a contract with a record company in the very near future."

Butch thought about Jesse's prediction for a good ten miles. "I hope you're right. So, Atty. Mory is the guy we created to teach us what we need to know about the music business?"

"Exactly," Jesse said.

Butch began rolling a joint. "I'll tell you one thing. He's the first guy who ever made me feel old."

"He's the first guy to make me feel like I need to be a lawyer," Jesse said.

"What do you mean by that?" Butch asked.

"I mean I didn't understand anything he said once he started talking about contracts. I did hear the word 'exclusive' and I'm not sure I like that. I also heard the word 'recoupable,' and that sounds like we've got to pay him back for putting us in the studio."

Butch shared Jesse's concerns. "What about his company owning the tapes? Does that mean he owns the songs?"

"I think ownership of a production, or the tapes, is different than ownership of the songs. But again, I don't understand it. These are things we need to know. Every band we read about has signed a bad deal, early on, that took them years to escape. I'd call my father for legal help, but he would just say go to law school. That's what he always says."

Butch saw the irony in the situation. "So, what? We need to hire a lawyer to make a deal with our lawyer?"

"Let's see how it goes," Jesse said. "For now, we've got three nights in Natchitoches and then we leave for Michigan. I don't think we can even pay for the gas to get there."

Butch moaned at the thought. "You're the one getting married on top of a sand dune in . . . what's the name of the town?"

Jesse turned to look at him. "Pentwater. It's going to be fun. The band will set up on a sand dune overlooking Lake Michigan and we'll have a great party."

"How much are we getting paid for the wedding?" Butch asked.

"A golden memory for the rest of your life."

Butch squirmed in his seat. "Why couldn't you guys get married in New Orleans, like normal people?"

Jesse turned to look at him. "You know why. All our family and most of our friends are up north."

Butch tried to put a positive spin on things. "You know the band will follow you anywhere. If we survive this so-called wedding tour, maybe Atty. Mory will put us on a fast track to a recording contract."

CHAPTER TWENTY-SEVEN

JAIL HOUSE ROCK

Jesse was alone and driving the band van to the gig in Natchitoches. The rest of the band was traveling in other vehicles. He looked in his rearview mirror and saw he was being stopped by the Louisiana State Police. A quick glance to the speedometer showed he was doing 75 mph in a 55 mph zone. He slowed down quickly and pulled over to stop.

He was glad he'd gotten his Louisiana driver's license when he handed it over to the trooper with the vehicle registration. An out-of-state license would have gotten him thrown in jail until the ticket was paid. He'd learned that lesson the hard way in New Orleans.

The trooper went back to his car but returned in short order to the van. Jesse could tell from the stern expression behind the reflector sunglasses that things were not going well.

"Out of the car, now," the trooper barked.

"What's the problem, officer?" Jesse asked as he began exiting the van.

The trooper had his hands on his hips. "No problem. You're going to jail. I don't have a problem with that, do you?"

The officer spun Jesse around and slammed him face first into the side of the van. Jesse knew better than to fight back. "I thought I was getting a ticket."

The cop frisked Jesse roughly." You got a ticket for running a red light in New Orleans. You didn't bother to pay it. You're what we call a scofflaw." He punctuated the word with two fists into Jesse's armpits as he continued the frisk. "You don't think the rules apply to you. There's a warrant out for your arrest, son. It's for failure to appear in court. Judges don't take kindly to people thumbing their noses at the court." He finished the search by yanking Jesse's hair up to check his neck. "Put your hands behind your back. I'm taking you into custody."

The trooper put the cuffs around Jesse's wrists.

"But I'm a musician and my band's got a gig in Natchitoches in three hours," Jesse pleaded.

"I guess I should have known that from all the hair you're throwing around. Maybe they'll give you a free haircut at the jail."

"What about the van?" Jesse asked. "All our equipment is in there."

"We'll have it towed to the jail at your expense," the trooper said as he escorted Jesse to the back seat of his car.

The handcuffs were cutting into Jesse's wrists. "Can you loosen these things? They're killing me."

"It's a short ride," the trooper said.

Jesse didn't say another word as he was driven to the Parrish jail. The trooper turned out to be a downright gentleman compared to the two jailors who pushed Jesse into a solitary cell like he was public enemy number one.

The fat jailor was missing lots of teeth. "Looks like we'll have to cut that hair for your own safety."

"How do you spell head lice?" The skinny jailor slammed the cell door much harder than necessary.

"You must be in one of those hard rock bands," the fat jailor said.

Jesse tried hard to be nice. "No, we play country music. You'd like the band."

Both jailors got a good laugh out of that.

"Nobody's going to like your band tonight," the fat jailor said. "You got a no bond warrant."

Jesse thought they were going to hang around to torment him, but they left without saying anything more. He looked around, through the bars, and didn't see any other prisoners. The silence was deafening. It was worse being alone than being harassed. He felt like a complete fool for forgetting to pay the red light ticket in New Orleans. The words to his song, "Red Light," echoed in his head. "It's so much fun running red lights. Specially in the dark without no headlights."

How could he be so stupid as to end up in jail twice on traffic tickets? Spending the day in the New Orleans jail should have taught him a lesson. He could end up forcing the band to cancel gigs for who knew how long. No way they could continue without him or the equipment. Most of the sound system was in the van, which was probably being hooked up to a tow truck at that very moment.

At least he hadn't been high or in possession of marijuana. By some unusual state of affairs, there was no contraband in the van. Jesse had run out the day before and he was due to score from Rene at the gig.

Knowing what Amy would say was the worst part. His irresponsibility drove her crazy. She wouldn't say, "I told you so." She wouldn't have to say that now. She had "told him so" a thousand times already.

Admitting to himself in the confines of a jail cell that she had been right was hard enough. Knowing he had let her down again was even harder. They were getting married in less than a month and here he was in jail again. Having a partner who cared was a good thing, he realized. It made him want to live up to her expectations. Unfortunately, he was living up to her worst fears.

Jesse spent the first half hour in jail on the pity pot, feeling sorry for himself. That proved completely unproductive. He had to think. He had to think his way out of jail. Or, maybe, he could sing his way out. He started singing the words to Hank William's song, "Jambalaya," at a fairly high volume. He guessed that country music might be his only connection with the jailors.

Sure enough, the skinny jailor came in and said, "I wouldn't think a long hair would know any country music, much less all the words to a Hank Williams song. And, I hate to say it, but you don't sound half bad."

We play lots of country music, even bluegrass. We've got a fiddle player who will blow your mind."

"What's he play?" the jailor asked.

"Orange Blossom Special, Foggy Mountain Breakdown, you name it, we play it."

"Foggy Mountain Breakdown's a banjo tune," the jailor said.

Jesse realized he was making a musical connection. "You should hear it with a fiddle and a screaming Hammond B-3 organ."

The jailer looked at Jesse like he couldn't believe the long-haired Yankee was making musical sense. "Tell you what. Sing one more Hank song. If you know all the words, I'll let you make a call."

"Are we talking about a musical bribe here?" Jesse asked.

"Call it whatever you want," the jailer said as he sat down on a metal bench for a good listen.

Jesse sang "Your Cheatin' Heart" for all he was worth, even throwing in hand gestures and dance steps. It sounded good. Not Hank Williams good, but good enough. The acoustics in the jail had a nice echo to them. Jesse was most surprised when the jailer started singing a wonderful high harmony on the chorus.

Jesse was amazed by how good they sounded. They laughed together when the song was over. Jesse stuck his head between the bars. "You've been doing some singing in your time."

The jailer nodded. "My brother and I been singing together and playing in bands since we were kids. We always wanted to take it on the road like you're doing."

"Why didn't you? Why don't you? You sound pretty darned professional to me."

The jailer was flattered. "Well, thank you very much. What happened was this. We both got married and had kids. And I'm not saying it happened exactly in that order if you know what I mean."

Jesse backed off the bars. "I'm getting married in about a month."

"Is she pregnant?" the jailer asked.

"Not that I know of."

The jailer stood up and put both hands on the bars between them for emphasis. "Then don't do it. Long as you can stay free, you stay free. Look what happened to me and my brother."

"It doesn't look like you're doing so bad," Jesse said.

"Don't let the badge and the uniform fool you," the jailer said. "I'd trade places with you in a heartbeat if I could."

"You do remember you've got me locked up here for who knows how long," Jesse said.

"Oh, don't worry about this. All you've got is traffic tickets. Get your people here with money and you'll be on the road again in no time."

"Does this mean you're not going to shave my head like you were talking about when you threw me in here?"

"We were just scaring you, seeing what you was made of," the jailer said. "Course, if you'd been a real asshole, we would have given you a trim you'd never forget."

Jesse got to make his call. He was hoping pretty hard that Rene's father would answer the phone. The rest of the band would be on the road and unavailable by telephone.

Mercifully, on the fifth ring, Burt picked up the phone.

"How the hell did you end up in jail?" he asked.

Jesse explained the unpaid ticket from New Orleans and the new speeding ticket.

Burt did not sound pleased. "What did you think would happen if you didn't pay the ticket or at least go to court?"

"To be honest. I forgot all about the red light ticket. I wasn't trying to play games."

"I'll be right there," Burt said as he hung up the phone.

In an hour and a half, Burt and Rene were welcoming Jesse out of jail.

Jesse was more than happy to see them. "How'd you get me out so fast?"

"It cost us almost four hundred to pay the red light ticket and the speeding ticket and the tow," Burt said. "Once we paid, you were free to go."

"Thank you so much," Jesse said as he hugged Burt and Rene. "It's good to be a free man again."

As they were walking out of the jail, Jesse stopped and turned around to say to the singing jailer, "Come on up to the show tonight. We'll put you on a microphone."

The jailer laughed and waved. "Sing 'em some Hank tonight."

"What was that?" Burt asked as they walked out. "Old home week?"

"Just call it a little jail house rock," Jesse said.

Rene didn't laugh at the joke. He gave Jesse a look like he was more trouble than he was worth. "We're going to have to hurry to make the gig. And don't forget, the four hundred for your fines came out of the band account. You'll have to pay us back."

CHAPTER TWENTY-EIGHT

RUNNING ON EMPTY

The gig at Natchitoches went well. By Sunday, the band had enough money to think they might be ready to survive the wedding tour to Michigan, even though they only had two gigs booked. Louisiana to Indiana was a long way between bookings.

The Lunch on the Lawn performance near the capital building in Indianapolis was better than Jesse expected. The downtown park was packed with at least five hundred people. The government workers were surprised by the intensity of the music. They were not quite ready to be jolted out of their dress socks at noon by a hard-driving band. The crowd loved the surprise and cheered wildly after every song. It was Friday and people were ready to party.

The gig had been set up back when the band was playing on Bourbon Street at Fritzel's. A half-drunk woman said she'd send a contract and, amazingly, the contract arrived in the mail about a month later. Jesse signed it, thinking the gig would be one of many on the band's northern tour. That was well before the trip was all about Amy and Jesse getting married.

The band looked particularly heroic on the stage in Indianapolis, which was a flatbed truck trailer between two tall Oak trees. The wind was strong out of the south and blowing everybody's hair like they were riding horses into battle. The Divebomberz had not had a gig or a rehearsal in more than a week, but they sounded tight and powerful. The time off had been an energizing break. Even Rick was complimentary after the gig. "I almost forgot how much fun it is to play with you guys."

That was quite a comment from Rick, who had been bitterly complaining about the impossible logistics of what he called the "tour of fools."

The performance was scheduled to last an hour, but nobody in the crowd seemed in a hurry to get back to work. The band played three encores, and people were still screaming for more when the organizers signaled the band to stop.

Amy was busy taking pictures of Jesse. Terri was doing the same with Butch, Loretta with Tim and Polly with Rene. Rick and Dale were the only two members of the band who didn't have their girlfriends on the trip. Even so, they did their best to be in all the photos.

Amy had the women of the band organized into a t-shirt selling machine. The shirts were wildly popular since they said The Divebomberz and New Orleans. It was t-shirt profits that would keep the band in food and gas for the poorly scheduled wedding tour. Plus, each woman had money of her own.

After the show in the park, a friend of Jesse's from college came up to say hello. He was wearing a coat and tie and seemed impressed by Jesse's wild lifestyle. "Man, you guys look like you're having so much fun up there, doing your very own thing. I envy you."

"It's not nearly as glamorous as it looks," Jesse said. "We've got ten people on the road to Pentwater, Michigan, and not enough gigs to get us there."

"What's going on in Michigan?" he asked.

"I'm getting married," Jesse said as Amy came up to join him. "And, here she is now, the girl of my dreams. Amy, meet Craig. We went to school together."

Craig ignored Amy and seemed flabbergasted by the news. "You're getting married? You've got to be kidding."

Amy did not appreciate his tone. "No. We're not kidding. And, no, I'm not pregnant."

"It's true love," Jesse said.

Craig tried to back pedal from his total amazement that Jesse would be getting married. "Congratulations to the both of you. And I must say, Amy, you are one brave girl."

"I know, that's what everybody says," Amy said to Craig. Then she turned to Jesse and asked, "Why do all your old friends act so surprised when they find out you're getting married?"

"They're jealous I found someone so beautiful as you," Jesse said.

"Good answer," Amy and Craig said in unison.

Two nights later, the band found itself playing an impromptu gig in a large event tent in Fort Wayne, Indiana, hometown of Jesse, Butch, Dale and Tim. All their old friends came out to see if The Divebomberz were as good as the rumor mill said they were. An organization called The Theatre for Ideas sponsored the tent as part of the city's summer festival. There was no pay for this gig. The band would have to pass the hat in order to make any money. Dale knew the people in charge and had set up the last-minute performance. It was a happening. All the old hippies came out to party. The sixties didn't die in the Midwest until 1979. Of course, they had been quite late in arriving.

As the performance got rolling, Jesse realized one of the fundamental truths about sound acoustics: everything sounds better under a tent. The cloth ceiling rising to a peak in the center gave the sound a gathered, rich feeling. Bass notes hung in the air like humidity. Tones from the guitar and fiddle wove dense, musical tapestries. The drums and vocals were perfectly compressed and mixed with the Hammond B-3 organ. Butch was playing a Les Paul guitar through a Marshall amplifier that was meaty and mean. The band filled the tent with all the power and joy of the rock revolution. Once they added their special blend of bayou funk and bluegrass to the mix, the musical canvas was complete.

"This is a dream come true," Dale shouted in Jesse's ear during an ovation break between songs. "Everybody's loving it."

Jesse felt triumphant and strangely vindicated. This was his hometown. He left town two years earlier as little more than an amateur musician. Now he was playing in a six-piece power band that sounded ready for the concert circuit.

All the band's friends were screaming in support of what seemed like a miracle transformation. The two Louisiana boys, Rene and Rick, seemed shocked by the crowd and its joyful response. In no time at all, there were two hundred people crammed into the tent with people standing five deep outside.

Word spread quickly that a great band was making a surprise appearance at the Theatre for Ideas tent. A television reporter and cameraman fought their way into the tent and broadcast The Divebomberz live on the late news.

Jesse introduced the band after the first fifteen songs. They needed a water break. It was a hundred degrees in the tent. People were soaked with sweat as they cheered wildly for their returning musical road warriors. Rene and Rick got roaring cheers of approval when Jesse introduced them. "We picked up a couple raging Cajuns from the bayou."

Dale addressed the crowd once they had quieted somewhat. "Down in New Orleans, they call us the hottest band on the bayou. But y'all know, and we all know, that The Divebomberz are from Fort Wayne, Indiana."

That drew a cheer that seemed to blow the roof off the tent.

The crowd started chanting, "Divebomberz, Divebomberz, Divebomberz."

Jesse decided it was a good time to pass the hat. "Okay, people, listen up for a minute, please. There's a hat coming around. It's a big cowboy hat and I can see we're already getting some contributions. We need you to give generously. It's the only way we're getting paid tonight. So, dig deep. We need the gas money."

Butch chimed in. "And don't forget the party tomorrow night at Goeglein's Barn. It's five dollars at the door and that includes all the beer you can drink. It starts at 8 p.m. We've got the fabulous Arvel Byrd playing fiddle with us. It's going to be a great jam, so come on out."

The band kept playing and passing the hat and promoting the party for another ten songs. The crowd was spellbound. Amy and Terri kept the band in beer until the show finally ended. They sold out of t-shirts early.

The wedding tour would have made a lot more money if Amy had stocked another five hundred t-shirts. As it was, once the first three hundred were gone, that was it. There was no way to make more on the road. Amy made each one by hand and her silk screens were back in New Orleans.

The crowd protested mightily when the band said goodnight. The police said the show had to end at midnight. Thanks to The Divebomberz, the night was one of the most peaceful nights in Fort Wayne festival history.

Jesse and Rene counted the money from the hat. It looked like more than it turned out to be. The grand total came to $373.75. It was mostly one-dollar bills and three quarters.

"Who throws quarters into a hat?" Rene asked as he picked the quarters out of the bottom of the hat.

Dale was disappointed. "I was hoping it would be a lot more money than that. I don't think we've ever had a better crowd."

Butch patted Dale on the back. "We sounded great tonight. My old buddies came up to me like I was some kind of rock star."

"You are," Tim said. "We all are."

"Not on three seventy-three a night for six guys," Rick said. "How are we going to divide it? I'm flat broke."

"How about fifty per man, split the rest between the two drivers?" Tim said.

"How about thirty per man?" Rene suggested. "We need at least two hundred for gas."

As the band was discussing the ugly reality of how little money they had between them, Jesse's mother and father came up to say hello. His mother threw her arms around him and said, "I can't believe you're really doing it. We're so proud of you. The band sounds so professional. Even your father is impressed."

As they hugged each other, his father said, "The band sounds as good as anything I've heard on the radio. Not that I'm any judge. But, frankly, it seems like you could do pretty well with this unit."

"We're so excited about the wedding," Jesse's mother said as she gave Amy a hug. "You are one beautiful girl, inside and out. And we love the t-shirts."

"Thanks for having the wedding at your place in Michigan," Amy said to Jesse's parents. "Do you know if the cottages we reserved are ready for the band?"

"Everything's ready and waiting," Jesse's mother said. "Everybody's excited about the wedding on Eagletop. It's the biggest sand dune around. It's like a mountain. You're going to love it. Everybody will be shocked to find out how great the band is. And you'll be pleased to know, the cottages are only twenty-five dollars a night no matter how many people you put in them."

"That's a lot for us right now," Jesse said. "Hopefully, the party tomorrow will raise some money. We're running on empty these days."

"One word of advice," Jesse's father said. He waited to see if Jesse was ready to hear it.

Jesse put his hands on his hips. "I'm ready."

His father put his arm around Jesse's shoulder. "Okay. I know you had to pass the hat, but don't let on like you need gas money to survive. You look like big stars up there until you tell everybody you're broke."

The party at Goeglein's Barn was standing room only. Everybody paid the five-dollar cover and got to drink free beer all night. From the size of the crowd, Jesse thought the band was making a fortune.

It was a huge hoe down with two fiddles screaming like ecstatic banshees all night. Arvel and Tim sounded like they had been born to play together. Arvel was the best fiddler in the area. Near the end of the first set, he took the mike. "Ladies and gentlemen, let's hear it for The Divebomberz."

Everybody stopped what he was doing to send up a massive cheer for the band. Arvel continued. "I can tell you from playing with them tonight that these local boys are now the hottest band on the bayou."

The crowd surged toward the stage and waved their hands in the air as they let out a deafening cheer.

The band finished the set with an inspirational version of "Orange Blossom Special." The band and the two fiddlers sounded like a steam locomotive coming down the tracks. No one was dancing. They were crowding around the stage to witness what sounded like musical history being made. Jesse wished he had set up a couple recording mikes so they could have the performance on tape.

The band took a short break and came back onstage stronger than they left. The crowd seemed delirious. Everybody was chugging beer in an apparent effort to keep up with the band.

Halfway through the second set, Jesse noticed the dancers were slipping and sometimes falling onto the floor, which was completely covered with beer. People were sloshing the free beer around because they knew they wouldn't have to pay for refills.

The band was playing so hard that Jesse broke a bass string. That had never happened to him before. Bass strings don't break as easily as guitar strings. He replaced the A string. Two songs later, his D string broke. The band kept playing while Jesse did his second string change. No one seemed to notice the bass had dropped out for two songs. Rick covered the bass line pretty well with his left hand on the organ.

The dancing area became so covered in beer that drunken revelers were diving onto the frothy wooden floor to see how far they could slide on their stomachs. The show reached an emotional conclusion about 1 a.m. The dance hall was flashing the lights as the crowd gathered close and gave the band a prolonged, good night cheer.

It took a while to clear out all the drunks. As the band began to pack up its gear, Jesse had a meeting with Tim's sister, Kate, who had helped produce and promote the party. She reported the band took in $2,565 at the door but spent $1,850 on the beer. After the beer bill and cost for the hall and posters and security, the band made a disappointing $115.

Rene immediately turned on Jesse. "I told you the free beer was a bad idea. That was our beer they were throwing around and sliding through. I knew this wasn't working out." He stormed back to his drum kit.

"What's wrong with Rene?" Butch asked as Jesse came back to the bandstand.

Jesse hung his head. "We didn't make any money."

Butch was shocked. "What? We packed the place. Everybody paid at the door, didn't they?"

"The beer cost us almost two grand," Jesse said as he shook his head and lowered it.

Tim's eyes and mouth opened wide in disbelief. "No way."

"Ask your sister, Kate," Jesse said to Tim. "She wouldn't lie to us."

Dale covered his face with his hands and then pulled them away. "People did get drunk as hell."

"I didn't think beer by the keg would cost that much," Jesse said.

"But you didn't check, did you?" Rene said as he came back into the conversation in a threatening fashion.

"Did you check, Rene?" Jesse shot back.

Rene was so mad his face was turning red. He took a step toward Jesse. "No, I didn't. As usual, this was all your idea. This party was about as hair-brained as the whole trip. We should let you go to Michigan on your own if you absolutely have to get married up there."

Dale stepped between Rene and Jesse. "Come on Rene. We just had one of the greatest shows of our lives."

"It's not a great show if the band doesn't make any money." Rene stomped off in a huff, slipped on the wet floor and fell into a puddle of free beer.

CHAPTER TWENTY-NINE

THE WEDDING

Things didn't get any better between Jesse and Rene as the band made its way to Pentwater, Michigan, for the wedding. Rene had to have his father loan the band four hundred dollars for travel expenses. That four hundred could have come from the band account had Jesse not incurred his unexpected jail expense. Jesse never considered asking his father for financial support, although it would have been forthcoming without question. He needed to prove to his father that he could make it in the music business on his own.

"Why does this band always have to be about you, Jesse?" Rene asked as the two of them looked out on the relentless waves of Lake Michigan.

Jesse was getting sick of Rene's constant criticism. "It's not about me. It's about us. And, in case you forgot, we're going into the studio in Dallas to make a demo tape and get a record deal."

Rene was not about to be placated. "I don't see us in Dallas. I see us blindly following you all the way to Michigan so you can get married. I see this band going broke because of you."

"Rene, you're on a beautiful beach, you've got a great band. The sunset is going to be perfect. Everybody's having fun except for you. Polly is having a good time being here. Does it ever occur to you that the only real problem is you?"

"I can't believe I let you get us into this mess," Rene said.

That was the last straw for Jesse. "This mess is my wedding. If you came all the way up here to make my life miserable, you can pack up right now and head back to Louisiana."

"That's the best idea you've had in a long time," Rene said as he turned away from Jesse. He walked down to the road like someone who was never coming back.

Amy overheard the argument and came up the dune to Jesse's side. She didn't say a word as she took his hand. The two of them gazed onto the vast beauty of the sun drenched waves. Lake Michigan looked awesome as any ocean. Not being able to see the other side made them immortal for the moment.

"Everybody's got a cabin?" Jesse asked after a long, contemplative silence.

Amy struggled to keep her voice even and calm. "Terri says her cabin isn't as nice as Loretta's. Rick and Dale don't like being so far from the lake. Your parents are worried about the weather. Most of the guests don't have any place to stay but the beach. I can't get hold of the caterer. Parking is going to be a huge problem. The older guests are complaining about having to climb a mountainous sand dune to see the wedding. Everybody seems crabby as hell. Other than that, everything's fine."

Jesse turned and took both her hands in his. They looked into each other's eyes, sparkling like water in the sun. It was a serene moment. Amy was the first to giggle. Jesse joined her as they held each other and laughed out loud at the wonderful absurdity of their situation.

Jesse remained optimistic. "At least the two of us can be happy. Tomorrow is our big day. We're going to go up there on top of that giant sand dune and make all our friends climb up and help us get married."

"I could not be more happy," Amy said with tears welling in her eyes. "Look at that lake. It's happy for us. It knows everything is going to work out better than ever."

"Yes, it does. And so do I." Jesse took her in his arms and kissed her tenderly.

"I wonder what the Voodoo voice thinks about the wedding?" Amy asked as she and Jesse took a breath. "You haven't mentioned the voice in quite some time."

Jesse didn't respond as he stared at the expansive horizon of the lake. Amy decided not to push the issue and joined Jesse's silent reverie.

He finally put his thoughts into words. "You know, I haven't heard the voice in some time, but I'm listening for it all the time. I think it might be more important to listen for it than to actually hear it."

Amy kissed his ear. "What do you mean?"

Jesse backed off the ear tickle. "Listening for the voice is a great thing to do. Most of the time we only listen to our own, never-ending stream of thoughts. By listening for something else, we break free. We recognize the universe is a lot bigger and better than our little selves."

"What do you hear when you listen?"

Jesse looked her in the eyes. "It's more of a feeling than something you actually hear with your ears. It's like musicians, listening for the muse. We don't actually hear music. We get a feeling about what kind of music we need to make."

Amy thought about that for a long time as they watched the sun begin to sink toward the water. "I love you, Jesse. And, believe it or not, I get what you're trying to say about listening for the voice, or the muse, or the universe."

"Thank you baby. I know you're with me."

Amy kissed him hard on the neck, then backed off into a face to face. "What I don't understand is why the voice won't talk to you on a regular basis. It seems like no matter how much you listen for it, it only comes to you when it's good and ready."

Jesse shuffled his feet in the sand. "You know, I wonder

about that a lot. And I try to see patterns in what the voice has said to me. It seems to be warning me away from the music business. It warned us that Pete was a slaveholder and it called Tony a thief."

"Anything else?"

Jesse smiled. He knew what she was after. "You know the voice has always urged me to team up with you."

"Team up?" She raised her chin and narrowed her eyes.

Jesse grabbed her by both shoulders. "No. Marry you. Make you my wife. Make you the happiest woman in the world so we can live happily after."

Amy bounced up and down on her toes. "That's what I'm talkin' 'bout."

Jesse returned to the reality of the unhappy drummer. "I hope Rene isn't packing up to go home to Louisiana."

Amy thought for a moment before responding. "He's not a happy camper. But he won't leave. We've seen him leave in a huff before. It's nothing new. I wish I'd seen him fall in the beer at the barn party."

Jesse and Amy were chuckling at the thought when they both had to shout for joy. It was Casey, hiking up the dune to surprise them for sunset. He had driven, non–stop, from law school in New Orleans to Pentwater, Michigan, for the wedding. He yelled out greetings and a reminder. "Don't forget it was me who paid Jesse's airfare so he could fly to Indiana and propose to you."

Amy ran into his arms. "And for that, my sweet Casey, I will be forever grateful. We're so happy you made it. And look, you're right on time for the pre-wedding beach party."

Casey rubbed his hands together. "In that case, it's time to build the pre-wedding beach fire. All our friends are here or on the way. It's time to party like sand fleas."

Jesse and Casey built a ten-foot bonfire near the water's edge.

They started with a shallow hole in the sand and a large circle of logs and filled the circle with dry grass and newspapers and small branches. On top they built a pyramid out of chopped wood. Jesse knew the fire would leap into the night with one match. The sun went down until it was on that magical place where the water meets the sky. Oranges and reds painted the horizon. The sun changed shape as it continued to sink. It became an egg, then a UFO and then a golden pancake.

"It's a sizzler," Casey yelled triumphantly as the sun appeared to sink into the water with a steaming fizz.

Jesse's mother led the party of family and friends in her traditional sunset rendition of the camp song, "Day Is Done." Everybody held hands around the unlit fire. Once the song was completed, Jesse held up a box of wooden matches. "Here it is, people. I'm going to use one of these matches, and only one, to turn this pile of wood into a living, breathing symbol of my love for Amy."

He struck the match and held it to the kindling. The fire started slowly at first but soon roared into the night, so big it reminded Jesse of the blaze at the Safari Club. Everybody danced around the fire until it got so hot they had to back away. Butch and Jesse broke out acoustic guitars and Tim got his fiddle going. Several guests had guitars and percussion instruments. The sing-a-long was enthusiastic and mostly harmonious.

Once the fireside jam got to "The Weight" by The Band, everybody jumped in on the chorus and held out the three-level vocal part like it had a life of its own. As the song ended, the impromptu band gave itself a rousing round of cheering applause.

The music sounded perfect around the crackling fire. The Lake Michigan waves rolled in a steady rhythm. A marijuana haze wafted in the gentle breeze as the beer and wine flowed. Jesse felt like the luckiest man in the world. By the end of the party, even people who didn't know each other were carrying on like old friends. There was some skinny-dipping but no naked fire jumping. The fire was too big and Jesse's mother would not have approved.

Rene and Polly did not attend the beach fire. Nobody had seen them all night. "He's been in a bitchy mood ever since he bailed you out of jail," Dale said to Jesse.

Tim came up to Jesse. "You don't think he'd go home the night before the wedding, do you?"

Rick overheard the question. "I wouldn't put it past him. This whole wedding tour has been driving him crazy. He might leave just to protest us not getting paid for playing the wedding. And, you know what? He does have a point. Actually, each of us should be getting a per diem."

"What's that?" Tim asked.

"It's a daily allowance," Rick said.

Tim thought about the concept briefly. "Where would that money come from? Who would pay it?"

"The record company pays it when you're on tour," Rick said.

Tim looked at Rick like he was joking. "You mean the record company we don't have?"

"Exactly," Rick said.

Amy broke into the conversation to get back to the Rene issue. "Are he and Polly getting along?"

Jesse was staring into the fire and worrying about Rene. He was barely hearing Amy's question about Rene and Polly when he heard the Voodoo voice, loud and clear. There was no mistaking the deep, African vocal tone.

"The drummer must die."

Jesse leaped to his feet in surprise at the ominous proclamation. He looked around anxiously to see if anybody else had heard what sounded loud as thunder. No one else heard it.

It was the kind of party where nobody was surprised to see somebody leaping to his feet. Jesse made a few dance moves to cover his shock and surprise. How could people not hear what sounded so loud to him? He walked away from the fire and into the darkness like he was going to take a piss. Hearing the voice talk in such a murderous tone had shaken him. He'd never heard it like that. He walked down the beach until his eyes adjusted to the darkness. The message kept ringing in his mind.

"The drummer must die."

Jesse tried to review what the voice had told him previously. It had evolved over time. At first, it simply introduced itself. Next, it told him to keep running. Then it saved him from the Safari Club fire by telling him to knock down the walls. It told him not to let Amy go during the hurricane at the Seashell Club. It revealed itself to Tim to warn against Pete, the short-time band manager, being a slave owner. It turned off the light in Rose's bedroom to stop Jesse from cheating on Amy. It warned him the record company agent from Los Angeles was a thief and it told the ship captain to leave his ship. The voice had issued warnings on many occasions, but it had never talked about death. Saying the drummer must die took everything to a frightening new level. Was the Voodoo voice capable of killing someone?

The party was still blazing when Jesse came back to the fire. He had no time to think about the voice. He was the man of the hour. Everybody wanted to talk to him. He didn't mind. He was truly grateful to have so many good friends. He tried to hug each person at the party to thank him for coming.

When, at last, the party began to fade, Jesse's father said goodnight and his mother had some typical advice. "Don't stay up too late, you've got a big day tomorrow."

She turned to Amy. "I'm glad my baby boy found such a

good woman to take care of him. Promise me you won't let him stay up all night."

"I promise," Amy said as she hugged her future mother-in-law in genuine affection.

Jesse didn't tell Amy about the voice as they gathered trash and coolers and headed up from the beach to his parents' cottage. People spread out their sleeping bags to sleep on the beach as the fire dwindled down to a huge pile of glowing coals.

Jesse and Amy had a tiny bedroom in his parents' small, summer home. As they were getting into bed, Amy said, "Jesse, I hope you realize how lucky you are to have such a loving family. Not everybody gets that, you know. Your mother and father have been so good to me."

Her voice trailed off. Jesse kissed her softly on the forehead and realized she was already asleep. He put his head back on the pillow and stared up at the ceiling, contemplating his last night as a single man. He listened into the night, hoping the Voodoo voice might have some words of wisdom for him besides, "The drummer must die."

Jesse had a terrible dream that night. He and Rene were chained together in the wretched hold of a slave ship in the middle of the Atlantic Ocean. Three hundred men were crammed into spaces smaller than coffins. Jesse was not prepared for the humiliation and the claustrophobia and the choking stench. It was hopeless and terrifying and evil beyond belief. The total darkness was disorienting. The sounds were even worse. Men and women were sobbing and screaming and choking and praying out loud.

Even in his sleep, Jesse realized this was something more than a dream. Everything felt much too real. It smelled like rotten meat. The man next to him was so weak he could barely be heard, crying out in pain. It took some time for Jesse to realize it was Rene. His voice was raw and his breathing sounded labored. From the terrible sounds he was making, Jesse knew that Rene was dying. He was delirious and calling for water. He was blaming Jesse for the fact they had been captured in the first place.

Rene moaned and managed a vicious whisper. "You said it would be safe to travel on the road. You said it would be safe. I believed you. I was a fool to trust you. I know better. I knew we should have stayed off the road. But, no, you convinced me. I hope you're happy I'm dying. I won't be able to tell everybody how stupid you are."

Jesse tried to console his friend, but the feverish rant only became more insulting. Rene's voice began to fail. His breathing became labored. Jesse could hear his friend dying and there was nothing he could do about it.

"Please," Rene said in a voice dwindled to a rasping gasp. "Please . . . water . . . that's the least . . . bring me . . ."

Jesse wanted more than anything to ease his friend's suffering. He struggled against his chains in vain. Then, he realized he could no longer hear Rene breathing. Then he heard the death rattle; a shuddering, gurgling, collapsing sigh. Rene was gone.

Jesse was sobbing when Amy awakened him. "Jesse, Jesse. Wake up, you're having a bad dream."

Jesse woke up and tried to get his bearings. He couldn't help but tell Amy everything. "I heard the Voodoo voice last night at the fire. It said the drummer must die. And, now, I just had a dream, so real it could not have been a dream."

"What happened in the dream?"

Jesse told her about the slave ship and how Rene died.

Amy was up on her knees. "Oh, my goodness. I hope he's all right. I don't know how powerful this Voodoo thing is. Could it actually kill someone?"

"I don't know. But I'm going to find out." Jesse got out of bed and threw on some clothes.

"Where are you going?" Amy stood up on the bed.

"I'm going to Rene's cabin to see if he's still here," Jesse said.

Amy hopped down to the floor and started getting dressed. "I'm going with you. I'm your wife. Or, I will be in a few hours."

"You've been my wife since the moment we met. And I've been your husband. We were destined."

"I love it when you talk like that," Amy said as she tried to keep up with him on the way to the band van.

Rene's truck was in front of the cabin as they arrived. Jesse sighed in relief. "That's his truck. He's still here. That's a good thing. Now, let's see if he's okay."

Rene answered the door in his underwear. "Jesse? Amy? What are you guys doing here? It's the middle of the night."

Jesse gave him a big hug. He was so relieved to see Rene alive and in good health. "I was worried about you. You weren't at the beach fire. I'm sorry I snapped at you."

"Oh, thanks, man. I've been having a tough time. The money thing had me down for a while. Don't worry. Polly and I took the night off and had a good, long talk. We know things will work out. And, don't worry, we wouldn't miss the wedding for the world."

Amy gave him a kiss on the cheek. "Good. We'll let you get back to sleep."

Rene was pleased Jesse and Amy had come over. "Thanks for the bed check."

The sun was shining for the wedding. Jesse's father was best man. Amy's sister was her maid of honor. Amy's niece made the wedding couple matching outfits, a dress for Amy and a peasant shirt and pants for Jesse.

The guests hiked up to the ceremony site on top of the sand dune. Even the elderly and those with health issues made it to the top. The view of Lake Michigan through the pine trees was nearly as breathtaking as the hike. The beach below stretched down the coast as far as the eye could see. The sky was as blue as the lake.

Jesse's brother-in-law, a Presbyterian minister, conducted a traditional ceremony, complete with wedding rings and simple vows. The service was short and sweet, but all who gathered were deeply moved. Amy and Jesse were crying and smiling at the same time, kissing each other when the time was right.

As the guests were lining up on a pathway down the forested dune to greet the happy couple, Jesse looked up at the tallest tree over the ceremony. Sure enough, there was Casey, mooning the entire wedding party. Everybody laughed. No one thought it inappropriate. This was a rock and roll wedding. The unexpected was expected. In fact, the traditional ceremony had been somewhat of a surprise to those who climbed the sand dune, not knowing what to expect at the top.

The band was set up on the lower sand dune. It was somewhat of a miracle that they had electrical power. Three extension cords, plugged together, were barely long enough to reach from the cottage. Jesse used the microphone to make a toast to his bride.

"This beautiful woman has shown me what it means to be in love. I knew from the day we met that she was the girl for me. Besides being the world's greatest living artist, she has been a huge help to The Divebomberz. I see some of you are wearing the t-shirts she silkscreened by hand. She helps everybody she can. And that is one of the many reasons I am proud to introduce my brand new wife, Amy."

Everybody cheered. The champagne began to flow. Amy stepped up to the microphone to thank her family for coming and to thank Jesse's family for throwing the party. She didn't like public speaking much but she spoke from the heart.

"I'm so happy. I want to tell everyone how grateful we are that you came and climbed the dune with us. I don't think any of us will ever forget this perfect day. I know I won't. It's so good to be here with Jesse and the band and my family and Jesse's family. I am so happy for us all, but especially for me. I want everybody to love everybody."

Jesse kissed her and lifted her over his head in triumph. She waved with both hands as the crowd cheered and applauded.

He put her down and strapped on his bass. He was itching to play. It had been a while since the last performance, and he was excited to see how the band sounded on a sand dune overlooking an endless body of water. They started off strong, shocking those who had not heard them before. This was a road-tested rock and roll band. The only thing missing was Rick's Hammond B-3 organ. It was too heavy to haul up the dune. He made due with an electric piano.

People kicked off their shoes to dance barefoot in the sand. Some had partners. Others went solo. It was almost impossible not to move to the music. The band was jubilant if not triumphant. Playing on a sand dune for such an uplifting occasion had inspired each and every member of The Divebomberz, even Rick and Rene. Children were dancing with their grandparents, husbands were dancing with their wives and Amy danced with her sisters and their husbands. Eventually, a giant circle formed with everybody holding hands. When they all came to the center, they shouted out whatever they felt like shouting, then fell back to reform the large circle. It was amazing no one was injured, considering how much chest thumping and body slamming was going on in the middle.

As he watched people having fun, Jesse continued to wonder about the message from the Voodoo voice. Was Rene the drummer who had to die? Or was the drummer merely a metaphor for something else that needed to end? But if it wasn't about Rene, why did he have the vivid dream about Rene? The dream was as Voodoo as the voice.

The raucous festivities kept his mind from dwelling on what the voice had said. Many a guest seized a microphone to boom out congratulations to the newlyweds. One of Jesse's college friends slurred an embarrassingly long salute to Amy for tackling the dangerous task of keeping Jesse in line. Amy grabbed the microphone from him before he became totally rude.

"Thank you, Randy, for your kind words," she said. "We don't even want to guess what you were going to say next."

The crowd cheered her impromptu censorship.

The band took a break for a picnic dinner on the cottage deck. The cake was cut. Guests, young and old, made long and short toasts. Some were serious, others funny. The generation gap closed quickly over the course of the party.

During the band's second set, Jesse began to realize an important lesson. It was such an obvious truth, it was a wonder he had not seen it coming. It was a simple lesson: Never play in the band at your own wedding.

Somehow, Jesse thought he could pull it off. After all, he could talk to everybody at once with the microphone. What he forgot was the importance of mingling and pressing the flesh. It's impossible to mingle over a microphone. Talking to everybody at once is not the same as greeting individual guests, shaking hands, hugging and kissing. Worst of all, he couldn't dance with his bride or his mother or anybody else while he was playing in the band.

He made sure the band stopped playing for the day after a long, second set. Rene was the only band member to complain. "What do you mean? We came all this way to play two sets? I was just getting warmed up."

The celebration went on without missing a beat. Tim kept the P.A. going with taped music. The party became progressively more reckless and wild as the alcohol and marijuana consumption continued at a record-breaking pace. Some of the more liberated guests began running naked down the dune. For raw entertainment, nothing beats flopping body parts and Tarzan yells streaking into the water.

Jesse's father took him aside for a private moment. "You know. I really like this girl. I think you've got a keeper. Look how happy she is. Look how she talks to everyone."

"She's a jewel," Jesse said.

His father had something to get off his chest. "I just want you to know your mother and I are proud of you. I'm proud of you, whether or not you go to law school."

Jesse hugged his father and felt a rush of incredible gratitude. He had two parents who loved him and who had done their best, and were still doing their best, to raise him. He wondered how people got along with no parents to love them. He had enough issues even with everybody wanting only the best for him.

Another beach fire began at sunset. Storm clouds were beginning to roll into view. The band made sure to pack up all its gear before settling down to some serious beach theater.

"Do you feel any different?" Amy asked Jesse when they caught a rare moment with each other.

Jesse pretended to slur his words. "Yeah, I'm feeling pretty damn loaded."

Amy punched him playfully on the shoulder. "You know what I'm talking about."

Jesse got serious. "I feel better than I ever felt in my whole life. And it's all because I married you."

"That's more like it," she chuckled as a new set of well-wishers came up to congratulate them.

The party began to blur for Jesse around midnight. Part of it was the booze and pot and part of it was the relentless socializing. During a break in the action, he grabbed his new wife's hand and led her into the shadows and away from the fire.

They were asleep in the cottage by 1 a.m. when a group of party marauders burst into their bedroom. Casey, of course, was leading the charge. "What's this? Are the newlyweds asleep on their wedding night? You two should be giving each other the performance of a lifetime."

"We'll get on that first thing tomorrow," Jesse said as the pranksters wisely decided to leave the exhausted wedding couple in peace.

Amy didn't even wake up. She had knocked herself out for days trying to make everyone feel welcome and included in the wedding celebration. The girl isn't lazy, Jesse thought. She had more energy than any three people he knew.

Jesse hugged her in her sleep. She let out a deep sigh. Once again, he felt like a lucky man. He knew he would take care of her. As he drifted off to sleep, he heard thunder rolling in from the lake.

The rain came down hard at 3 a.m. Only a few people on the beach had set up tents. The rest got soaked.

CHAPTER THIRTY

THE TAPE

Nine weeks after the wedding, The Divebomberz finally made it to the recording studio near Dallas, Texas. Attorney Steven Mory was paying for the session to see if the band was good enough to warrant his representation. The band had been playing four nights a week since the wedding. They were well rehearsed and ready to record. The steady work had also helped them get back on their feet financially. The experience in the studio turned out to be vastly more productive than the ill-fated recording session many months earlier, sponsored by Pete in New Orleans. The only similarity between the two sessions was that the person paying for the time was not present.

Two engineers had the band miked up, plugged in, and ready to sound check in less than an hour. After a few minor adjustments, each member of the band had a good sound mix in his headset. Rene got to play in the big room with everybody else. All the instruments went to the mixing board by way of a direct box so there was no drum bleed on the guitar tracks. Dale's lead vocal was a dummy track so it didn't matter if the drums came through in his microphone. He would sing his lead vocal on a later track in an isolated vocal booth.

The lead engineer was a thin man with a little grey in his beard. He looked like Beatle George Harrison. "You guys sound like the real deal. I can tell you've been gigging a lot. We've got rhythm tracks on four songs in less than three hours. That's what I call a road band."

Butch was more than pleased by what he was hearing on the playback. "You guys are the best. This studio is sounding better than anyplace we've ever played."

"Thanks for letting us play together like we do at a club," Rene said.

The engineer was satisfied. "These are basically live tracks. They sound good enough already. But just wait until we put a little fairy dust on them."

"I like the sounds of that," Dale said.

The engineer got the band together. "We'll start with Dale's lead vocal. Then, we'll do harmony parts and group backing vocals. We can layer as many vocal tracks as you want."

Tim was sober for this session. "Can you make us sound like the Norman Block and Tackle Choir?"

Everybody laughed except the engineer.

No matter, spirits were high. Jesse felt better than ever. It was a huge relief to finally be making a record with someone who really knew how to do it.

Dale recorded his vocal, then Butch, Jesse, and Tim. The engineer blended the voices perfectly. Nobody had to ask for more of himself.

The engineer surprised them with a suggestion. "Okay, here's what we'll do next. I want all six of you to stand around one microphone and sing on the choruses."

Rene started walking out of the room. "I'm not a singer."

The engineer coaxed him back. "Everybody's a singer. Don't worry about finding a harmony part. Just sing the song like you would in the shower."

The first time through, singing as six, the band was blown away by how good they sounded. Rene found himself a nice part on the low end of the layering. Rick added a surprising harmonic high line. The track sounded good by itself. It sounded even more rich and full when mixed with the other vocal and instrumental tracks.

Tim spoke for the entire band. "Holy shit. We sound like a hit record."

"Muscle Shoals got nothing on this, baby," Rick said, referring to the legendary studio in Alabama. "These boys in Texas are breaking us into some new territory."

Tim was excited. "We're a six-headed vocal monster. Looks like we'll have to get a vocal mike for Rene when we play live."

Rene didn't like that idea. "I don't know about that. I hear myself on tape and it doesn't even sound like me."

"Everybody feels that way at first," the engineer said. "You'll get used to it."

By the end of the recording, Jesse knew the band had passed its electronic audition. He also knew the lead engineer would tell Atty. Mory he had a potentially hot act on his hands.

Jesse sat in the control room and didn't say a word while the engineers did a rough mix. It kept sounding better and better until the lead engineer stood up to speak. "That's good enough for now. How do you like the way you sound?"

Dale dropped to his knees in mock worship. "We sound better than we ever thought we could. You guys have done an amazing job."

The engineer was pleased as the band showered him with congratulations. "You guys did the job. I haven't seen any band put down four original songs faster or better. My personal favorite is 'Hurricane on the Bayou.' That should be your first single."

"Too bad we couldn't put down 'Red Light,'" Jesse said. "That's been going over great everywhere we go."

Rene laughed at Jesse. "Just because you wrote it doesn't make it good."

"I wrote them all," Jesse said. "Butch and I wrote them all. Don't laugh at me just because you can't write your way out of a paper bag."

Butch stepped between Jesse and Rene. "Now, boys. Let's stay on our best behavior here."

Dale jumped into the mix. "Don't forget. I helped write a few."

Tim held out his hands as if in prayer. "More importantly. We all play them. The songs only sound good because we sound good together."

His comments helped the band move on without the usual squabbles about song selection, copyright and what to do with all the money they had yet to make. Afterword the band packed up their gear and loaded it into Jesse's van, Rene's truck and the homemade trailer. They were tired and more than a little cranky. Playing four nights a week for several weeks in a row had been tiring and stressful. Adding the recording session to their schedule was definitely working overtime. They were ready for a break.

The engineer gave the session tape to Jesse as the band was leaving the studio. Without thinking, Jesse got in the van and drove off with Atty. Mory's tape, completely oblivious to the problems this would cause.

Two days later in New Orleans, Jesse got an angry phone call from Atty. Mory. "We agreed the tapes belong to me. I paid for the god damned session and you ran off with my recording. I can't believe you would do this to me. I thought you were a man of your word."

Jesse was caught off guard. "Wait a minute. I didn't run off with anything. I've got the demo tape right here. I know it's your tape. I'm not stealing it. I can drive it over today if that's what you want."

The attorney dialed down his angry tone a couple notches. "That won't be necessary."

"I didn't mean to piss you off," Jesse said. "They offered us the tape so I took it. Did you hear it? They made us sound great."

Atty. Mory sighed in exasperation. "No, I did not hear the tape. You took the tape. How could I listen to it when you have it in your possession?"

Jesse continued on the defensive. "Oh, I thought what they gave me was a copy of the original."

The attorney tried to be patient. "No, you have the original tape. There are no copies. Now, listen to me carefully, Jesse. You own the copyright to the song, I own the copyright to the production of the song; my production, the one I financed. That means the tape stays with me."

Jesse didn't understand what the attorney was saying. Nonetheless, he agreed to ship the tape that afternoon, by U.S. Mail.

Two weeks later, Amy called Jesse in Shreveport to tell him a package had arrived from Atty. Mory.

She was out of breath. "I opened it, Jesse. I was so curious. It's a contract. He wants to represent The Divebomberz. He wants you and Butch to sign it as key members of the band. This is so exciting."

Jesse tried to contain himself. "What does it say? Can you read it to me?"

"It's thirty-five pages long, Jesse. I tried to read it and I don't understand it at all. It seems like he gets twenty percent of whatever he makes for you but it doesn't say how much he's going to make you."

Jesse realized she wouldn't be able to explain the contract over the phone. "Is there a date on it?"

"The letter is dated September 2, 1978. It states you have twenty days to consider the offer."

Jesse made a trip to New Orleans the next day, which was Sunday. It was going to have to be a quick trip. He had to be back up north by Wednesday. The band was playing a four-night stand at the Barmuda Triangle, the club where the assistant manager had been shot and killed on ladies night.

Jesse had two things to do in New Orleans. One, read the Mory contract with Casey and see if it was worth signing. And, two, go see Carmen about the Voodoo voice.

Finding Casey was easy. One phone call and he came over to the Tchoupitoulas Street apartment within twenty minutes. He read the entire contract out loud to Jesse and Amy, pausing here and there to explain certain points.

Casey's tone was low and lawyerly. "This contract is pretty one sided. First of all, it's exclusive. That means anything you do from now on must be through him, except for bookings. I like that he doesn't get anything on gigs you book for yourself. What I don't like is he's the only one who can try to get you a record deal. What about that guy from Capitol who was going to put you in that famous studio in Muscle Shoals?"

"He's waiting for a demo tape." Jesse thought back to Tony and how the voice called him a thief.

Casey put down the contract. "The tape you no longer have."

"Right," Jesse said.

Amy turned to Jesse. "I thought the attorney was going to mail us a copy?"

"He was but he hasn't," Jesse said.

Casey looked at Jesse. "Why didn't you make a copy before you mailed it back to him?"

Jesse hung his head in frustration. "I don't know. He made

it sound like I was stealing from him. I didn't want him to think that."

"Okay, I get that. But can't you do another recording somewhere else?"

Jesse held his hands up. "Who's going to pay for it?"

Casey looked at Amy and Amy looked at Jesse and Jesse looked at Casey.

Casey stood up from his chair to summarize. "All right, I'm no entertainment attorney. But I don't like the exclusivity this attorney is giving himself. I say don't sign the deal until you get that exclusive bullshit out of there. Besides, we don't really know what this guy can do. How many artists do we hear about who sign bad deals with people who can't deliver?"

Jesse looked at Amy. She shrugged her shoulders at first but then responded. "I have to agree with Casey. I don't know this guy from Adam. Why put your career in his hands when he's not even saying what he can do for you?"

"He did make us a killer demo tape," Jesse said.

Amy stood up. "A tape I have yet to hear."

"How did you not listen to it when it was here?" Casey asked.

Jesse held his hands in the air. "It was on a reel-to-reel tape and I never got it to a machine that could play it."

CHAPTER THIRTY-ONE

BOX OF TIME

The door to Carmen's shop was open. Jesse walked in slowly so as not to make the floor boards creak too loudly.

Carmen heard him enter. "Come on back, Jesse."

Jesse walked through the beaded doorway and saw Carmen and Ruthie the duck lady waiting for him like he was late for an appointment.

Jesse hugged Carmen and Ruthie together. "How could you possibly know it was me?"

Carmen answered with a broad smile. "We've been expecting you."

"The person you call the mystery man told us you would be coming today," Ruthie said.

Jesse was confused. "How would he know?

Carmen looked at Ruthie as she began speaking. "The Voodoo world is abuzz about The Divebomberz. As you know, the band is at a crossroads. There is trouble in the air. Death is stalking the band."

Jesse was surprised Carmen and Ruthie knew what the voice had told him. "That's why I'm here. The Voodoo voice told me the drummer must die. What's with that? If it's telling me I have to kill somebody, I can tell you right now I'm not going to do it. What I'm really worried about is that the voice might kill Rene. Is that possible?"

Carmen tried to soothe him with a new calm in her voice.

"The power of Voodoo has taken many, many lives. Where were you when the voice spoke to you? What were you doing? What were you seeing?"

Jesse told the two magical women about the wedding and the beach fire and the dream about Rene dying on the slave ship.

"What did he say in the dream just before he died?" Ruthie asked.

Jesse was surprised to have Ruthie playing such an active role in the Voodoo diagnosis. He hadn't realized until that moment that Carmen and Ruthie might be two separate visions of the same spiritual force. The thought was so heavy it made him want to sit down. Ruthie and Carmen were sitting in the only two chairs in the room and neither one of them seemed inclined to help him find a chair of his own.

Carmen reached up to take him by the arm. "What did Rene say in the dream?"

"He was blaming me for getting caught and sold into slavery and dying on a godforsaken slave ship." Jesse leaned back like the forces of Voodoo had him up against the wall.

Ruthie pressed for details. "How real was this dream? Could you smell things in the dream?"

The horrible odor came back to Jesse. "The dream was the worst experience of my life. It was even more terrible than the dream of the Voodoo slave uprising. And, yes, I could smell shit and puke and rotting blood and flesh."

He was becoming upset and agitated as the visions of the slave ship became real in his mind once again.

Carmen tried to settle him down. "The first thing you need to understand is that these are not just dreams. These experiences are not something you wake up from and forget halfway through your morning coffee. You can die in these altered states of reality."

Ruthie stood up. "What makes you think right now is any different than the Voodoo dimensions you have been allowed to visit?"

"I'm still myself," Jesse said.

"And that is the problem," Carmen said. "The Voodoo voice is trying to show you a way out of your self. Right now, the drummer is part of your personal prison. No doubt, he's fighting you for control of the band."

Jesse nodded that she was correct. He was amazed at her intuition about the power struggle. He had not discussed the Rene situation with either Carmen or Ruthie.

Ruthie tried to explain. "You don't need to kill the drummer. You need to stop trying to control things. The voice said the drummer must die. That might be as simple as finding another drummer. Or it might mean you need to stop fighting with your notion of who the drummer is and what he represents. It doesn't mean you need to take any action."

Jesse began to calm down. "I get that. I don't need to be in charge. What I don't get is why I'm hearing the voice in the first place."

Carmen closed her eyes like she might be going into a trance. "The voice and spirit and power of Voodoo are there for everyone at anytime."

"Seek and you shall find," Ruthie said.

Jesse was relieved to see Carmen open her eyes. He spoke to Ruthie. "That sounds pretty Christian. Is Voodoo the same thing as God?"

Carmen and Ruthie looked at each other as if trying to decide which one of them would address the issue. Carmen accepted the challenge. "We live in a box of time and space. Our minds cannot understand the infinity of space or the eternity of time. Think of the Voodoo voice as an angel, leading you out of your mind's box of time."

Ruthie picked up where Carmen left off. "Into something you can't understand. But something you don't need to understand. Trying to understand things causes most of the world's problems. People make up all kinds of ridiculous rules and reasons to explain who God is and what God does."

Carmen concluded. "God is that which we cannot understand."

"That's just about everything," Jesse said.

Ruthie tried to help. "Voodoo helps connect you to everything you don't understand so you don't worry so much about not understanding it."

Jesse began to feel uncomfortable. "What about the ship captain? The Russian we helped jump ship. I guess he heard the voice too, didn't he? How's he doing?"

"He's having a ball, being gay in the French Quarter and cooking at Rod's," Ruthie said.

Carmen raised her eyebrows. "And don't you want to know that Dupre heard the voice and paid attention."

Jesse was so surprised he straightened off the wall. "Dupre, with the Wheelers?"

Ruthie raised her right index finger. "Not anymore. He quit dealing and drugging. He even quit the motorcycle gang and left town. He's off with some Buddhist woman in Boulder, Colorado."

Jesse was having trouble with his timeline. "That can't be. I just saw him in a bar brawl in Shreveport."

"This just happened," Ruthie said. "He was in this very room less than a month ago."

Carmen seemed pleased to add another surprise to the mix. "And Gypsy's working on a fishing boat in Alaska."

It took Jesse some time to respond. "No, you've got to be kidding me."

"We're not kidding," Ruthie said. "So, let me ask you. Are you seeing any patterns here?"

"Between me and the ship captain and Dupre?"

"Right," they said in unison.

"I guess we're all in the process of changing direction in our lives."

"Bingo," they said.

Jesse returned to the topic of Rene. "So what about the drummer must die stuff?"

Carmen spoke to him like a mother speaks to a child asking too many questions. "The voice was speaking to you, not to the drummer. But I'd have to say that Rene had better change some habits in a hurry if he wants to stay alive."

"He does get high and drive like a maniac," Jesse said. "We've been afraid he'll kill us all someday."

"My guess is the voice is telling you to end your relationship with the drummer," Ruthie said.

Carmen disagreed. "I feel it is more ominous than that."

Jesse was relieved to see that neither of them knew exactly what the voice was really saying.

Carmen opened her arms. "The interpretation is up to you. Remember, the signs have no intrinsic value. They mean different things to different people."

"They also mean different things to the same person, depending on when he is interpreting them," Ruthie said. "It's all up to you. We can't tell you what to feel."

Carmen added another thought. "Trust your feelings. You know how to listen now. Trust how the voice makes you feel and act accordingly." She bent close to him and wiggled her nose as if beginning to taste a fine wine. "I sense a major change coming your way soon. It will be a good one."

"What makes you say that?" Jesse asked. "Is it something about the way I smell?"

"It's not about smell like you smell hamburgers on the grill," Carmen said. "It's more like what you call pheromones. Sometimes we know things on a visceral level before the concept makes it all the way up to our brain."

Jesse decided to accept that explanation without asking any more questions. He hugged Carmen and Ruthie and thanked them as he said goodbye. He felt like he was floating on air as he walked out the door and into the drunken clown parade that was Bourbon Street.

CHAPTER THIRTY-TWO

THE END

Jesse and Tim were playing warm and friendly music on the front steps of Tim's house on Annunciation Street in New Orleans when the news arrived like a bucket of ice water tragedy.

They saw Butch walking down the sidewalk and right through the gaggle of children, who were dancing to the music. He didn't even acknowledge their presence. That wasn't like Butch. He had his head down and he was walking fast. Something was wrong. He walked up the four, wooden steps and sat down next to Jesse without saying a word.

Jesse let him sit for a minute before asking, "What's wrong?"

Butch didn't speak.

Tim moved closer to Butch and put his arm around him. "What's wrong, Butch? Come on, you can talk to us."

Butch sighed deeply and looked across the street without focusing. Jesse and Tim could tell he had been crying. They waited for him to gather himself.

"Rene is dead," he finally said as he dropped his head on his knees.

Jesse and Tim looked at each other in shock, unable to speak. How could Rene be gone? He was a huge part of their lives.

Jesse had told Tim weeks earlier about the Voodoo voice saying, "The drummer must die." They'd had long talks about it. Neither one of them expected the morbid prophesy to become reality.

Now, Butch and Tim and Jesse sat on Tim's porch in disbelief. Butch lifted his head and put his hands over his face to hide his tears. "I just got the call from his father about twenty minutes ago. Rene lost control of his truck on a curve. He was going too fast, probably. Anyway, the truck spun around and slammed into a tree, backwards. Rene hit his head on the back window and died at the scene."

"Was there another car in the crash?" Jesse asked.

Butch uncovered his face and looked at Jesse. "No, but there was a passenger in Rene's truck. And here's the weird part. The passenger wasn't hurt at all."

Tim leaned in for more information. "When did this happen? Where did it happen?"

Butch shook his head like he really didn't know much. "I guess it happened yesterday afternoon on some back country road near Shreveport. His dad told me some particulars, but he's so upset he's not making a lot of sense. I can't remember much of what he said. I guess I'm not able to process any of this."

Tim kept asking questions. "Who was the passenger? It wasn't Polly was it?"

"No, it was some guy helping Rene move a couch or something. I can't remember his name but it was nobody we know."

Tim stood up. "Shit. Shit. Shit. How could this be happening?"

Butch and Jesse stood up and the three band members hugged each other in silent mourning. Tim's girlfriend, Loretta, came halfway out the front screen door. "What's the matter? What happened?"

Tim was grim. "Rene was killed in a truck crash. We'd better call Dale and Rick."

Loretta gasped and put her hand to her mouth. The screen door slammed shut behind her as she ran back into the apartment to get to the telephone. The children stopped dancing on the sidewalk below. They could tell something very bad had happened. They walked away without saying a word.

It was the middle of November, 1978. The band had been bouncing back and forth between the same old clubs since the wedding. They had performances booked through the spring of 1979. Rene's sudden death changed everything. The band's immediate future had been in doubt anyway. The crowds at Johnny's had been getting smaller and smaller each time the band went back to play there. The last thing Johnny said to Jesse was, "You can't play the same place too much. People find out your shit stinks."

The Divebomberz held a meeting at Tortilla Flats the day after hearing the news of Rene's death. Rick wasn't there. He surprised everybody by saying he was quitting the band anyway, and that he'd made the decision even before Rene died. Actually, it wasn't that big of a surprise. Rick had been threatening to leave for months. He said he didn't see much future in being on the road without a record label promoting and supporting the tour.

He was right, of course. Everybody was more than tired of being broke, stumbling from one gig to the next. Jesse was beginning to feel like he couldn't keep going much longer. He knew Amy's patience and support were wearing thin.

Dale wondered aloud. "So, what do we do? Go back to Fritzel's?"

Butch took a long swig of beer. "No way. What we do is we get another drummer and another keyboard player. Bands go through personnel changes all the time."

Jesse was pretty sure Butch knew it wouldn't be that easy. "I don't know any drummers who aren't already with a band. Let alone any drummers with a truck and a father who's ready and able to help a band stay on the road."

Dale grabbed Jesse's shoulder. "What about Atty. Mory? He could help us, couldn't he?"

Jesse stared into his beer. "He doesn't want anything to do with us if we won't sign his contract."

Dale waited for Jesse to look up at him. "So, why don't we just sign the contract?"

Butch sighed and answered the question one more time. "Because we don't want just one guy in charge of the rest of our lives."

Dale took his hand off Jesse's shoulder and slapped it on the table. "How bad is it. We finally get a demo tape done and then we can't do anything with it."

"Sounds like you're siding with Rick and Rene," Jesse said.

Butch waited a moment before leaning in to the table. "Nobody's siding with Rene."

They sat in mournful silence for a moment until Jesse recovered enough to propose a toast. "Here's to Rene. He was a great drummer. He took us to new heights. We didn't always agree on everything but we're sure going to miss him."

The band cheered half-heartedly and then settled back into an awkward silence.

Tim got practical. "Looks like we'd better cancel our bookings and fall back for a while to regroup. We can't do those gigs without a drummer. It's going to take a few weeks, anyway, to put a new lineup together."

Dale poured himself another glass of beer from the pitcher. "Oh, man. The worst thing we could do is start cancelling gigs."

"It doesn't look like we have much choice," Butch said.

The band kept kicking around possibilities for another couple rounds of drinks. The wind had been sucked out of their sails. They heard a train rumbling down the nearby tracks. Nobody felt like jumping it.

Jesse was more than shaken by Rene's death. In some weird way, he felt responsible for causing the tragedy. After all, it was his Voodoo voice that predicted it.

Amy was quick to correct him. "That is so self centered of you, Jesse. In the first place, the Voodoo voice does not belong to you. You said it yourself. The voice is there for anyone who knows how to listen. Do you think the sun rises and falls because of you?"

"Maybe I could have done something to prevent it once I heard it was going to happen," Jesse said.

Amy stayed on him. "You're the one who always talks about escaping the prison of self. Then you jump right in and take the blame for something you had nothing to do with. Stop feeling sorry for yourself. Self pity is still self centered."

Jesse was groping for answers. "Do you think the Voodoo killed him? I mean, it was such a freak accident. Even his passenger has no idea what happened. That guy wasn't even hurt. He told Rene's father the impact didn't feel strong enough to injure anybody. He thought it was a fender bender until he reached over and found out Rene was gone."

Amy switched into a more comforting tone. "All the voice said was the drummer must die. It didn't say Rene must die. It didn't say when or how anybody was going to die. And, what the heck, everybody dies. That's not exactly news."

Jesse spoke with desperation in his voice. "Come on, Amy. My Voodoo voice says the drummer must die and, before we know it, Rene is killed in a freak truck accident. How much more connected does it have to get?"

Amy handed Jesse a beer she had just gotten out of the refrigerator. "Again, it's not your Voodoo voice. And the only thing that killed Rene was his own crazy driving. I'm just glad you weren't in the truck when it happened. How many times have I said that man was going to kill the whole band with his crazy driving? Did anybody do a blood test on him after the crash?"

Jesse almost laughed at that notion. "I don't think so. But I'm sure he was all smoked up."

Amy knew he was right. "So blame the marijuana. Why blame the Voodoo voice? We both know what killed him. It was drugs and reckless driving."

Jesse wasn't looking for something to blame. "Let's say it was the drugs. That doesn't change the way I feel."

"And how is that?" Amy asked.

Jesse pronounced his emotional verdict. "Guilty."

Amy stood up and looked down on Tchoupitoulas Street as if that would clear her head. "You feel guilty because you've been mad at him for so long. You can feel bad about that. Don't feel bad about something you didn't do."

"Maybe what I really feel guilty about is something else," Jesse said.

"What?"

Jesse hung his head. "I guess I'm feeling guilty because I'm thinking about quitting the band. It's starting to feel like I'm leading them down a long road to failure."

Amy was smart enough to remain silent.

"I keep thinking about that white horse I tried to jump on in Minden."

"You mean the one that almost broke your leg after you crashed its ass and slid down its tail?"

"That's the one."

Amy nodded her head. "Are we talking about the little things of today predicting the big things of tomorrow?"

"Exactly," Jesse said. "I keep thinking that horse might be the music business and I'm the fool trying to ride it without reins or stirrups or a saddle or even a blanket."

"You're lucky that horse didn't kill you."

The day after Jesse finally admitted to himself his doubts about the band, he went to Butch's apartment to talk. He was surprised to find that Butch was feeling a lot the same way. They both needed a break from the road and the band in general.

Butch made a pot of coffee and the two of them sat down on his second-story veranda. "If you leave, Jesse, the band is over. We lost Rene and Rick and we were getting sick of Dale's singing. Tim won't have any trouble finding another gig. You'll go to law school like you swore you never would. What I worry about is me. What am I going to do after The Divebomberz?"

Jesse loved the way Butch could cut through the crap and get right to the point. "We keep writing and recording songs. We don't need a band to do that. We can hire the players."

Butch took a slow sip of coffee. "How are we going to pay for that?"

"We'll get day jobs and save our money," Jesse said.

Butch laughed as he put down his cup. "Oh, we'll have to get jobs, for sure. That's long overdue. But I doubt we'll be able to save enough to pay for studio time and musicians."

"It might not happen overnight," Jesse conceded.

Butch gazed into the leaves of the Magnolia tree. "You know. I was wondering if you getting married would be the beginning of the end for the band."

Jesse got defensive. "It wasn't getting married that did it.

Amy never asked me to quit the band. It was the going nowhere that did it. Going nowhere and getting older."

Butch looked at Jesse. "I know. That's a bad combination. I've been thinking about the same thing. And I'm not saying Amy killed the band. It's just that once a guy gets married he starts thinking about his future."

Jesse stared into the Magnolia leaves. "I have no idea what I'll do without the band. It's going to be hard, for sure. We can't just give up on all our hopes and dreams."

Butch got up to get the coffee pot. "Hopes and dreams change. We'll be all right."

"I'm not ready for law school," Jesse said.

Butch poured him another cup. "You've been saying that a lot lately."

Butch and Jesse got all coffee'd up and rehashed the band's greatest escapades for a couple hours. Later that day, they met with Tim and Dale. Everybody agreed it would be best to take a break from trying to keep the band on the road. It had been like rolling a giant stone up a steep hill for months. They would get day jobs and try to save some money. Nobody talked about breaking up the band. But everybody knew it was the end.

CHAPTER THIRTY-THREE

PEOPLE

Three months after The Divebomberz unofficially disbanded, Jesse found himself nailing down roll roofing in the warehouse district of New Orleans. It wasn't a bad job. It was hot and dirty, but it was steady work. The roofs were enormous. They stretched out as long as football fields.

He was learning the roofing trade from his friend, Paul. The pay was seven dollars an hour, which was fine with Jesse. He and Paul were working time and materials for a landowner who wanted them to stretch out the job for as long as possible. Their employer wanted to continue collecting from his insurance company for storm damage repair and loss of rent.

Amy and Jesse met Paul more than a year earlier in New Orleans' Audubon Park, near the zoo. The Divebomberz were still playing at Fritzel's. Jesse had just been talking about adding a banjo player to the band when Amy spotted Paul walking in the park by himself, carrying a banjo over his shoulder.

"There he is," she squealed. "There's your banjo player. How amazing is that? "

"Don't bother the poor man," Jesse said.

Amy ignored him and ran over to the man with the banjo. "Hey, mister, can you play that thing?"

"No, I just like to walk it in the park," Paul said.

Amy and Jesse laughed. They introduced themselves and sat down to have a chat. Paul was pleased to play a little banjo for them. He was quite good. After two songs, Amy had heard enough to make him a job offer. "Jesse here has a band on Bourbon Street. They're looking for a banjo player. They've already got a fiddle player. They're really good. You'd fit in great. I'll bet you could sit in tonight."

Jesse and Paul had to laugh at her forwardness.

Amy was undeterred. "Where do you live?"

Paul looked at her and smiled. "In my van."

"You sound like my kind of guy," Jesse said.

That was the start of a fine friendship. Paul did sit in with the band that first night. He sounded great, but he would not be persuaded into joining a band on Bourbon Street. He'd already been in too many bands.

Paul and Jesse had long, philosophical talks while they put down miles of roofing together. They talked about their fathers and mothers and what they wanted to do with their lives. They talked about music and the music business. Jesse talked about The Divebomberz and what a heartbreak it had been to see his dreams go up in smoke. "I hate to say it. But I didn't even see it coming. One day, we were plotting our musical careers together. The next day, we were all going our separate ways."

Paul was blunt. "Bands break up. What did you expect? Even The Beatles broke up. Don't worry about it. You can always start another band if you're a glutton for punishment."

Starting another band was the last thing on Jesse's mind. He felt like he was still getting over four divorces and a funeral. He still went over to Butch's apartment to write songs. He still went over to Tim's to play music on the porch for the kids on Annunciation Street. He still went out for drinks with Dale in the French Quarter. He even had a couple good talks with Rick. But it wasn't the same and he knew it never would be. The

Divebomberz had been Jesse's first real band. Watching it come apart at the seams had been nearly more than he could take.

Working with Paul on the roofs turned out to be the perfect therapy for Jesse. He could tell it was good for Paul too. They were both coming up on thirty years old and beginning to wonder what they could do to make some sense out of the world. They took a lot of breaks so as not to make too much progress on the job. The roofs turned out to be the perfect place to play Frisbee, even though a few disks a day went over the edge and had to be retrieved.

One day, while resting after an extended Frisbee session, Jesse asked Paul, "What's the most important thing in life?"

"People," Paul answered without hesitation.

Jesse thought about the answer for a minute. "Yes, I suppose that's right. Without people, life would get pretty lonely and boring."

Jesse was drenched in sweat and half covered with tar when he looked up and into the sun. Wincing from the brightness, he heard the Voodoo voice again. It was as loud and clear in his mind as it had ever been.

"Time to move on."

Jesse's head began to swirl as he received the message. He closed his eyes and felt completely surrounded. He was afraid to open his eyes again. Instead, he looked into some dark recess of his mind that was gradually being illuminated.

In the trance vision, Jesse was surrounded. Paul was there. The Voodoo witch doctor was there. Marie Leveau was there. So were Gypsy and Dupre. Carmen, Ruthie the duck lady, and the mystery man were all there. Butch and Rene and Tim and Rick and Dale were there. Dutch was there. Amy was there with his mother and father. Dr. John was there with Professor Longhair and Allen Toussaint and Aaron Neville. Casey was there. The last person to come out of the shadows of Jesse's mind and into the circle of his enlightenment was the biggest surprise of all. It was none other than Johnny from Johnny's Cimarron Club.

Nobody said anything. They didn't need to. They just stood there and stared at Jesse like they were waiting for him to come to an inevitable conclusion. In an epiphany, Jesse realized that all these characters had been teaching him lessons far more important than the selfish pursuit of pleasure. It was all part of the directive he had just heard from the Voodoo voice.

"Time to move on."

He realized that the rock band from New Orleans was a level of education he had to pass through in order to get to the next curriculum. Events had been slowly turning his head in a new direction. From going to jail a couple times to negotiating with the Wheelers and the Gypsies to realizing he needed a lawyer to deal with his lawyer, Jesse was beginning to understand that his new level of education would also be his next adventure. Much of the sorrow he had been feeling about losing his band melted away in the message of the moment.

Jesse felt a warm glow inside. He knew what he had to do as he opened his eyes. The only person he actually saw was Paul, who was staring at him like he was afraid his friend might be suffering from heat stroke.

"I'm going to law school," Jesse said.

Paul sat down beside him. "Just like that?"

"Just like that," Jesse said as he looked back up at the sun for confirmation.

Paul waited for a long moment before he began asking questions. "Don't you have to apply and be accepted and all that? Doesn't it cost a lot of money? And where will you go?"

"I'll go back to Indiana with Amy and everything will work

out," Jesse said. "It's time for me to get back with my family. I guess I was starting to realize that when I dragged the band back to Indiana and Michigan to get married."

Paul looked at Jesse to make sure he wasn't fooling around. "Are you sure?"

"Absolutely."

Jesse couldn't wait to tell Amy the news. He called and asked her to meet him at Tortilla Flats as soon as she finished teaching her painting class.

"What's up?"

He took a deep breath and let it out carefully. "I'm going to law school."

Amy was slow to respond, like she wasn't sure if he was serious. "Oh, my goodness. Good for you, I guess. I hope I'm going with you."

Jesse raised his volume. "Of course you are. We're going to live happily ever after."

Amy had to cut the conversation short. "I can't talk now. Besides, this is too important for a phone call. Tell you what. I'll see you at 4 p.m., Tortilla Flats. Hold that thought. Don't be late. I love you."

Jesse was waiting at the bar when she came rushing in the front door to hug him with all her might. "What the hell is going on? One day you're trying to be a rock star and the next day you're going to be an attorney? Isn't that completely switching teams?"

Jesse sat her down and poured her a glass of Sangria. "Not at all. It's all about people and getting back to the ones we love and seeing what we can do to help. We're going back to Indiana. That's where our people live."

"What about our new people in New Orleans?" Amy asked.

"They can come visit us," Jesse said. "I haven't told anybody yet."

Amy was beginning to bounce on her bar stool. "Wait until Casey hears the news. Wait until your father hears the news. Oh, my God, Jesse. What happened?"

Jesse told her about the Voodoo voice and his epiphany on the warehouse roof with Paul. "The more I think about going to law school, the more I realize I was always going to do it. It started to feel like the more I said I wouldn't do it, the more I knew it was what I have to do."

"I suppose life is all about doing what you say you're never going to do," Amy said.

"So true," Jesse said as he took her by both hands. "How many times did we say we were never getting married?"

"That was mainly you."

Jesse squeezed her hands. "You said it too."

"I know I did, but I didn't mean it."

Jesse kissed her softly and whispered in her ear. "Looks like I didn't mean it either."

"What about my job?" Amy asked as she let go of Jesse's hands and grabbed her drink. "It took me a long time to get this gig teaching painting at Delgado University."

"We'll wait until the end of the semester. I'll keep working. We can save some money. And then we'll be off on the next exciting chapter of our lives."

Amy grabbed him by both shoulders and looked him in the eye. "I know you're not giving up as a song writer."

"I'm not done with music by a long shot," Jesse said. "But I am done with reading contracts I don't understand. Who knows? I might end up representing people like us."

Amy was so happy she could barely remain seated. "Think of all the good you can do. You can help musicians and artists and writers and I'll be a painter and a teacher. We can make a stand together."

Jesse was pleased to see her getting excited about their future. Making her happy was becoming more and more important to him.

They clinked glasses as Jesse toasted. "Here's to all the creative souls. With any luck at all, we'll be able to help them save the world."

Amy put her drink down on the bar and looked Jesse in the eyes. "I know this is the right thing for us to do. I've known it for some time. But I still have to ask what made you come to this new conclusion? What happened to make you want to take this new direction?"

Jesse thought about her questions while finishing his glass and pouring himself one more from the pitcher of Sangria in front of them on the bar. "You know, I don't want to say it was the voice that made me do it, but it was definitely the things I heard the voice saying that made me come around to this new way of looking at things."

"What new way?"

Jesse spun himself completely around on the bar stool for dramatic pause and emphasis. "I'm starting to see the connection between the getting high and the thrill seeking and the need to be the center of attention."

Amy's eyes widened as she waited for him to elaborate.

"I started getting the picture when Carmen was interpreting the Voodoo slave uprising where I killed the old white plantation owner who turned out to be me. I realized the connection between the slave and the slave owner, and how that connection is the battle going on inside of everyone."

Amy poured herself another glass of Sangria. "What battle are you talking about?"

"The battle to be less selfish."

Amy took a slow, thoughtful sip of her drink. "What's that got to do with the slave and the owner?"

Jesse began snapping an imaginary whip. "Oh, you know, we whip ourselves into getting what we want and then we do whatever it takes to get it. We give the orders and we take the orders and, in the end, we get no satisfaction and wind up feeling lonely and confused about why we're so unhappy."

"Wow," Amy said. "I didn't realize you were so unhappy."

"Neither did I until I found you."

Amy put her drink down and threw her arms around Jesse, spilling his drink. "Oh, Jesse, I love the way you sweet talk me. You know it works every time. So, what was it Carmen said about the obstacle course of life?"

"She said life is a spiritual obstacle course, designed to see if you can get over your self."

"That's it," Amy said as she began wiping Jesse's drink off his shirt and pants. "Now, I hate to say this, but it doesn't feel like you've become a completely selfless soul."

"It's a process, not an event," Jesse said. "I'm a work in progress. That's all I'm saying. I'm a work in progress and there's a lot of room for improvement."

"I'll show you a work in progress," Amy said as she slipped her hand up his thigh.

Jesse grabbed her hand and looked through the twinkle in her eye, deep into her soul. It wasn't something he intended to do. He slipped and fell in. He saw her strength and kindness and sadness and fear. He felt himself floating on the river Carmen had been describing. He lost himself in her eyes. Amy didn't blink or flinch. She was being swept away by the current.

Jesse could feel the presence of the Voodoo voice in the freedom of the moment. It was silent as a smile and satisfied as surrender to the universe. Visions of his New Orleans life with Amy flashed through his mind like a psychedelic newsreel.

He and Amy were hanging the Voodoo cow skull on the brick wall of their apartment, they were slow dancing on New Year's Eve at Raceland Music Hall, they were holding hands on the promenade overlooking the Mississippi River.

It was always about Amy. She was the star of every scene. How could he have missed it for so long? She held the key to his lock before he ever thought about escape. Jesse raised her hand to his lips and kissed their wedding ring. She was all he ever needed.

The Divebomberz: The band that inspired the novel Rock and Roll Voodoo

Back row left to right: Dale and Renee
Front row left to right: Jesse, Tim, and Butch

ABOUT THE AUTHOR

Mark Paul Smith is the author of *Hitchhike, Rock and Roll Voodoo,* and *Honey and Leonard*. After an around-the-world hitchhike, he became a newspaper reporter and then played in a rock band on Bourbon Street and on the road. He has been a trial attorney since 1982. Mark and his wife, the artist Jody Hemphill Smith, own Castle Gallery Fine Art in Fort Wayne, Indiana.

Excerpt from Honey & Leonard
by Mark Paul Smith

To Release in November, 2019

Honey and Leonard *(Excerpt)*

ONE

HONEY REMOVED HER EYEGLASSES and blinked in disbelief.

The tree-lined street in front of her house was jammed with fire trucks, police cars, an ambulance and several governmental vans. Uniformed people were everywhere. Most of her neighbors had come out to see what was happening. Honey felt her heart begin to race as she noticed the yellow police tape being stretched around her two-story, brick home.

"Leonard!" she screamed as she began running toward her front door. "Leonard! Oh, no!"

She made it through the crowd and the yellow tape and halfway up her front steps before a burly detective in a brown suit grabbed her with both arms. "Oh, no you don't, lady. This is a crime scene. You can't just come charging in here."

"But this is my house!" she cried as she realized the futility of struggle.

The detective released her from his bear hug and held her by one wrist so he could get a better look at her. "Is that you, Mrs. Waldrop?" he asked.

"Yes, it's me. You know it's me, Davey. You delivered my newspapers for ten years. Now, let go of me," she wiggled out of his grasp. "What's happened to my Leonard?"

"He's going to be fine. The medics are with him now. I'll take you to him if you promise to stay with me and not rush in like you own the place."

"I do own the place."

"Bad choice of words on my part. It is a working crime scene at the moment. I'm still Davey but you'd better call me Detective Perkins for now. I'm in charge of the investigation."

"Crime scene? Investigation?" Honey raised her voice. "What have they done to my Leonard?"

As she waited for the detective's explanation, Honey noticed all activity around her home had come to an abrupt standstill. Everyone was staring at her. Detective Perkins offered her his arm and began escorting her into the home.

"Why is everybody staring at me?"

As if in answer to her question, the front door banged open and out came two medics carrying Leonard on a gurney. He looked quite pale and was strapped down for safety. He managed to raise his head slightly when he heard Honey calling his name.

"What happened?" Honey asked as the detective let her get close enough for conversation.

Leonard looked confused and alarmed as he shook his head and said, "I have no idea. They said I have to go with them."

"Where are you taking him?" she demanded as the medics continued toward the ambulance. "You've got him all doped up. What's going on here?"

The detective had to grab her arms again as she attempted to grab the gurney. "Come on now, Mrs. Waldrop. He's going to be fine. You've got to let him go so they can take him to the hospital for testing and observation."

"Don't you 'Mrs. Waldrop' me. And take your hands off me, Davey. This is police brutality."

The detective let her go as Leonard was taken away and loaded into the ambulance. Honey didn't try to follow. A tight circle of uniforms had gathered to see if she was going to make enough of a fuss to get handcuffed. Being surrounded, Honey wisely decided to change her approach.

"Davey," Honey said, "I mean Detective Perkins. Perhaps you and I could go inside so you could tell me exactly what is happening."

The detective appeared relieved by Honey's more cooperative attitude. "That is an excellent idea. Let's do go inside. But let me warn you, there are quite a few folks in there and they're searching your home."

"Can they do that?"

"Yes, I'm afraid so. We've got a search warrant signed by the judge. Here it is. Take a look."

"How can they take Leonard out of my house if he doesn't want to go?"

"Adult Protective got a court order to have him removed. Here, look."

Her eyes glazed over the documents in emotional shock..

Honey was glad the detective had warned her about the search. Once inside, she was devastated to see people in hazardous materials suits with masks and plastic gloves going through her every drawer and cupboard. She was disoriented by the time she and the detective settled into the breakfast nook in the kitchen It felt like aliens had invaded her home.

"I'm sorry," she began, "this is all just too much."

"No, no. There's no need to apologize. I know how hard this must be for you, and let me start off by saying I don't believe a word of it. Not one word."

"Believe a word of what?"

Detective Perkins took a long look into Honey's eyes and sighed deeply. "Okay. Here it is. Leonard went in for some blood tests recently, and it looks like he's been poisoned. That's why they sedated him and put him on a stretcher. Apparently, the doctors wanted him immobilized for the trip to the hospital."

"What?" Honey's eyes widened. "Who would poison Leonard? He doesn't have any enemies. Neither one of us do. We've only been dating a year come Halloween. He's been a farmer his whole life."

The detective waited for her to continue with a look of sympathy in his eyes. Suddenly, Honey realized what was going on. "Oh, my God, you can't think it was me."

"No, I don't think it was you," the detective attempted to calm her. "I've known you and Doc Waldrop, rest his soul, my entire life. And I know you and Leonard have been having a wonderful time together these past few months."

"All of North Manchester, Indiana, seems to know everything about us," Honey scoffed. "My husband was the finest doctor this town ever saw. I loved him dearly, but he's been dead nearly five years. And now, Leonard Atkins is the best thing that ever happened to me. You can put that in your report. Everybody else seems to be taking notes. You'd think people would have better things to do than gossip about a couple of old folks falling in love. It's 1992 for heaven's sake. Old people are taking over the world."

"This isn't about gossip, Mrs. Waldrop. Leonard's been poisoned. The blood tests prove it. Don't worry, I'm not going to arrest you today. I just need to ask a few routine questions."

"Arrest me today?" Honey gasped. "That sounds like you might arrest me in the near future."

"No, at this point, I'm not even saying you're a suspect."

"So what am I?"

"You're what we call a person of interest."

"Oh, good Lord," Honey began to cry. She wasn't one to break down easily. She'd seen a lot of sorrow in her day. Tears were getting the best of her at this point. It felt like everything she loved was being taken away. "This is like some terrible television program," she said as she wiped her eyes with a cloth napkin.

As the detective took her hands in his to try to comfort her, a person in a hazmat suit came up and said, "Detective Perkins, we've searched the kitchen and the living room and the bathrooms. We've got samples.

"Better check the basement," he said.

"Oh, yes," Honey said, "by all means, check the basement. That's where I keep all the poison."

"Now, Mrs. Waldrop . . ." the detective began.

Honey removed her hands from his and began to regain her composure. "No, I'm fine. Go ahead. Search anywhere you like. I'll help. This is preposterous. There is no poison in this house. Come on; let's check my closet upstairs. That's where I keep my makeup. If I had any poison, which I don't, that's where I would keep it."

"Good idea," said Perkins. "That's more like it. We do appreciate your cooperation."

"It doesn't look like I have much choice," Honey grumbled as she and the detective went up the carpeted steps with one of the hazmat suit people.

Her walk-in closet was the size of a large bedroom. It was filled with a long lifetime of a wealthy widow's clothing and accessories. She had more than two hundred pairs of shoes and a hat for nearly every day of the year. Each side of the room had a vanity desk with a large mirror and drawers filled with make-up and lotions and perfumes and hairsprays.

"This ought to keep you and your boys busy for a good long time," Honey said as she looked up to the detective. "I've got shoes in here older than you."

"I'm sure you do," Perkins said as he took Honey back downstairs to the kitchen nook.

Honey and Leonard *(Excerpt)*

"I know who's behind all this," she said once they sat down.

He waited for her to continue.

"It's Gretchen. Gretchen Atkins, Leonard's niece. She's been taking care of his money. Or should I say stealing his money. He gave her Power of Attorney once he started having problems with his memory after his wife died. He's rich as Croesus, you know."

"I've heard that."

Honey paused, catching herself. "Now don't you dare think I would hurt my Leonard for his money. I've got more than enough of my own, thank you. The doctor left me well off when he died, and I've been doing quite fine by myself. You can ask my broker."

"Why would Gretchen be behind this?"

"She doesn't want me in the picture. I ask too many questions. I told Leonard he never should have signed over Power of Attorney to her. And I told Gretchen he could revoke it any time he wants. That's why she's trying to get guardianship on him. She wants him found mentally incompetent, so he can't revoke her Power."

"How do you know all this?" Perkins asked.

"Leonard's at my house more than he's at that pathetic nursing home she put him in. She calls it independent living. I call it independent dying. I know he has some problems with his memory, but he's getting better. I'm taking good care of him."

She looked at Perkins to make sure he was paying close enough attention. "Anyway, Leonard brings his mail over for me to help him go through it. I saw the petition to establish guardianship over Leonard that Gretchen filed with the court. Her lawyer sent him the legal notice."

"How long ago did this happen?"

"It wasn't more than a week ago. And I'll tell you what. Leonard's prepared to fight it. He doesn't need a guardian as long as he has me. And if he does need a guardian, it'll be me, not her. She's stealing his money. She doesn't care about him. She just wants his money. Look at the car she's driving. It's a brand new Toyota. I've been told her big new house is paid for. She doesn't make that kind of money teaching fifth grade."

"So why would she want to poison Leonard?"

"He doesn't have a will. Gretchen's the only family he's got left. If he dies, it all goes to her. Leonard and I were going to get a lawyer to do a will and revoke that Power of Attorney, but now she's trying to say he's not competent to sign anything."

"Is he competent?"

Honey's face lit up as she formulated her response. She was still a beautiful woman. She had Liz Taylor in her eyes and Katherine Hepburn in her shoulders and hips. Her family came from Mobile, Alabama, where she'd been the queen of her high school senior prom. It was a storybook life until she lost her only sibling, her brother, on a bombing run over Germany in World War II. After that terrible loss, she started volunteering in the hospital, treating many returning veterans. She was a good worker, but she got in trouble a time or two for flirting with the patients. The doctor was tall and handsome. He swept her off her feet at a time when she was looking for a hero. They married after the war and moved north to his home state, Indiana.

Honey could pour out Southern charm like maple syrup turns Southern grits into a decidedly Northern dish.

"I'll tell you how competent Leonard is," she told the detective. "Last Saturday night, he showed up at my door with a dozen roses and took me to dinner. His shirt was clean, his shoes were shined and his hair was strictly Valentino. We had a perfect, Italian night out."

"Did you drive?"

"No, I let him drive my Cadillac. I hate to drive, and he's still an excellent driver. He sold his Oldsmobile two weeks ago and he's looking for a new one. He's between cars."

Honey and Leonard *(Excerpt)*

"How did he get to your house?"

"He walked. He's in good shape, I'm telling you, mentally and physically. The nursing home is right down the street from my house, about a quarter mile."

"I know he's got a valid driver's license," Perkins said. "He got a ticket last month for running a red light."

"That was that stupid light out on South Mill Road. I was with him. We were in his old car. There was nobody on the road. He always runs red lights when there's nobody coming. He's got a mind of his own."

"There was somebody on the road."

"If you want to say that policeman was on the road. He was hiding behind the gas station, just waiting for someone to run that light."

Perkins laughed. "Let's get back to the point. How do you suppose Gretchen would poison Leonard?"

"I have no idea."

The detective waited patiently for her to continue. Honey knew what he was doing. He was waiting to see how she would attempt to incriminate Gretchen and unwittingly shine light on her own activities and motives. She wasn't going down that road.

"What makes you think Leonard was even poisoned?" she asked. "He didn't look that bad on the stretcher. He was fine last night and this morning when Dorothy Anderson picked me up for our Wednesday bridge luncheon."

"We have blood test results that show he's been poisoned."

"Poisoned with what?"

Perkins shook his head and said, "I'm not supposed to tell you that."

"Why, Davey Perkins. Don't you Sherlock Holmes me. You can't come in and tear my house apart and call me a murderer and then not tell me what kind of poison we're talking about. Besides, if I did it, which I most definitely did not, and wouldn't even think about even if I hated him, which I don't—I love the man dearly . . . Now wait, where was I going with that?"

"You were saying, 'If I did it.'"

"Oh, right. If I did poison Leonard, I would already know what the poison was, now wouldn't I?"

The detective smiled slightly as he said, "I guess that's right. And, anyway, I know you wouldn't poison anybody. So I'll tell you. It was arsenic."

"Arsenic!" Honey was visibly shocked. "That sounds so positively evil. Where would I get arsenic?"

One of the hazmat suits interrupted to ask, "How much of the medicine cabinet do you want us to analyze?"

The detective got up to supervise the search and said, "Don't worry, Mrs. Waldrop. It won't take much longer. I'll make sure we don't take anything you need on a daily basis. By the way, are Leonard's meds in the same cabinet as yours?"

"Mine are on the right, his are on the left. You can read the names on the bottles. And, Davey, please, stop calling me 'Mrs. Waldrop.' You make me feel as old as I am. You're a full-grown man now. You may call me 'Honey.'"

"Yes, of course, Mrs. Waldrop . . . I mean, Honey."

Perkins chuckled in embarrassment and went off with his people, leaving Honey alone with her thoughts. She was more than worried. She was being accused of trying to murder the man she loved. She knew she hadn't done anything wrong, except maybe let too many people know she and Leonard were happily in love and living together.

What makes people so nosey? And why do they love a scandal? Oh, that's right. It's good old-fashioned entertainment.

How could she prove her innocence? And what about Leonard? She was more worried about Leonard than anything else. She kept seeing the confused look on his face as they took him out on the stretcher. The more she thought about it, the more she realized there was only one thing she needed to do. Go find Leonard.

She got up to make some Earl Grey Tea for herself. She needed to think. Going to see Leonard might be problematic. For one thing, she hated driving. For another, there must be rules against attempted-murder suspects going to see their alleged victims in the hospital.

She could get in to see him. They would have taken him to Wabash County Hospital, fifteen miles away. She knew everybody there except the new folks. She had been president of the Women's Auxiliary when her late husband had practically run the place. She got on the phone to call Dorothy, her bridge club friend.

Dorothy answered after the first ring and said, "My goodness, Honey, what's going on over there? I had to drop you off a block away. I should have stayed with you. Now, I hear Leonard's been murdered and you're the number one suspect. How could anyone even suggest such a thing? Don't worry. I'm your alibi. So are all the girls at bridge club."

"Dorothy," Honey said. "Leonard is not dead. The police say he's been poisoned but they know it's not me. They're still here, searching the entire house."

"Oh, thank God! Is he going to be okay?"

"I'm pretty sure he will," Honey said. "Now, listen. I need a ride to the hospital right now. I've got to be with Leonard. He needs me."

There was a long pause on the line.

"Honey, I'm not sure I can do that. I'm not sure you should do that. Are you under arrest or anything like that?"